The Soulmate Prophecy

— BOOK 3 —

THE REVELATION

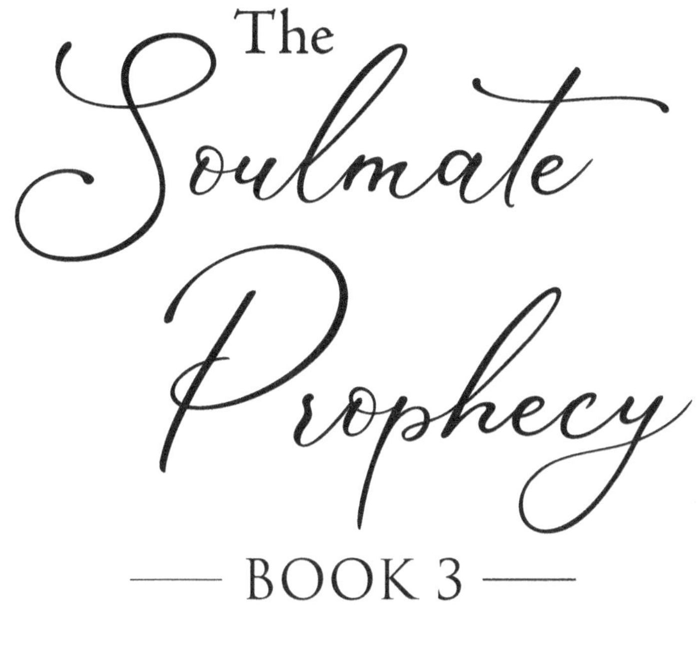

The Soulmate Prophecy

BOOK 3

THE REVELATION

YASMINA HAQUE

MainSpring Books

Printed in the United States of America
ISBN 978-1-946854-23-0 (paperback)
ISBN 978-1-641336-46-8 (hardback)
ISBN 978-1-946854-22-3 (ebook)
Library of Congress Control Number: 2021910344

MainSpring Books
5901 W. Century Blvd
Suite 750
Los Angeles, CA, US, 90045

www.mainspringbooks.com

Prologue

"I so fucked it up. I can't let this little girl go. They are just babies."

"It's just a kitten, right?" asks Jay taking the black and white tabby in his arms. He cuddles her as she licks his nose. I want to tell him she's more than a kitten, but I decide to show him instead.

"Mia, where is Tia?" I casually ask.

The little kitten turns into a baby bunny right in Jay's arms within a blink of an eye. His entire body stiffens. I would be scared, too, but I've seen this a hundred times already. It's not affecting me anymore.

"No way!" screams Michael. Jay turns ten shades of white and shakes. Michael pats the bunny's head to see if it's real. She puts her front paws out and her eyes glow red as if in love.

"Here, give her to me," I say to Jay. "You're going to make her sick with all your trembling." Jay seems paralyzed in place so I pry Tia out of his hands.

"Are you ready for more?" I asked my two assistants. Michael nods his head exuberantly while Jay shakes his.

"Tia, where is Leah?" I ask. The little black and white bunny turns into a baby kangaroo instantaneously in my arms. Her warm brown eyes glow as it looks at me. The little girl knows that I am her creator. That I am her Master.

"What did you do?" whispers Michael. Jay holds onto the table for support looking a bit green. It's probably how I looked when I first witnessed what I created.

"I created a shapeshifter. Unintentionally. It's a schizophrenic kitten, bunny and joey combined. I don't have the heart to destroy her. She wasn't supposed to turn out this way."

"That is wicked, wicked, Bro!" says Michael. "Do you know what the military could do with technology like that? Do you know what Zenith could do?"

"Then it's not going to find out! Understand?" Both my assistance nod their hands. The little joey snuggles into me, scared up on my words. I cradle her letting her know that no harm will ever come to her. I've turned into such a sappy scientist. Where the fuck that came from, I have no clue.

"Will she survive in the Rainforest? She's so little. How big will she grow?" asks Jay.

"This is it," I say. "I've stopped all growth patterns."

Michael takes the little joey in his arms. She rests her head on his chest as if it's naptime.

"Can I keep her?" he asks.

"Leave her in the Rainforest during the day and I suppose you can take her to your place at night. All three of them use a litter box." Jay gives a quizzical look in his green hue.

"Unless you want her?" says Michael to Jay. Jay violently shakes his head.

"Thank goodness Christoph's allergic to cats," says Jay taking a seat. His green demeanor slowly changes back to his normal color.

"She's hypoallergenic," I smirk winking at him.

Chapter 1

August 30, 2015 @ 10:00pm
Kaelyn's Apartment
Lovelin

"Shhh, sweetheart."

I can barely breathe. Too many sensations. Not just around me, but within me, bombarding throughout my…soul. It's in my fingers and toes. It's in my waist and all over my chest. My thighs and calves paralyze at every one of his touches. My brain's on some sort of extended vacation. I have no idea where it went and nor do I care.

I hope it never comes back.

"My Lord, please," I whisper into his neck. I convulse at my waist. I've never felt like this before. I never knew such sensations existed. His body on top of mine makes me shudder all over.

When he touched me between my legs, I arched and cried out. He eases me back down onto our mattress, but with a force I want to feel over and over again.

"Shhh, sweetheart, I'm here," he whispers into my ear.

Where is here, I have no idea. I cannot even recollect where I've been. Some part of my mind tells me we are at his apartment. Some part of my mind tells me we are in some sort of unknown

Heaven. Then some part of me tells me we are far, far away in some beautiful sandy land that doesn't exist.

Without any warning, he enters into me. I cry out again. I throb around him and I can feel him getting harder and harder. It's painful and exquisitely pleasurable in the same breathe.

Our breaths mingle as one around us.

"Shhh, sweetheart. I know it's hard, but inhale." I breathe his magnificent essence that has haunted my dreams. He smells ever so musky. He smells ever so sweet. He smells like the sand and the Rainforest surroundings that I will never ever get enough of.

I then forget to breathe again.

He's been inside me for a few moments, a few minutes, but not long enough. It will never ever be enough. This man. This Lord. I can't believe he's going to be my husband.

"Just stay with me, precious. Just stay with me," he whispers heavily into my ear as he tries to command. I try to obey. I want to obey. He doesn't move. I want him to move. I find myself praying for him to move, but he's cruel and just lays within me while I breathe his hot Rainforest scent at his neck while he suckles on my breasts as if he has had no nourishment in weeks.

Our bodies are wrapped around us completely. It's not enough. I want his skin infused within mine. Just to have his skin on top of mine will never be enough. I want more. I want to be deep beneath his skin and bones and live there. Not just now or for the next moment, but for all eternity. Nothing else will do at the moment. Nothing else will do unless it's forever.

"Kaelyn, please!"

"Shhh. I'm right here. Nothing will ever take you away from me." He whispers into my ear again, "I promise," as he moves onto my other side.

He's cruel, keeping himself from shuddering on top of me for so long. I don't know where it all started and I hope it never ends. I remember the first time my body and soul were all his.

"My Lord Kaelyn, Kaelyn," I say gasping, whispering out of breath. His weight's heavy on top of me. Heavy, burning and soothing at the same time. He lifts his head up and looks into my eyes.

"Spread your wings, Love," he says. "Let us soar where nobody's ever gone before."

I do as he desires. He plunges into me again and again like a starving bear that has hibernated far too long. For the first time in my life, I feel whole and complete. Every time he exits me, I cry out in agony from the loss of him although our bodies are wrapped around each other.

I then feel the greatest plunge.

"Love!" he cries out as he enters my soul.

Our soul.

His body shakes uncontrollably upon mine. I've lost every one of my senses. I've lost all sense of everything.

His breathing comes in gasps. I know the feeling because I was just there moments before when he was caressing my face, suckling my breasts, kissing my belly, parting my thighs.

"Easy, Love. I'm here," he says. He tries to dive deeper into me. As long and thick and as luscious as he is, there was no more room to dive deeper. Life is not fair in many aspects. I sink lower into the mattress and wrap my legs higher around his waist to give him more access. The pressure brings me to oblivion.

"My Lord! Please, not now!" I cry out. I want this to go on forever and ever.

He laughs softly into my ear, into my hair while he gives soft kisses on my earlobe and then trails his tongue down my neck.

"Let it be now, Love. Then we will have more time to do it again and again." With those words, he exits out of me and then plunges in again, over and over. I hold on tight around his neck.

His hands wrapped around above my waist.

"My most beautiful Master Kaelyn," I whisper, tears streaking my face.

He kisses me softly. That only makes me shake more. His tender kisses are so soft and gently that I just want to explode.

"Kaelyn," I bury my neck into his face whispering; I don't know when my voice will ever function again and nor do I care. He gets up and entwines my hands into his above my head and thrusts deeper than I can withstand into my soul.

Our soul. Once again.

The sensation's so exquisite that I cannot even scream out in ecstasy. More tears stream down my face. He starts to tear. Within moments, his body pounds into mine. At first, it is a need, going over and over again in beautiful harmony as we enjoy each other.

The next second, it is desperation, a longing, a wanting, that has been there forever. Since time started.

"Kaelyn," I sob into his lips as he gives me tender kisses over and over again as his soul goes in and out of mine.

"Love! Lovely!"

I am in this world and then I am not. I can feel his life bursting into my body. It's thick and wet and warm and beyond the most miraculous sensation that the world we live in has to offer. He collapses on top of me and sobs softly into my hair, my neck, my ear.

I hold him ever tighter. My fingers through the back of his damp hair, my lips upon his slick neck giving soft kisses.

"I'm here, baby," I say sobbing with him. I'm finally home.

Chapter 2

August 31, 2015 @ 9:00pm
Sector Nine - Female Dormitories
Lucinda

"You won't believe what happened to me today," I say tossing my backpack at the foot of my bed. All four of our cats sleeping from all directions of our apartment enthusiastically and then lazily pounce onto me with their loving greetings.

"Darby, the sea lion kissed you again," says Paris not looking up, absorbed in her reading as usual. She's propped up on her bed with a dozen pillows wearing just her underclothes scrolling through an electronic magazine. I'm sure it's about drone technology. Tech stuff is all she ever reads. She works in the Maintenance Section and creates the drones that service the *Underground*. She's one incredible seventeen-year-old engineer.

"Better!"

"Better than your boyfriend, Darby?" asks Shika. My other roommate, Shika's just a common girl that works in one of the shops in Mid-Section. Her parents have a soap store. The soaps her parents and Shika design are second to none. They are used throughout the *Underground* in all the smart showers and spas. They keep us one hundred percent bacteria-free as well.

"Jay Ahmed asked me out on a date for tomorrow night."

All four of our cats cuddle into me. Thor, my black and grey Persian, brings me his toy mouse to play with. Kenya, our Bengal, carries his feather wand in his mouth to me. Lilly climbs up my hair onto my head and Pricilla purrs in my neck.

"No way!" exclaims Jazmin. "He's engaged to Samantha Stonebridge, Zenith's other golden child. He would never!"

Jazmin's parents have a shop in Mid-Section as well. Her father, Nicolai Toretti, owns the only jewelry store down here. He can create the most beautiful pieces. All you have to do is give him an idea and it's done for you. He can get whatever stones and gems from the *Surface*.

Zenith provides everything to him. Zenith provides everything for us.

"That's what I thought, too. Apparently, they are not together anymore," I say. Well, at least that's what I think, otherwise Jay would not have asked me out.

"I haven't heard of a break up. Everybody knows they have been betrothed since they were babies. I wouldn't go," says Paris placing her tablet on her nightstand. "You don't want to step on toes. Samantha's a nice girl. She's crazy super smart and has helped me many times in class. It's hard not to like her."

"What does she have to do with anything?" Jay asked me. "It's just a harmless evening at the *Holoplex*."

"The *Holoplex*!" they all say together.

"Tomorrow's the first," says Paris. "Everybody's going to *Prizes*. It starts in three hours."

"I'm not spending the entire twenty-four at *Prizes* this year. I've been going since I was five and I only have a penguin and a bear to my name. I'm going out with Jay."

"There's nothing harmless about a date at the *Holoplex*. The movie theater consists of seventy queen-sized, reclinable beds, not chairs, remember?" says Shika. "I suggest you don't go either, but if you do, not in your pajamas like you do with us."

"The *Holoplex* has a very conservative dress code. What are you so worried about? It's just a movie. And Jay's so brilliant," I say trying to convince them. "Do you have any idea how hard it is to find a significant other down here? Our choices are so limited, and divorce is forbidden."

"That's why we are here," says Jazmin. "Only to work. With no distractions." I'm ignoring Kenya so he takes his wand over to Jazmin.

"A bed is a bed," says Paris. "It doesn't matter what setting it's in. Almost everybody that goes to the *Holoplex* is in a team. Only married couples are seen sharing one bed. There are generally three to five of us sharing popcorn and hummus with carrots all comfy in one of them."

"I'm going," I say. "He offered so what's the harm?" The three of my roommates look at each other. Lilly's now crawling down my hair. Pricilla has fallen asleep in my neck.

"I'll go with you," says Jazmin.

"Hell, no, you won't!" I shout back. "I'm not giving him an idea of some sort of threesome!" Pricilla looks up at me from my hollering as if I'm right and then goes back to sleep again.

"She's right," says Paris. "She's going to have to go alone. Just don't get your hopes up too high, Cindy. You don't want to tangle with Samantha Stonebridge. You know her Uncle is Kaelyn Stonebridge, Zenith's true golden savior. I'm surprised they didn't name him after one of the Greek or Egyptian Gods. That family is way out of your league."

I don't want to tangle with Samantha, I think to myself. I want to tangle with Jay.

August 31, 2015 @ 9:00pm
Sector Nine - Male Dormitories
Jay Ahmed

What the fuck possessed me to ask Lucinda out, I don't know. Maybe it was her smile. Maybe it's just because I feel so lonely lately. I've never really even spent much personal time with Sam except for dinners with our roommates, but I miss her. I feel detached. Maybe it was the euphoria of my breakthrough and I needed someone to share it with.

Kato's still up in front of his holographic 3D screen as I walk in. "How was your day, Bro?" he asks hearing my presence.

"It was not a *good what a day*, but a *great what a day*; however, I think I made a mistake," I say flopping onto my bed.

"That's okay." He scribbles equations with his finger, the stylus in his mouth. "You'll fix it tomorrow." I put my backpack away and change out of my work attire into shorts and a t-shirt.

"It's not work or laboratory related." Now I have his attention. He walks over to me.

"How did you fuck up this time?" he questions sitting on my bed. "What did you do to Sam now?" I reluctantly tell him I asked Lucinda out for a movie tomorrow night.

"Did you not eat all day? Was your blood sugar low? You let go of Sam just days ago and you're on the bandwagon? You told me you weren't interested in anyone else. What's wrong with you?" says Kato slapping my head. I knew he wouldn't be too happy with me.

"Lucinda was excited about my day! She actually cared to ask me! I've felt so alone lately. It felt good to have someone ask about my day!" I curl up in a ball on my bed and cover my face with my forearm. "And for your information," I say in my fetal position, "I didn't let go of Sam! She let go of me!"

"I ask you about your day every day! What? I'm not good enough for you?" I give him a funny look from under my covers.

"That's not exactly how I wanted that to come out." I sulk into my mattress even further. "Everybody's going to *Prizes* tomorrow. It starts in three hours. You won't be there? You and Sam go every month."

"She hasn't mentioned it and I don't feel like getting my brain deep-fried without her," I say covering my head once more. I know I should eat, but I don't feel hungry. As usual.

"I'm going," says Sal. "Dr. Winkle gave me the day off. It won't be the same without you, Jay. I heard Zenith added *Surface* and *Underground* trivia as one of the categories and it's going to be a game played against one another, not just individually."

"Sorry, little brother, but I just can't." Sal goes back to reading his electronic book. He's got sushi by his bedside and eats with chopsticks while he reads. I wish I had some sort of appetite right now. I've heard the expression that girls can drive you crazy, but I never thought I would ever fall into that trap.

Chapter 3

August 31, 2015 @ 2:00pm
Cryogenics Lab
Samantha Stonebridge

I read Zareen's entire toxicology report. She wasn't pregnant herself. She wasn't even sexually active. There was a bit of alcohol found in her system, not nearly enough to sound an alarm. The startling fact, however, was the trace amount of potassium cyanide found. The funny thing is that we don't stock potassium cyanide in our pharmaceutical closet. It obviously came from the *Surface*.

Did Zareen order the cyanide? I doubt that she committed suicide. Cyanide would be an easier method than slicing your wrists or hanging yourself. Maybe that's what the murderer wants us to believe. But why in the bath? It had to be murder. However, whoever murdered her had to have known we would find this. Now I know why I was chosen for the autopsy: to carry out the President's command. He's obviously behind this.

Zenith is behind this.

Who could murder in the *Underground* to carry out Zenith's commands? Their security team comes to mind. They are beyond devoted.

I cannot second-guess Zenith. My first allegiance has always lied with Zenith. I thought Uncle Kaelyn's was, too, but now I'm not so sure. I'm going to have to let this one go. Obviously, Zenith knows something we don't. I start pacing around Dr. Kai-af's lab.

Is it really our business to pry into their affairs? We were brought down here for a job. I was bred for a job. Can we start second-guessing Zenith now? I'm at a battle within myself. Uncle Kaelyn took matters into his own hands to find answers. Maybe he shouldn't have done that and just let it go as well. I don't know. I'm so fucking confused.

Maybe Zareen wasn't the upstanding citizen of the *Underground*? Maybe her path turned for the worse? I've never known it happen, but it could be possible. I wonder what her teammates in the cloning sector are like. Are they in on it, too? Will there be more deaths?

I press my wrist and tell Uncle Kaelyn about my findings. He didn't say much except to keep him in the loop.

August 31, 2015 @ 3:00pm
Genetics Laboratory
Kaelyn

I remember August fifteenth close to midnight when the President first spoke to me about Zareen. Her bosses were straying away from protocol is what she told him. Zenith knew. Zenith obviously killed her to keep her quiet. But why? Who's baby? It wasn't hers.

I try to concentrate on my work. "You okay, Bro?" says Michael. "You look really worried. Not frustrated, but worried."

"I'm fine. Something's just not adding up."

"The story of our life," says Michael peering into his own microscope.

"Where's Jay? I didn't think he had class this afternoon."

"He's working on his own independent project. He says he's close. I'm fine without him. He works eighteen hours a day and has his own dreams. I hope they come true."

I hope they come true as well. After all, dreams created our civilization down here. I try to concentrate on my own work, but my mind keeps traveling to Samantha's words.

Maybe the cloning sect is cloning a baby. But who? Why?

I recall my earlier conversations with others. Just three days ago, my mother asked me about Adolf Hitler. At that thought, I start pacing around my lab. It was so out of the blue when she mentioned him, I really didn't pay much attention. I was so distraught over Krista's behavior and Lovelin's happiness that I dismissed it as nothing. Now I wonder why she would ask me about that evil inhumane monster.

Cloning Adolf Hitler? How can they anyway? Even if they could, why would Zenith want to have Hitler cloned? He killed millions of Jewish people. Zenith's mission is to save Mother Earth, not radical religious messes.

Kaelyn, you're pulling at straws! I throw my lab coat off and head into the Rainforest. I need some fresh air. I can't concentrate on my work anyway. Maybe a break and some artificial sunshine will give me the relaxation I need to work and concentrate again.

Pressing my wrist, I call Lovelin just to hear her voice while inhaling the Rainforest scents. We talk about nothing. We talk about everything. I wish I could kiss her through my wrist. Seeing her lovely face in front of me isn't good enough anymore. Dr. Chowdury's going to have to make some enhancements to this technology.

Before I know it, I'm at my sandbox. I take off my boots and let the sand wash over my feet. It's hotter than usual today, and I relish in it.

"Love you, sweetheart," I say ending our conversation.

"Love you more." We argue back and forth for a while. I wish I could understand why I act like such a teenager with her. Maybe because my teenage love was genes and DNA rather than girls like a normal human male. I hate our sappiness and can't get enough of it at the same time.

"Hi Papa," Loopy says gliding onto my shoulder. She tumbles and flies slower than usual. "Say hi to Mama for me!" I press my wrist disconnecting the line before I hear her words. Her face frowns and she turns blue all over in one breath.

"Are you okay, Loopy? You're flying slow," I say examining her. Nothing looks out of the ordinary.

"Found a new anthill, Papa!" she exclaims turning light orange as she speaks. "Had a big lunch," she says patting her tummy.

"Any survivors?"

"Nope. It was a clean sweep!" she says happily changing into a bright orange hue with golden wings. Survival of the fittest. Darwin lives within the Rainforest walls. Darwin lives all over and within Mother EARTH.

A clean sweep? I think about that for a moment. I hope I'm wrong.

"Are you okay, Papa? You look worried," Loopy says cocking her head as she sits on my shoulder.

I smile at her. "You needn't worry about Papa. I'm fine. I'm with you, aren't I?" She turns pink all over at my words. That's definitely a better sign than blue.

"Love you, Papa."

"Love you more."

"No, you don't," she argues back turning a bit red.

I'm not having this argument twice in the same hour so I give into her. She flies away looping in the sky in a soft orange glow. I bet she's going to tell Zara. Zara's the only other one I have the 'who loves who more argument' with these days. Lovelin started it. A part of me wished she never started it, but most of me can't get enough of it.

I lay in the hammock soaking up the makeshift sun. My shirt's already half drenched. It doesn't bother me. I'm used to it.

I think about Loopy's words. I think about clean sweep. I should be uneasy about Zenith's plans, but I'm not. I'm safe in the

Underground with my loved ones. I'm safe with my creations and Lovelin.

Without Loopy's insight, I couldn't have understood, but now it's sapphire crystal clear.

The *Surface* is headed for a clean sweep. Zenith's taking drastic measures in population control.

It should scare me, but it doesn't. That's not my agenda.

Chapter 4

September 1, 2015 @ 6:30pm
Sector Nine - Male Dormitories
Jay Ahmed

"Hey, little buddy, I need a favor."

"Name it," says Christoph engrossed in his studies. I'm surprised he heard me. I peer into his tablet. He's studying for a geology exam tomorrow. "How in the world do you lose 1.2 billion years?"

"Ah, you're studying the *Great Unconformity.* Unbelievable, isn't it?"

"That's insane!" says Christoph absorbed in his reading.

"Mother Earth's full of mysteries."

"I wish I could go to the Grand Canyon and see it." Christoph can't take his eyes off his tablet scrolling with his fingers as he reads.

"Jake, pull up the section of the *Great Unconformity* in the Grand Canyon on Christoph's wall."

"Dr. Ahmed, there is only one *Great Unconformity* on our benevolent Mother Earth, and I know where it is," responds Jake. I smile to myself. This sassy part of Jake is the first I've heard and I love how he's evolving.

A most spectacular image of the canyon appears. Jake displays the image live in 4D rather than 3D. We can hear the canyon sounds that are happening this instant. There's a warm breeze. Unfortunately, we cannot hear the Colorado River. Christoph gets up and runs his fingers over the two rock layers that have over a billion years' erosion in-between them.

"What happened? I want to know what happened! Where did all that time disappear to?" I think Christoph's passion is geology. Sometimes it's too bad he's never going to be able to leave the *Underground* to see all of Mother Earth's wonders firsthand.

"I need to you to come to the *Holoplex* with me," I say changing the subject.

"Tonight? I have an exam tomorrow. And I went to *Prizes* earlier. My brain's exhausted as it is. I'm no prodigy, remember? I just go to hang out with my friends."

I tell Christoph how I somehow wound up asking Lucinda out, and wish I hadn't. Last night with Sam in the Rainforest gave me a glimmer of hope that the two of us will eventually get back together. I can't ruin a nine-year betrothal over one fight. I've got to make things right between us, but I don't want to cancel on Lucinda. She didn't do anything wrong.

"You're going to owe me big time," says Christoph waving above his tablet to shut it off. He leaves his wall the way it is.

"Name it, little buddy."

September 1, 2015 @ 6:50pm
Holoplex
Lucinda

It's almost seven and Jay hasn't shown up, yet. Maybe he's not coming. I press my wrist. There are no messages that I may have missed. I sit straight in one of the leather recliners as I wait in the lobby. I don't put the massagers on. A few of my friends wave at me. I see Professor Harding holding Professor Sanchez's hand. I smile at them. Professor Sanchez is so sweet. I didn't know they were a couple.

I hope after tonight Jay and I are a couple.

After Jay asked me out, I set up a hair appointment at *Mystic Creations*, one of the *Underground* spas. Noah spent close to two hours creating ringlets with slight dark red streaks down my back that came out flawless. I don't know how he got my hair to shine like this. I love it. I then went to the *Devil's Playground* for a new outfit. I got a cashmere black body fitted V-necked sweater with grey leggings, and low-heeled silver sandals. My blonde hair shines even more so with the black background of my sweater.

Jazmin loved the outfit. My other two roommates thought it looked too sexy for a first date. They commented that Jay might not like the forward type. He's a professional doctor and scientist after all. I took the chance and stuck with the new clothes. Forget the doctor - scientist. He's still a young man nonetheless. That's what I'm banking on.

There's only five minutes left before the movie starts. He's not coming. I can feel it in my stomach. Maybe Samantha and he are still together. I'm going to wait until seven and then leave. There's hardly anyone in the lobby this close to show time. Most have already gotten their food, popcorn, and drinks and are in the theater getting comfortable and cozy in the beds and blankets. Who doesn't love to watch television in bed? Zenith has thought of every luxury for us. I hear the last call announcement before doors close.

Featuring at the *Holoplex* this week is the *Fast and Furious* marathon. I've seen all eight of them. I heard only six or seven of them have been premiered on the *Surface*. I wonder if Jay has seen them. The problem with a movie date is that you don't get to talk a whole lot. I don't receive any messages in my line of vision. It's almost show time. He's apparently not coming. I can't believe I got stood up! How am I going to face my roommates? Just as when I'm about to get up and leave, I see Jay saunter in carrying a child on his back.

"Sorry, we're late. Christoph wanted ice cream."

"No problem," I say trying to smile. I couldn't very well say anything else. I was too surprised to ask who the little boy is.

Jay and Christoph order nachos with extra jalapeños and juice at the concession counter. By the looks of their camaraderie, they must be roommates. I meekly ask for apple juice at the end of their order because they don't ask me what I want. We're able to scurry into the theater just as the automatic doors close behind us. The theater's only a little less than half crowded tonight. Most are at *Prizes* this evening.

"Where do you want to sit, little buddy?" whispers Jay to Christoph. He whispers in Jay's ear. Jay finds a bed in the center top row and Christoph engages himself off of him down right in the middle of it. Jay then places their drinks on the right side of the bed and their food in the tray next to it. Christoph gets comfy propping up his pillows. He adjusts the bed with the remote so they are half-sitting, half-lying. They cover themselves with the silver duvet. Jay snuggles up next to him as I stand still watching them get settled.

That's just fucking dandy! Jay doesn't ask me which part of the theater I want to watch the movie from. He doesn't ask me what side of the bed I would like either. I feel like a third wheel in their guy's night out. Maybe Jay already had an evening planned with Christoph and asked me to tag along. Who knows? I decide I'm not going to be a baby about it. I get comfy with my pillow, but I don't get under the covers with those two. It's a good thing my sweater's keeping me warm. The temperature at the *Holoplex* is always set to a cool sixty-eight degrees.

As the movie starts, Christoph summons me with his index finger and I hesitantly lean into him. "You're very pretty," he whispers into my ear. I lean back taken by surprise at his sweet comment. He couldn't be more than ten years old. Jay's engrossed in the movie. Christoph smiles at me. I then forward into him.

"Thank you, you're real cute yourself," I whisper back.

"Want some nachos?" he whispers offering me some. I take a couple and eat. I wish I could be feeding these to Jay.

Christoph puts the nachos between us cuddling into me a bit. I sip on my juice and share the nachos with him. Jay doesn't seem to care to eat. He didn't eat throughout the entire movie. At the funny parts, Christoph has the cutest laugh. I find myself enjoying his company. He whispers comments to me throughout the entire show.

"If you could have a car, what would you drive?" I've never thought about that so I just shrug my shoulders. "I'd love one of those fast Lamborghinis. They're so bad for Mother Earth, though."

"I think I'd rather have a luxury boat and sail around the world," I whisper after a while. I'm a marine biologist after all. I'd love to see the world's sea life. Christoph gives me a double thumbs up sign.

The movie went by slow and fast at the same time just like the cars we were watching. As overhead lights go on, silver drones enter the theater and place the empty containers and trays into their baskets. Some people take their tubs of popcorn home with them. As soon as Christoph and Jay get out from under the covers, golden drones strip the bedding and replace it with fresh ones before the next showing. The duvets are all sprayed with a freshener unless stained from food. Then they strip them off for wash also and replace the comforters with fresh ones. We try not to get messy, but accidents happen.

As we exit the *Holoplex,* Christoph's again riding on Jay's back. We take the train back to Sector Nine.

"Thanks for a great time, Lucinda," says Jay. "We'll have to do that again sometime."

Really? He wants to go out with me again? Well, it's not like he went out with me this first time.

"I'd love that," I say not really knowing what else to say in front of his adorable little roommate. Christoph winks at me.

What the hell. I wink back.

September 1, 2015 @ 2:00am London Time
Sector Two - Quantum Physics Laboratory
Zachary Briarwood

"I'm taking the Spear for a second test run," I say.

"Where are you going?" asks Kieran wiping down my Spear.

"I'm going to London."

"Homesick, are you? Bring me back some of that amazing Indian street food."

"It's 2am London time. Unfortunately, no street food." He frowns at me. "I so wish myself."

I use the *SuperNet* to find the latitude and longitude lines that I precisely want. I hope I got them right.

"What are you going to accomplish at 2am?"

"That's the point. Hopefully, everybody's sleeping," I say taking off my navy blue lab coat revealing casual blue jeans, sneakers, and a Cambridge sweatshirt. I debate whether to take a jacket or not since it's probably cold and raining in London this time of the year as in every time of year, but I doubt if I will leave the building so I decide against it. Kieran hands me the Spear. It's practically glowing.

"Jake, video encrypt everything please."

"As you wish, Dr. Briarwood," replies Jake.

Kieran's in front of his holographic computer monitoring me as I turn the Spear and press the button. As before, a whirlwind forms around me. Within moments, I'm flying again through a dark tunnel. So this is what Superman feels like. I could get addicted to this. This journey seems longer than the one to Washington, DC. It makes sense since London's farther away from the *Underground* than Washington.

This time, however, I'm not thrown into a chair, but land on my feet right into a closet. Yes! I got the coordinates right! I just hope this is the old apartment that I grew up in and not Lady McPherson's flat next door. She's such a sweet old lady, but definitely not the grandmother type. She babysat me a few times as an infant, but when I spoke in complete sentences at nine months, she told mum it's best she find another babysitter. It frightened her that I would rather read than play with blocks.

And when I did play with alphabet blocks, I spelled words from them.

The first time I spelled out 'milk' for Lady McPherson, she behaved like she saw a ghost and ran out of her apartment screaming. The first time I spelled 'milk' out for my mum, she just went to the refrigerator and then handed me a bottle. I remember I was about seven months old.

I quietly open the closet door. There's a boy asleep in the corner of the room comfy in his bed. His comforter is adorned in footballs and he cradles one while he sleeps. He looks my age.

My room's now decorated in a football theme. There are posters of Beckham and Pele on the wall. The ten-shelf bookcase that used to hold hundreds of my books is now filled with football trophies and model airplanes. There are flags of the World Cup decorated on the walls as well. My walls were always decorated with my achievement certificates.

Obviously, this is not my room anymore.

I don't hear anybody talking so I leave the boy's room and walk down the hallway a bit. I peek into the guest room, which has another child asleep in it. I creep towards the bed. The yellow star nightlight radiating in the corner casts a glow upon a little girl with blondish brown hair.

She couldn't be more than seven or eight years old. She must be the little sister. Her room's decorated in the *Little Mermaid* theme. She has a mural of mermaids dancing around her light pink walls in a faint glow through her nightlight. Her bookshelves are filled with fairytale books.

I walk to her dresser. Rather than adorned with stuffed animals and dolls on top like I anticipated, I find a stethoscope, a pulse ox, a blonde wig, catheters, needles for drawing blood, blood tubes, gauze, and tourniquets. The contents before me make me sad. This little girl seems to have some sort of health condition.

Without any warning, the lamp next to the little girl's bed clicks on and the room illuminates. Oh, fuck! I'm caught!

I slowly turn around and look at the cute little girl struggling to sit up in her bed.

"You're not my brother," she says gazing at me. For some peculiar reason, she doesn't seem to be afraid. I stare at her beautiful warm blue eyes before I speak.

"Hi, I'm Zachary," I say approaching her bedside kind of wobbly at my knees. "I won't hurt you. I used to live in this flat. I just came to visit." I hope she believes that. I wouldn't if I was her. I'm perspiring through my hoodie. I sit hesitantly on her bed. Thank goodness, my feet have stopped tingling as they rest on the floor.

"Do you have the key to our flat?" she asks wide-eyed. Oh, Mother shit! What do I tell her?

"My mum used to keep a spare hidden in the building." The girl glances at my Spear. "This is one of my martial arts weapons. I like carrying it around with me. It's only for self-defense." I lay my Spear on the floor. The girl coughs a couple of times. My armpits drench even more so. I hope she doesn't call her parents or the police. I'd have to disappear immediately and I don't have the *Underground* coordinates programmed into my Spear, yet.

"What's your name?" I ask all friendly.

"I'm Clarissa," she says taking a swig from her water bottle.

"You're very pretty, Clarissa. How old are you?" She gently puts her water bottle back on her nightstand.

"I'm ten and I'm not pretty anymore," she says taking off her wig. Her head's completely bald. Her small action makes me nervous and ever so sad.

"You're still very pretty. What kind of cancer do you have?" She coughs a couple more times. She drinks some more before answering.

"I have leukemia. I'm not going to live very long," she says softly. "I hardly ever leave my flat. My immune system's not strong at all."

Oh, how I can relate to that.

"Leukemia is curable." I see her chemo port beneath the side of her neck.

"Not the kind I have. The doctors say I have only a twenty percent chance. I'm in hospice care now. I can't even go to the hospital. I'm definitely going to die."

I'm stunned upon her soft, unafraid words. That's so unfair. No, it's so fucking unfair!

I want to cry for this sweet little girl. Even without the wig, she's so cute. Clarissa puts her wig back on. Now she sneezes a couple of times. She grabs tissues from her nightstand and blows her nose.

"May Mother Earth bless you. How's Lady McPherson?" I say trying to change the subject. Clarissa doesn't seem to be afraid of death. She must have accepted it. I don't believe in God and don't believe in the Devil, but childhood cancer, if one has to believe, is the Devil's work at play.

"Thank you. Lady McPherson died last year. How long have you been away?" More fucking bad news. Now I wish I didn't choose London for the second test run. I shy my head away.

"Almost three years. I've known Lady McPherson since I was a baby. Literally." Clarissa waits a few moments before speaking.

"So you're the genius boy she always talked about," Clarissa says smiling. "I've heard so many stories of you! You're a doctor, too! Mrs. McPherson loved you."

Really? I thought she was afraid of me. She could never comprehend my brilliance. I don't know how much more sadness can wash through me.

"I'm not a medical doctor. I have double PhDs each in Physics and Astronomy."

"Wow! I always wished I could meet you! One of my wishes actually came true!" she says with glowing dark blue eyes. They shine like sapphires. They are not icy as before.

Now I'm happy that I chose London as my second test run. A part of me is angry that Clarissa will probably pass away within the next year. I don't know how I'm happy, sad, and angry all at the same time. This little girl's playing on my emotions telling me I made one of her wishes come true. She gazes at me like I'm sort of superhero. I wish she wouldn't do that.

"What else do you wish for?" Maybe if she wants something, I can get it for her.

"I don't want to die, but it will happen. I don't have very good odds," she says with acceptance leaning back into her pink pillow as she clutches onto her Ariel mermaid doll. I was hoping she wished for a game or something fun to play with. I start shaking within me. I don't want Clarissa to die. She didn't do anything to deserve her fate. Maybe I can change her destiny.

"I'm not going to let you die," I promise her.

Where the fucking fuck did that come from?

"I know a doctor that can cure you." What in the world am I doing? I can't take her to the *Underground* with me? Zenith will never allow it.

"No doctor in the world can cure me. That's what my parents were told."

"This doctor's kept very secret. The problem is that if I take you to him, you will never be able to see your family again."

Hello, Char! Shut the fuck up!

"Why?"

"I can't tell you. I've taken an oath to secrecy. You can never return, but you will live and can have a happy life." What am I saying all this to her for! Zachary, get a fucking hold of yourself!

"Will you be there? Is it where you live?" She looks ever so hopeful with her sapphire eyes pleading me.

"Yes, I will be there. There are a lot of special people that would take care of you."

Some force has taken over my mind.

Some force has taken over my soul.

"I'll think about it. Can I get your phone number?"

"You can't call me where I live. There's no signal from your phone, unfortunately. Clarissa, you can't tell anyone I was here. I work for the government now. You were supposed to be sleeping. Do you understand? This is a top secret classified mission."

"I understand Zach," she says nodding her head.

"Char."

"What?"

"My nickname is Char, not Zach."

"That's cool! It makes sense that you would have a special nickname," she says with a smile. There she goes again, idolizing me.

"I'm no more special than you are."

"That's not true. God gave you everything. I'm not special to him whatsoever," she says taking her wig off once more.

I want to cry at her words. I want to tell her that I don't believe in God. There is only our precious Mother Earth to believe in. I want to tell her that she's the cutest little girl I've seen, but I know she won't believe me. I have to get out of here before I become even sadder, if that's even possible.

"I have to go, Clarissa. May Mother Earth bless you with the sweetest dreams."

"Will you come back and visit? I like you Char," she says coordinating the wig back on top of herself. She has such a sweet disposition. I like you, too, Clarissa.

Unknowingly, I put my arms out. Clarissa crawls out of her bed and onto my lap. I give her a long hug. Her body's so frail and thin. At one point, I thought I would break her from my embrace.

"I will be back. I don't know when, but I'll be back to see you," I say kissing her forehead like a big brother would. I don't know what possessed me to do that either, but she didn't shun away from my affection. Clarissa crawls back into her bed. I pick up my Spear, turn off her lamp, and exit to the bathroom on the left. I input the coordinates back to my lab, and activate my Spear.

Soon enough, I find myself thrown into my lab chair.

"No, Honey, I'm home?" asks Kieran.

I shake my head as my tears hit the floor.

Chapter 6

September 1, 2015 @ 7:00am
Sector Four Apartments
Lovelin

I awake to the aroma of raspberry and spice. My Lord has gone, but an 18th century teacup sits on the nightstand. This dainty cup alone in its perfect porcelain of ivory and red has to be worth a fortune. I wonder if it was Jake's or Kaelyn's idea. Kaelyn's not a big fan of flavored tea; he sticks to *Darjeeling* and *Prince of Whales*. I take a sip without brushing my teeth. Just the perfect amount of sweetness. The *Underground* drones are amazing. Tea and coffee are always better in china than mugs and paper cups; the revolution of *Starbucks* is truly a nightmare. The *Underground* definitely has it all together.

The tea's divine as I try not to gulp it down, but savor it. I'm not doing a very good job. I finish my delicious tea and get out of bed.

Kaelyn knows exactly how to love me.

The marble beneath my feet immediately starts to heat. It's a luxury I'll never get used to. My toes are always happy. The soles of my feet die in joy every time they touch the floor.

All of me seems beyond happy down here.

All *Underground* inhabitants take so much for granted. If they only knew what *Surface* life was like. It's such a struggle to earn a living on the *Surface*. Struggles down here are of a different variety. I don't know which one is easier. I doubt it if there's an answer. What's the point of thinking about it anyway?

As I get up to start my day, the wall suddenly glows. We fell asleep to a soft, warm breeze and view of the Egyptian dessert. Kaelyn has beautiful aquariums and bowls filled with all sorts of colorful sand and white flowers in his apartment. He's more addicted to sand than I am. It's basically the only color in this place besides his black bedsheets. No designer on the *Surface* could have ever created a more perfect home for us.

The wall suddenly changes from its beautiful warm view to a stark, dark one. I didn't ask for this. I doubt it if Kaelyn's sending this. It's just not our style. I sit back and wrap myself around our black comforter again.

It's raining and very dreary upon the wall. I suddenly feel ever so cold in just my dark red camisole and underclothes although our comforter should keep me cozy. Grey clouds cover the entire sky as heavy tears fall from within them.

Mother Earth seems to be mourning someone.

There are hundreds walking wearily dressed in various shades of grey, dark blue, and black. There are hundreds of umbrellas covering their heads and faces. I can't seem to make out who they are or where they are going. What a sad scene. I can't understand why I'm witnessing this. I pull up the comforter to my neck believing it will shield me from all harm.

The grounds look like some sort of eerie park. There are beautiful fresh-cut flowers enamoring our Mother Earth. I see a white van.

I cannot make out what the writing on the van says. Two people come out of the van with umbrellas. They don't seem happy about all the rain and dampness.

"Jake, what's going on? On the wall?"

The images magnify in front of me. The van reads Channel 4 Action News. I still don't understand until she decides to get to work which is a while. Her make-up's running and that's more of a tragedy than the one she's supposed to broadcast.

"What can you tell the world about Lovelin Khan?" says the news reporter. Two people raise their heads with red and puffy eyes from underneath their umbrellas. Tears fall from them.

I know they've been falling for days. I can feel it in my heart. I can now feel it in my soul.

They look tired and dreary. It's Rave and Mickaela.

"You couldn't have had a better friend," says Mickaela through her endless tears. "I don't know how I'm ever going to be able to live without her." Mick holding Rave's hand squeezes it ever so tighter. Mick lays her head on Rave's shoulder. I now realize that she hasn't slept in days. I now shed tears with them.

"She was fun and caring and loving and everything you would want in a friend, in…in…a sister," says Rave through her sobs. "We could never get enough of her," says Rave trying not to fall apart. I sob violently with her. Suddenly, I miss them so much.

I've been so caught up in Kaelyn and my wonderful life down here that I haven't even thought about anything else since we came together. Guilt relishes throughout me making my heart ever so miserable. I never thought I would be so missed. I've been so wrapped up in my new life that I haven't even missed my past. I don't want to see this. I want to be selfish and turn this off, but a part of me grieves with them. If they only knew.

"She's with us though," says Mick. "I can feel it. She will always be with us." She looks up at the sky with her words.

"No, Mick, I'm here, sweetie," I say through my sobs. I tumble out of bed somehow and try to reach out for her. I touch her beautiful face softly with my fingertips upon the wall. The wall doesn't seem to mind. I kiss both their faces on the wall. "I'm alive and kicking. Not up there, but down below."

"Can you hear me, Love?" says Mickaela gazing at the dark grey sky as rainwater showers down upon her beautiful face. "I'm not going to do it. I promise I won't. I'm not going to do it, Love."

Oh, Mick, I'm so proud of you.

The sky darkens and raindrops shower harder.

"Look down, Mick! Look down!" I scream banging my fists on the wall. They walk away before me because the interview is over.

There's no coffin. There's no burial or cremation site. Hundreds enter the mausoleum and pray. There's no body or ashes to mourn. I sob throughout my entire funeral ceremony with all those that attended. Many fans that I wasn't even aware of, spoke, saying what beautiful escapes I brought to their world. My mother held Penelope as she said her prayers for my happiness in Heaven. Daddy fell to his knees as he covered his face with his hands as mom said her prayers.

That's when I fell apart. Daddy has always been my hero. That's what a Daddy is and he played the role perfectly throughout my life.

"STOP, JAKE, STOP," I scream. "WHY WOULD YOU DO THIS TO ME?" I yell beating my fists into the wall over and over again. "I'VE ONLY BEEN EVER SO GRATEFUL FOR YOU!"

"It wasn't I, Miss Lovelin," says Jake.

"THEN WHO THE FUCK WAS IT?" I cry, but the words barely come out of my mouth due to my anguish. I cry out for the loss of my family and friends. Not only my loss, but theirs.

Silence.

"I am learning. Forgive me for making you so distraught, but I'm not at liberty to say," he replies. I sob into the pillows on the bed. I wish Kaelyn was here. I need him so badly, but I refuse to burden him with my anguish. He has work of his own. He has an agenda down here and I'm not going to interfere with it.

The wall glows again. All the images disappear. Then one black sentence writes itself very slowly in the middle of the wall.

You don't belong here

September 1, 2015 @ 7:00pm
Sector Four Apartments
Kaelyn

This was not a *good what a day*.

It was a *fucked up, fucking miserable what a day*. A miserable day at the lab.

A disastrous day in general.

The only silver lining was waking up in Lovelin's arms. Now I can't wait to fall back into them. Only she will be able to take the weariness away.

I enter our apartment expecting some sort of delicious aroma to greet me.

Nothing.

The entire apartment's dark and silent. This is not what I'm used to coming home to since Lovelin moved in with me. I was expecting *Brass Monkey* to be blaring while she dances around the kitchen preparing our evening meal. Something's dreadfully wrong.

Overhead lights come on as I walk into the kitchen. The kitchen hasn't been touched. A fear goes through me. Maybe she had an accident! The worst thoughts rush into my head. I haste into our bedroom with the force of a hurricane, although a hurricane is calm and peaceful compared to what I feel. Lovelin's still in what she wore last night. She sleeps in a fetal position upon the comforter. She's scared and cold.

I run my fingers through her hair as I put her face up against mine and body up against me. Her eyes look swollen and red. It doesn't seem as though she has left the bed all day. What in the world happened?

"Love, Love, wake up!" I say shaking her. I cradle her in my arms. She stirs and then cries. "What is it, Lovely? What happened?" I say trying to get her to look at me.

"Jake," she says through her wet, closed eyes. "Show him." She then nuzzles into me and cries some more as I watch her funeral unfold.

When I see the words, I shake from anger. I kiss her head and tell her that she's home and that no one will ever harm her. She weeps, holds me tighter, and just nods in my chest.

My wrath will be painful, brutal, and exhausting. They will be begging me to put an end to their lives.

Chapter 7

September 2, 2015 @ 7:45am
Sector Nine - Male Dormitories
Christoph

Jay left me and hasn't come back, yet. I've been asking Jake for updates on Kato, but even Jake can't give me a definite answer about his condition. All I know is that he's still alive. All I know is that Kato's in distress. I don't know if I should go to class or not this morning. If I don't, I'll miss my geology exam. I was up until past midnight studying for it since I went to the movies with Jay and Lucinda yesterday evening. Lucinda's nice, but I'm sure she was disappointed. She wanted to be with Jay and got me instead.

I should go to the waterfall. Sal's all alone. I'm sure he's a total mess, too.

I press my wrist texting my professor if he will give me a pardon since my roommate had a terrible accident. I'm very much prepared, but if I can the take the exam later; whenever he wants me to. He relays that I need to take care of myself, my Sector Nine family, and can return to class when I'm ready. I knew he would understand. The *Underground* always understands.

I take the train to the Maintenance Section. I try to eat on the train, but nothing goes down my throat. Not even the buttery crispy chocolate danishes. I forcefully sip on mango juice to get some calories and energy into me.

45

I depart at Platform *Horizon* half walking, half running into the surveillance section where Sal is. There are dozens around him watching Kato's surgery on the screens before them. I walk over, push everybody aside, and curl up into Sal's lap. Nobody knows who I am since I don't interfere with Sal's work, although I can see from their expressions that they understand. I need my brother, Sal, today as he needs me. We don't say anything, but just hold each other for support.

"I should have come to get you, but I couldn't leave my post," Sal whispers to me. "I should have told Jake, but it's been so hard," says Sal in tears I've never seen before.

I know. I understand his role down here so I just nod.

Together we watch the horrors unfold.

And then we cry together.

And then we hold hands and pray to Mother Earth together.

September 2, 2015 @ 7:45am
Infirmary Operating Theater
Samantha Stonebridge

There were already half a dozen physicians trying to save Kato when I ran into the operating theater. Kato was immediately put on life support as a precaution. I see Grand Sister unfolding a mediblanket from Kato's chest as I rush in. His sight made me stop in my tracks. His exposed torso made me gasp. I can't move. I'm too shocked to cry. I could throw up, but I tell myself not to, for anything. I've never seen anything like the horror before me.

I stand paralyzed for a few minutes as Grand Sister coats his chest cavity with salve. He's just another patient, after all, to her. She's just going through the motions emotionless and concentrating on her work. Sauri always has it so together. I wish I could be more like her.

Everything seems to happen in slow motion in front of me. Kato's torso's completely open. I can see his heart, lungs, and ribcage; or at least what's left of his lungs. There's no way he could be breathing on his own. His hands are bloody and charred. Two other physicians attend to the third degree burns on his hands.

A couple of the other physicians immediately start mending his ruptured aorta with a laser. They fuse Kato's severed heart in an instant. That was the easy part. I finally get the courage and slowly approach the table. There are four 3D images around us. Kato's blood pressure has stopped dropping.

Grand Sister's applying massive amount of salve into what's left of Kato's lungs. Even I know cellular repair isn't going to work that fast on this kind of damage. They have bombarded nanites into his chest cavity for repair as well.

"What do you want me to do?" I whisper gazing at my brother's dying form.

"There are twelve charred bones in his frontal ribcage. They aren't completely broken, but apply *Magic Bone*. Maybe we can repair some of the chips and fragments. It may help on top of the nanites. *Smoke Guard* is already being applied through his I.V. line since there's no place to put patches on him," says Sauri.

I do as I'm told. Right as we start to reconstruct Kato's open chest cavity, he starts convulsing. The salve's not working like we hoped it would. The nanites can't work fast enough. He's body's going into shock. We all stand back and just watch. None of us know what to do.

"Jake! Call Kaelyn! He's needed in the O.T. immediately! We need help with reconstruction!" yells Grand Sister. I hold Kato's bandaged hand.

"Do something!" I scream. "We can't let him die!"

The others try to hold him down from falling off the surgical table. Instead of relying upon my colleagues, I run out of the operating theater to our pharmaceutical closet. I frantically rummage through each and every one of the drawers and cabinets hoping to find something that might help. Something that we may have overlooked.

Then in the back of one of the armoires, I find convulsion patches. I didn't know we even had such patches. The creation date says November 1999 on them. Nobody in the *Underground* has had a seizure or convulsion in years. I hope they still work. Our medicinal methods generally don't have an expiration date, but there's always a half-life we need to account for. I don't know what the life expectancy of these patches are, but I grab all of them anyway.

I sprint back into the O.T., Uncle Kaelyn's already there administering a grey liquid over Kato's chest cavity. I don't know what it is. I've never seen it before. Kato's still convulsing, but not as badly. I slap on six of the patches, three on each side of his torso with whatever room I could find. His convulsions stop after the sixth one. Thank goodness because there were only ten in total. His vital signs slowly stabilize.

After all that could be done to repair Kato's insides, it then takes two hours to reconstruct Kato's chest with an artificial skin graft. After the entire four-hour procedure, his breathing is present, but shallow. Blood pressure's stable. The worst seems to be over. Blood count levels are within normal limits.

Kato then gets transported into one of the infirmary's post-surgical rooms by medi-drones. The physicians decide on constant twenty-four-hour surveillance and care, and set up six-hour shifts amongst themselves. I want to help, but Sauri won't let me. She says my classes and lab work are more important for me. They can handle it. A tear falls down my cheek because I'm not wanted.

My Uncle Kaelyn puts his hands out and I crawl into them for the millionth time in my life. I softly sob in his strong arms.

"He's going to be just fine. Proud of you for not panicking. I know he's your friend. Those convulsion patches helped. Even I forgot they were there and I rarely forget anything. I'll teach you how to make more. I created them before you were even born."

"I'm so drained," I say holding on to my Uncle's neck.

"I'm so proud of you, Sam, and a bit jealous, too," he says cradling me tighter. "You may have saved him, not me."

"That's the most preposterous, fucked up, ridiculous thing I've ever heard! I know you're just saying that to get me to stop crying!"

"I can't pull one over you, can I?" I don't want to laugh, but a small giggle with tears escapes my mouth.

"I've never had a simulation exercise like that before. Maybe the simulator is better than cadavers. I'm going to start programming all sorts of scenarios hoping they will never happen, but if they do, we can be better prepared," I say through my sobs. My Uncle kisses my forehead.

"Well done, Dr. Stonebridge. Well done," he says cradling me.

September 2, 2015 @ 8:00am
Mid-Section Waterfall
Sophia Cambridge

Although religion isn't forbidden in the *Underground*, nobody believes in it. It's truly a man-made stupid entity to bring about our homo sapiens dark side. An avenue to segregate Mother Earth's children for no reason. A reason to fight over our inner turmoils.

In the *Underground*, we do not segregate ourselves down here as humans on the *Surface* do. We are one community born on Mother Earth. It doesn't matter what part of Mother Earth we come from. We may look different on the outside, but we are all made of the same flesh and blood on the inside.

We consider ourselves slaves to Mother Earth and slaves to each other in our own community. We do not rely upon a higher entity that we can't see to salvage our wants and desires.

We pray to Mother Earth and we pray for our people to show we care and love when times are in utter distress.

Today is one of those most needed times.

There were already many gathered at the Mid-Section waterfall by the time we arrived. There were already a hundred rose petals or more swimming around in the little lagoon at the bottom. Each rose petal a prayer for Kato's health and life. I know most of the Maintenance crew and wait staff don't personally know Kato, but they're here this morning sending well-wishes his way.

A little girl kisses a yellow petal before her throwing it to the waterfall. "Please, Mama Earth, may he come to no harm. Whatever he did, he did it for you." Tears fall from all around as we hear her words. I don't know who this little girl is. She doesn't live in Sector Nine. She probably lives in Sector Six or Eleven with her family. She couldn't have said it any truer.

There are two flower shops in the *Underground*. One is Fancy Florals and the other is Forget-Me-Not. Both have been incredibly busy with the upcoming wedding. Many of the flowers are grown in the *Underground* greenhouses. Many are also brought from the *Surface* if needed.

Today, drones have been sending all the roses and lilies in supply from both shops to the waterfall upon hearing the level one trauma emergency.

Ari and Zen pull yellow and pink petals from two of the roses. Jay plucks from a red one. They all get down on their knees and say a prayer before tossing their petals into the lagoon.

There is no Lord of Death. There is no Lord of Life. There is no higher entity beyond Mother Earth. There is only us, the children of Mother Earth. We pray to you, our Mother, to salvage our brother today, to bring melody and harmony to our souls.

The three souls hug each other as the petals wash away into the swirling water down the basin.

I take the longest stemmed white rose I can find to the waterfall. I kiss every petal and say my prayer. I don't ask Mother Earth for Kato's health or for his life. I only ask her for his comfort. I only ask to give him a world without pain and suffering. I then throw the entire rose to the waterfall, stem and all. I don't leave until it is devoured by the beautiful swirls of blue and green.

"You love him, don't you?" says the little girl that said her sweet prayer earlier.

"What good is my love if it can't save him?" I say with tears falling from my eyes. She takes my hand in hers.

"Love conquers all," says the little girl. "Not wishes or prayers."

September 2, 2015 @ 8:30am
Rainforest
Lovelin

There's no church in the *Underground*. There's no chapel either. There's no mosque, no synagogue, no temple, no place of worship. Kaelyn says all that they worship is Mother Earth. We are all one and the same with our one true Mother.

This morning I know this is definitely where I belong.

Kaelyn takes the *Range Rover* to the Rainforest waterfall. When he found out it was Kato that was in serious trauma, he was completely distraught. I asked him why he doesn't go and help, but he explained that he's not a part of the surgical teams as he was as a child and young adult. Zenith wants him only working for himself. There are other physicians to take care of emergencies.

Kaelyn told me how Kato found Loopy. He told me how Kato helped him in a time of need when he didn't even have to. Kaelyn told me that Kato's a special boy. I think everybody's special down here. That's why they are down here and not above.

"We don't throw money for wishes like *Surface* people, since we have none down here." I don't say anything, but just listen.

"Money is materialistic. It's man's evil device. How's it supposed to grant you wishes?" he says picking two of the largest, brightest hiscasuckle flowers from a bush. He hands me one. "It's not Mother Earth's way. It's not our way."

We are at the top of the waterfall looking down into the lagoon. It's misty and not too hot this time of morning. Kaelyn gets on his knees. I do the same beside him. I don't know what he says, but I can see his lips quiver as they softly mumble a prayer. He then throws the flower into the waterfall.

There is no Lord of Death. There is no Lord of Life. There is only us, the children of Mother Earth. We pray to you, our benevolent Mother, to salvage our souls.

It's a beautiful cascading descent down to its death.

A sacrifice.

One soul for another.

I say my prayer to Mother Earth for this young brilliant boy. I pray for his health and happiness and prosperity. I wish I knew him better. I pray that I will get a chance to know him better. I kiss the flower before throwing it to the waterfall.

Kaelyn told me that all go to the Mid-Section waterfall for well-wishes. I've come to realize that that's their place for celebration and prayer. It's not some man-made building for comfort and solace, but nature's way; Mother Earth's way for comfort and solace. The waterfall is Mother Nature's temple of worship. It's a place of forever peace and sanctuary.

We just hold each other looking as our flowers tumble and swirl around in the lagoon. They look like they are dancing with one another until they disappear below.

The flowers dance with one another to their deaths.

"Dr. Stonebridge, you are needed immediately in the operating theater," says Jake. "Dr. Park is in ultimate distress and everyone is asking for your immediate assistance."

Kaelyn releases me immediately. "Let's go!"

We can't get into the *Range Rover* fast enough. Kaelyn drives like a complete maniac through the jungle terrain. I wish I had a second seat belt. I've never seen him like this. He's always so respective of the Rainforest. It's his place of worship. It's his home. It's a part of our benevolent Mother Earth. He parks upon the little pond that holds his cancer-curing agents. I don't get out of the jeep, but I see him scoop up from the pond with his hands and return.

"Hold them!" he commands me. "Don't let them slip away!"

I cup the two tiny creatures into my hands. They squirm and fight trying to flee away from me. "Kato doesn't have cancer."

"I know, but they have regenerating properties. It's a shot in the dark," he says driving through the lush jungle before us disrupting all its foliage and all its inhabitants.

I hear a squeal crying from them as they try to squeeze through my fingers for freedom.

"They hate being out of the water for so long. They need the hydrogen from the water to breathe," he says rushing back to his laboratory. "Hold them tight!"

"They'll die without the water then. I don't want to crush them and make it worse."

"Love, they are going to die anyway. I need their blood to try to save Kato."

The creatures cry and squeal some more upon his words. My teardrops fall onto the creatures in my hands.

A sacrifice of a soul to save a soul.

Chapter 8

September 1379 BC
A little village in Egypt
Maya

"Baba." He doesn't look up at me. He's engrossed in his work as usual. He's trying to decipher something. He has such a puzzled expression on his aging face. His forehead has a dozen creases in them. I see him writing figures on parchment. I don't understand what it says. I wish I understood what it says. All I know is that those are figures and not symbols or pictures.

"Baba!" He's too lost in thought. I hope I don't lose my pregnancy temper. I adore my father-in-law.

Amir and his brother know how to read pictures and do figures. Fatima was insistent that she learn everything. She always had a passion and fascination for learning. She has learned so much on her own without the help of the men. She's even trying to devise her own writing method. She has such a phobia when it comes to domestic work. She should have been born a boy. Mina and I were never taught. Mama and Mother say it's not necessary for a girl. Our work's in the kitchen and tending to family. Our work's at home, where the heart is.

I wait standing for my Father to notice me. I'm five months in term and look larger than a camel. How he doesn't realize I'm in front of him is beyond me. I must be taking up more than half the room. I clear my throat loudly. My Father looks up. His face goes from a frown to an instant smile and then to a frown again.

"Maya, everything all right? The little ones?" he says with a worried look on his face. I've never bothered my Father before while he's working.

"Everything's fine, Baba. I've come to ask for a favor."

"What is it sweet child?" He puts his ink and parchment away.

"I want you to teach me how to read and write." My Baba has even a larger puzzled look on his face than the one from just a few moments ago. His forehead is creasing ever more.

"Whatever for?" he questions.

"I want to pass the story of my children to others." I leave no other explanation.

"What story? The little ones aren't even here, yet."

"Baba, please. Teach me!" I plead. My Father sighs. Everybody knows I've become more irritable as my babies grow.

"Maya, when will I have the time? Reading and writing cannot be learned overnight. You are older now. It will be difficult for you."

"Please, Baba. I will then in turn teach my children." He contemplates a while and then nods his head.

"Very well, come here. Let's start."

September 2, 2015 @ 7:30am
Cloning Laboratory
David

"He's beautiful, David. Can you tell?" says Kaiser looking at the computer screen. The artificial chamber is completely dark but there's a camera within it. The little boy swims around in the artificial amniotic sac. His picture on the monitor is a happy one.

He's going to grow up to be one ugly mother fucker is all I think. Maybe the *Underground* barber will do a better job with him this time around.

What if he doesn't turn out the way Zenith wants?" I ask.

"Of course, he will. We know his leadership skills. Zenith will channel him in the right direction this time. Millions still will follow. He cannot fail with Zenith behind him."

"He's still at least twenty years in the making."

"Quit being such a pessimist! What's gotten into you?" says Kaiser slapping me at the side of my head. I want to slap his head back, but keep my composure.

I don't know what's gotten into me. Maybe Zareen's death still haunts me. The day of her roses ceremony, almost everyone that lives in the *Underground* was at the waterfall at some point in the day. Her beautiful face was displayed on the three large screens by the waterfall. The one with Barney and Dorry was my favorite. She was genuinely happy. So many were distraught by the accidental tragedy. Zareen had so much potential and so much to live for.

I haven't been sleeping well at night. I haven't been with my usual girlfriends lately. My life in the *Underground* has changed.

I don't know if I was cut out for this project. Cloning was supposed to bring out different ramifications.

Not widespread death.

I don't know if I want to be a part of ending a significant portion of the world's population. I have to admit I'm all for population control. I just don't know if mass destruction is the way to go. This time it's not about religion.

This time it will be on a more global scale. Unfortunately, it is necessary according to world figures. Our Mother Earth's already beyond capacity. Yes, it's the right thing to do. Zenith knows what it's doing.

"I'm the Father and you're the Mother, understand?" I say looking at Kaiser. I've been trying to decipher this section of Kaelyn's report on Loopy for the last hour.

"What?"

"Yes, I don't do doody duty and I'm definitely no fucking wet nurse. You either raise him yourself or get Zenith to bring a mother down here," I say staring at my boss. Kaiser doesn't have the strength to beat me. I can put him over my shoulder and throw him into the *Fathoms Above Fitness* pool in a heartbeat. I'm expecting a screaming competition. I've never spoken to him in such a tone before.

"Hmm, you're right. I have a hard enough time disciplining Harvey. I'll talk to Zenith."

He doesn't want to fight me.

"Be quick about it," I say boldly. "He doesn't have much time until his birth. What does the chamber say?"

"Forty-five days, three hours, seventeen seconds."

"Well, you better do something by then or you'll be up with a screaming baby and numerous nighttime feedings.

"How do you know he will be a screaming baby?"

"He was a fucking screaming madman in his older years. I'm sure he was quite the terror as a child."

Kaiser looks at me with horror in his eyes. He presses his wrist and calls the President. "Hello, Dr. Shue. Everything going according to plan?"

"Yes, Sir. I do have one favor to ask you."

"Anything."

"I need a mother for our project."

"Zenith has been interviewing. We're sending one to you before his arrival."

Barney covers his eyes with his paws.

"I'm hungry!" squawks Dorry.

Chapter 9

September 3, 2015 @ 8:30am
Underground Infirmary
Samantha Stonebridge

Before starting classes this morning, I checked on Kato at the infirmary. I could hear Sophia softly sobbing throughout the night. At 2am when I couldn't take it anymore, I left my bed, crawled under her covers, and just held her. She was asleep within minutes. I finally slept as well.

Sophia asked if she could go with me this morning, but the other surgeons won't allow any visitors right now. Not until Kato awakens. We're keeping him unconscious until his severed aorta and lungs heal further. The blast did so much internal damage. We all hope he can recover from the extensive burns within him. He has a fifty-fifty chance of survival right now. I tell Sophia his prognosis looks hopeful and not to worry. He's my number one priority.

Kato's not kept in the twelve-bed infirmary, but in a post-surgical room. It's a single, private, glass-encased room. We have six of these rooms. They are more sterile than the infirmary itself. I walk towards this section and see Kato in Room One. I can see Dr. Rossie attending to him. I love Dr. Rossie. She's our number one Veterinarian down here. I've learned so much from her. She changes one of Kato's hydration patches. There's someone in Room Six.

That's odd. Nobody else was here last night.

I walk down the hall to check who's in Room Six. The glass door says "Dr. Zachary Briarwood - Quarantine." Quarantine! That hardly ever happens in the *Underground*. I can see he's sleeping. There's water and a box of tissue on his night stand.

In quarantine, only smaller medi-drones fly in and out within a retracting glass window with whatever the patient needs. This is to minimize contamination. It's usually just meals and medicine. I wonder who Char's physician is. There's nobody at the computer console in the adjacent room where Zachary is monitored. I walk in and check the screens. Dr. Kieran Mersa admitted him.

His heart rate's steady. His bronchial tubes and nasal cavity show some congestion. His sinuses don't look completely clear either. I exit the monitoring room and head for Room Six. I shouldn't go in, but I do. I sprayed *Surgical Mist* all over myself before leaving my dwelling. It should give me a few minutes protection.

"Char?" I say approaching his bed. His eyes flutter open. He squints towards my direction. "Sam? You shouldn't be here. I don't want to get you sick."

"What's wrong with you? How'd you get like this?" I ask not coming any closer.

"I have the common cold."

"Hello, Char, but the common cold is not common in the *Underground*. How in the world did you get sick?" I question as I hesitantly approach his bed. I sit at the foot of his bed. He shoves his palm out telling me not to get any nearer.

"I can't tell you Sam. It's classified," he says staring at the ceiling. "You really should go. I don't want you to catch this. It's no fun. Our immune systems are really compromised living down here."

"Yes, I know. I'm a medical doctor, remember?" He just stares at the ceiling. "Char, I promise I won't tell anyone. You have my word. Zenith will never find out if that's what you're scared of. You can trust me." He still stares at the ceiling. Then he sits up in his bed.

"I got sick from a little girl." I think about that for a while.

"Which little girl? I don't know of any sick little girl in the *Underground*," I say all confused.

"She doesn't live in the *Underground*. She lives in London." Char's soaking up the expression on my face. My jaw must be sitting on the bed right now.

"You went to London? When? How? Does Zenith know? You left the *Underground*? Are you fucking crazy?" I must have said all that at lightning speed. I hope Char got it all.

"Yes, Zenith knows," is all he says. I gesture with my hand for him to continue. "Kieran and I have discovered teleportation." I stare at him completely speechless. Now I know my jaw is on his bed. My stomach feels like it took a dive bomb to the floor.

"You can teleport! No fucking way! How? How? Tell me everything!" I scream.

"Keep your voice down, Sam," Char whispers looking all the way to Room One where Dr. Rossie still is.

Jay now sits in a chair next to Kato holding his hand. I don't know when he walked in. He's looks my way with red eyes and the saddest expression. "It's by Spear and it's a long story. When I get better, I'd rather show you. It's complicated." I turn my eyes away from Jay.

"Where else have you been?" I say all excited.

"My first journey was to Washington. I visited the President of the United States," he says smiling and winking at me. I scream, laugh, and clap my hands all at the same time.

"Zenith has to be loving it! This is exactly what we are meant to do!" I say more than exuberantly.

"Yeah, they are extremely excited. My second trip was to my old flat in London. A part of me still misses my life on the *Surface*. That's where I met Clarissa. She's ten and has an incurable leukemia. I got sick from her." Char's saddened upon mentioning her name.

"Char, that's awful. How so sad for her." He just nods. Then all of a sudden, he starts rambling.

"I want to bring her the *Underground*. I want your Uncle Kaelyn to cure her! She's so sweet, Sam. I know you'd like her if you meet her. She has a pretty smile and a cute perky nose. She doesn't deserve this!"

Char's all emotional over this little girl. He's no longer the insecure, shy boy I had lunch with the other day. Something's changed him. He seems more confident and even more mature than just a few days ago. I guess when you discover teleportation, confidence grows within yourself.

"Childhood cancer is not fair, Char, but Zenith will never allow it. That's not our mission down here."

"I know, I know, but I have to be able to find a way to convince them or maybe I won't tell them at all and just do it!"

He's all hostile.

"How can they punish me? I have all the secrets to teleportation that they want!"

Wow! Char's really changed. Nobody dare goes against Zenith. I then think about what Dr. Kai-af and Uncle Kaelyn told me about their own dreams. What Zenith doesn't know won't hurt them. I think about it.

"You should do it, Char! You have my full support. She'll never be allowed to return, but she'll be alive. I'm sure her family would be willing to sacrifice her presence for her life." Char relaxes in his bed.

"Thank you, Sam. You're a true friend." I smile at him.

What Zenith doesn't know won't hurt them.

"Char, will you do me a favor? Once you're out of here."

"Of course, Sam, name it."

"It requires a trip to Egypt?" I say hesitantly.

I didn't know anybody could smile so wide.

September 3, 2015 @ 8:45am
Infirmary
Jay Ahmed

Why's Sam so happy? My brother and best friend's dying and she's all smiles. She's making me angry. She's making me beyond angry. Doesn't she have any consideration? What's she doing with Zachary anyway? I didn't know they were friends. He's a physicist. They don't have anything in common.

I guess she has moved on.

The other night at the waterfall, I thought her sweet caress in my hair was telling me something. She's obviously a great actress and only did that so I couldn't say no to her request to help her. Jay, you're such an idiot! I wonder if Zenith programmed the acting abilities into her.

She laughs and claps her hands screaming like a monkey although I can't hear her through all the glass between us. What in the world has gotten into her? I look away from her. Kato lays motionless. His breathing's incredibly shallow. He has oxygen and hydration patches on him. Something erupts within me.

"Dr. Rossie, go home. You've been here for hours."

"Thanks, Jay. Missed you in the O.T. yesterday, but everyone understood. Samantha was great. She acted like a true physician and was all business."

She's not acting great today. She's acting like a complete fucking moron.

"I'll be back tonight. I'm going to stay on as his nighttime physician. Dr. Khalid will be in this afternoon. Call him if you need any help." I say my thanks as Dr. Rossie leaves. I check all of Kato's vitals. I add another oxygen patch on Kato's chest as Sam walks in.

"How is he?" I want to say 'What's it to you? Go back to your new boyfriend', but I don't.

"Stable," I say quite harshly.

"Are you upset with me, Jay?" She walks over to Kato and holds his hand. I don't say anything for a while. I don't want to start a fight.

"What's with you and Zachary?" You two look like you've been best friends for years."

"Really, Jay? You're jealous?"

"No, I'm not jealous," I lie. "It's just that I've never seen you with him before."

"Do you know how incredible he is, Jay? He makes me feel stupid. He's going to help us."

"Help us? What do we need his help for? For what? Kato? He's a physicist, not a physician!"

Sam then goes on to explain how he discovered teleportation and his trip to Washington and London, and then how he got sick. She says he's going to teleport to Egypt and bring back the archeologist and scrolls. Zenith wants him to travel the world to test out the Spear anyway.

He wouldn't be going against their orders except for the fact that he will be bringing the archeologist back with him. Minor detail. What Zenith doesn't know won't hurt them. I sat completely dumbfounded through her entire speech.

"No way! I can't wait to see this Spear!"

"Me, too! I don't know which is more remarkable, Uncle Kaelyn finding the cure for cancer and his creations, or Char's teleportation method." Even I have to agree that's a tough one.

They are both so different. They are both so special.

"I'm sorry, Sam. When I saw you clapping and laughing while my brother's in here fighting for his life, I kind of blew up inside me. I was so mad at you for such inconsideration." I shamefully bow my head. I should have known better than to think Sam doesn't care. She was even here before I was this morning.

"Jay, I'm sorry, too. It's just so exciting and I couldn't contain myself. I know Kato's your brother, but he's my friend. I'd like to consider him as my brother, too. We are all miserable about what happened. None of us slept last night. I'm sure you didn't either. Sophia's still crying."

"I took a melatonin for the first time in my life. It knocked me out. It was either that or three beers."

"I would have taken the beers."

Chapter 10

September 3, 2015 @ 8:00am
Sector Two - Design Studio
Sophia Cambridge

I want to make him outshine the groom. I shouldn't but I want to. Would it be wrong? Guess what? I don't care!

Kato could walk into the *Underground* Ballroom in ripped jeans and a stained lab coat and still outshine all the other men.

'Dress you up in my love' comes to mind.

"Chaz, Tara, give me an incredible outfit for a young man. Not something suitable for a prince or groom. It needs to be above and beyond all that. I'm so distraught I cannot think today."

My drones come over and hug me from both sides. I didn't know they were capable of doing that. I can sense that they actually feel my pain, but that can't be right. They are just reacting to my words.

"How tall?" asks Tara.

"Six feet"

"Weight?" questions Chaz.

"One hundred eighty pounds?" I think. My drones frown. "He's not fat. That's pure muscle." They fly around the room talking in whispers to each other.

"Jake," says Chaz. "Please bring up Dr. Kato Park's measurements." I look completely in awe at my drone.

"How did you know?" Tara flies in front of me.

"Of course, we know, Miss Sophia," she says. "We were designed for you."

September 3, 2015 @ 8:00pm
Infirmary - Room One
Kaelyn

Jay sits in a small golden leather chair with his head on Kato's infirmary bed. Kato's not completely lying flat, but raised a bit. I can understand why Jay wasn't in class and at work today. I don't know how I'm going to tell him that he can't live here until his roommate wakes up.

If he ever wakes up.

I told all the surgical physicians to keep him in a constant state of unconsciousness until his insides heal more.

If they heal more.

Kato's lungs were seventy percent burnt and his aorta severed upon the blast. The other physicians were able to mend his heart to stop the bleeding, but the explosion took out too much of his lungs. I was summoned yesterday evening for help. All ten of the attending surgeons were desperate to save this boy. He's one of us, after all.

When I first saw Kato on the operating table, even I was at a loss what to do. His lungs weren't working much. The surgical team kept him on artificial life support. Some artificial organs are still in its final stages according to the biomedical engineering team. Many have been perfected. Their works on lungs aren't self-functioning, yet.

After extracting blood from my creatures, rather than using an I.V. line, I directly administered it all over Kato's lungs. I don't know if his lung cells will regenerate and grow. It's a long shot.

I've never used my creatures this way before.

Zenith said to do whatever it takes. Replacing him will not be easy.

They have no idea. Kato's more Saint than Savior in my book.

I check Kato's vitals. He looks stable. His lungs haven't changed much. Only two percent according to the computer. At least it's a step in the right direction.

"Dr. Stonebridge," asks Jay raising his head from the bed. "He hasn't moved one bit all day."

I wonder when Jay ate last. His eyes are red and his face hollow. "That's good. He can't heal if he's exerting himself. He won't mend overnight. It will be days, Jay, maybe weeks. His lungs were badly destroyed." Jay puts his head down on the bed once more and reaches placing his hand on Kato's heart.

"I wish I could do something. How about a lung transplant? I could give him one of mine."

I don't believe I have ever heard more loving words. If Michael were in this situation, what would I do? Would I offer a lung to him? It sickens me not to be able to answer my own question.

"Let's just wait and see what happens. Hopefully, it won't have to come to that." Jay just stares at Kato's sleeping form. "Excuse me for a moment." Jay doesn't even realize I have left the room.

I walk down the hallway into Room Five and call Samantha from my wrist. She's studying and I tell her to come to the infirmary to take care of Jay whether she wants to or not. He hasn't eaten all day. I would do it myself, but I need to get home to Lovelin. I walk back into Kato's room and tell Jay that he needs to return to work and class by tomorrow afternoon. It would be better for him to keep himself occupied. He sadly nods his lying head.

September 3, 2015 @ 8:30pm
Room One - Infirmary
Kaelyn

"Any improvements?" asks Sam sauntering in.

She bloody well took her sweet fucking time getting here!

"Not really. I'll stay here until Dr. Rossie arrives. You take Jay to eat. He's dehydrated and needs nourishment." Samantha nods her head.

"C'mon, Jay," Sam says helping him up from his chair. "You heard Uncle. Don't bother arguing with the big boss."

Sam knows me all too well. I can't understand why I hear such sarcasm in her voice. Maybe I'm hearing things. Jay reluctantly gets up from the bed as Sam reluctantly tends to him. She doesn't look worried and shows no sign of sympathy for Jay. I've rarely ever been annoyed with Sam, but this evening she's making my blood boil. The thought crosses my mind that Jay's too good for her and he's better off without her.

I look at Kato's sleeping form. I was never a praying man, but I did pray for this young man today. He reminds me of myself at his age; all full of ambition, longing and desperate to change the world for the better. I run my fingers through his silky black hair. He's one of Zenith's children just like myself. He found my Loopy, and was shattered to pieces when he believed she had died. He didn't even have to help at the Rainforest that night, but came because he was worried.

And I never even knew him, just vaguely aware of who he was.

I'll never be able to do enough for this boy. He's all caring not only about his own work, but the work of all others as well. I bow my head.

His selflessness puts me to shame.

September 3, 2015 @ 8:30pm
Ten Thousand Leagues Café and Bakery
Jay Ahmed

"Eat, Jay," Sam says spooning lemon rice soup into her mouth. She doesn't bother looking at me, but just into her crystal bowl. "You need to keep up your strength. Starving yourself won't make Kato recover any faster."

Should I tell her I have basically stopped eating because of her? Adding Kato to the mix isn't going to change much. I do as she tells me anyway. I can barely taste the soup I once so loved. I just go through the motions.

Samantha slams her golden spoon down and asks the drone for chicken kabobs and rice. She's mad about something. She's been scowling at me all evening. She didn't say one word to me the entire train ride here. I don't know why she's bothering to have dinner with me if she doesn't want to. I could have had dinner brought to the infirmary if Uncle Kaelyn wanted me to eat.

I've got to stop thinking of him as my Uncle.

"Are you mad at me?" I ask with a sneer. "What did I do now? Is mourning for my brother pissing you off?"

"No, mourning for OUR brother is not pissing me off," she says all annoyed. This time she's shouting in my face. Some people around us glance our way.

"What is it then?" I say trying to eat my soup. She doesn't say anything for a while slumped back into her chair.

"How was it in bed with Lucinda?" she says in rather a loud voice staring directly at me crossing her arms. Now most of the others around us stop eating and talking and glare towards us.

Fuck! So that's it. She knows.

"I took Christoph with me to the *Holoplex*, Sam. He watched the movie between us," I say in a low voice. "Lucinda and I are just friends."

"I really don't care, Jay. It was just a question to make conversation. Seems like you've had an interest in her for some time since it didn't take long for you to move on."

She's the one that broke up with me and she's complaining? She sounds mad and jealous. I wish I knew what's going on in that super brain of hers. Just yesterday, I had her in my arms sitting in the train comforting me. Just this morning, she was telling me about Char and his teleportation method. She seemed happy with me and still included me in all aspects of her life. Now if she had a chance, I bet she would kill me.

"Well, if you don't care and it's just your way of making conversation, then the bed was very comfortable," I say smirking at her. "Very comfortable!" Maybe I didn't need to emphasize the comfort part, but I'm upset with her for no longer caring.

Between Samantha and Kato, I don't know if I can cry anymore. I feel as though all of my reserve has left my body and then some. No wonder I'm so dehydrated.

Samantha's food arrives. She just stares at it for a while before taking a forkful of rice into her mouth. She doesn't say anything further and refuses to make eye contact with me. I get up from the table to leave.

"Thanks for dinner, Sam," I say throwing my napkin on the table.

"Don't thank me. Thank my Uncle. He made me," she says stuffing chicken into her mouth.

And when I didn't think I could possibly be more miserable.

September 3, 2015 @ 8:00pm
Infirmary - Room One
Samantha Stonebridge

I can't believe Uncle Kaelyn called me to feed Jay. I'm not going to be his fucking babysitter! He's a big boy. Let him take care of himself. Let Lucinda take care of him. That's what I wanted to tell my Uncle, but I didn't. If Uncle Kaelyn only knew the gossip traveling through the grapevine. I bet he doesn't know that Jay and Lucinda are a couple now. At least that's what I heard. Lucinda has been telling everyone what a great time she had with Jay and that they'll be going out again soon. It sure didn't take him that long to find a replacement for me.

I can't believe it! That pretty little blonde doesn't even have a fraction of my brain!

At the infirmary, I could see that Jay was all bent out of shape over Kato. A part of me felt miserable looking at Kato's lifeless form. If that were any of my roommates lying there, I probably would have looked worse. I get Jay up not for myself or Uncle Kaelyn, but for Kato. I know he would want me to take care of his brother in times like this. If Uncle Kaelyn only knew, he would have summoned Lucinda, not me.

I had a pretty bad day myself apart from Kato's tragedy. I had to put a little pug down today. He was old and suffering from pain. I need to come up with a way to create a longer lifespan for our precious pets. I should put a word into Zenith that it should be one of our missions. The little pug looked at me with his big brown eyes pleading for help, and what the fuck did I do?

I killed him.

Mercy killings are awarded according to the *Underground* inhabitants and Zenith. Lifelong pain and suffering is not a way to live, whether above or below the *Surface*. I wanted to see it that way, but today I couldn't. I felt like a failure again. I didn't want to take my miserable day out on Jay, but I did.

He told me he and Lucinda are just friends. I didn't know he had taken Christoph with him on his date. Lucinda seemed to conveniently leave that part out when telling everybody about her amazing time with Jay. Apparently, they shared nachos. Their fingers touched every so often. I don't know what to believe. All I know is that he was the one that asked her out. If I really mattered to him, he wouldn't have asked her. That's my theory.

Jay left me eating alone. He has never done that before. Our fingers never touched one another while eating before. He has no right to be upset. I'm not the one asking other guys to go to the movies with me. Maybe I should. Maybe I should give him a taste of his own medicine, but then again, why would it matter? It's over between us. I have to get on with my life.

I finish the entire plate of chicken and rice by myself. I'm not going to let anything or anyone let me down anymore.

I'm Samantha Skylark Stonebridge after all. Zenith's golden child. I slam the fork into my plate.

Chapter 11

September 4, 2015 @ 7:00am
Sector Four Apartments
Kaelyn

Already up and dressed sprinting for the door, Lovelin grabs me across my waist from behind. She was sleeping so soundly earlier that I didn't want to wake her. Her days writing her latest novel, playing with the children, and cooking keep her incredibly busy. This morning, her body in her black camisole and white laced panties against my back is making me lose every one of my senses. We both wore just our necklaces to bed last night.

"I hate it when you run away from me," she says burrowing her entire body into me a bit further. "At least you could have woken me up to let me know you're leaving." I know I shouldn't, but some force overtakes my body, not my head and I turn around and kiss her fully on the mouth. She smells like hiscasuckle flowers. I'm at peace once again.

"I didn't want to wake you, Love." That wasn't a complete lie. I knew if I had woken her, we would be tumbling in the sheets and I wouldn't be able to get any work done this morning.

"Do you want breakfast?" she says kissing my nose. It wasn't a soft kiss, but a wet kiss. This woman is a demon dressed like an angel.

"No, I need to get to the lab. I'll eat on the train," I say completely out of breath. That was a lie. Lovelin's breakfasts have already put ten pounds on me and I need to stop eating for at least the next few days.

She looks up at me with the naughtiest look, washes her fingers through my hair, and kisses me. I don't know how she does it, but her kisses set my soul on fire. I hold her tightly around her waist for support, otherwise I'll be on my knees before I know it. My mind tells me I need to get to work, but my body tells me I need to take her back to bed.

Jake makes the decision for me.

"Attention, all surgical teams. Severe level one trauma emergency in the infirmary, post-surgical Room One, life support failing. I repeat, attention, all surgical teams. Severe level one trauma emergency in the infirmary, post-surgical Room One, life support failing."

Lovelin and I look at each other. Kato.

"Oh, no!" Lovelin whispers. She releases, pushing me away. "Go save him, Kaelyn!"

September 4, 2015 @ 7:00am
Sector Nine - Female Dormitories
Samantha Stonebridge

Zen's playing When You Wish Upon A Star on her harp. This morning I need her to play her drums and her electric violin both at the same time. I can't seem to wake up and get motivated. Maybe a cold shower would help. I snuggle under the covers as

Chika sleeps in my tummy. I have no desire to get out of bed. I can hear Sophia in her washroom. She purposely stays super busy with the wedding attire. Thank goodness there's going to be a wedding soon. A spark of happiness. Sophia's work keeps her mind off of Kato. Ari's up getting ready for class. She has to work tonight at the bakery although she doesn't consider it work, but playtime.

"Attention, all surgical teams. Severe level one trauma emergency in the infirmary, post-surgical Room One, life support failing. I repeat, attention, all surgical teams. Severe level one trauma emergency in the infirmary, post-surgical Room One, life support failing."

I go numb upon Jake's words at first. I can't seem to move or get out of my bed although I desperately need to. I hear Sophia's anguish from her washroom. Zen and Ari rush over to console her. I know Jay hears this announcement as well as all of the other *Underground* inhabitants. His brother's dying and he believes he's too weak to save him. That thought gets me out of my trance.

I hastily get out of bed tripping to my closet. Fuck my hair! I brush my teeth, throw on surgical scrubs over my pajamas, spray myself, and I'm out the door.

September 4, 2015 @ 7:00am
Infirmary - Room Six
Zachary Briarwood

Jake's announcement wakes me. I get up from my bed and look over to Room One. I cup my face and peer through the glass wall squinting to see what's going on. Although there are four other glass-encased surgical rooms between us, I can see Kato convulsing. Dr. Rossi's at a loss what to do.

I want to leave my room to help, but I can't. Infecting him even with the common cold could kill him. I wouldn't be much use anyway. I'm just a physicist, not a physician. I press my wrist and call Samantha. Even though I still live in Sector Eleven, I was given wrist technology because I am one of Zenith's scientists. Sam has to be up with the announcement.

"You have to fly like a windstorm, Sam! He's convulsing like I've never seen!" Dr. Rossi places a mediblanket on Kato's chest. I can't tell if he's hemorrhaging or not.

For the first time in my life, I get down on my knees and pray to Mother Earth.

September 4, 2015 @ 7:00am
Sector Nine - Male Dormitories
Jay Ahmed

Instead of taking a melatonin last night, I had three beers. Thank you, Samantha! I don't know whether to love or not love her. I went to bed feeling sick and miserable, but I slept like a baby. I felt as though my whole life fell apart after Sam's accusations.

I've never met Polly until yesterday evening. I went straight to Cave Dwellers after my fight with Sam. I wanted to be alone. I knew none of my friends would be there. It's not where Sector Nine hangs out. Two fights with Sam in the last month. We have never fought before. Apparently, relationships are more complicated than they need to be.

Polly introduced herself after I asked for my first Blue Moon, and I liked her right away. She's the grandmother I wish I always had. She could actually be my great-grandmother I suppose.

I called her Nani Polly after my first beer. She loved that. I poured my heart out to her at the start of my third Blue Moon. I learned she has a soft spot for my boss, Uncle Kaelyn, and that I should listen to him. I told her about my breakup with Samantha. I don't know why. I guess I needed someone to talk to. My brother's fighting for his life. She shed a few tears holding my hand. I can't imagine the stories bartenders hear. Thank goodness, I'm a scientist and not a bartender. I would hate to be in Polly's shoes listening to my own pathetic sob stories.

I've decided to go straight into work today rather than the infirmary this morning. Kato would want it that way. I don't want to disappoint Uncle Kaelyn either. My head doesn't exactly hurt, but it's heavy.

I hear Jake's announcement. Numbness, shock, and anger battle with one another throughout me. I throw the crystal frame of Samantha's into my opaque wall. It's the picture of us by the waterfall. Sam sent it to me the evening of Sophia's studio unveiling. It was the first thing I could find. Christoph and Sal huddle together. The Maui waves are dying at the shore upon sunrise at my wall. I can hear the warm water diminishing and falling asleep upon the sandy shore. The frame breaks, but my wall remains intact.

My heart broke first.

September 4, 2015 @ 2015
Sector Four Apartments
Sunny Kai-af

We're both naked asleep, wrapped up in one another. It's been a long time since I slept with him. At first, it just started as a once in a while affair fifteen years ago, and then it became a regular once a month get together. His marriage needed something to keep the fires burning and I was the spark that set the flames. Now, it is back to the casual relationship we once had. I love it nonetheless. Missing each other makes our time together even more incredibly amazing than before.

His cock is hard against my ass. He holds my cock and strokes to awaken me. He tries to penetrate into me as he strokes. His wife still sleeps on his back. I've never been inside his wife. I've thought about it and as much as I love and cherish her, I don't want to. She loves to watch her husband and I make love to one another. She also loves to watch her husband and I fuck each another.

Just as my lover drives deep into me, Jake's announcement goes on. I then receive a call in my line of vision from Jake. I press my wrist.

"Dr. Kai-af," says Jake.

"Yes, Jake," I say as my lover retreats.

"Upon reviewing all of Dr. Park's vitals, I have concluded that you are needed in the infirmary for preservation purposes."

I couldn't get my clothes on and out the door fast enough.

Chapter 12

September 4 @ 9:00am
Underground Operating Theater
Kaelyn

"He's going into shock!" screams Dr. Rossi as I rush in with an I.V. bag. There are six physicians in the O.T. Four are just trying to hold Kato down so he doesn't fall off the table from all his convulsing. Samantha administers convulsion patch after convulsion patch on his head and legs. I start an I.V. line and administer my cancer-curing agents. I need to find a way to administer without a line. Another project. We can all see Kato's eyes roll into his head.

The nanites within Kato are obviously not doing much cellular repair. His trauma's far above their capacity to reconstruct at the speed we need them to.

Kato's blood pressure rapidly falls and his heart gives out. His convulsions diminish somewhat, but he flat lines anyway. "No!" hollers Samantha. She takes the syringe filled with salve and immediately injects it into his heart. After ten seconds, Kato starts breathing again. His convulsions slowly stop.

"His body temperature's 96.5," whispers Samantha as she inhales. She's trembling and scared.

"It will go up. Be patient," I say as I slow down the drip of Kato's I.V. line. He seems a bit stable at the moment.

"I'm at a complete loss what to do," says Dr. Rossi with her eyes closed raising her head to the ceiling. Many of the other physicians are also dumbfounded what to do and we are the supposed to be the most brilliant physicians. "Mother Earth, please help!"

"I know someone that can help," I say. I leave the operating theater for the Rainforest.

* * *

I walk back in the O.T. holding Jasper's hand as he waddles beside me. Sam smiles at us, but with a distraught look. All the other physicians look in awe at Jasper.

"Everyone, this is Jasper," I say pointing to his orange mange.

"Hello Jasper," says all six of the physicians.

"Hello everyone," says Jasper giving all the physicians a salute. Stunned silence fills the air and then everyone starts talking all at once.

"Yes, he talks. So do you. Don't be so surprised," I say picking up Jasper in my arms placing him next to Kato on the operating table. "We need his prognosis. Tell us what to do to save him."

Jasper stares at Kato's comatose form. He then emits white headlight-like beams from both his eyes scanning Kato from head to toes. Sharp intakes of breaths can be heard around me as Jasper evaluates his condition. Even Sam's eyes bulge with wonder.

"Master," says Jasper as his eyes turn off bringing back his serene hazel glow. "In his current condition, he only has a twelve percent chance of survival. The damage is far too intensive. Cellular repair with even our technology looks grave."

"No!" yells Sam quietly. She covers her face with her palms silently sobbing.

"Tell us what to do," I ask Jasper.

"He needs an immediate lung transplant." I knew that was necessary, but I wanted his opinion. "That would increase his chance of survival to seventy-eight percent. After that his chances of complete recovery goes down."

"I'll contact Zenith with the specifications," says Dr. Rossi as she leaves the room immediately.

"Master, I also think keeping him on a couple of convulsion patches whether he's having a seizure or not. Just as a preventative measure." I can see the others give a why-didn't-I-think-of-that look.

"What about cryogenics? Do they store organs?" asks Samantha.

"No, they only store intact, complete species," I say collapsing into a chair.

"What about prosthetic organs?" Sam questions.

"We have some, but bio-medical hasn't perfected the lung, yet. I checked."

"How long will it take to get a lung?" she asks.

"Hopefully, within the week." The other attending physicians put a mediblanket and thermal socks on Kato. I just sit watching Kato. There's nothing more I can do right now. Jasper jumps off the table and crawls onto my lap.

"Master, a week at the most. With every day thereafter, his chances of survival go down five to seven percent per day."

"A week! He doesn't have a motherfucking week! We'll be lucky if he gets through today! How come we don't harvest organs down here?" screams Samantha.

"Dr. Stonebridge, get a fucking grip on yourself! It is what it is. We're lucky he's still alive and I've never known Jasper to be wrong. If he says Kato has at least a week with our current methods, then we have at least a week. And you know very well why we don't harvest organs down here. We don't need to. Our nano technology has always sufficed. Kato is an unusual circumstance."

"I'm sorry. I just feel so fucking useless!" she says throwing her hands up in the air stomping her feet at the same time.

"Being frustrated isn't going to help him any. Come here," says Jasper holding out his arms. I hold Sam on my lap with my left arm around her and Jasper lays against my right.

"I need you to be strong for Jay," I say. Jasper nods his head. "I need you to behave like the professional physician that you are. Not some teenager whose hormones are all out of control." Jasper nods his head again. Everyone tries not to laugh at the comment. Sam weeps upon my shoulder. "Promise?"

"Do I have a choice?" she says between her sobs.

"Of course, not." Jasper shakes his head.

"I promise, Dr. Stonebridge," she says wiping her tears away.

September 4, 2015 @ 2pm
Mid-Section
Samantha Stonebridge

"Can I see him?" says Sophia as she slides into the booth across from me at Ten Thousand Leagues. She's an absolute Hollywood Bollywood mess. She's in sweatpants and a sweatshirt; clothes she only wears in our apartment at bedtime. I never thought Sophia would be ever caught dead wearing such attire in public. It's just not her. She's always dolled up.

Her hair's in a messy bun rather than a fashionable one. Her nail polish is chipping away. There's no soft make up on her face as usual. I've never seen her in such a disarray.

"No, I already ordered lunch for both of us."

"Why not? And how can you eat at a time like this when Kato's fighting for his life?" I can feel Sophia's frustration. I threw the same temper tantrum just a little while ago.

"You and I both have to keep our strength up. Kato would want it that way." I don't know whether or not to tell her he's still critical. It would just worry her more. "You stay busy and let the doctors do what they can. They're talking about a lung transplant. It looks hopeful so don't worry." I definitely don't tell her that the lung might not be here for a while.

"I love him, Sam!" She covers her hands to her face crying. "If he dies…" I slide out of my seat and next to her. I wrap my arms around her as tightly as I could, as a true mother would do to a grieving child.

"I know you do. That's why you have to stay strong. You know all of us are doing our best to save him. You have to believe in us. Zenith said whatever to save him."

"I believe in everyone in the *Underground*. I do have faith in all of you," she says all teary-eyed. "It's just so fucking hard!"

"He's going to be fine," I say trying to convince myself of my own words. A drone with our food hovers to us. "Just put everything on the table. We're sharing." The drone does as it's told.

"Spinach pies are Kato's favorite," says Sophia.

"I know. Eat for him. Don't let them go to waste. He wouldn't be too happy with you if you did."

"You're such a fucking devil, Sam," she says eating one of the pies with her head on my shoulder. "I love you so much."

September 4, 2015 @ 10:00pm
Infirmary - Room One
Samantha Stonebridge

"You need to go home. Now." Jay's laying his head on Kato's bed. I bet he hasn't eaten anything all day so I brought him a shaved prime rib sandwich. Sal and Christoph called me fifteen minutes ago to let me know Jay hasn't come home, yet.

"I can't leave him."

I don't know who's the bigger mess, Sophia or Jay. Jay's also dressed in casual street clothes rather than in professional attire. He looks like he hasn't shaved in days. I wonder when he washed his hair last. It looks oilier than shiny. I bet he ignored his classes and work today.

Again.

"Get up! Now!" I command. "Dr. Everette's got this."

"Jay, you've been here all day. Get some rest. I promise I'll keep you in the loop if anything changes," says Dr. Everette. I pull Jay up from the chair.

"I have a sandwich for you to eat on the train."

"Not hungry," he says wearily walking out of the room clinging onto me for support.

"Don't care. You're eating or I'll call Lucinda to come over and feed you. I'm sure she would love to."

"Why do you care for me so much all of a sudden? Did Uncle Kaelyn summon you again? Yesterday, you wanted to have nothing to do with me," he says pushing away from me.

"You want to move on. Fine. I can accept that and still be just your friend. It's what friends do. They take care of one another," I say boarding the train handing him his sandwich. "You're going to class and work tomorrow. Kato would want it that way. Case closed. No more mourning for him like he's already dead."

Jay nods unwrapping the sandwich.

September 4, 2015 @ 10:20pm
Sector Nine - Male Dormitories
Jay Ahmed

I don't want to move on. I know I should move on. Sam's obviously made up her mind about our relationship. She wants me to move on. She sounded so jealous yesterday. I took that as a good sign that we still have a chance. She obviously doesn't want me seeing other girls.

Now my former betrothed is acting like a mother to me. I don't know if I like this or not.

Sal and Christoph are still up when I enter my apartment. I change into shorts and a t-shirt without bothering to brush my teeth and curl up under the covers. Sal and Christoph come under the comforter and cuddle on each side of me.

"Can we all sleep together?" asks Christoph. He puts his head on my shoulder.

"Of course we can, little buddy," I say hugging an arm around him.

"How's Kato?" asks Sal. He's got his head around my other shoulder and his hands around my neck.

"He's stable, but still unconscious," I say putting my other arm around him. "Don't be afraid. He's going to be great." I say trying to convince myself holding onto my honorary little brothers.

"Can we go to the waterfall tomorrow?" asks Christoph snuggling and crying into me a little bit.

I haven't visited the waterfall since Kato's accident. I've neglected my little brothers to fend for themselves. As independent as they are, they are still children after all and need a support system. The den mothers do a great job coordinating the younger children of the *Underground* with the older ones. Guilt washes over me like a tsunami.

"Not only are we going to the waterfall tomorrow, but we are also going for ice cream. Kato would want that."

"Thanks, Jay," the both say together.

"Mint chip is Kato's favorite," says Sal.

"Mint chip it is then all around."

Chapter 13

September 4, 2015 @ 10:00pm
Kaelyn's Apartment
Kaelyn

"What a day," I say flopping down onto my bed. I feel Lovelin wash her hand through my hair the moment I lay beside her.

"Is it a *good what a day* or a *bad what a day*?" I chuckle a bit.

"So you've caught onto the *Underground* lingo. Both. Kato seems to be stable, but my laboratory work is another story."

Lovelin massages my forehead and scalp. She knows exactly how to relax me. She knows exactly how to love me. I close my eyes and just let the wonderful sensations take me over. Shit! I see an incoming call in my vision even with my eyes closed. It's the President. I press my wrist.

"Yes, Sir."

"How's Dr. Park?"

"Not critical, but not exactly stable. I hope you can acquire a lung soon." I hear Lovelin take a sharp breath.

"We are in the process of acquiring his needs. The problem is that it may take some time."

"I understand. I know you'll do your best, but time is precious for him," I remind him.

"What is your upcoming *Showcase* miracle?" Damn! I don't have anything ready, yet.

"It's a surprise," I say all relaxed. Lovelin's massage is drifting me to slumber.

"I understand that you are recently struggling. Is that true, Kaelyn?"

"Who the fuck told you that!" I say sitting up wide awake. Lovelin leaves the room.

"I have my sources. Is it true?" Yes, it's true, but I'm not going to admit that to you.

"Of course not! Everything's on track. You needn't worry about me," I say reassuringly. I wish I could truly spit in his face.

"How's Miss Khan? I hear you're spending a lot of time with her."

"She's fine. She's writing another novel to occupy her time. She would like her own bookstore in Mid-Section. Sounds like a good idea, don't you think?" President or no president, he better not go against me.

"Splendid idea," he says agreeing. "Ask her to take a survey by all the *Underground* inhabitants. If she has over sixty percent positive feedback, I'll allow it. As long as there's space in Mid-Section for her shop."

"I'll let her know. I'm sure she'll be thrilled that you allowed her the opportunity." I wish I didn't have to kiss his ass and feet, but for Lovelin I'll do anything.

"Keep me posted. Good night."

"Good night, Sir," I say disconnecting the line. I flop onto the bed once more.

"Everything okay? I brought you some warm milk."

"Trying to put me to sleep, are you?" I say downing the milk in one sitting.

"I just want you comfortable and relaxed," she says massaging my temple once more. Where did this amazing girl come from? I get comfortable on her lap while she continues.

"The President wants you to take a survey of all the *Underground* inhabitants. If you have over sixty percent positive feedback, he will allow you to have a bookstore in Mid-Section," I say all drowsy.

"Seriously?" I get up, change my clothes, and fall back onto Lovelin's lap.

"Yes. Jake can administer the survey to every sector. Make it short and sweet. Let them know you live in Sector Four with me. Everybody has a great deal of respect for those who live in Sector Four.

"I don't want to use you, Kaelyn, for my own personal gain." I pull her into my arms and kiss her tenderly.

"I want you to use me. I want you to use me for anything you want and need," I say nuzzling my head into her chest.

"As you wish," she says pulling the covers over cuddling into me.

September 4, 2015 @ 11:15pm
The White House
President of the United States

I make my second phone call. He answers immediately.

"Good evening, comrade. I have a delicate matter for you to handle."

Chapter 14

September 5, 2015 @ 7:00pm
Sector Nine - Female Dormitories
Samantha Stonebridge

"What a day!" I say face planting into my bed. I'm sure I could go to sleep right about now in my lab coat and all. It wouldn't be the first time.

"Is that a *good what a day* or *bad what a day*?" asks Zen. She's playing on her clarinet a song I've never heard before. It sounds lovely nonetheless. I wonder if she'll also play the clarinet at the wedding in addition to the piano or just practicing for the *Showcase*. I'm too tired to ask.

"I don't know, yet," I say in a muffled voice from my mattress. Chika jumps on my back and tugs on my hair. She wants to play and I don't have the energy to. I grab her elephant squeaky toy from underneath my pillow and throw it blindly towards the kitchen. She dashes off. Ari's not home, yet, and neither's Sophia. Everybody seems to be working late tonight.

Well, I guess I shouldn't be lazy either. I change into pink pajamas, grab an iced espresso from the refrigerator, and start researching on birthmarks again. I need some downtime from the cryogenics lab, my studies, Kato's health, and all the stresses of my *Underground* life, which I can't get enough of.

Within the hour, I find a picture of a stone tablet. It's a boy and a girl sitting with their feet outstretched in front of them. They're wearing rags about them pointing to their feet. I enlarge the picture to get a closer look at their toes. The stone tablet looks extremely old and faded, but I can see that they both have identical marks between their last two toes on their left foot. It looks somewhat like a horseshoe. The stone tablet is dated 479AD Persia. There's no article to go with the picture. It's a stone drawing found over a hundred years ago that now resides in the Smithsonian.

479AD is about sixteen hundred years ago and falls within my four-thousand-year-old timeline. I want to be surprised by this picture, but I'm not. Now I'm just waiting for everything to fall into place. I just hope I can find all the pieces to this crazy jigsaw puzzle.

I gulp down the rest of my espresso. It's eight o'clock when Sophia walks in. The first question she asks is how's Kato.

"No, I haven't had dinner. How about you?" She's not happy with me as she sits on my bed. "You know he's stable. I told you just a while ago."

She frowns at me because I don't give her any more information. I don't tell her that Kato had another round of convulsions this afternoon, but his physicians got him through them. I don't tell her that Kato's lungs are not regenerating like we hoped they would. She asks when she can see him and all I say is soon. She annoyingly gets off my bed and heads into her closet.

"How's the wedding attire coming along?" I say trying to find other articles.

"Fucking stable!" she yells from her closet.

September 5, 2015 @ 7:00pm
Landing Dock
Kaelyn

The elevator up to the landing dock took longer than I remember. I want to make sure she's the right breed; otherwise, I will have to send her back. Zenith has only gotten my requests wrong once. I questioned what imbeciles were working for them. I was twelve years old at the time. Ever since then, they haven't gotten my requests wrong, but I still take all my deliveries personally rather than having them transported to my lab. I keep forgetting how cold the landing dock is, which is stupid of me because I should remember everything. I should have worn a jacket.

"Good evening, Dr. Stonebridge."

"Good evening, Brooks." He hands me a cage. She's sleeping on a pink blanket. She's smaller than I expected.

"Cute little thing," says Brooks. "She was babbling all the way through the submarine ride. She just fell asleep a few minutes ago."

I smile softly at his words. Babbling is not my agenda. I want to tell him she'll be talking in weeks, but I don't.

September 5, 2015 @ 9:30pm
Sector Nine - Female Dormitories
Samantha Stonebridge

"What a day!" says Ari crashing down onto her bed. I can smell the cinnamon and spices soaked in her all the way to the corner of my bedroom.

"A *good what a day* or *bad what a day*?" the three of us say in unison. We're eating chicken wings and pizza for dinner. Sophia and Zen are on my bed with me. We don't have a dining room on purpose; Zen's piano takes up that intended area. Chika's fast asleep on one of my pillows with her elephant toy cuddled in her tummy.

"My science test was a *bad what a day* and my molten lava chocolate cake was a *good what a day*," Ari says cuddling into her pillow.

"Ari, I can help you with science," I say picking up the last piece of steak and fried egg pizza. "The stuff you're learning, I did back in pre-school." No answer. "Ari?" She's already asleep in her chef's attire.

"I'm whipped," says Zen. "Going to bed."

"Me, too," says Sophia. She leaves our pizza and chicken boxes outside our door and asks Jake to have a drone retrieve them.

I'm now wired on my second espresso so I decide to do some more research. I have to admit, researching this stuff for Uncle Kaelyn has been fascinating and very frustrating at the same time. I want answers, but I know I have to be patient. I just hope Char will be able to bring me back the information that pulls all this together. It's a gut feeling that I'm banking on. Uncle Kaelyn has gotten me to be a patient one. We are scientists after all. Patience comes along with that title I suppose.

It's close to eleven o'clock before I find another drawing. It's dated May 30, 279BC Sahara Dessert. I pull up a map of 279BC on my wall. It's really not much different than our world today. Our continents are separated rather than one big glob like they used to be millions of years ago. This picture could be from anywhere in the dessert. It's an oasis of some sort. Two women are next to two babies. One's a boy and the other's a girl. They seemed to have just been born. They sleep with their arms around each other. The young women have smiles on their faces. I can tell they are the mothers.

They had to have been born at the same time. The date gives it away. It saddens me because I'm no longer surprised by my findings.

It also crazy excites me.

Chapter 15

September 6, 2015 @ 11:00am
Rainforest
Kaelyn's Creations

"I'm bored," says Seth. He tosses his banana peel into the sky while swaying on the jungle gym. A multi-colored bird comes out of nowhere and grabs it.

"We can do algebra equations in the sand," says Jasper.

"Seriously?" says Seth. "You haven't moved beyond algebra?"

"Let's go for a swim!" says Zara. "Let's go for a fly!"

"I can't swim," says Seth.

"We can teach you," says Loopy. "It's easy."

"What's so fun about swimming? Your fur gets all wet," says Seth. "As for flying, do you see any wings on me?"

"I don't have fur," says Loopy. "I have…I have…" She looks all around her. She even picks up her feet one by one and looks underneath them.

"Scales," says Jasper. "You have scales. That's why you can change color and we can't. You have chameleon sliced into you."

Loopy looks all around her body over and over again. "What sliced? I'm not cut anywhere," she says looking under her wings. The boys shake their heads.

"Didn't Master ever tell you how you were created?" asks Seth. Zara and Loopy look at each other in confusion. "Haven't you noticed that all the movies we watch in the sky, animals can't talk like we can?"

"That's not true," says Zara. "They all talk in Dr. Doolittle." Loopy nods her head.

"And in Babe," says Loopy giggling. "I love that little pig. Wish we had one here."

September 6, 2015 @ 11:15am
Rainforest
Kaelyn's Creations

"I'm bored," says Seth swinging in the hammock.

"We can do algebra equations in the sand," says Jasper. Seth shakes his head.

"Let's go for a swim!" says Zara. "I bet once you try, you'll love it."

"Let's try to find that new kitten and bunny," says Jasper.

"What new kitten and bunny? I've only seen the new baby kangaroo," says Seth.

"What new baby kangaroo?" says Zara.

"Let's go into Papa's lab," says Loopy.

All three of them stare at her utterly confused.

"We can't get into Master's lab," says Seth. "We don't have the code to the door."

Jasper and Zara nod their heads.

"I have the code to the door. Papa takes me all the time!" says Loopy.

"I don't like going through Master's door," says Jasper. "It means he's going to poke me. I'd rather be here."

Seth and Zara nod their heads.

"We can go at night when Papa's not there," says Loopy. "He goes to his apartment to his bed that doesn't smell."

The other three nod and shake their heads at the same time.

September 6, 2015 @ 9:00pm
Genetic Laboratory
Kaelyn's Creatures

"It's dark," says Seth.

"Mr. Jake, can you please turn on the lights," says Loopy. The overhead lights go on. "Wow," whispers Loopy. "He listened to me."

"What's that?" asks Zara looking at Kaelyn's huge microscope.

"Papa doesn't like that, so stay away from it," says Loopy. "It makes him mad."

"Then why does Master have it?" asks Jasper.

"Hmm," says Loopy putting her front leg up to her chin.

"What's that?" asks Zara looking into Michael's aquariums.

"Don't know?" says Loopy. "But I bet they taste delicious!"

Seth bites into one of the green fruits. "No bad," he says plopping the entire fruit into his mouth. The others follow his lead.

They're all asleep in seconds.

Chapter 16

September 7, 2015 @ 8:00am

Genetics Laboratory

Kaelyn

I find all my creatures asleep at Michael's side of the lab the moment I walk in. What the bloody fucking fuck! How did they get into my lab!?

I smack Seth's head. "Wake up!" I command. Seth's groggy, but immediately wakes holding his head. He seems a bit out of it and disorientated. "What's the meaning of this?" I say most annoyed. "How did you all get in here?"

"It's my fault, Papa," says Loopy. Seth, Zara, and Jasper huddle into each other. They know I'm angry. I don't know if I've ever been angrier with them.

I shouldn't be surprised how Loopy knows the code to the door. I've brought her into the lab hundreds of times on my shoulder. I'm going to have to change it weekly. She's far more observant than I give her credit for.

"Get back into the Rainforest! Go do your chores!" I yell pointing to the door.

"Jake, no *Holoplex* movies for a month!" They all put their heads down and scramble towards the door. "I'll determine your punishment later."

106

They leave to do their commands.

I press my wrist. "Hey, Bro, what's up? By the way, I'm taking your girl down this morning on the tennis court. She may need a shoulder to cry on. Hope you're available."

"What are you growing in your aquarium?"

"Fermented wineberries. Should be ready in the next twenty-four hours to make some sweet wine. I'm presenting the first bottle to you and Lovelin."

No wonder they were all sleeping so soundly. They fell asleep drunk.

September 7, 2017 @ 8:30am
Fathoms Above Fitness
Michael Shapiro

"You are going down, sister!" I say swishing my tennis racket around all over the place. How hard can this sport be compared to racquetball? I got this. I think. I'm trying to adjust to the weight and length of the racquet. It's just going to take me a few minutes to adjust. I've got this though. I think.

Lovelin looks at me for a while from her side of the court. She should be warming up, but isn't. She leaves the court.

Maybe she has to use the little girl's room. That's it! She's all nervous watching my moves! I warm up some more and jog in place. The ladies in the court next to me give me a look. I can tell they've never seen such an athlete before.

Lovelin returns placing a box of tissues down behind my side of the tennis net.

"I got you a welcome present," she says smirking at me.

Oh, let the trash talk begin! She's dressed all professional in navy blue and white. She had to have played tennis in college. Did she? Kaelyn never mentioned such a thing so I dismiss her intimidation.

"I believe you will need those at the end of the match so just help yourself," I say acting with a great deal of confidence. She starts the game off with an Ace.

This is going to be a long morning.

* * *

It actually wasn't a long morning.

Lovelin beat me six to nothing. Probably in Olympic time. Does the Olympics even have tennis?

"So, why does my boss love you again?" I ask taking one of the tissues. Lovelin kisses me on the cheek.

"Your court next time or rematch?"

I pick up the box of tissues smiling at her.

"You're going to want to hold on to these," I say handing her the box of Kleenex. She hands them back to me.

"I'll take my chances," she says with a smile bumping purposely into my shoulder.

Now I know why my boss loves her so.

September 7, 2015 @ 12:00pm
Genetics Laboratory
Kaelyn

I hit my microscope again. The little monkey then hits it as well. She smiles at me.

"No, you don't do that. Only Papa can do that." She extends her hands for me to pick her up. Seth, Jasper, and Zara never behaved this way. She wants to be clingy to me. She doesn't understand that I am her Master.

Damn! I called myself Papa. I've got to stop doing that.

I scoop her up and put her back in her cage. I can see a frown on her face. She cuddles into her little black teddy bear.

"Master is working, understand?" She doesn't move. Apparently, her first cranial inject hasn't affected her, yet.

"You're my Pah-pi! Not Master!" she says holding her bear tight cuddling into her pink blanket for a nap.

Holy Mother Earth!

Chapter 17

September 7, 2015 @ 10:00am
Sector Two - Physics Laboratory
Samantha Stonebridge

"Are you sure you're no longer contagious?" I question mesmerized looking around Zachary's drop dead gorgeous laboratory. I'm beyond jealous right now. I could only dream to have one of these of my own someday. How did he get this? How did I not get this?

I may be Zenith's prize child, but since I haven't concluded what branch I want to expertise in, yet, I have not been given a laboratory of my own. I'm leaning towards cryogenics, but I haven't decided, yet. There are too many fields to choose from. I'm not into genetics like Uncle Kaelyn is. He has had his own lab since he was five years old. Everything's a passion right now. I'm sure I'll narrow it down soon.

I sprayed a double dose of *Surgical Mist* all over me just as a precaution from *Surface* infection. Jay told me he did the same. Char and Kieran's lab is nothing like we have ever seen before, but then again, we haven't been inside all the laboratories down here.

There are huge depictions of almost every wonder of the world on their walls: the Great Pyramids, the Grand Canyon, the Hanging Gardens of Babylon, Earth's moon, Stonehenge, the Great Barrier Reef, and the Mayan and Aztec ruins. I remember reading about them years ago. They have six opaque walls in their lab. I thought these walls only existed in Sector Four and Nine in our private dwellings. Jay and I look at each other puzzled. We don't know of any other laboratory designed like his. There are beautiful glass cabinets at the far end filled with all sorts of stones and rocks. Two large tables are at another corner of their lab along with some sort of simulator. There are pieces of equipment I've never seen before.

"Dr. Khalid has given me a clean bill of health," Char says. "Zenith told us to take a heavy duty dose of antibiotics before every teleportation trip. There's too much airborne contamination on the *Surface*. I got lucky with the first one."

"Where are you getting antibiotics from? We don't even keep much of a supply in the infirmary. They are hardly ever needed," I say.

"We received our first shipment a few days ago," says Char. "They're stored in a lab cabinet. Hawke Enterprises above makes them easily for us." That makes sense.

"Have you been anywhere else?" I ask.

"Kieran's taking his precautionary treatment right now. His first time will be on the thirteenth," says Char. Char makes it sound like that Kieran's going to lose his virginity. Precautionary treatment. First time. I try not to giggle.

"You have moon rocks!" exclaims Jay peering into one of the glass cabinets. I rush over to Jay's side to see myself. The rocks are labeled. There are quite a few of them. I didn't know the *Surface* had such a supply. It's incredible what Zenith supplies for them.

"All those rocks helped make the Spear," says Kieran. He brings out the Spear from a mahogany armoire. Jay and I stare at it. It's gorgeous! There are intricate carvings along the entire length of the Spear. There's a serene glow around it. It's mesmerizing. It almost looks…alive.

Char demonstrates how it works. There's an electronic keypad within the Spear head. The head opens with a twist. Jay and I jump back a little as it snaps open. He explains how the coordinates are inputted and then its activation method. It's all so simple and fascinating at the same time.

"I can't believe you only need one," says Jay. "Did you see the movie *Stargate*? Even that futuristic traveler needed two gates for teleportation."

"*Stargate*, as classic as it is," says Kiernan, "is still primitive technology. We had to device a way to go beyond that. Even *Star Trek* members can't teleport the way we do and they are supposed to be far into the centuries than we are. They have to go into a teleportation chamber within the Starship Enterprise. We can teleport from anywhere around the world! Space travel is next on our agenda."

Jay and I stare widemouthed at each other. "You two rock!" I say. "No pun intended!" All of us laugh.

"Want to see a demonstration?" Char asks.

"Heck, yeah!" Jay and I say simultaneously.

Jay and I can't contain our enthusiasm. This is the first time Jay has some life spark in him since Kato's accident. It's the first time

I've seen him smile all week. I hope he can find some peace soon. He looks like he's lost at least ten pounds. His hair's even longer and the stubble on his face more prominent. He shouldn't look so incredibly beautiful, but he does. I wonder why he no longer grooms himself. He has always been so professional. I guess Kato's state has taken him away from the routine in his life. I'm not complaining. Savage has a different sort of beauty.

I'm surprised a bit at how Jay and I think alike, and then I'm not. I've spent practically my whole life with him. Apart from Uncle Kaelyn and my roommates, Jay has always been actively involved with everything that I'm involved with and what I have accomplished. I could always turn to him when needed.

Char holds the Spear at his side and activates it. He closes his eyes. There's a whirlwind of a tornado forming all around him. That has to be uncomfortable. I lean into Jay for guidance. He puts his arm around my shoulder saying not to be afraid, he knows what he's doing. I'm surprised he's putting his arm around considering everything we have been through lately. Maybe we have a chance together after all. I wish I could tell him 'let's start over again', but I can't. I'm too scared he will say 'no'.

Char doesn't look worried at all with the tornado all around him. The wind gets faster and faster and there's hardly any noise. All I can feel and hear is a faint summer breeze. Within moments, Char disappears.

I look at Jay. I've never seen his eyes and mouth so wide open. "Where did he go?" Jay asks Kieran.

"Hi guys!"

We turn around. Char's sitting on one of the tables in the corner of the lab behind us. The Spear's still in his hand. He looks exactly the same.

"That's amazing! You two are going to be the bomb at the *Showcase* this year!" I say. Kieran explains how they can't reveal their work this year. Zenith wants long-term results.

"It doesn't hurt, does it?" asks Jay. "Those whirlwinds would kill the average human being."

"No," says Char. "I can't explain it. It's truly a supernatural phenomenon."

Jay and I look into each other's eyes and smile at his last comment.

September 7, 2015 @ 10:30am
Sector Two - Physics Laboratory
Zachary Briarwood

"So why am I going to Egypt to bring back this archaeologist?"

It takes Samantha over an hour to tell us about Lovelin Khan and her connection with Dr. Kaelyn Stonebridge. She talks about her research and the couples she has found throughout time with the same birthday and birthmarks, and incredible same birth times and deaths. I couldn't believe what I was hearing. Even Kieran tries to soak it all in motionless in his chair while she speaks. We don't want to miss a single word. Samantha believes that there's some supernatural force reincarnating them. She's determined to find the source. At the end of her long scenario, Kieran and I just sit speechless for a while.

"How do you it's this archeologist that holds the key to all of this?" I ask.

"It's a strong feeling, Char. Just like when you and Kieran designed the Spear. You must have done months of research and have had gut feelings as well," she says. The two of them could only nod their heads.

"It's a personal matter. It's not even work-related," says Kieran.

"Yes," says Jay. "It's completely personal. Uncle Kaelyn's one of the greatest minds on this planet. Samantha and I want to help him find out what's going on. He has done so much for us and we want to return the favor for all his support over the years. My breakthroughs could have never happened without his insight. We believe he and Miss Lovelin deserve this whether Zenith does or not. I know it's straying away from protocol, but we could possibly unravel something amazing. Something beyond science amazing!"

"He's really scary," says Kieran.

"Once you get to know him, you'll realize he's a good guy. He's so above everybody else. He can't communicate with just anyone," says Jay. "And he's beyond dedicated to his work. He's impossible to please, but that's the part that makes him so great. Trust me, I've learned firsthand as his assistant. It's an honor to work for him." That makes sense. Kieran even agrees with that.

Sam looks at Jay with glowing eyes and the dreamiest smile. I've never seen her look so happy. It looks like love in her eyes. Jay smiles at her. They're obviously still betrothed.

"So when's the wedding?" says Kieran. He knows about Jay going out with Lucinda. I guess he's trying to get some information out of them. Even I could tell Sam and Jay have feelings for each other.

"Oh, us?" Jay says looking towards Sam. She looks away. "We haven't thought about it. So busy and what's the rush, right?" Kieran seems somewhat satisfied with that answer.

There's an awkward silence. Jay and Sam no longer gaze at each other. They must feel embarrassed in front of us.

"I know we are all servants of science," says Sam breaking up the tension between them. "I've never known anything else, but there's another realm on the *Surface*. A realm worth discovering. A realm that's not taught down here. Your entire Spear exists because of the belief of this realm. If anybody can understand, it's you two. Will you please help us?" Kieran looks at me and smiles.

"Of course, we will, Sam. Mother Earth has many faces. We are all here to save Mother Earth after all," I say.

September 7, 2015 @ 11:45am
Sector Two - Physics Laboratory
Jay Ahmed

I've never seen Sam look at me that way before. It looked like she was idolizing me. And then I realize, of course, my idolizing her uncle, would make her happy. I only said the truth.

"So when's the wedding?" says Kiernan. My stomach drops into the beautiful tiled stones of his lab upon his words.

I didn't know how to answer. Suddenly, my throat felt dry. Sam looked away. She didn't tell them that we are no longer betrothed. Does she still want to be betrothed to me? If she didn't, she would say something, right? I took her silence as a sign and told Kieran we have been too busy to set a date. Sam doesn't oppose to my answer. I take it as another good sign that we still have hope. Kieran and Char agree to help us.

"We just don't need the archeologist," says Sam. "We need those scrolls as well. Without them, he's absolutely useless. You're going to have to convince him somehow, Char."

Sam then explains my restoration process and how there's no such process on the *Surface*. The archeologist should be excited about it. My restoration process will serve as bait.

"I can give you a can," I say to Char. "It will have a minute amount of capability. Just enough to quench his thirst. Just enough to restore a couple of symbols or a few pictures. I bet he will travel with you anywhere. He will probably think you're from another time, maybe even another planet. It should be fascinating for him since he's an archeologist."

"Your Spear is full of hieroglyphs and depictions of *Underground* images he's never seen before. He won't be able to get enough of it. He will be putty in your hands if you play the cards right," says Sam. I nod my head agreeing.

"Don't worry. I'll find a way. I won't disappoint you, Sam," says Char looking at her with a soft smile. I should be pleased with his confidence, but I'm not.

No wonder Samantha worships this guy.

Chapter 18

September 7, 2015 @ 9:00am
Room One - Infirmary
Sophia Cambridge

I've never been in the infirmary before Kato's accident. I've never had to. If I got a cut or scrape, Sam would always bring supplies to our dorm room and take care of me herself. One of the perks of having a physician for a roommate. Ari has burned herself on more than a few occasions and Sam was always there to heal her as well. *Burn Be Gone* is an incredible salve; however, it can only be used up to third-degree burns. All the restaurants in the *Underground* keep it in their pantries for emergencies.

I know what a hospital is supposed to look like by watching episodes of ER and Grey's Anatomy with Sam when we were younger. According to Sam, those shows are primitive medicine, but the drama's fun to watch. This place is nothing like a *Surface* hospital. Kato's in a beautiful glass-encased room. His bed looks palatial through the glass door. There's nothing hooked up to him. His body, however, is covered in patches.

"Hello," I say. "May I come in?" The doctor with holographic computers all around him lifts his head up and smiles at me. I can see Kato's chest cavity in front of a 3D image. I want to gasp, but try to remain calm. Seventy percent of his lungs are missing.

"Come in, dear child," he says. I don't know who he is. He waves his hand and the images disappear. It's sweet of him that he doesn't want to worry me.

"I'm Sophia Cambridge," I say extending my hand for a shake. "I live in Sector Nine and is Kato's friend."

"I'm Dr. Kavanaugh," he says shaking my hand. "His girlfriend?"

"No, Sir," I say blushing. I wish I was his girlfriend. "Just a friend. Kato's a brilliant guy. It's hard not to admire him."

"You're not a physician," he says motioning me to take a seat by his bed. I hold Kato's hand. He doesn't move and my heart sinks to the floor.

"No, Sir, I'm *Underground's* latest fashion designer. My studio is in Sector Two. I'm designing the attire for the upcoming wedding."

Dr. Kavanaugh blows a long whistle swirling in his chair. I like his curly blond hair. He looks like he's in his twenties. There's no ring on his finger. He's not incredibly handsome like Kato, but has a fun demeanor about him.

"Impressive! How old are you? Thirteen, I'm guessing?"

"Fourteen at the end of November."

I gaze at Kato. His breathing's shallow and his face pale. Without even thinking, I kiss the top of his hand in front of Dr. Kavanaugh. Neither of us says anything for a while. I just gaze at Kato's face. He looks like he has lost weight, but I know they are keeping him well-nourished and hydrated with patches.

"Sophia, do you mind if I use the little boy's room? Can you watch Kato for me? He's pretty stable right now." I have a feeling Dr. Kavanaugh wants to give me some alone time. "Call me through your wrist if anything happens."

"Of course, Sir. Take your time."

He leaves through the glass door. I get up and run my fingers through Kato's beautiful black hair. It's not silky shiny as I have seen. I'm sure it's just being washed by a dry shampoo. He smells ever so sweet and musky at the same time. I inhale his beautiful scent over and over again.

"Kato, can you hear me? It's Sophia," I say massaging his temple. "You have to fight and get better. Do you understand? There's no way I can live without you." I only say these words because I know he can't hear me. He's unconscious after all.

"Kato, can you give me a sign?" I say squeezing his hand running my fingers through his hair. He doesn't squeeze my hand back. No movement. Nothing.

I can feel tears well up in my eyes. I lean in and kiss him gently on his lips. "I love you, Kato. Please come back to me," I say as the tears slip down my face onto his lips. I should wipe them away or kiss them away, but I don't. I can hear footsteps behind me and I wipe my tears with the back of my hand as Dr. Kavanugh enters the room. He hands me a tissue.

"How many times have you been to the waterfall?" he asks me taking his chair. I tell him the truth. He doesn't say anything at first.

"Just remember, love conquers all. Not prayers." I nod smiling up at him.

"I know," is all I say back. "I've been told."

September 8, 2015 @ 2:00pm
Cryogenics
Samantha Stonebridge

I hang my backpack in the closet before approaching Dr. Kai-af.

"Any developments?" I ask rushing to his side. His sandwich is untouched. His soup is cold. He looks up from his computer.

"I don't have good news, little one," he says swirling around to face me. "I'm going to have to put Zareen away. There haven't been any changes. She's stopped communicating." I slump down in the leather chair across from him.

"I understand. You have your own work to do as well. I'm sure you're disappointed as much as I am."

"Very. I was so hoping to bring her back somewhat even if not completely. It's hard to find bodies to work on down here. My methods just aren't working. My equations are off. I'm going to have to start from scratch."

"Are you going to cremate her?"

"No, I'm going to keep her in a cryogenic coffin and bring her out in a year or two. See if we can get some answers then. Let her body heal some. Hopefully, by then I will have found a way."

"Does everybody go against Zenith's rules?"

"We do everything they ask, little one. There's nothing wrong with having our own dreams as long as we don't hurt anyone. You must follow your passions as well."

"That's the problem. I can't figure out what my passions are just yet. I enjoy everything. That's why I haven't presented at a *Showcase*, yet. I don't know which way to turn."

"You are always welcome at my door." I smile at him.

"Thank you, Sir. I'll think about it. Need help with Zareen?"

"Sweet little one, thank you, but you get back to class. My assistants and I can take care of her."

Sam gives me a hug and I kiss her forehead. I gaze at Zareen. I so wanted to know her story, but I guess it will have to wait.

September 8, 2015 @ 2:05pm
Cryogenics
Jake

"Dr. Kai-af, may I have a word with you?"

"Jake?"

"Yes, Dr. Kai-af, it is your servant Jake speaking."

"What is it, Jake?"

Unfortunately, he tells me.

Chapter 19

September 9, 2015 @ 9:00am
Rainforest
Lovelin

I've hardly seen Kaelyn all week. He's up early in the morning and comes to bed late at night. So this is what being married to our Earth's savior is going to be like. A part of me feels beyond blessed; the selfish part of me just wants to keep him all to myself.

I look back on my *Surface* life. A forty-hour workweek is a part-time job for children down here. Everybody in the *Underground* makes me feel so lazy. I decided to keep writing and plan to have my own electronic bookstore in this second life, my *Underground* life. I'm still waiting for the results of the survey. Every doctor and scientist can have their own section regarding their written work if they like, but my bookstore will be primarily for pleasure reading, fiction and non-fiction. It's not thousands of square feet like a *Barnes and Noble* because everybody here only believes in electronic versions of everything, but paper thin tablets will be readily available for readers to take home, keep for themselves, or return after they are done.

I'm going to use the *SuperNet* to order paper formatted books. If there's a particular genre someone wants to read, I will be able to make recommendations since I've always read what's on the bestseller's list and other lists. Although I still ache to be with Kaelyn, my new hobby has kept me thoroughly busy throughout the day. He's still forever in the back of my mind. I wish I could understand our pull towards each other. As brilliant as he is, he can't figure it out as well. I suppose time will tell.

I visit the Rainforest mostly every morning. I either make breakfast for all of us or have Jake send it to the lab. By five o'clock, I'm generally back home in Sector Four and prepare a meal for Kaelyn and I. If he's not home by eight, I have it sent to his lab. We generally visit the Rainforest once more in the evening before retiring.

Kaelyn said he had a great breakthrough in his work a couple of days ago. Ever since then, his lovemaking has been keeping me up for hours the last two nights. If his successes at work are going to spill into his enthusiasm with me, I hope he has an off day or two just so I can recuperate. Although I'm never going to get enough of him, I'm exhausted this morning.

Kaelyn's been at his lab since seven and now fast asleep in the canopy. The children want me to play 'find me' with them. I'm tired, but I don't want to disappoint them so I play. I'm going to lose anyway. No matter where I try to hide, Loopy and Zara always seem to find me. I know Jasper has x-ray vision, and that's the confusing part why he's usually the last to show up.

I've gotten to be quite the tree climber. I hide in one of the larger trees. There must be at least a hundred massive branches extending from it surrounded by a hundred more vines. The view of the lagoon and waterfall is serenely beautiful from up here. I sit down to rest on a thick branch. I, too, want a nap. I wish it could be on Kaelyn's chest in the hammock, but I'm happy to suffice for a tree right now. Just as I'm about to close my eyes…

"Found you, Mama!" squeals Loopy with delight. I wake up in a startle as she swoops in loops and lands on my shoulder.

"How do you keep finding me so fast? It's not fair! What's your secret? Out with it!" I say poking her tummy. Loopy turns pink all over. There are streaks of golden in the wings.

"Papa told me I have the nose of a German shepherd. Whatever that is. It makes me smell everything! I can usually smell your perfume the moment you enter the Rainforest!"

Incredible! "You little cheater!" I say laughing and tickle her tummy. She giggles so much she falls off my shoulder.

"Hi, Mama," says Zara flying into my lap. She gives me a hug with her hands and wings. I gently hug her back. I don't want to hurt her beautiful falcon wings. Zara looks up at me with her big brown eyes. She's ever so sweet. Loopy flies to my shoulder again.

"Why doesn't Papa dress you?" I ask Zara. "He dresses Seth and Jasper, but not you."

"Mama, I can't fly if I wear clothes. My wings get in the way," she says softly. That makes sense.

"Can't Papa have clothes made for you?"

"I don't know, Mama."

"Would you like some pretty dresses?"

"Oh, yes, Mama, yes! Like the pretty dresses you wear!" she exclaims. Loopy looks back and forth as we speak. She claps her webbed paws with Zara's happiness.

"Let me see what I can do. C'mon, let's go find the boys."

"Seth and Jasper are at the canopy eating. I can hear them from here," says Loopy.

"Yes, Mama, so can I," says Zara nodding.

The canopy's at least a half a mile away. I'll never win with this amazing bunch and nor do I ever want to.

September 9, 2015 @ 3:00pm
Sector Two - Sophia's Design Studio
Sophia Cambridge

Katia's wedding dress is complete.

"What do you think Chaz?" I ask as I drape the gown on Katia's mannequin. I had mannequins of the bride and groom created to their exact measurements. They look exactly like them. I hope neither one of them gains or loses any weight before their wedding day. I even programmed the simulator to see how the gown flows when Katia dances with her husband to be. The lace flutters like butterflies around her.

"I did do a phenomenal job, didn't I?" Chaz says winking at me. I roll my eyes. I have to admit he did do a phenomenal sewing job and added the pearls flawlessly. I don't want to give him a bigger ego than he already has.

"We did a phenomenal job!" said Tara correcting him. "If I didn't cut the fabric so perfectly, you would not have been able to sew it." Those two fight like lions and tigers more and more as the days go by. They obviously like each other. I didn't think drones could have emotions, but these two surprise me with something or another on a daily basis.

"Yes, you both did an amazing job, but it couldn't have happened if I didn't design it. We make a great team!"

"You're not crying today. Is Dr. Kato all better?" asks Tara. I wish she didn't remind me of Kato, but they both have been worried about my emotional state lately. I didn't know drones were capable of sympathy, but these two are. I don't know if that's good or bad, yet.

"He's stable, Tara. Thank you for asking." I look at the mannequin of Kato decorated in the wedding attire I created for him. The silk tail tuxedo with soft leather accents would look extraordinarily handsome on him if he awakes to wear it. I order Chaz and Tara to store it in one of the armoires until needed. My only wish this *Showcase* season is Kato's health.

There are no religious holidays in the *Underground*. Only birthdays, anniversaries, and the main festivity, the *Showcase*, are celebrated.

The *Showcase* is grander than all the *Surface* religious festivities combined together. It's a two-week celebration. Every *Surface* awards show is sheer crap compared to the miracles of the *Showcase*. The beauty here is that no one competes with one another. Everybody's genius and talents are celebrated and appreciated. There are no trophies awarded. There are no tiaras crowned. We celebrate each other and our contributions to Mother Earth.

It's Zenith's favorite time of the year.

"Miss Sophia," says Jake. I'm surprised to hear Jake's voice since he has never called me before. My first thought wanders to Kato.

"Yes, Jake. Is everything all right?" I ask worried. Tara and Chaz fly back to me. "Start the groom's leather tail jacket. I'll be right there," I say looking at them. "It's a leather and lace theme. The leather to make his tuxedo jacket is stored in armoire two." Tara and Chaz fly away to do their bidding dancing along the way. We have Taylor Swift's "Style" playing in the background.

"Miss Lovelin would like to know if it is possible for you to visit the Rainforest today. There's something she would like to show you," replies Jake. Oh, I love Miss Lovelin! If she didn't want to open her own bookstore, I would have asked her to be my assistant. I just adore her fashion sense.

"More than happy to. What time?"

"At your convenience, Miss Sophia," says Jake.

"Please tell Miss Lovelin I'll be there in a half an hour." I don't know why I'm nervous. Sam tells me that Dr. Stonebridge and Miss Lovelin have fallen head over heels in love with each other. I can't blame Dr. Stonebridge. Miss Lovelin's ridiculously beautiful and talented in her own way.

"Your laboratory clearance has been approved," says Jake.

"Thank you, Jake."

"You are welcome, Miss Sophia," he replies and ends the conversation. I wonder what Miss Lovelin wants to show me in the Rainforest. It's such a beautiful place. The last time I was there was with Kato. It's a happy memory finding Loopy. It's a sad memory, too.

That's where my love for him all started. A part of me is sad, but I could use a good nature walk. I've been doing nothing but working from dawn to dusk to keep my mind off of Kato with no luck.

"Chaz, Tara, I have an appointment to get to. See how much you can get done. I've got ideas for the bridesmaids' dresses and groomsmen attire in the computer. Tell me tomorrow what you think. Go ahead and make alterations if necessary. Don't work all night like yesterday. Make sure you recharge."

"Bye, Miss Sophia," they both say in unison working away.

September 9, 2015 @ 3:30pm
Genetics Laboratory
Sophia Cambridge

The Genetics lab is massive and absolutely beautiful. I can see Dr. Stonebridge working behind a glass door. He peers into a microscope and uses a laser at the same time. He's beautifully dressed in dark grey pants and a lavender dress shirt. I can see the beautiful silver buttons glistening from here. His attire surprises me. I always thought he lived in his black lab coat.

"Hi, Sophia. What are you doing here?" says Jay. He and Dr. Shapiro are both in their lab attire. There's a tremendous amount of foliage on a table in front of them. There are flowering pots with leaves along the back wall. There are tiny aquariums of foliage all around as well.

"Miss Lovelin called me. She wants to show me something in the Rainforest," I say walking forward. Miss Lovelin comes into the lab from the Rainforest door upon my words.

"Ready, sweetie," she asks smiling at me.

"Ready," I say smiling back. Miss Lovelin extends her hand and I take it. I wave bye to Jay and Dr. Shapiro.

The Rainforest is warmer than I remember from the last time I was here searching for Loopy. Maybe it's because it's daytime now and it was nighttime then. I should have changed out of these leggings into shorts. Miss Lovelin's beautifully dressed as usual in black dress shorts accompanied by a golden rhinestone belt, a white buttoned down shirt with golden buttons, and mid-length lace up boots with a golden zipper in the back.

"Dr. Stonebridge looks mighty sharp this morning," I say. Lovelin smiles.

"I now shop at Mid-Section for him and order other clothes off the *SuperNet* as well. My favorite designer is Bugatchi. He only uses Hong Kong tailors. He claims they are the best in the world."

"That's not true. My drone, Chaz, is the best in the world. No man or machine can stitch as flawlessly as he can. He has a big head about it, too," I say laughing.

"That's wonderful, Sophia. I'm so happy for you." We have a few minutes of silence between us as we soak up the warm rays and the harmony of the animal and plant life that surrounds us. I love the feeling of the outdoors, although I know I'm not really outside.

"How's your Kato?" she asks me as we leisurely walk. I blush.

"He's not mine. He's more stable now, but still hasn't woken."

"Sophia, I see Jay almost every day. He has told me you and Kato care for each other dearly."

"Really? Jay told you Kato cares for me?"

"Yes, really, and you needn't be shy with me. I'm not the gossiping type." I tell Miss Lovelin how brilliant and beautiful Kato is. He's such a gentleman, too. She lets go of my hand and hugs me around the shoulder. "He's going to be just fine." I don't want to cry, but a tear slips down my face. Lovelin plucks some hybrid fruit for us. I've never eaten such delicious fruit.

"Oh! There's a baby kangaroo in the jungle!"

"Come here, Leah," says Lovelin as she sits on the earth. The sweet little creature climbs onto her lap. "Ready to see Kaelyn's magic?" I don't know what she's talking about so I just nod my head. "Where's Mia?" The cute little baby kangaroo turns into a kitten. I think I just peed my pants. "How's Tia?" The kitten now is a baby bunny. Lovelin and Tia rub noses together.

"How's that even possible!" I exclaim as Lovelin hands me the bunny. It's ever so furry and soft with the prettiest pink eyes.

"Kaelyn calls her a shape-shifter. Don't ask me how. His report is ten times the size of *War and Peace*. If you really want to know, go for it."

The little bunny jumps out of my lap and hops away. We resume our nature walk. The sounds of the Rainforest are so soothing. I can hear a variety of chirps and whistles. This whole place sounds like a choir singing in delight. Loopy flies in loops toward us and stops in front of my face just hovering in the air. She's orange and green with golden wings. She hasn't grown much since I saw her asleep last in a hiscasuckle flower.

"Who's that, Mama?" she says. I stare speechless at her. My mouth must be on the Rainforest floor. Her voice is another sweet melody adding to the harmony of this Rainforest.

"Say 'hello' to Miss Sophia."

"She talks!" I try to exclaim with a hoarse voice. I don't know which is more amazing, the little kitten-bunny-kangaroo or Loopy speaking.

"Yes, she started the night of her shedding. Highly classified. Keep whatever you see here to yourself. Understood?"

"Of course, I completely understand. I would never reveal Dr. Stonebridge's work. We all know the laws down here." Loopy sits on my shoulder.

"Hello Miss Sophia, you're awfully pretty," says Loopy. This little creature just stole my heart. Well, maybe Kato stole it first.

"You're damn incredibly pretty, too, Loopy!" I say. Loopy then turns about ten shades of pink all over and acts all shy. She's blushing!

My feet walk from dirt and foliage into sand. I'm in a giant sand box. I've never been to this part of the Rainforest before. There seems to be a jungle gym in the corner with three monkeys. One is drawing in the sand.

"Oh! More beautiful creatures!" I've always wanted to see Dr. Stonebridge's creations. There has always been dozens of speculations throughout the *Underground*, but he refuses to reveal them. Only Loopy and Zara have been shown at the last *Showcase*.

"Prince Seth, Prince Jasper, Princess Zara," she addresses, "this is Miss Sophia."

"Hello, Miss Sophia," they all say in unison. Jasper comes forward to me.

"You are ever so lovely, Miss Sophia," he says. He talks, too! I shouldn't be surprised. I want to pick him up in my arms and never let him go. I hesitantly put my hands out and Jasper crawls right onto my lap. His golden orange mane is silky soft. His eyes are full of emotion.

"You are incredibly lovely yourself." Jasper has a bashful expression in his eyes as he wraps his arms around cuddling into me.

"Princess Zara, come here," says Lovelin. The little monkey with the gorgeous brown and grey wings crawls up onto Lovelin's lap. "Sophia, Princess Zara needs some beautiful clothes fit for a princess of her caliber. She's not a worthless *Surface* princess, but a true *Underground* princess. I'm sure you can see that," Lovelin says winking at me. "I believe you are the only one that can help her?"

I look at the sweet tiny monkey in front of me. She's grown a bit since I saw her last year. Her feet are webbed and there are the most glorious wings adorning her back.

"She's going to need something practical so she can fly and play and sleep in. Something perfectly engineered for her to stay cool in the Rainforest heat like her brothers wear," says Lovelin. "Above all, it has to be incredibly stylish!"

I laugh and cry at the same time. "Incredibly stylish is all I know! I would be honored to make a new wardrobe for the princess!"

"I know you're busy with the upcoming attire, but maybe after? This could be your next project? She won't need much."

Zara looks up at me with awe. She's so precious.

"Jake, please send all of Princess Zara's measurements to my computer at my design studio."

"Done, Miss Sophia," says Jake.

Zara comes up to me and kisses my cheek. She then puts her arms around my neck from behind and lays her head on my shoulder. "I love you, Miss Sophia."

I don't know when I've ever felt more cherished.

Chapter 20

September 10, 2015 @ 8:00am
Kaelyn's apartment
Lovelin

I wake up alone. I slept on his chest all night and didn't even realized when he slipped out of bed this morning. We made love twice last night. I stretch as I relive last night's escapades. I'm still exhausted from round two.

"Miss Lovelin?" asks Jake. This is the first time Jake has addressed me.

"Yes, Jake. Everything all right?" I ask sitting up in bed.

"The results of your survey are in. May I give them to you?" I'm scared, but I want to make this quick, like ripping off a band aid.

"So appreciative, Jake. Please go ahead," I say shaking inside myself. I pull the covers around me a bit more and close my eyes.

"You have a seventy-two percent approval rate. Would you like me to breakdown the specifics for you?" I breathe once more. I didn't even realize I was holding my breath until Jake stopped speaking.

"Please."

"Eighty-two percent of the scientists would like you to reference their work in your store. Ninety-eight percent of the wait staff and maintenance would like you to carry fiction and non-fiction novels both in electronic and non-electronic formats. They would also like your recommendations. The same panel would like a top one hundred list of your favorite authors, and a top five hundred list of your favorite novels in each category: romance, biographies, science fiction, drama, fantasy, erotica, personal health, classic literature, cooking, etc. In addition, the survey reveals that eighty percent would like for you to determine age groups: years one to five, six to ten, eleven to twelve, thirteen to sixteen, seventeen to twenty, young adult, and adult. Understood?"

Oh, my dear Lord, what have I done! I'm not a *Barnes and Noble* or *Amazon*! "Yes, Jake, understood. Thank you for everything."

"Best wishes, Miss Lovelin."

"Love you, Jake," I say slipping under the covers into the bed.

"As you wish," says Jake.

I smile to myself melting beneath my comforter. I got this!

September 10, 2015 @
Cloning Laboratory
David

"You really think everybody is going to follow him this time?" I say. I haven't had sex since Zareen's death. I don't know what's wrong with me.

"Why not? He's quite the leader," says Kaiser. I don't know what he's reading. I gave up upon Kaelyn's report on the creation of Loopy. It was too over my head.

"He was a madman caught up in religious turmoil. How do you know he will follow Zenith's path?"

"The mentally ill, the sick, and the diseased are worse than any religious turmoil. Who doesn't want to get rid of them? We just have to brainwash him to take care of the parasites on our Mother Earth. We can do this. It's what Zenith wants and we will carry it out. He will save our planet."

"I would love to see a population of pure health as well." The ramifications for our population as a whole would be incomprehensible. Barney licks my hand. It's his way of saying 'let's go for a run'. A run sounds good. I haven't been sleeping well at night. I need to get all this extra energy out. I still have no desire to hook up with even one of my regular girls. I have to find a way to get out of this slump somehow, but I haven't a clue what to do.

I take Barney for a run.

September 10, 2015 @ 9:00pm
Sector Four - Kaelyn's Apartment
Kaelyn

"Doesn't anybody read down here?" Lovelin questions.

"What are you talking about? Everybody reads down here. Learning is most of our life."

"But nobody reads for pleasure?"

"Love, when do we have time? Everybody works down here 24/7. I tried reading one of your books once without even knowing it was you. I didn't have the time to get past chapter three. We don't have the luxurious lifestyle of *Surface* people."

"You think the *Surface* is luxurious? It's a struggle, Kaelyn, for most. You're all pampered and catered to down here. You don't have to worry about making a living."

"Love, it's a tradeoff. We all have our sacrifices. The *Surface* is counting on us to make it better for them, although they have no clue we exist. We are the fairy Godmothers nobody knows about and we can't even brag about it. We work harder and sacrifice far more than any *Surface* earthling. And for what? Ourselves? No. We do it all for our Mother Earth to keep our species beautiful and alive. You think we are privileged just because we don't have *Surface* problems? There's far more on our shoulders than any *Surface* person could imagine. That's why we are protected down here."

"Forgive me, my love." I pull her into my arms and kiss her gently.

"You will never have to ask for my forgiveness," I say. "Remember your past life, but let go of it. Work for us and Zenith. In return, it will work for all humanity."

Chapter 21

September 10, 2015 @ 8:00pm Egypt Time
Sector Two Laboratories
Zachary Briarwood

"Why couldn't the archeologist she seeks live in Argentina or Australia or even the Antarctic? Do you have any idea what Egypt is like right now? It's an incredible fucking mess," says Kieran. "And what do all the *Surface* nations do? They just stay in their own little world, under their own little rocks and watch from satellite television."

I want to say that we live under our own little rocks, too, (no pun intended) but I don't.

I know Kieran's worried about me, but I don't want to disappoint Sam. I'm just as curious to know what those scrolls say as much as she does. Maybe it's nothing. Maybe it's something. It's such a long shot. If it wasn't Samantha, I would dismiss it. Zenith created her like her Uncle and he's amazing. I'm sure Sam will follow in his footsteps. They are the same blood after all.

Samantha webbed a fascinating untold tale before us.

I want to believe in it. I want to believe in something other than the death and destruction and fear embedded in the *Surface* world. As beautiful and as glorious as our planet is, too much hate surrounds and lives within it. I want to believe in love and in miracles. I know Sam wants to believe in that, too.

"I'm teleporting right into the archeologist's work site and back. I don't plan on being part of the war. I doubt it if he is. He's remotely away from the bombing area. I'll be back soon," I say trying to put my partner's mind at ease.

"If you are not back in twenty-four, I'm coming after you." I slowly look up from inputting my coordinates. His words take a moment to register. He softly smirks at me.

"Your Spear is done?" He nods his head. "Where is it?"

"It's in its final stage in the chamber. I placed it last night after you left. Zenith has no idea, and they won't until necessary."

"Did it take your…"

"Very well." I want to jump up and down like some Peruvian monkey, but I withhold my enthusiasm until I see Kieran and his Spear for myself.

"How much longer?" I question as I finalize the coordinates into my Spear. I hope I got them right. It's the trickiest part of the teleportation process. A thousandth degree off could land me in harm's way or worse like falling off a cliff. We have to rely on *Google* maps. Kieran checks the chamber.

"Digital read says six hours, two minutes, and twenty-three point four eight one two five seconds."

"I'll be back before then." I'm ready for takeoff. "Wish me luck." I stand in the middle of our lab like before the start of every journey.

"Stay safe," Kieran says monitoring the control panel. "Your heart rate's elevated. Calm down."

I need to do some yoga and meditation exercises before every trip. I wish I didn't get so anxious. I breathe in and out for a couple of minutes. I close my eyes and listen to soothing sounds of rushing water in my head. I hear birds flutter by and visualize dragonflies dance on beautiful red flowers. I don't stop until Kieran gives me his approval.

"That's better. You're ready."

I open my eyes and activate the Spear. Within moments, a soft warm breeze flows all around me. I close my eyes once again and find the waterfall I earlier left in my mind. The white water thunders ending at a beautiful cascading river two hundred feet below. Toucans fly down and out with me. The greenery is lush and sways in the wind of the descending waters. The Milky Way's glorious sun is just about set.

So this is what soaring like an eagle feels like.

The ride's fast and thrilling, calm and peaceful at the same time. It's even more exhilarating than the previous one to London. The flows of rushing cascades are within me as I land. It doesn't feel like the warm sand that I expected.

I tumble in the warmth and wetness. I should have landed in the archeologist's office near his dig site. I'm having a difficult time breathing and I hold my breath the moment I realize I'm underwater. I'm no longer in my meditative calm, but in a rocky swift whirlwind that's beckoning me to the bowels of the Earth.

The Spear in my hand burdens me, but I hold onto it as if it is my lifeline for it is my lifeline. I struggle to swim against the strong current. I cannot see anything except for a black abyss trying to pull me further below and away from my destination. I spiral faster and faster, deeper and deeper into a deep dark grave.

This is not the way I want to die. This is not my time.

I fight to reach the surface. The currents are strong and keep tumbling me back. My Spear breaks apart from me once, but I am quickly able to recover it. My lungs and calves and arms burn as I break the water's surface. I gasp for air when I reach the humid air of this foreign land. I cough up much dirty liquids as well. I open my eyes to majestic brown mountains in the distant and the fading golden Egyptian sun.

I wish I wasn't so mesmerized by all its beauty because that was the moment nature took advantage, and had one of its children carry me downstream washing me away down the Nile.

September 9, 2015 @ 9:00am
Genetics Laboratory
Jay Ahmed

"I can't get it to work on a cellular level!" I say annoyed with myself taking my frustrations out on a red leaf, which is in shreds at my feet. I start tearing another one. Michael's not going to be too happy with me. Thank goodness, he's in the Rainforest working. I yell into the air hoping my Uncle will hear me. Sometimes he gets so absorbed in his work; the sounds of a hurricane can't pull him out of his concentration.

Uncle Kaelyn looks up from his petri dishes. "Jay, did you say something?" He watches the tiny red fragments flutter down as they fall out of my hand.

He leaves his workspace and sits next to me. I'm on the verge of tears. Again. When I saw Kato this morning, I thought I was going to have an emotional breakdown. He has lost weight although he's on nutritional supplement patches. Samantha hasn't spoken to me since our time in Zachary's lab either. My project's not going as I want.

"It only works on a molecular level. I've learned to enhance it, but only molecularly. It doesn't work on a cellular level. It won't work on anything organic," I say reaching for a green serrated leaf this time.

My Uncle stops me and asks me what I've tried. I tell him. He tells me about his trails. I don't think I can do that. No, I know I can't do that. I'm not that kind of scientist.

"Jay, do you know how many of my creatures I have had to destroy before I succeeded?"

I try not to think about it. I don't want to think about it.

"You have no problem shredding leaves apart. They're alive, too. If you want to help Kato, you have to conduct cellular research at the animal kingdom. Their cellular structure is different.

You know that. Trials on plants and vegetables aren't going to help you even if you succeed at it."

He makes sense. Of course, he does. I knew that, but I was in denial about it. I immediately stop tearing at the leaves. I don't know if I hurt them or not. Although I can't hear them cry out, I'm sure they do. All in the name of science.

"Start small. Work with mice. It's the only way. If you want to try saving your brother, you have no choice; otherwise, let's just wait and see if we can acquire a lung soon."

I pictures Kato's lifeless form just lying in the hospital bed.

"Where can I get the mice?"

Chapter 22

September 10, 2015 @ 8:15pm Egyptian Time
Zachary Briarwood

The Spear's far heavier underneath the waves and I can't adjust it as I need for survival. Now at the surface, I struggle to place the Spear between my legs. The current keeps beckoning me down beneath the torrential waves as the sun fades faster than I want. On my fourth try, I'm able to place the Spear and sit while turning another section of lock below its head. There are some villagers in the distance, but the sun has almost retired for the evening as I pray that the locals don't see me. Even if they do, I will be gone before they even realize what took place before their eyes.

"Fly!" I command. "Fly fucking hard!"

The Spear rises into the warm Egyptian air with me upon it. Water drips and evaporates from my entire entity. I lean forward onto my vessel and turn to my right. I guide my Spear the way I want to drive.

No *Surface* sport cars could ever have the dreams my Spear is spoiled with.

I fly low over the Nile. The water brushes against my boots as I speed through a velocity unknown to mankind through the sandy dusk. My black jeans and grey shirt are soaked, but I'm not cold from the desert heat. My dark brown hair flows behind me as the stars come upon to greet me.

I don't know where I'm going. I couldn't have been that far off my mark, could have I? It takes me about five minutes before the archeological dig that I intended to land on comes before me. There's a small building in the midst. A dim light's still on within its structure. It's barely visible through the broken window.

"Halt," I command. The Spear slows at first and then stays suspended in front of the building. I check my perimeter. Nobody's around the dig site.

"Down," I command once more. The Spear, now dry from our ride, slowly settles me until my feet land upon the sand. I then take my Spear out from between and hold it in my right hand. I input the *Underground* coordinates into it before entering through the rotting, sand mite infested, dilapidated door.

A tall thin man stands over a table mumbling to himself. There's no one else in the room. He paces back and forth along the table gazing upon a parchment in front of him every so now and then. He puts his hands to his hair as if trying to tear it out and then mumbles louder this time. I wish I knew what he was saying. I make a note to myself to study the local language before each journey.

The doctor's dressed in typical Egyptian clothing with a long brown tunic and flowing cotton pants. He wears a black vest and black boots rather than sandals. He's clean-shaven.

There's a scar across his left eye. He's a handsome man nonetheless from the side with his long hair past his shoulders. I can see dozens of broken artifacts adorning other tables and a cabinet. The overhead light bulb's not going to last another week. It's barely illuminating now.

I slowly walk around. The floor doesn't make a sound even with my wet shoes. The sand is soft. I then creep to the back of the table to face the archeologist. He looks up mumbling and then quickly stops. He gazes first at me and then the Spear in my hand. I lay out the Spear in both my hands horizontally for him to view. It glows in all its scriptures and symbols as I hold it tighter and tighter.

Astonishment washes all over his face.

He just stares at me dumbfounded for a while taking it all in. I don't say anything nor do I move. He walks back from the table. Instead of running, he gets down on his hands and knees and bows his head as if in prayer.

"Dr. Takbare, I have come from far, far away, and you have been chosen."

I thought he would crumble upon my words. I want him frightened so I could get him to do my bidding. I want him scared so he wouldn't resist. Instead, this brave man lifts his head and looks directly into my eyes.

"Lead me to your people, oh, Holy One," he says before bowing to me again.

September 10, 2015 @
Sector Two Laboratories
Jay Ahmed

"God damn it!" I say throwing the mouse across the wall. It bleeds all the way down to the floor. I don't know if it's dead by the time it travels all the way down to the crown molding that dresses this laboratory.

I hope it's dead.

I don't want him to suffer just because of my frustration. A drone immediately comes and cleans up this innocent mouse. The half a dozen other students cease what they're doing and just stare at me. I've never been one to lose my temper during trials.

"Jay?" says Dr. Shu Yen. "I think you need a break. Let's order some lunch for you."

"I'm not hungry," I say ignoring him with a wave of my hand.

Where did I go wrong this time? I go through the equations on my holographic screen suspended in air in front of me. I change a couple of the figures. Yes, that has to be it!

"Jay," says Dr. Yen again, "you won't be able to accomplish anything without nourishment."

I pick up another mouse to mutilate just as Samantha's pretty face comes into my line of sight. I press my wrist. The archeologist has arrived. Char really did it! I don't know whether I'm happy or sad about this. My project seems insignificant compared to what he has accomplished. No wonder Sam can't get enough of him.

"I think I'll go out for lunch," I say looking up at Dr. Yen. The others have resumed their experiments.

"Take your time. Take the day off, Jay. You've been at it since dawn. Tomorrow with a fresh brain and a pair of relaxed eyes."

I put the frightened mouse back into its cage. It huddles up with the others in the corner. Somehow, they all know they are going to die. Better them than my brother.

I can't understand the monster that I've become. We are here for Zenith and Mother Earth to create, not destroy. I hate it and love it simultaneously.

I grab my stuff and head for the train.

Chapter 23

September 10 @ 3pm
Sector Two Laboratories
Samantha Stonebridge

I catch up with Jay on *Platform Archive* going to Sector Two. We get in and find a bench for us. We gather our belongings on the train floor and talk about our day as we settle in. Neither of us had a chance to grab lunch. Jay gets up and makes us both roast beef sandwiches on sourdough bread with sweet horseradish sauce. Jazmin and Paris board the train taking seats adjacent to us. Jay gives me my sandwich and I sit just a bit closer to him as they store their backpacks in the overhead compartments. We both bite in at the same time. I see he has a bit of horseradish at the corner of his mouth so I wipe it away with my napkin. I can see Jazmin and Paris looking at me from the corner of their eyes as I do so. Jay just says he's so hungry and sorry for eating like a starved dog.

He's finally hungry. I've been watching him withering away into nothing these past weeks.

I'm going to miss an exam in Neurology and then a mock surgery in the O.T. afterwards. I haven't come up with an excuse, yet, to tell my professor. I wish I could tell them I'm sick like *Surface* children do. Unfortunately, that one doesn't work all too well down here. I can't very well tell him the truth that I have a meeting with an Egyptian archeologist that just happens to be in town.

After we devour our sandwiches, I put the plates in the bin for washing. The drones immediately take them away. I stumble upon Jay's backpack in front of him and fall into his lap. I did it on purpose.

"Sorry, wasn't paying attention," I lie.

"Sorry, Sam. Shouldn't have kept it in your way," he says moving his backpack to the left of him. I sit closer to him than before upon returning to our bench. Jay's backpack is full. Not with books, but with his miracle spray.

"Have you named it?" I whisper looking dreamily up into his eyes.

I could never be an actress. This is too much work. Jazmin and Paris are engaged in their own conversation.

Jay's probably wondering what's gotten into me. We haven't said much to each other these past few days. He has been working on perfecting his method and Uncle Kaelyn keeps him extremely busy as well. Kato's always at the back of our minds, but he seems to have stabilized.

"Named what?"

"Your invention, silly. You have to call it something."

"I don't know, Sam. Haven't really thought about it. What do you think?"

I wonder if he's going to ask Lucinda the same question later. I wish I could stop thinking about her when Jay's with me. Just as

I look at Paris and Jazmin, they smile on cue and then avert their eyes away.

"How about Reverse," I say laying my hand on Jay's knee. From the look on Jay's face, he's not too gung ho about it.

"Too simple. It doesn't reverse everything," he says putting his hand on top of mine. "I was thinking As Good As New." He has a smile on his face. Paris and Jazmin notice us holding hands. Well, somewhat holding hands.

"Could you be any more boring?" I spit out before thinking. Jay puts his head down and then retracts his hand from the top of mine. I'm positive the entire train heard us. Oh, fuck! I didn't mean it that way! I don't think he's boring. What is it with boys and their lack of egos these days? He slides a bit away from me as if I have burned him.

Jazmin and Paris are questioning what just happened.

"I know," I whisper summoning Jay to my ear. He leans in, but I pull him closer with my fingers in his hair at the base of his neck. "How about Time Warp?" I then release him.

A smile crosses Jay's lips as he leans back. "I like that. That's really creative, Sam. Didn't know you had it in you."

Now I sit back and away, a bit annoyed. "You never thought me as creative?"

"No, no, it's not that. It's just that Sophia's always been the creative one. You know, with her incredible imagination and designs. We, generally, are just the bookworm and play-by-the-rules type."

"We?" I question again. "I thought you were pretty creative for coming up with your restoration process."

"Thank you," he says and nothing more. Jazmin and Paris still pretend not to eavesdrop.

I haven't started to design a project, yet. I don't know what's taking me so long. My Uncle Kaelyn already had a half a dozen new medical techniques by the time he was my age. The *Surface* still doesn't possess his technology. I guess I'm not as brilliant as I think I am. I'm obviously not focused enough. I need to start a project of my own, and fast. I feel like such a failure again.

We arrive at Sector Two. "We're here," says Jay. He grabs his stuff. "Let's go."

He can't get off the train fast enough. I saunter off behind him. I can't imagine what Paris and Jazmin are thinking, but I know what I'm thinking.

Something obviously went wrong when Zenith and the *Underground* physicians designed me.

September 10, 2015 @
Sector Two Laboratories
Zachary Briarwood

When did a Holy One ever wear designer black jeans?

I land back into my laboratory with the archeologist and the scrolls intact. We belted the metal case that contained the scrolls around his waist before takeoff. He was hesitant to transfer them, but the small basket they were found in was too frail. I was afraid it would not survive the journey and the scrolls would be lost between there and here.

"You got him!" says Kieran. I just nod. I don't have the energy to tell him about my life-ending, life-saving journey just yet.

Dr. Takbare looks around our lab. He's definitely not the shy type. He gazes into our cabinets with bewildering eyes.

"May I?" he pleads with extending hands. We just nod our heads. I put my Spear back into its armoire. I administer the safe lock. Zenith couldn't open it in a million years.

Kieran has spaghetti and meatballs waiting for me on standby. My earlier swim made me famished and I devour it all in a matter of minutes. I order another plate and one for the doctor through Jake.

Dr. Takbare cradles the Mayan stones as if they were newborn children. His eyes become glassy. He puts them away and then worships the artifacts of each cabinet one by one. I've never seen a man appreciate a bunch of rocks the way he does.

"What is this holy mess?" asks Dr. Takbare as he eats.

"It's just spaghetti and meatballs," I say. He nods his head. Then he nods his head some more, moaning as he eats.

"So this is the food of the Gods," he says trying to twirl more spaghetti around his fork.

I nod my head too tired to argue.

September 10, 2015 @
B Line Train to Sector Two
Jay Ahmed

I know what she's trying to do. She wants Paris and Jazmin to believe that nothing's astray between us. All of me is happy about the fact that Sam's jealous of Lucinda. I don't think I planned for it to be that way. Maybe I did it subconsciously.

I can't believe she's jealous. I didn't think Zenith programmed jealousy into their golden child.

I'm kind of liking it. No, kind of loving it. She was such a bitch the other day. They say payback is hell. I just don't know if I want Sam to feel that or not. I don't want to hurt her anymore. This cycle has to stop.

I board the train with her like we've been best friends all along. We both haven't eaten so I make us a couple of sandwiches. Roast beef with horseradish is one thing we have in common. For the first time in a long while, I'm really hungry. Maybe it's because I'm sharing a meal with Sam again on a positive note. Maybe it's because Kato's also stable. As we start eating, I see Jazmin and Paris look our way. I try not to notice and just keep eating. Sam brushes away some sauce from the corner of my mouth. I'm so hungry I guess I wasn't paying attention to my manners. I should do that more often. I apologize out of politeness.

After we are done and Sam puts the dishes away, she stumbles on my backpack right into my chest. I instinctively grab her. I hold her a bit longer than necessary. We both apologize simultaneously. Even after the apology, I don't want to let her go.

"Have you named it?" she says.

She looks like she's going hypoglycemic, but that can't be because she just ate. Her eyes are all glassy and she looks like she's going to fall again.

"Named what?"

"Your invention, silly. You have to call it something."

I think she's joking when she called me silly, but I'm not sure. I tell her I honestly haven't thought about a name. We go back and forth for a while trying to come up with something suitable. Then she tells me I'm boring. I'm silly and boring within the last few minutes. I move away from Sam. She's on her high horse again.

She suggests Time Warp and I actually find myself liking that name. The more I think about it, I find myself loving that title. I try to tell her how much I like it, but it doesn't come out right.

Now she thinks I find her uncreative. I'm caught in that never ending loop again. I can't get off the train fast enough.

Chapter 24

September 10, 2015 @ 2:00pm
Sector Two - Physics Laboratory
Samantha Stonebridge

"Dr. Briarwood, Dr. Mersa," says Jake. "Your laboratory has a security breech."

"No, it doesn't," says Char. "I have a new colleague working with me."

"This new colleague is not an *Underground* inhabitant according to facial and skeletal recognition. He appeared into my system out of nowhere recently," says Jake. "Protocol tells me that I must contact Zenith."

Oh, shit!

"Jake, you're not allowed to view our laboratory. It's private footage," says Kieran. "I have been given limited capabilities after Dr. Zareen Kalli's death," says Jake.

Oh, shit! Didn't know that. Jake should have made an announcement, but he didn't. "I never heard such an announcement," I say.

"It was posted on *Show Off* recently," says Jake.

We all sigh. Apparently, the four of us haven't checked *Showoff* lately.

"Jake, you cannot contact Zenith. I forbid you," says Kieran. "He's vital to our work. He will not be leaving our laboratory. His visit will be a short one."

Silence.

Oh, shit! Jake is completely devoted to Zenith.

"Very well, Dr. Mersa," replies Jake.

We all find ourselves breathing a sigh of relief. Jay sprays his glowing light blue aerosol all over the three-thousand-year-old parchment. The mist looks like sparkles dancing to a waltz until it falls upon the paper. Once the mist slumbers itself into a sleep, its color dims and dies.

I can't understand why Jay created such a boring can to put his prized work into. The can is pasty white and looks as ugly as a decaying corpse. If it was me, I would have created a beautiful spray bottle of vibrant colors. I bet Sophia could do much more of an amazing job in the design. Some boys just don't have any visual creativity.

My mind tells me I love Jay nonetheless, designer boy or not.

I glance upon the parchment-type thin cloth. I'm surprised this type of paper hasn't disintegrated by now. It looks like it's going to crumble apart at any second. It looks browner and browner by the minute. The parchment's lace thin and withering away by the moments in front of me. How it survived all these years with the erosion around it is unbelievable.

I want to touch it, but I don't out of respect. I don't want to harm it. Jay doesn't even touch it. He runs his fingers over it in the air above. He looks at it with love in his eyes.

I wish he would look at me that way.

I only sit back and wait for instruction. There's nothing much I can do right now. The ball's no longer in my court. Jay's the ringleader in this show. I wish I didn't feel like the clown at the halftime performance.

Mummification is unbelievable and cannot be duplicated. I wonder if anyone in the *Underground* has tried. I suppose their paper is made the same. I wish I could take it and analyze it, but then I would have to destroy it to do so. I cannot destroy this parchment. I have a feeling if I do, I will destroy my Uncle and Miss Lovelin. I look at Jay. I know he's thinking the same.

Is he? Maybe I'm grasping at straws for some sort of connection. I look at him again. No. I'm right. His face tells me he wants to analyze the cloth paper lying in long sheets in front of him.

Jay stands back after the first spray and watches. Nothing happens. Dr. Takbare looks annoyed, but still stands ridged with hope. He looks like he's caught between worlds of believe and make believe. I have faith in Jay so I just wait patiently. It's not just Jay. I have faith in everyone in the *Underground*.

I'm so fidgety, but I try to not let it show. I want to bite my nails, but I hold back keeping my hands underneath my butt while sitting in the leather high back chair in Char's lab. Jay gives me a funny look while I squirm around with my hands under my ass. I try to avoid his glares. It's hard, but I wait. Dr. Takbare folds his arms and taps his feet as I squirm around. I want to follow Dr. Takbare's lead in my chair, but restrain myself. My bottom's getting too warm with all ten of my fingers under them.

Within minutes, the parchment goes from an old dusty yellow brown to a bright shade of yellow brown. There's a glow upon it as it changes color. The parchment seems to be getting sturdier and stronger as well, not the frail thin material once in front of us. All of us look in awe except for Jay.

Of course, he has seen this before.

I hesitantly get up from my seat, but keep my hands firmly by my side. I peek at the unraveling before us.

More of the symbols and pictures become visible, although I have no idea what they mean. I don't think my eyes could get any wider. I should have brushed up on ancient Egyptian languages and hieroglyphs before this, but then Zenith would be wondering what for. I'm a modern doctor and scientist after all. I didn't want to bring up any red flags. Now, I wish we didn't have to take Zenith's permission for everything we want and do. Then again, Zenith's our fail-safe. Their security lets us live in peace down here.

Dr. Takbare mumbles to himself watching the scrolls come to life as it once was. He pulls on his own hair once in a while talking in circles watching the scrolls transform to their yesteryears. He looks like an animated monkey as the scrolls bounce back some three thousand plus years. He smiles, then laughs, then hoots, and then hollers. He's definitely a doctor and scientist like we are.

I slump back into Char's comfortable chair watching the parchment come alive moment by moment.

It's a bittersweet afternoon with such mixed emotions. I like this Egyptian man. He has an amazing passion for his work like we do. Jay stands tall like a Prince next to him. He has such a proud smile on his face. I smile at his smile. He looks, turns, and winks at me.

Without thinking, I blow him a kiss with my fingers to show him how proud I am of his achievement. He grabs my kiss from the air and puts his hand on his heart. His eyes look dark and beautiful as he gazes at me when he does so. I sit back and close my eyes.

I don't vision the miracle happening in front of me with the scrolls. I don't vision the wedding day I wish would happen between us.

I vision only more sorrow between us, and it makes me want to scream.

How am I going to tell my beloved Jay that Dr. Takbare will have to die?

September 10, 2015 @ 3:00pm
Sector Two - Physics Laboratory
Samantha Stonebridge

Jay gives the scrolls a second coat of his spray. Dr. Takbare seems to be in some sort of trance watching the scrolls get brighter and brighter. More figures appear on the parchment out of nowhere. I wish I knew the story embedded in the thin fabric.

I can't believe he actually did it. I knew Jay was a brilliant physician, but he's more than that. He's an incredible scientist as well. I feel so insignificant compared to him right now. He came upon this idea on his own. It just hit him one day and he flew with it.

He should have been Zenith's golden child, not me.

"It's like the words are reborn," Dr. Takbare whispers. He puts his hands out to touch them, but Jay holds them back. He holds the doctor back.

"Don't!" says Jay. "It's still reconstructing."

The doctor gets on his hands and knees and prays to Jay as if he is some sort of God. I'm ready to get on my hands and knees and worship Jay, but I hold myself back. We are Zenith's children after all. This is what we are meant for.

"Did you hear what he said?" I ask looking at Jay. I can see Jay's expression as he goes from comprehension to understanding. At the end, we both look at each other with exuberant smiles.

"REBORN!" we say in unison. Char and Kieran smile inquisitively at us.

Without a second thought, I run into Jay's arm and hug him around his neck. When he picked me up, my legs wrapped around his torso somehow. I don't think I meant to do that. I don't know if Jay meant to do that as well. I'm positive some force guided me, or guided us, to link ourselves together.

The soft kiss upon my lips came out of nowhere. It was so quick, I didn't even know what was happening until it was over. Did he really kiss me or did I just imagine it?

"Praise to all the Gods!" say Dr. Takbare. Jay releases, dropping me to the floor. I try to stay standing, but my knees still shake and now I understand the feeling of butterflies in my stomach.

"Such a miracle!" he exclaims deciphering the scroll. His eyes go up and down the parchment at lightning speed.

You have no idea, I think falling to my knees. I can't even feel my toes. I don't know if I like this. How am I supposed to get any work done on my knees? How am I supposed to get any work done with my brain in a complete disarray?

So this is love.

* * *

"Jay?" He turns around.

"Yes, Sam." He doesn't look affected in any way. I don't know what to say.

"Everything working according to plan? How long before the scrolls are read?"

"Doctor says a couple of days. Some parts of the scrolls are taking longer due to decomposition. The restoration process will take a bit longer on some parts than others. It's truly a miracle they have survived this long!"

The miracle is that he kissed me. If he truly did. I'm still trying to figure out if I dreamt it. "So, what's the next step?" Not really for the scrolls, but for us.

"It's a waiting game at the moment."

That's what I was afraid of.

"Sam, Char has a bed coming in for the doctor and he wants more spaghetti for dinner which has already been ordered. I've got to go. See you tomorrow, okay?"

He's leaving me? Well, there was obviously no kiss and I just imagined it all.

"No problem, Jay. You go do what you gotta do. I'm not the ball and chain sort of girl," I say somewhat wincing at my last statement, but it needed to be said.

September 10, 2015 @ 4:00pm
Sector Two - Physics Laboratory
Jay Ahmed

When she ran into my arms in all the excitement, I didn't know what to do, but it just came naturally. I wanted to kiss her. I've been wanting to kiss her. So I kissed her quick, not the longing I've been dreaming about.

She raised her arms a bit to bring herself closer to me since we have a bit of a height difference, but I wasn't expecting her to wrap her legs around me, to wrap her body around mine. I thought I would drop to the floor and beneath to the underworld when she did, but I held myself steady the best I could and let go immediately. She was affecting me like nothing before and found myself going tense all over.

I don't even know if I kissed her or not because everything went by so fast, but at the end I know I did because my head couldn't function anymore.

So this is love.

We had some sort of conversation after the doctor prayed in front of me. Why he prayed at my feet, I don't know. I was still living in the moment of Sam around me discovering a name for my invention. She seemed happier than me. She didn't seem jealous at all that I had a breakthrough before her. I guess she's not all businesslike she wants me to believe.

Then maybe she's just happy because all of this is for her Uncle. I wish that thought never popped into my head. With that thought, I drop her as if burned by a flaming bunsen burner without meaning to.

Chapter 25

September 13, 2015 evening
Sector Two - Physics Laboratory
Kieran Mensa

My Spear is done. It's not like Zachary's spear of black, grey, and gold entwined with hieroglyphs. Mine is black and red with depictions of flowers and birds and Ivy and waterways. I've always been fascinated with the Hanging Gardens of Babylon. Many say it never existed, but I believe it did once upon a time. Mother Earth is full of beautiful mysteries.

"Scared?" questions Char. He's in front of the 3D computer screen this time. "Your heart rate is up."

The Spear is heavy in my hand, but I feel as though I am one with it. Nothing ever felt more serene. "The journey? No," I say inputting the coordinates. Char nods his head.

"Breathe Kieran. It will be fine."

I inhale deeply and exhale slowly. Within moments, I feel the soothing effects of a meditative trance. "I'm ready," I say. I stand in the middle of our lab and activate my Spear. Within moments, I feel a soft, warm breeze all around me. I could fall asleep in this heavenly feeling. I can see Char smile through the wind. He waves 'bye' with his hand.

Then I see only darkness.

I am floating and then I am flying. I want to fly faster. "Ride!" I command. My Spear takes off at lightning speed. What a rush! Universal Studios could never ever duplicate this! Char told me about the exhilarating travel, but this is beyond anything and everything I've ever imagined. I can go on like this forever.

With that thought, I land in the middle of a small apartment. The journey was faster than I imagined it would be. Char apparently did not command his Spear to take him to his destination at its capacity. We are learning along the way.

There is one lamp on. The rug underneath my feet is torn and faded. I remember the day Abba brought it home. The beautiful red and golden threads brightened our dreary apartment immediately. Simba lays sleeping on the frayed sofa. He doesn't even realize that I have landed. He has aged since I saw him last. His beige and ebony fur, nonetheless, is as beautiful as ever. I know Kavita has been taking good care of him.

I don't know what Zenith gave my family in exchange for me. They don't seem to live any differently as I did as a young boy so many years ago. The room is clean and smells sweet. There are fresh-cut flowers on the two end tables.

There are also three pairs of eyes staring at me in horror and bewilderment. I did find the most beautiful brown ones. There are tears welling up in them. Her face is all aglow.

"Ma, I'm home."

September 13, 2015 afternoon
Post-Surgical Ward - Infirmary
Sophia Cambridge

Sam told me this morning that Kato's eyes opened, but he is still in a semi-unconscious state. I begged her to let me see him. His attending physicians gave me permission.

There is no attending physician when I enter Kato's room. He must've stepped out for a moment.

I see at least six holographic screens in the room showing his insides and how they are healing. I can see how the insides of his body are repairing or if they aren't. He has to have at least six tiny nano cameras within himself if not more.

The first screen shows his hands. They are still bandaged, but almost healed. He has lost his left little finger. Sam says that they will either make a prosthetic finger for him or will take a real finger and do a transplant.

The second 3D screen shows Kato's heart. It is pumping steadily. His aorta looks almost completely healed. His blood pressure is a normal 110/70.

The third screen made my heart sink into the floor and beyond. His right lung seems to be recuperating and repairing itself with whatever salve and medications needed. His left lung looks almost nonexistent. I don't see any cellular repair whatsoever. Sam says they will do a lung transplant if needed. Zenith has been trying to locate a donor that matches his. I know Jay volunteered, but he doesn't match Kato's blood type.

I walk over to Kato's bed. His beautiful blue-black eyes are open. His hair needs a wash with some proper conditioner. Medi-drones have been trying to keep it fresh and clean as possible. An enzyme tablet is put in Kato's mouth daily to eliminate tartar buildup and keep his mouth fresh and healthy. His urine catheter shows clear liquids so I know he is well hydrated.

I hold his hand. It is warm, but dry. I take hand lotion out of my purse and apply it on the parts that are not bandaged up. Underground lotions are one hundred percent bacteria free. It shouldn't hurt him.

He doesn't move when I hold his hand or apply the cream along his fingertips and wrists. He has lost weight, but doesn't look malnourished.

My phone beeps. I pull it from my purse. Tara and Chaz are arguing over the groomsmen attire. Tara wants me back at the studio immediately or she will not be held responsible for her actions against Chaz. He may not live to ever sew another pearl again is her last sentence. The text message was electronically signed by Jake. As much as I love them, I'm going to have to talk to engineering about those two. They behave more human than drone.

"Kato, can you hear me?" I say. He doesn't know. I run my fingers through his hair. He still doesn't move. I doubt it if you can even hear me. "I have to go now, but I'll be back. There are a dozen of white roses in the waterfall for your health."

I kiss him softly on his lips. "I love you," I whisper inches from his face. Kato still has no response. A tear from my eye falls onto his lips. I turn around and walk out of the infirmary because there is nothing else I can say.

September 13, 2015
Iran
Kieran Mersa

Mother is too emotional to move. She must think she's dreaming. I can see it in her face. Kavita is the first to run and give me a hug. I have missed my little sister terribly. She was just a baby when I left. I remember swaying her in my arms and rocking her to sleep. I didn't know if she would even remember me, but she knew who I was the moment I landed. We are the same blood after all.

"I knew you would come home! Ma and Abba said you never would, but I knew!" she says all excited not letting me go.

Ma and Abba get up and hold me with a force that I've only felt once before. The day Zenith took me away.

"Praise Allah that you have returned to us!" exclaims my Abba, all choked up. I can feel my mother shake as she holds me.

"It is not Allah that has brought me to you. It is I that has brought me to you!" I say. My family lets me go. Simba is now sniffing at my heels. He wags his tail immediately and reaches his paws up to my knees. Of course, he remembers me. I was the one that picked him up from the gutter and brought him home. Ma and Abba were so annoyed that day. He was another mouth to feed which they couldn't afford. I told them not to worry. Ever since, I shared my meals with him.

I pick Simba up and cradle him like the puppy he once was in my arms so long ago.

"Allah made your brilliance happen," says my mother. I'm not in the mood to argue with my family. Their religious beliefs drive me crazy.

"I'm hungry, Ma. Feed me," I say sitting on the sofa with Simba. He now sleeps in my arms. My mother and sister rush into their tiny kitchen. They will be feeding me chicken and rice in no time.

My Abba holds up my Spear. I can see he is at a loss for words. "I can go anywhere in the world with it," I say. "In time, I will be able to go anywhere in the universe with it."

"Inshallah," says my father.

"It won't be God's will, Abba. It will be mine if I decide to do so," I say. "Your God doesn't exist in my world."

My Abba frowns. "Where does your peace come from, my son?" he asks.

"My peace comes from within. What do you all know about peace in Iran? All you know is hate and war. The world can't stand any of you. It is all because of your religious nonsense that you have no peace," I say. "You all live in fear. That's not a way to live if you truly have a wonderful God."

My Abba shakes his head. I know he will not be able to understand or comprehend what I say. He does not know anything about the harmonious world I live in.

"I don't expect you to understand, Abba. I'm far more open-minded and educated than you are."

My father now has an angry look on his face. "You think you are better than me?" he asks. His voice is not angry, but calm.

"I didn't come home to argue with you Abba," I say. "But please understand that my greatness does not come from superior beings. My greatness comes from our home. This Spear that I created to teleport is all from the natural wonders of our wondrous Earth and from myself."

"And who created our home?" says my father with an annoyance and raised voice.

"Do you really want to argue the creation of the universe with me? I am a man of science. You know that. For once, can we have an amicable conversation?" Simba still sleeps in my arms. He hasn't moved. He seems so at peace and so am I with him.

Kavita comes to me with a tray of samosas. I bite into one. "I made them myself. Ma taught me," she says smiling.

They aren't very good. The food in the *Underground* has spoiled me. "Absolutely delicious, sweet one! I think it's the best I've ever had!" I lie trying to swallow down my second bite. Kavita shrieks in delight and runs back to the kitchen. "Want one?" I asked my father.

He smiles and shakes his head.

* * *

My mother's chicken and rice was delicious, just as I remembered it as a child. Simba slept in my lap throughout the entire meal.

"I have to go," I say. "This visit was a test run."

"Oh, please, bhai jan, don't go!" says Kavita crying. She runs to my side and wraps her arms around my neck. My parents look ever so sad.

"We understand," says my father getting up from the table wrapping his hands around my mother. I can see that they are both fighting tears. I wish I could miss my parents, but I'd rather be in my true home where I am happy, the *Underground*.

"When will you come back?" asks my sister.

I know the answer, but I don't tell her.

Simba still sleeps in my arms. I gaze down at his beautiful, peaceful form. How am I going to let him go? I massage his head. He doesn't open his eyes. "Simba, I have to go," I say. His eyes remain closed.

"Simba, give me a lick before I have to depart," I ask. He still doesn't move or open his eyes. Kavita starts sobbing with her hands still around my neck. My parents hold onto each other even tighter. I put my ear to Simba's heart. There is no beat. I can now feel his body getting colder and colder. He has the most peaceful look up on his face.

My best friend has been waiting for me to come home to die in my arms.

Chapter 26

September 13, 2015 Evening
Sector Two - Physics Laboratory
Kieran Mersa

The ride back was miserable. I told my Spear to take its time. I needed a slow rush to mourn. When I landed in my chair back at the lab, the first words I heard were "What? No *Honey, I'm home*?" Char was all smiles that I arrived home safely.

Simba's still in my arms.

Then my tears flowed.

September 13, 2015 afternoon
Genetics Laboratory
Samantha Stonebridge

I get through security at my Uncle's lab. I don't even say hello to Jay or Dr. Shapiro, but walk straight to the side of the section my Uncle Kaelyn's working in. I enter through a glass door.

"Why haven't you pushed me?" I scream at him. "I should have had some miraculous breakthrough by now!" I yell stomping my feet all over his pristine laboratory.

He's not in his lab coat. He's dressed in a *Burberry* midnight blue shirt with black dress pants and black dress shoes. He doesn't look like some incredible doctor-scientist, but instead like some runway supermodel with his unruly platinum locks. His hair hasn't been cut in a while and it's flowing inches past his shoulders. I don't know if I like what Miss Lovelin is doing to him. I hope he hasn't lost focus in his work dolling up for her every day.

"I'm not your fucking professor, Sam." There's a tiny monkey lying on his table. He's unconscious. My uncle's injecting something into his brain. I haven't seen this little monkey before. Zenith must have recently brought him in at my Uncle's request. No, my Uncle's command. They give him everything.

"Nor am I your fucking babysitter," he says in a calm voice. "Nor am I your fucking father," he says a bit harsher this time as he pushes the six-inch needle further into the monkey's cerebellum.

"Yes! You're my fucking Uncle and I have idolized you from the day I was born! I remember the day I was born just like you! You are supposed to guide me, you fucking jackass! You are the only one I have ever worshipped! The only one I have ever believed in!" I scream as I take his seat in his high-back, white leather chair. I cross my arms all huffy and puffy. I doubt it if Loopy could ever get as red as I am now.

My Uncle picks up the little monkey and places him in a soft, blanketed glass box. I can see Jay and Dr. Shapiro from the corner of my eye watching my temper tantrum. After my Uncle situates his monkey, he takes his sweet time slowly walking over to me.

He crouches down eye level in front of his chair and then slaps me. Hard. I've never been slapped before. I don't cry. I just stare at him and then he slaps me again, even harder. I'm not upset with my Uncle. I know I deserve it. I think subconsciously I've been waiting for some tough love.

"Zenith never programmed 'humble' into us. It is a trait we have to learn for ourselves."

I slump further into my chair.

"You've already lost Jay due to your arrogance and mightiness. I shouldn't be the one to spell it out for you. You are smart enough to figure it out yourself." I slump further. I'm practically on the floor. "As for me pushing you? Was there anyone there to push me?" I open my mouth to speak, and then my Uncle slaps me again. "You should have been pushing yourself all this time. Nobody babysits anyone down here, but how could you see that? You've been too high on your pedestal lately to notice the little ants below."

"Yes, Uncle. I understand." I get up and walk out of his lab. I don't say anything to Jay or Dr. Shapiro as I leave the laboratory. Speechless, they just watch me leave.

I still have no idea what amazing I want to do.

By the end of the evening, I'm convinced I'm not amazing whatsoever. I cry myself to sleep.

September 14, 2015 morning
Sector Nine - Male Dormitories
Jay Ahmed

I can't believe Uncle Kaelyn slapped Sam, not once, not twice, but three times. Physical abuse is not tolerated in the *Underground*.

We are supposed to be a superior race of humans. I can't even understand what Sam was so upset about with her Uncle. She has always shown him the greatest respect. We all do.

I only caught bits and pieces of her emotional outburst: worshipped and only believe in you is all I got. Whatever her Uncle said was too softly spoken through the glass door and walls between us. She must have said or done something intolerable to deserve the punishment. I still feel bad for her. My sleep was on and off. I received no visions, and no communication from my wall. Sam has not reached out to me. Maybe she's embarrassed. Maybe's she's still on her high horse.

I call her through my wrist. All my roommates still sleep. She has facial recognition off.

"Yes, Jay, what is it?" I can tell she's been crying.

"Meet me for dinner? Wherever you would like?"

"No, Jay." My heart sinks into my knees. "Wherever you would like. Just text me when and where." Sam disconnects the line.

September 13, 2015 @ 10:00pm
Cryogenic Lab
Kieran Mersa

Char was the one that contacted Dr. Kai-af. It is late, but he's excited about the opportunity.

"I don't know really when he passed away. It can't be more than two to three hours." I don't tell Dr. Kai-af I brought him from Iran. He presumes he's been my dog in the *Underground* all along.

Dr. Kai-af takes Simba from my arms and places him in some sort of incubator. He draws Simba's blood from the back of his left leg and chest. It pains me to watch him do so, although I know Simba feels no pain.

"Thank you for the opportunity. Zenith doesn't allow preservation of pets in the *Underground*. They take up too much space in our limited city down here. However, since you are one of us, I will do it for you. I won't tell them. It's better what Zenith doesn't know; then it won't harm them."

Char and I nod our heads. Everybody has secrets down here.

Chapter 27

September 14, 2015 @ 5:00pm
Rainforest
Sophia Cambridge

"Do you like it?" I ask Zara.

Today I wore a short white skirt and a white sleeveless laced shirt tied to my waist rolled at the sleeves with black hiking boots. I learned my lesson over the past month about practical, fashionable Rainforest attire. Zara just stares at the dress all wide-eyed in a glow. She softly puts her webbed paws on it.

"This is mine? It's so soft," she says ever so sweetly. "It will tear while I'm climbing." She looks at me with a weary look on her sweet face.

Seth and Jasper both nod their heads.

"No, it won't. I promise. It's made from our *Underground* cotton. It won't rip and will maintain you at a cool sixty-five degrees while you're playing."

Seth and Jasper both nod their heads again.

Zara smiles up at me. She then extends her little arms. Her beautiful wings are four times the size of her arms. I put the navy blue dress on her. She puts her arms through them like a lab coat and her wings fit perfectly through the slits at the back of the dress. I help her clasp on the silver buttons in the front. There is a silver lace that trains all along the ruffled skirt. I made a round neck t-shirt collar for simplicity; a winged collar would have been too cumbersome for her. It's also sleeveless for mobility.

"You truly look like a princess," says Lovelin washing her toes all over the sand. "All she needs is a tiara right now." Jasper's sitting on her lap while Loopy dozes on her shoulder. She's yellow with golden wings this evening. Lovelin says she's a bit tired from playing all day.

"Yes, Nicolai is working on one as we speak!"

Lovelin smiles out loud. "Try it out, princess," she says to Zara.

Zara flaps her wings and flies through the sky. I had built-in shorts sewn under her dress that stays put as she flies. She soars through the air and lands up in a tree. She then nosedives down towards us super-fast landing softly at my feet.

"She's incredible!" Lovelin just smiles.

"You have no idea how incredible they are," Lovelin says caressing Jasper's mane. He lays cuddled against her. "All the world's animals would be jealous of these four."

"I love it!" squeals Zara as she twirls around in circles in her new dress. "I love it! I love it! I love it!"

"I will make you more as soon as I'm done with this wedding," I say pressing my wrist. "Pictures, please," I say taking a few pictures of Zara while in my line of vision.

"Wedding!" screams Seth, Jasper, Zara, and Loopy looking up at Lovelin.

"Mama and Papa are getting married! Mama and Papa are getting married!" squeals Loopy jumping up and down on Lovelin's shoulder. She's now wide awake.

"Oh, dear. No, no sweetling. Not just yet. Calm down. It's a different wedding," says Lovelin. All four of them stop jumping up and down in exuberance and frown.

"You're getting married!" I shout out to Miss Lovelin.

"Shhh, nobody knows, yet. Kaelyn just proposed the other day," Lovelin says pulling out her necklace from underneath her shirt. "Kaelyn hasn't set a date so we haven't told anyone."

"Oh, my! That's exquisite!" I scream.

All the animals start hooting, hollering, and chirping. They seem to have picked up on our excitement.

"What will be exquisite is the wedding dress you will design for me," says Lovelin with a wink still washing her toes upon the Rainforest sand.

I scream some more. "Really! Really, Miss Lovelin! You will let me design your dress!" I collapse onto her, giving her and Jasper the biggest hug.

"Of course, who else would I want?" she says hugging me back.

"Miss Sophia," gasps Jasper. "I can't breathe!" I immediately let both of them go.

"I'm so happy for you! Can I tell Sam? Can I tell my roommates? Oh, please, oh, please!" I've never found myself so out of control.

"Sophia, I think it would be best if Kaelyn makes the announcement. I need you to keep this a secret until then, please," she says holding Jasper. "I think Sam would be sad if she didn't hear it first. Kaelyn said she had some sort of an emotional breakdown at his lab yesterday.

He even said that he had to discipline her for the first time in his life. He hated doing it, but had no choice."

I calm down, a bit disappointed. She's right. Sam really should have been the first to know. She's more her Uncle's daughter than niece. "That's why she cried all night long. I thought she had another fight with Jay. She didn't want to share so I just let her be."

"I don't know the details either, Sophia. I don't pry. It's not my place to come in between them. I only listen to what Kaelyn tells me." Seth, Jasper, Zara and Loopy all seem sad learning about Sam's state of unhappiness.

"Oh, all right. I won't say anything, but I'm going to start designing your dress right after I'm done with this wedding. I can't wait to get started! Whenever you get a chance, just tell me your colors and theme."

"Zara will be my flower girl and you and your roommates will be my bridesmaids. I like the idea of midnight blue and ivory.

Kaelyn looks like a mighty Lord in midnight blue." She winks at me again. I think I saw some sort of a blush in her light honey-colored cheeks. I collapse onto Jasper and Miss Lovelin again. Jasper has had enough of me to last him the rest of the year.

"Will I get a new dress for the wedding?" asks Zara.

"Most definitely!" Zara beams twirling around again.

"You look very pretty, Zara," says Loopy with a yawn. She's now even more tired from all the excitement. "The color suits you." Miss Lovelin gives her a soft kiss on her cheek. Loopy turns bright pink all over.

"Would you like me to make something for you?" I ask Loopy.

Loopy shakes her head. "I have an amazing wardrobe! I can change colors whenever I want. You don't have the bells and whistles like I do," she brags changing from gold to green to pink to orange. Lovelin and I laugh at her. Seth and Jasper just nod their heads.

"You are very lucky. Your Papa's amazing!"

"I'm more amazing!" says Loopy going into her fluorescent yellow zooming through the branches.

"No way!" I say in total awe watching her weave in and out of bushes and trees. Seth and Jasper just look at each other.

"What's wrong?" I ask them.

"What's with girls and new clothes?" says Seth.

"I don't get it either," says Jasper.

Lovelin sighs. "As incredible as they are," she tells me. "Unfortunately, they are still typical boys."

September 14, 2015 @ 8:00pm
Underground Landing Dock
Samantha Stonebridge

Jay wants to have dinner at the landing dock. I didn't know we were even allowed at the landing dock. That place is reserved for security and those delivering supplies from above. I don't even know where it is. I wear a simple pink cotton dress with black leggings and short black lace-up boots. Will I need a jacket? I don't even know if the landing dock's temperature-controlled.

"Jake, what's the temperature in the landing dock?"

"It's fifty-five degrees," replies Jake. Damn, that's cold. I search my closet for something warm. I wish I had a cute jacket, but all I have are sweatshirts. I've got to start being a bit more fashionable socially and not just professionally. Now I see why my Uncle Kaelyn's always sharply dressed. He finally has someone to come home to.

My pink sweatshirt's going to look ridiculous over my dress so I head for the *Devil's Playground* and take a faux white leather jacket off the mannequin in the window. Sophia's going to be so upset because it's not real. I know she'll be making a fine leather one up for me the moment she sees this.

I have Jake input the direction to the landing dock in my line of sight. I didn't realize how far beneath the Earth's surface we really are until I take the elevator up to the landing dock. The ride seems at least a thousand stories. I feel misty air touch my skin the moment the doors open. This air smells different than what I am used to. It smells cool, sweet, and a bit musky. The dark grey stones beneath my feet are wet. There are three submarines docked. One of the docks is empty. The water's calm with very soft waves.

I feel as though I'm in a very large cave with a pond in front of me. This water's from the Pacific Ocean itself. This is the first time I've ever seen ocean water. The entrance to the docks are closed. The camouflaged garage doors are made from the same stone as beneath my feet.

Soft music plays around me. Jay has a small bonfire burning off to one side. There's a picnic blanket set with an array of food. Two drones pour juice into the champagne flutes. Fire torches burn upon the stonewalls that surround us. The setting's absolutely beautiful by the water. I sit on my knees taking in the lovely sight. Jay went through a lot of trouble to set this up. I don't know what to say.

"Am I still too boring for you?" asks Jay handing me a flute of orange juice. He takes a sip.

"I never thought you were boring Jay," I say staring into my flute. "Believe it or not, but I have a lot of admiration for you."

"Your Uncle is the only one you admire. His private cubicle isn't soundproof," he says calmly.

I drain my orange juice and then throw the champagne flute onto the wet stones in front of the submarine docks. Some of the shards fall into the water. The drones immediately start cleaning up the broken glass. I didn't know they were able to swim as well.

"You brought me here to fight? Well then, let's fight! I've been quite miserable lately. I thought I had it all, but I don't. I can't seem to do anything right with my life these past few weeks!

Apparently, these past months and years!"

Jay finishes his juice and a drone pours another. "What do you want to do, Sam?" he asks calmly.

"I want to make a difference!" I scream. Jay eats one of the peanut satays. "That's what I was bred for."

"You know what your problem is?" He's half-sitting, half-lying starting on his second satay. His shirt's crisp and white and adorned with one of Sophia's ties. "You put too much stress on yourself being Zenith's golden child. You also think that everything should land in your lap because you are Zenith's golden child. You don't appreciate yourself because what you can do comes easy and naturally to you. You don't work at making a difference. You believe it will just happen." He finishes his second satay lecturing me.

I want to tell him that he shouldn't eat and talk at the same time, but I don't. He obviously doesn't care what I think about his manners right now since I seem to have none myself. I've lost my appetite completely because his words are true. He's just reiterating what my Uncle told me yesterday. I haven't put much effort into creating something new.

"You also think you're too good for everyone except your Uncle because you are Zenith's golden child," he says forking Indo-Chinese chicken fried rice into his mouth. I wince at his last statement. "Everyone likes you because you are helpful and caring, nonetheless, but deep down inside you do it just to show off." I think I'm going to cry again. That remark hurt more than the others.

Jay doesn't love me. He only likes me. I doubt it if he even likes me now.

"The older you're getting, your head's getting in the way. And not in the right direction," he says softly again eating a piece of tofu. Now I know he doesn't even like me. I want to get up to leave. I don't know how much more criticism I can take. I wanted the fight. Jay's words were far more painful than my Uncle's slaps.

"Dr. Stonebridge," says Jake.

"Yes, Jake," I whisper looking above. I seemed to have lost my voice.

"You have been summoned to the infirmary. Impromptu surgical conference. Zenith has acquired a lung for Dr. Park."

Jay stops eating as I take in a sharp breath. Within that moment, one of the doors to the landing area rises. Flows of waves come in as a submarine emerges to the water's surface and docks itself. The door closes behind it. Two men appear out of the stealth submarine. One is Percy Mink. I don't know who the second one is. He's bald, wearing tiny round glasses, and has a sweet smile on his smooth small face. He appears with a stainless steel case in his hand. Jay and I get up and introduce ourselves.

They both look upon what seems to be a romantic date.

If they only knew.

Chapter 28

September 15, 2015 @ 6:00am
Sector Nine - Female Dormitories
Samantha Stonebridge

"Are you okay?" asks Sophia as I dress in my surgical scrubs. "You've been crying two nights in a row. How are you going to be able to perform in the O.T. this morning in your emotional state?"

I throw my pink lab coat over my navy blue scrubs. "I'll be fine the moment I'm there. I'll go straight into doctor mode rather than the fucking idiot mode I've been in."

"Whenever you're ready and want to talk." Zen and Ari still sleep. Chika wearily with heavy droopy eyes goes from my bed and cuddles into Sophia. Chika nuzzled into me all night trying to comfort me as I sobbed every couple of hours. She probably got less sleep than I did. I don't believe I deserve her unconditional love, but I took it. She made me feel wanted.

"You want me to talk. Okay, here's the short and long story. My Uncle's probably most disappointed in me." Chika's now slightly snoring. "No, scratch that," I say with a wave of my hand. "My Uncle is second most disappointed in me. Jay is first and foremost disappointed in me," I say putting my footies on. "There's a far better chance of our planet blowing up than Jay and I ever getting back together."

"C'mon Sam," says Sophia with a sigh.

"Jay basically told me last night that I'm nothing more than a self-centered fucking bitch who looks down upon everybody."

"That's not true, Sam. You're very loving and caring, always there to help others. I could never have gotten through bio-chemistry without you."

My tears start to form again. "Didn't you know? I only help others to show myself off."

I wipe my tears with the back of my hand and leave for the infirmary.

September 15, 2015 @ 2:00pm
Sector Two - Physics Laboratory
Samantha Stonebridge

Kato's transplant took six hours and was highly successful. He's completely off life support, and breathing normally on his own. His vital signs look good. Jasper evaluated Kato once more after the transplant and stated that Kato will pull through. My Uncle Kaelyn was deemed a savior once more for Jasper's creation.

I really didn't do much except carry out my superior's orders. I learned and observed. I stayed quiet and as humble as I could. I had a variety of tools at my reach including convulsion patches if anything went astray. We were far better prepared this time.

Char summoned me that the scrolls have been completely deciphered. Dr. Takbare has been pacing back and forth in his lab all afternoon mumbling to himself and throwing his hands up in the air every so often. When I walked in, the doctor was beaming. He also seemed to be in a lot of distress.

"It's not possible!" he shouts. "It's just not possible! She's wrong!"

"What's not possible?" Char, Kieran, and I ask in unison.

The archeologist then tells us the story embedded within the scrolls. At the end of it all, Char, Kieran, and I smile with bittersweet sorrow.

Holy Mother Earth! We know she's not wrong.

September 15, 2015 @ 10:00pm
Cadaver Lab
Samantha Stonebridge

I needed a place to carry out this situation in secret. I knew nobody would be at the cadaver lab so late at night. I contact Percy Mink through my wrist. I explain the situation to him. He promises to carry out my orders and keep my secret.

Second, I ask Jake to send an apology note to my Uncle's wall. I don't care if Miss Lovelin reads it or not. She should know what an ungrateful brat I've been. I hope she can forgive me for treating the man she loves so badly with such disrespect.

I don't tell Jay the story within the scrolls. I don't tell him about my conversation with Percy Mink either. It's not the time. Actually, I haven't told Jay anything since that disastrous evening except that Kato's expected to make a full recovery. All he said was 'thank you for letting me know'.

Even Char and Kieran don't know about my plans. I will tell them in the morning. I have no choice. Dr. Takbare's death is only to protect them, Zenith, and the inhabitants of the *Underground*. I hope in time I'm forgiven for my actions.

September 15, 2015 @ 10:30pm
Sector Four - Kaelyn's Apartment
Lovelin

I wake up to the softest kisses on my lips. My fingers instinctively fly into Kaelyn's hair. I must have fallen asleep waiting for his workday to finish. His kisses become deeper and more demanding. I then remember what I read earlier and throw him off of me onto the marble floor.

"Love, it's me! Jake, turn the lights on." Overhead lights come up and I try adjusting to its brightness.

"I know it's you! I'd know your scent and touch anywhere! How could you, Kaelyn? How could you hurt her like that? She's just a little girl!" I point to his opaque wall as he gets up off the floor and turns around to face it.

> My Dearest Uncle, I know I deserved what I got from you. I obviously have a lot of growing up to do. I want you to know how sorry I am. I am awfully disgusted with myself for disappointing you. I appreciate your truthfulness and I hope I use your words right to never disappoint you again. Please tell Miss Lovelin I am also terribly sorry for hurting the man she loves and cares for.
>
> I have been insecure and frustrated with myself lately and needed a scapegoat that I wasn't the

one to blame. I was wrong to do that. I know I hurt you, but you hurt me, too. It wasn't all those slaps across my face, but your words that you are not my Father. I know you are only my Uncle by blood, but you have been more than Father and Mother to me combined, and I will always cherish and respect you as a parent.

I hope one day you will find it in your heart and your soul to forgive me. Love you always, Samantha

Kaelyn sits on his bed, bows his head, and runs all ten of his fingers through his hair. "She's not an ordinary little girl," he says massaging his temple.

"She may be some genius super child, but emotionally, she's just a child nonetheless, and you had no right to lay your hand on her! There are other ways of discipline," I say sharply. He turns his head gazing at me straight lipped.

"Don't tell me how to treat my niece," he remarks coldly. With that, he gets up and heads for the washroom.

Will he treat our children that way? We haven't discussed it, but I want to have children with him some day. Maybe his creations are enough for him. Has he ever slapped them?

"I'm going out," he says harshly exiting the washroom heading toward the platform.

I knew I should never have come in between them.

Chapter 29

September 16, 2015 @ 7:00pm
Sector Four Apartments
Kaelyn Stonebridge

I spent the night in the Rainforest and the entire day in my lab. Zara and Loopy kept asking me where their Mama was as I tried to sleep in the canopy. I snapped at them and told them to go to sleep. None of them stayed in the canopy with me that night, but out in the Rainforest trees. It was the worst night of my life. I barely slept and when I did, I dreamt of myself slapping Sam over and over again, and Lovelin scolding me for my behavior.

It's the first time I haven't spoken to Lovelin in almost twenty-four hours and it's eating me up alive and tearing me limb from limb. When I returned to my apartment this morning for a change of clothes, she was already gone. I could have had a change of clothes sent over to me, but I wanted to see her. I needed to see her. There was no breakfast waiting for me and none was sent to my lab.

The only bright side in my life this moment is that my new little chimp is doing beautifully. I decide to go home early, but I first stop by my parent's place in Sector Four. The moment I walk through their door, my mum greets me with a long hug.

"What's wrong K K? You sounded most down when you said you wanted to visit tonight."

194

My father hands me a tall glass of scotch. I don't know if I can drink this. I haven't been drinking much lately. This one glass will put me under their diamond platinum table. I take a swig of the drink anyway. There's a sharp burn down my throat that hasn't been there in a while.

I sit on my parent's plush grey sofa and take another sip. "I actually have good news," I say taking out my necklace from underneath my shirt. The pink and white diamonds glisten in the lighting. "Lovelin and I are engaged."

My Mum hugs me screaming while my father pats me on my back far too enthusiastically. I can already feel myself going black and blue.

"Married! Married! You're getting married! Tell me everything! Tell me all the details! When? Where? No, that's stupid. I know it will be in the Ballroom." She's talking a hundred miles per hour running her fingers over my necklace.

"Actually, Mum, it won't be in the Ballroom. Lovelin and I want to marry at the Rainforest waterfall," I say taking another sip of my drink. My Mum screams again. I knew she would be excited, but she's lost all her prim and properness completely. You say the word wedding and girls seem to lose their sanity.

"That's perfect! That's absolutely perfect! When K K? Soon, right? This year I hope. Please say yes, oh, please."

"Sauri, let the boy speak!" commands my father refilling his glass. My mother puts her head down and quickly goes into a submissive state. Father has always had such an effect on her.

"Hopefully, soon, yes. We haven't set a date, yet. I've been extremely busy with my latest project, but I see a pot of gold at the end of the rainbow now," I say almost finishing my drink. My father wants to pour another, but I put my hand over my glass. I'm already relaxed to the heat and calmness of the intoxication.

"I understand. You don't want to wait long to have a baby. I completely agree," says my father. "You both are already old. Be grateful she looks the way she does." I wince at his comment. Thoughts of Sam and Lovelin flood into my head. I've got more apologizing to do. I've never apologized so much in all my years combined compared to these last three weeks. I don't think another Rainforest picnic is going to do the trick this time.

The apartment door unexpectedly opens and Dr. Kai-af walks in. He's in black leather pants, a white t-shirt, and a black leather jacket. I slowly stare at him from head to toe. He has the code to my parent's apartment? My mother's trying to look somewhat surprised, but not my father.

"So nice of you to join us for dinner," says my father. I look over to the kitchen. There's no aroma coming from the ovens or stove. There's nothing prepped on the granite counters either.

"We're going to *Cave Dwellers*," says my mother. He could have just met you there, I think to myself. I wasn't born yesterday. Even if I was just born yesterday, I could have figured this one out.

"Kaelyn's getting married," says my father as Dr. Kai-af takes a seat next to him. Quite closer than he should have. He then takes a sip from my father's scotch glass.

"Congratulations!" he says slapping my father's knee. "Who's the lucky girl?"

"The girl from the plane crash. Lovelin is ever so lovely," says my mother.

"You obviously know what you want," says Dr. Kai-af. "That was very fast considering she just arrived. I read her story on *Show Off*." He's holding onto my father's knee longer than necessary.

"Well, I've got to get home to my bride to be. Enjoy dinner," I say heading for the door. I don't think I can stomach this. The scotch feels like bile rising into my throat.

As I stand at the platform waiting for the train to arrive, my mother runs to my side. "It's not what you think, Kaelyn." I take a deep breath, feeling agitated. Lovelin does yoga and meditation exercises. She's teaching me, but I think I'm going to need a double dose tonight.

"Mum, I really don't care. Everybody has skeletons in their closets. I just wish I didn't know nor have to experience it," I say quite disgusted. "Threesomes aren't my thing."

"We are not lovers, Kaelyn. I promise," she says kissing my cheek, then my forehead. "You're not?"

"No, we are just friends. Very special friends," she says hugging onto me.

"Well, that's a relief," I say as the train approaches. "I don't think I could handle it if you ever hurt Father."

I board the train and just before the doors close, my mother blows me a kiss.

"We are friends, but they are lovers," she says with a smile on her face waving bye. The train door shuts.

Meditation and yoga won't even do the trick.

September 16, 2015 @ 7:30pm
Sector Four - Kaelyn's apartment
Lovelin

I get off *Platform Sphinx*. Today had to be the most miserable day of all my life. Kaelyn didn't come home last night and I barely slept. It's the first night he spent away from me since I moved in. Even if it was very late, he always came home.

He always came home to me.

At six in the morning, I went to the gym to get all my frustrations out. I then spent the day roaming around Mid-Section. I didn't even visit the Rainforest because I didn't want to run into him. I didn't know if he wanted me there or not. He obviously didn't or he would have come home last night. I'm more miserable because I didn't get to see the children. I hope they aren't upset with me. I had a drone send them strawberry tarts with a note saying that I have a predicament that needs attending to. Seth and Jasper are smart enough to understand. I hoped my little lie worked. I feel even more miserable telling them false truths.

Fuck you, Kaelyn!

I haven't drank for a while, but tonight I need a bottle of wine. Maybe more than that. I should meditate instead.

I enter the apartment to the smell of roses. No wait, that's lilies. There are red rose petals scattered on the marble floor in the hallway. I enter the kitchen. There must be at least a hundred stargazer lilies in a variety of colors and a hundred calla lilies adorning the kitchen countertops in beautiful diamond vases. There are red rose petals on the floor leading to the bedroom and living room. There are another hundred or so roses in crystal etched vases along the fireplace mantle and end tables. There are white flower petals all over our bed; they look beautiful against the black comforter.

I run back to the kitchen and go through every single vase. There are no notes in the flowers in the living room or bedroom. I run into the bathroom. The sight makes me gasp. Meditation is definitely off the venue.

There has to be at least a hundred different types of orchids lying all around: in the tub, on the counters, in the shower, and on the floor. There are no stems, just flowers. I couldn't find a note amongst them either. I enter my bedroom and search for anything that I may have missed.

And then the wall glows.

There's a picture of daffodils and tulips and dahlias swirling around in a menagerie of colors. There are only four black words in the middle of it all: I'm sorry, my love.

"I'm sorry, too, my love," I whisper to myself.

Strong arms squeeze me from behind across my waist. He kisses the side of my neck. I couldn't even hear him walk in. I was too mesmerized by the sight of it all. He smells like hiscasuckles and scotch. "I haven't eaten all day, but I want you first," he whispers into my ear.

"I haven't eaten all day, and I want you first," I say unwrapping his arms as we tumble onto the beautiful white petals on our bed.

He falls on top of me and kisses me with all the desires of the day and last night.

Today's also one of the best days of my life.

September 16, 2015 @ 7:30pm
Sector Nine - Female Dormitories
Samantha Stonebridge

I received word from Percy that the archeologist has been taken care of. It wasn't easy telling Char and Kieran what I did, but they understood. They don't want any chances of our home revealed either.

Collateral damage, they called it.

I checked in on Kato earlier. He was sleeping at the time, but Dr. Rossi said he spoke. I didn't ask what he said. I was so excited that he spoke that I forgot to ask. I watched his sleeping form for a few minutes and then left. He still needs his rest. I told Sophia that she got permission to visit him tomorrow.

"What a day," I say throwing my backpack down and flopping on my bed. I think I could sleep for a year.

"Is that a *good what a day* or a *bad what a day*?" asks Zen as she stops playing the piano. Canon in D.

"I need a drink." I've never ordered a death sentence before. I may need two. No, make that three.

"Oh, dear. That means a *bad what a day*," says Zen. She starts playing *Just the Way You Are* to cheer me up. They're so sweet to me. Their love for me makes me sad. I wish I could be more like them.

"There's iced tea in the refrigerator," yells Ari from the kitchen. She's got all sorts of cooking concoctions on her counters. The floor's a mess as well.

"I was thinking of something stronger," I yell back over Zen's piano playing. Chika comes and cuddles into my chest. I'm still in my lab coat. I pet her head and give her a tummy rub.

Everybody should have a pet. I truly believe your life can't be complete without one even though you know you will outlive it.

"I can make espresso!" says Ari again yelling from the kitchen. I can smell the baklava from here. I laugh inward at her tries.

"Where's Sophia?" I ask. Her side of the apartment is off.

"Still working," says Zen. "She's been playing referee and fashion designer at the same time." I don't ask, but just nod. I'm too drained to ask.

My wall then glows besides me. I get up from my bed and take off my lab coat. A beautiful depiction of Mother Earth appears.

It glows as it turns on its axis in the Milky Way. I will never get enough of her glorious sight.

Then the words appear in white across the screen: You are forgiven, kitten, Father Kaelyn. I get down in child's pose in front of my wall. I hesitantly lift my head and read again.

It's now a *good what a day*. A *very good what a day*. I ask Ari for iced tea and baklava.

Chapter 30

September 17, 2015 @ 7:30am
Post-Surgical - Infirmary
Sophia Cambridge

Kato sleeps soundly in his post-surgical room as I walk in. He's even lightly snoring. That's okay. He's beautiful enough to get away with it. There's a new doctor working at the computer. Maybe not a new doctor, but one that I've never met before. There are only two 3D images displayed now; one is his heart and the other his lungs. The bandages on his hands are off. The bad news is that he still has no little finger on his left hand. The good news is that his hands look like nothing ever happened to them.

"Hello doctor," I say. The pretty red-haired lady turns around and gazes at me. She's quite striking. I wonder why I haven't seen her before, then I realize that's she's probably always working and doing her own amazing down here.

"Wow! I love that outfit! Where did you get it? The *Devil's Playground* or *Sweet Darlings*?" I smile at her. I've got on leather black boots over my knees and a short black skirt with a short white crop top and a black leather jacket with gun metal accents that match the accents on my boots.

"Neither, I made the ensemble myself. Zenith gave me my own design studio in Sector Two. I hope to open my shop soon in Mid-Section. I've just been so crazy busy with all the upcoming wedding attire."

"Little you is designing the upcoming wedding clothes?" she asks astonished. "Damn, girl, you must be good! No! You must be more than good! Zenith does not give that role to just anybody. I heard that they shunned Vera Wang's designs for the last wedding down here.

How old are you, ten, twelve?" I must have blushed a dozen shades at her comment.

"I'm actually almost fourteen and it's always been a dream of mine to be a fashion designer."

"Fourteen? I was a physician at that age. I'm Dr. Rossi," she says getting up from her chair to shake my hand. "Such an honor to meet you. I want that outfit you've got on when you're ready." I laugh at her comment and nod my head.

"Of course, and the honor's all mine. Thank you for taking such good care of Kato. I'm Sophia," I say extending and shaking her hand.

"Oh, so you're Sophia," she says smirking at me. "At first I was surprised, but now I'm not."

"What? Is there anything wrong?"

"No, sweetheart, nothing wrong. It's just that the first words out of Kato's mouth when he woke up was I love you, too, Sophia."

September 17, 2015 @ 2:00pm
Sector Two - Sophia's Design Studio
Samantha Stonebridge

I saunter into Sophia's design studio unannounced. She gave me the code to her door in case I ever wanted to grab her for lunch. That's how she put it. I've already had lunch. Hope she did, too.

"The tailcoats should be in silk and wool ivory," says Tara. "With black leather piping."

"Are you blind?" says Chaz. "The tailcoats should be in black since the shirts are in ivory."

"The pants are in ivory, you dimwit, and the shirts are in black so the tailcoats need to be in ivory!" says Tara flying around flailing her mechanical hands in the air.

"The pants were never in ivory! They are in black! There is a glitch in the computer!" screams Chaz. "Isn't that right, Miss Sophia?"

Sophia's at one of her machines sewing a golden satin and laced dress. She doesn't seem to be paying any attention to the screaming match behind her.

"Hey, Sophia," I say, "Chaz needs you." Still no answer. I walk over to her and put my hand on her shoulder. She jumps.

"Sam!" she squeals loudly taking the wireless earbuds out of her ears. "What a great surprise!" She gives me a hug. Chaz and Tara hover above with their mechanical arms crossed frowning at her. I've never seen drones frown before. All the ones I know are straight lipped. "What is it now?" Sophia says looking at them.

"We seem to have a discrepancy in the color combination. There are two to three design sets in the computer," says Chaz.

"Ah, yes. Since neither of you dolls could agree on the color palette, I decided to split it. Who says all the groomsmen have to look the same anyway?"

Tara and Chaz exchange glances. "So, three of the groomsmen will wear black tailcoats and pants with ivory shirts. The other three will wear ivory tailcoats with black pants and black shirts. All of them with golden bows and belts. Should look striking! Got it!" says Sophia.

"Got it!" they both say in unison and go back to their lasering and sewing.

"I told you I was right," says Tara bragging to Chaz.

"I was right as well Miss-Know-It-All!" says Chaz. They both fly to the back of the studio and start working.

"I swear those two argue for the sake of hearing their own voices," says Sophia. "These earbuds have been a lifesaver."

"That's a gorgeous gown," I say feeling the golden satin. The lace is ever so intricate.

"All six of the bridesmaid dresses are in gold to match the groomsmen's buttons on their shirts and boot buckles. They are going to be a simple elegance. It's the guys that are going to look like elegant rebels."

"Boots?"

"Trust me. It's going to look fabulous! So what's up?"

"Kato had surgery at eleven this morning to reconstruct his little finger. I observed the whole transplant. It came out perfect. You would never be able to tell his finger once blew off. Just wanted to let you know," I say mesmerized at how fast Chaz can sew a tailcoat so flawlessly. The leather piping would have taken hours with our hands and he's sewing it in minutes.

"Zenith found a real finger?"

"It came in the same case with the lung," I say watching Tara's laser finger cutting fabric perfectly.

"Do you know who the organ and appendage donors are? It's hard to believe Kato will be walking around with someone else's body parts in and on him. Like some sort of extremely cute Frankenstein," she says with a small laugh.

"Sophia, I know whose body parts he has, but I don't think it would be a good idea for Kato to know. It might make him sad or it might make him hostile. Some things are better left unsaid." I wish I took my own advice sometimes. Then maybe I wouldn't be such an emotional mess.

"Why would he be hostile? It's not like he knows these *Surface* donors, right?"

"Sophia, did you know that Kato's parents were happy to give him away in exchange for a better life of their own?"

"No, he told me his father was a very poor fisherman and there were always tough times so Zenith took him because his parents wanted a better life for him. He was only three years old and extremely smart."

"It could go either way. Who really knows the whole truth? Zenith will say anything to make sure we function well down here."

"What are you saying, Sam?" She has a worried look on his face.

"You're not supposed to know this. Only the surgical team does. The lung is his father's and the little finger is his mother's."

"No way! They donated themselves for their son that they haven't seen in fifteen years and never ever will!" she exclaims. "That's a parent's love, isn't it?"

"I don't think it was a love donation. I think Zenith sacrificed them."

September 17, 2015 @ 8:00pm
Post-Surgical - Infirmary
Kato Park

I look at my left hand in front of my face. I've been flexing all my fingers for the last fifteen minutes. I can't believe they were able to find my little finger and construct it back on. It has to be my own finger. It looks exactly the same. There's no tissue damage or charring. The surgical teams must have been working on cellular repair all this time.

"Jake, what day is it?"

"It's September 17, 2015 at 8:02pm, Dr. Park."

I've been here for two weeks. I can't believe I've been unconsciousness for that long. I must have really been in bad shape.

"You're awake," says Sophia. She looks absolutely beautiful in her outfit, but I can tell she's tired. Her eyes look tired. She must have had a long day. She still looks more beautiful than any fairy princess ever could. Memories of a wedding announcement come back to me. She must be very busy just days before the wedding. I've been waiting for her to walk through that door.

"You're the one that woke me." She gives me a quizzical look as she sits on my bed.

"You were already awake when I walked in."

"Ever seen *Snow White* or *Sleeping Beauty*?" Her eyes widen.

"Of course, everyone has, haven't they? They are masterpieces according to the *Surface*."

"C'mon, Sophia. Stop playing with me. It was your kisses and tears that brought me back to life. I don't want to pretend anymore. I got a second chance."

"We are not a *Disney* movie Kato. I'm no princess and you're no prince. I don't have such magical powers. This is reality," she says all fidgety. I take her hand in mine and kiss the top of her knuckles softly.

"We are princes and princesses down here. We are all Zenith's prize servants, and you do have magical powers, Sophia. You were the first reason why I wanted to come back," I whisper. "I don't know what spell you've cast on me, but I hope we can be together forever." She doesn't move at first, then she leans over and gives me a hug.

"Well then," she whispers in my ear. "No more unsupervised experiments." She then kisses me softly on the mouth. I sigh.

"As you wish your highness," I say kissing the tip of her nose.

Chapter 31

September 29, 2015 @ 7pm
Mid-Section Waterfall
Samantha Stonebridge

Happy birthday to you! Happy birthday to you! Happy Birthday, amazing Samantha! Happy birthday to you!

Everybody's terribly off key, even Zen, as I blow out the fourteen pink candles on my fourteen-tiered birthday cake. I climbed a holographic ladder to blow the candles out.

Jake made a morning announcement for my birthday. All of us scientists get our birthday announced. Everybody has been bombarding me all day with birthday wishes. I had no idea that my roommates planned a surprise party for me the last few weeks. Everybody's dressed in various shades of my favorite colors of pink and white. Sophia had a casual dress code sent out to all the guests, but specified the color theme. I'm wearing my white jeans and a pink sweatshirt. Sophia lured me to Mid-Section wanting a birthday picture of us at the waterfall before dinner.

There must have been at least most of Sector Nine present as well as most of my professors. Grand Sis and the rest of my family shouted 'Happy Birthday' as I arrived. Dozens of tables with pink tablecloths and white napkins were set up in front of the waterfall.

Ari and her family outdid themselves with the cake. It's all done in pink and ivory with a raspberry filling and fresh strawberries and rawbleberries throughout.

Dinner was exceptional as well. Ari's family and many of the other chefs made so many of my favorites: hummus, chicken kaftas, lamb chops, rice pilaf, cabbage rolls, samosas and pakoras, dragon and firecracker rolls, sweet and sour shrimp, pepperoni and mushroom pizza, etc. I didn't know where to start.

"Happy Beautiful Beyond the Moon Birthday, my darling little pink and white love!" he says giving me a hug that's knocking me unconscious.

"Hello, Sir," I say pushing him back a bit. I don't know this guy.

"Dr. Stonebridge, my precious all-too-adorable Sweetheart. I am Valentino, your Master of Choreography for your first *Showcase* presentation," he declares bowing to me. His crew bows to me behind him with such beautiful smiles. Their words and small gestures make me feel like royalty.

Oh! I knew of the three amazing Masters of Choreography, but I didn't expect Valentino to be here tonight. Apparently, he takes care of many other events in the *Underground* besides the *Showcase.*

"Thank you, Sir! What a fabulous birthday display!" I hug him back, but I can't quite get the exuberance he gave me. Now he pushes me back.

"No, my sweet ever so darling incredible beyond our glorious Mother Earth and beyond, I am not Sir. I am Valentino and beyond blessed to be at your service," he says bowing once more. His crew bows with their hands fisted in the air behind him.

I think I'm going to cry.

"I have a gift for you, Sam," says Sophia. Valentino and his crew leave to their work. Sophia's drone, Tara, brings over a large bright pink box with a golden bow on top. She's dancing to the music overhead as she flies to me. Drones can now dance?

"Sophia, I don't need anything, but thank you." I hug and kiss her.

I open the box to find a gown. Dozens of oohs and aahs go up in the air as I pull it out. The full-length flowing skirt is done in ivory-colored silk with hundreds of pink crystals swirling throughout. They are actually swirling! What kind of fabric technology is this!

There's ivory-colored netting underneath to bring about the flare. I actually have to slip into the thinnest silk pants attached to the skirt for comfort. There are large crystals glistening like diamonds. The blouse is full sleeves with a low neckline made out of the same silk fabric. The top is completely plain as it falls right before my waist, but the veil sash is the most gorgeous thing I've ever seen. It must be at least twelve feet of the sheerest ivory fabric bombarded with hundreds of small pink crystals embedded throughout. These crystals are swirling as well!

"I'll drape the sash on you before the wedding. Half of it will be at your back and the other half will drape around the front over your shoulder." I've never seen such a beautiful gown in all my life.

"You're going to outshine the bride," says Miss Lovelin winking at me. Uncle Kaelyn has his arm draped around her quite possessively. He kisses the side of her temple. I've never seen him show any sign of public affection. I don't know who that man is anymore, but I couldn't love him more than I do just now. Everybody nods their heads agreeing with Lovelin.

Everyone except my parents; they don't smile at me.

They know Jay and I broke up. I told them it was all my fault. I didn't say much more. My mother said to call her if I ever wanted to talk. I haven't really talked to my mother in years.

We just converse about work-related stuff every now and then, nothing personal. I feel we both do it out of obligation rather than anything else. Why would I want to start having a heart to heart conversation with mother now? I don't mention that, but just say thank you. Maybe she's trying to reach out. I don't know if I'm ready to reach out.

"You are the best friend anybody could ever have," I say giving Sophia another hug. She's dressed in a lovely rose-colored Indian outfit with little white shimmering roses all over her scarf and leggings. The roses blossom and close every so often. Miss Lovelin's wearing the same, but in reversed colors.

The drones bring all of us a round of lemon drop shots. My Uncle Kaelyn winks at me this time. I can't believe he's wearing a light pink shirt. Miss Lovelin must have gotten him to wear it, or dressed him in it. I've never seen him anything in more than black, white, grey or blue.

He won't even wear khaki or green.

Ari and Zen refuse the shots and stick to their iced teas. Another round of *Happy Birthday* is sang while we dig into the cake. The serving drones offer others passing by if they would like a piece of cake. There are at least a dozen drones serving at my party. I'm sure this cake could feed half of the *Underground*.

"Sam, I've got a gift for you, too," he says shyly. I look up behind me with a ridiculous mouthful of cake and vanilla ice cream. It's Jay. He gets on his knees.

Oh, Mother Earth! Oh, my! He's going to propose!

I try to swallow, but seem to have forgotten how. I wipe my mouth with a napkin and gulp down as gracefully as I can. He opens the box himself and takes out a bracelet. The charm has the letter "S" on it. He wraps it on my wrist.

"The charm's made of sapphire, your birthstone. I hope you like it." I don't say anything at first, but just stare at the beautiful silver bracelet on my wrist. I wish I could be excited about it.

"Thank you, Jay, but you shouldn't have," I say quietly.

I don't like it. I saw Uncle Kaelyn's and Miss Lovelin's necklaces. I want a necklace with the letter 'J' on it. I'll even settle for a bracelet. I want to tell Jay he got the letter wrong, but I don't. I'm sure everybody heard the disappointment in my voice. He goes back to sit with his roommates and others from Sector Nine. I know Sophia can sense what I'm feeling because the next minute she grabs my hand.

"Jake, we need some Taylor Swift music," she says twirling me around in front of the waterfall. *Shake It Off* starts blaring and everybody's up dancing. Miss Lovelin tries to get Kaelyn to dance; he refuses to get up at first. I've never seen my Uncle dance before. He doesn't attend *Underground* weddings. He's not the dancing type, but she gets him on his feet to join in on my birthday celebration. She's so perfect for him. Everybody's having a great time and we dance for quite a while.

Char grabs my hand as I'm just about to sit down to rest. I really wanted another piece of cake, but I let him lead me to the menagerie on the dance floor.

"Jake, play *Every Woman in the World*," says Char. I dance hand in hand with Zachary. I don't know what possessed me to put my arms around him to dance, probably the lemon drop, and I find myself enjoying his attention. After a few moments, I see Jay and Lucinda dancing the same way on the other side. Jealousy hits me like a train crash. Jay says they are only friends. I wonder if Lucinda knows that.

"He loves you, you know," says Char gazing their way.

"What?" I say not looking into his eyes. He then turns to face me. Our noses are almost touching.

"Jay, he loves you, not Lucinda," says Char picking up my chin with his finger. "I could see it in his eyes when he was looking at you in my lab."

"Doesn't seem that way," I say glaring at them. They both have smiles on their faces. Jay doesn't even look our way. He's too engrossed in their conversation. A part of me wonders what they're talking about, another part of me doesn't want to know.

"I know you care for him, too. I don't know what happened between you two and I don't need an explanation, but let me help you. I know how a guy's mind works," he says. I hate the way Lucinda clings onto him dreamily gazing at him with her effervescent smile.

"Okay, Char, lead the way." Char and I dance and twirl around all the way to Jay and Lucinda. We bump into so many along the way. As we arrive next to them, Char asks if we can switch partners. He takes Lucinda from Jay in a flash swirling her away before either one of them could object. He may only be fourteen, but his height and dark black eyes make him look older. Jay and I stand before each other. We don't really look at each other, but then he extends his hand and I fall into them.

My mother, dancing in father's arms, smiles at me.

September 29, 2015 @ 7:30pm
Mid-Section Waterfall
Jay Ahmed

"Give it to her," says Kato.

"I'll give it to her in private. It looks like crap compared to that gorgeous gift Sophia just gave her," I say. I try to picture Sam in that gown. The poor bride-to-be is all I can think of. I can't imagine how Sophia's going to outdo herself creating the bride's wedding dress.

"Give it to her, Jay. In front of everybody. She'll love it. How could she not?" says Sal on his third piece of cake. Christoph even encourages me along with his hands not speaking. He's got too much ice cream in his mouth to talk.

I reluctantly get out of my seat and walk over to Sam's table. She's sitting with her family: her parents, her Uncle Kaelyn, Miss Lovelin, Michael, Grand Sis and Grandfather Victor, her Uncle Shaun and Aunt Sasha with their baby, Sarah. Sam gave Sarah the entire fourteenth top layer of the cake to eat. She's elbow deep into it eating with both hands. She feeds her parents as well; her mother with her right hand and her father with her left, sitting on top of the table herself. Her beautiful pink lace dress has frosting all over it. It's the most precious and funny sight. I know Jake's taking pictures for memories.

Sam's eating her birthday cake so I get on my knees to get eye level with her. I don't want her to make an effort to stand. She didn't seem all that happy when I put the bracelet on her wrist. It really pales compared to the gown Sophia gave her. I wish I had given her my gift first.

Sophia gets the dancing started and I'm in no mood, but I go with the flow because Kato makes me. As soon as I see Sam wanting to take a break, I head towards her to ask her to dance. I've got to make things right between us. Those lemon drop shots give me the liquid courage I need. Char intercepts and gets to her before I do. A wave of jealousy goes through me and I ask Lucinda to dance just to retaliate.

"So, how's your boyfriend, Darby?" I ask as I lead her to the floor. Lucinda starts cracking up with her head back to our makeshift sky. It's so easy to make her laugh. She's always smiling anyways. I glance over to Sam and Char. They're so close that if somebody bumps into them, they would be kissing. I wish I didn't feel so jealous. Sam told me they were just friends. I wonder if Char knows that.

"He's fine and as adorable as ever! How are your projects going?" she asks then staring at me all dreamy. It's really getting warm for some reason. We engage in small talk. Lucinda's really easy to talk to. Char comes out of nowhere and asks if we can switch partners. Sam's before me and I put my hand out. We dance to Taylor Swift's *Love Story*. I have a feeling Sophia or Kato had something to do with choosing this song.

"You don't like the bracelet, do you? You didn't seem happy when I put it on you."

"I love the bracelet, Jay. I was just expecting something else," she says with her hands on my shoulder. My hands are at her waist.

"I'm sorry. What were you expecting?"

"Jelly beans," she says with half a smile. Last year, I got her a champagne bottle filled with her favorite pink cotton candy jelly beans. She loved it and finished all of them within the month.

"I guess I really messed up this year," I say with a small laugh.

"You have no idea," she says shaking her head.

September 29, 2015 just before midnight
Sector Nine - Female Dormitories
Samantha Stonebridge

"So what did you say?" Sophia asks.

"I said jelly beans. It was the first thing I could think of. I couldn't very well have told him the truth now, could I?" I say flopping down onto my bed. I've awoken Chika up from a deep slumber.

I put her in her pink polka-dotted pajamas before leaving this evening. She walks over to me from her pillow and flops down on my chest nuzzling her face into my neck. I need to change, but I just let her sleep on me for a while. I rub her back and tummy as she softly snores into my neck.

"Sam, you two have been going in circles for weeks," says Zen getting into her bed. She changes her wall from swirling music notes to a picture of a baby grand piano covered in rose petals. "Say you're sorry and get on with life. Jake, please turn off my lights." Her overhead lights dim to darkness immediately.

"Easier said than done," says Sophia with a mouthful of toothpaste. She brushes her teeth in her bedroom while changing into her pajamas. Ari crashed on her bed, still in her pink sweater and white leggings, the moment she came in. The poor darling must be exhausted.

Apparently, she's been cooking for days for my party. I don't know how I'm ever going to be able to thank her and everybody else. I haven't had a birthday party since I was eight and living in Sector Nine. My parents used to have one for me every year until I wanted to live on my own.

I press my wrist. I send a text to my parents thanking them for attending. They text back 'Happy Birthday' once more and that they love me. I don't say I love you back, but send them an emoji of a pink heart. It's the most emotionalism my mother and I have had in years.

My wall has Happy Birthday written in the middle of it. So many of the *Underground* inhabitants have had Jake send me their birthday wishes; I have their blessings and signatures all over my wall. It's the *Underground* way of sending a birthday card. There must be over three hundred of them. I even received a gift from my immunology professor although he didn't attend my birthday party. He changed my immunology test grade to one hundred percent. I text thanking him for the birthday gift and telling him I missed seeing him at my party. Now I feel awful about throwing that temper tantrum. He's still my superior after all. I've got to get off my high horse. That's why Jay no longer wants me.

I gaze up at my wall to see if Jay sent a message, he would send it in blue writing, his favorite color. Before I could try, I see a little package sitting next to my bed. A drone must have brought it in. I scoop up Chika and lay her next to Ari. They immediately cuddle into each other.

I open the card attached to the package. Happy Birthday from Zenith. I open the beautiful golden box to find a crystal black sphere. Within the sphere is our Mother Earth in its brilliant shades of blue, green, brown, and white. There are snowflakes, stars, and comets dancing all around the earth. They glow in the black background.

"How incredibly beautiful," whispers Sophia standing in front of me. I hand her the snow globe.

"It's my birthday gift from Zenith. Our world is truly magnificent, isn't it? I wish everybody knew how to take care of it." The Earth spins on its axis within the globe itself as the beautiful snowflakes rise and fall all around it.

"I've never received a birthday gift from Zenith, but the design studio I have is worth a million birthday gifts and more. We are the lucky ones."

"Lucky, yes, but I'm the idiot for letting Jay go. I never realized it until now, but I feel incomplete without him. I felt it the moment we broke apart from dancing tonight. I bet Zenith didn't have this in mind when they created me."

"We don't realize a worth until we lose it. It's human nature," says Sophia placing the globe on my nightstand next to the pictures of the four of us. I put Jay's photograph away. It's too heartbreaking to wake up to.

The theme song to Zippity Doo Dah plays. Sophia and I stare at each other.

"Who could be here?" I ask getting up from my bed. "It's past midnight." I open the door to find a little drone hovering in front of me. In its steel basket is another gift.

"Present for Dr. Samantha Stonebridge," says the little green drone in its mechanical voice. I take the silver box and open it at my bed with Sophia.

"Who's it from?"

"No clue. There's no card," I say undoing the pink ribbon. "Maybe it's inside."

"Ah, mystery admirer." I roll my eyes at her. She's such a romantic lately. I open the lid and we both giggle.

It's full of pink cotton candy jelly beans.

"He cares about you, Sam. You wouldn't have received this otherwise." I hand her a few and we both plop some in our mouths.

"I care for him more than anything, but am I deserving of him is the question."

Chapter 32

October 1, 2015 @ 6:00pm
Underground Ballroom
Samantha Stonebridge

There's over eight hundred people attending tonight's wedding. Tears have been flowing all evening: when the bride and groom walked into the Ballroom, when they said their vows, when they shared their first kiss as man and wife, when they danced, and when they cut their seven-tiered cake. I still think the cake looks like shit, but the new Mr. and Mrs. love it. That's all that matters.

Champagne glasses have been tinkling all evening. The newlyweds kiss to each one of them. Many of the other couples also kiss to each one of them. Kato kissed Sophia by surprise once. She blushed all over.

I wish Jay would kiss me to each one of them.

The food's beyond imaginable. Ari and her family really outdid themselves. There had to have been food represented from almost every *Surface* country. Zen played their wedding song flawlessly on the piano. Everybody's having a magnificent time. The bride and groom look ever so in love and happy. They can't stop gazing into each other's eyes. The eight hundred or so at their reception could just poof and disappear and they wouldn't even notice.

I hope I look like that one day.

The dress Sophia designed for me even outshined the bride. I'm sure Katia's pretty pissed off with me. She really should be pissed off with Sophia. Katia looked at me once when I shook her hand to congratulate her during their reception line hours ago and then never looked my way again so far.

Jay kept gazing my way every ten seconds or so throughout the entire ceremony. He looks incredibly gorgeous in his black and red tail tuxedo. The leather accents make me want to drool. The boots that adorned his feet were even more striking than the groom and all his groomsmen.

When the dancing started, Jay didn't ask me first. Zachary did. He looks ever so handsome in his black tuxedo and maroon shirt. I took his hand and he led me to the dance floor.

"Is Jay not the dancing type?" Char asks swirling me to *Just the Way You Are*.

"My roommates and I dance all the time because of Zen. It's really unstoppable because of her playing all day and night. Unfortunately, there are no dance classes in the *Underground*."

"Dancing comes from within," says Char twirling me around some more. "It's either in your soul or it isn't. My parents dance all the time in our apartment just for the sheer fun of it. It's a way to relax and unwind. I usually read when they are dancing, but they grab me every once in a while and I have no choice. I do enjoy it once I'm up and about. I should appreciate my parents more than I do. We are of two different worlds."

He's so lucky. I always feel like I am of two different worlds as well and not just the *Underground* and the *Surface*. I wish I knew what my parents do.

October 1, 2015 @ 7:00pm
Underground Ballroom
Jay Ahmed

My eyes refuse to release themselves of her beautiful form, no matter how hard my brain battles for it. Her black flowing ebony hair cascading down her back to her ivory and pink gown looks more radiant than the Milky Way galaxy itself. I want to get up and ask her to dance, but my feet can't seem to move, paralyzed at her soft beauty.

Zachary takes her to the dance floor and their swirling and twirling makes my blood boil. Sam hasn't looked my way all evening. She can't seem to peel her eyes off of Zachary as well.

"Cut in," says Kato. So many are on the dance floor. Christoph and Sal are having a blast. They dance with everybody around them. They don't seem to care who's from which sector. Wish I wasn't so in love with Sam and could dance with whoever.

"How can I compete with Char? If you only knew of his accomplishments. It's hush-hush right now," I say slumping into my seat.

"She's dancing with him just to make you jealous Jay," he says smacking the back of my head. "Can't you see that? Don't you understand girls?"

Girls will be a lifelong mystery for all times.

October 1, 2015 @ 7:00pm
Underground Ballroom
Sophia Cambridge

"This is a ridiculous amount of food, Ari," I say dipping chicken shawarma in tahini sauce and stuffing it in my mouth. "I feel as though I've gained five pounds already and the reception just started."

"Every single chef in the *Underground* contributed their talents for Mishka and Katia. Apparently, a lot of people like them in Sector Eleven," says Ari eating ras malai. "I love the pearls on the table. Don't you? The simple white calla lilies as the centerpieces are perfect. Definitely not overdone like the wedding last year."

"Probably the best decorated wedding I've ever seen," I say. "I like simple elegance. I'll never get enough of looking at the diamond chandelier hanging in the center of the dome. I can't imagine what Zenith paid for that."

"I wish you had left some room in this gown for me," says Sam. "It already feels snug and there are still desserts I want to try."

"That's why I wore a sari," I say.

"Your black and pearl sari is stunning by the way," says Zen licking her fingers from the Chinese garlic chicken wings.

"Wait 'til you see Miss Lovelin's dress. I wish I had her dynamic figure," I say eating a piece of falafel.

"Want to dance ladies?" says Christoph and Sal. Their tuxedo jackets came off hours ago.

"You two have not taken a break since the dancing started," I say. "Eat a bit first. The food's amazing."

"We can eat anytime and the food's always amazing," says Christoph. "We don't get to dance in the Ballroom every day."

"He's got a point," says Ari wiping her hands on the pink pearl-infested black cloth napkin taking Sal's hand.

"Let's see if you can keep up with me," says Zen to Christoph as they leave for the dance floor.

"What do you say Fairy Princess?" asks Kato. "Can this Prince have this dance?" he says extending his hand.

"I have to be home by midnight though," I say as he leads me away to a fairytale evening that even *Disney* could never come up with.

Chapter 33

October 1, 2015 @ 10:00pm
Underground Ballroom
Kaelyn

I tap the groom's shoulder. He turns around perplexed and then wide-eyed. "Dr. Stonebridge, benevolent Sir," he says bowing at my feet. I think he wants to kiss them, but restrains. "What an honor to have your gracious presence at my wedding. My wife and I are ever so touched that you have taken the time from your busy life to attend our happiest day. It truly is an honor, Sir!"

I know, I want to tell him, but I don't. Lovelin and I didn't attend the wedding ceremony and we both missed the reception line. "I am having the most wonderful evening. Congratulations to you and your lovely bride. I know that this is your day, but I am wishing to make a personal announcement with your permission if you would kindly allow it."

"Of course, you may!"

Yes, I know.

"My wife and I would be absolutely thrilled!" I know that, too.

Mishka motions for the music to stop and takes the stage. "Ladies and gentlemen," he says with his voice echoing throughout the Ballroom. It takes a minute for the eight hundred guests to take their seats and simmer down. "I hope you are all enjoying your evening." Everybody claps and cheers. "Thank you all for attending. You have made this day a dream come true for my bride and I." More enthusiasm. "Zenith has made this day come true for my bride and I."

Everybody now stands on their feet kissing, clapping, hollering, and cheering, a few even whistling.

"Dr. Kaelyn Stonebridge would like to make an announcement so if you please give him your undivided attention." They know that. All guests attending sit down immediately.

"Thank you, Mishka. You do know you'll never be good enough for Katia, right?" I say smiling. Everybody laughs to my question.

"Yes, Sir, I have been told by all my friends and almost everyone in Sector Eleven." Everybody roars, clapping at my remark. Katia blows Mishka a kiss.

"Well, you have a lifetime ahead of you to try. Congratulations to you both and I hope you have a most wonderful life together as man and wife." Everybody cheers once more. "I want to share with everyone that a wedding day is in my horizon. My bride-to-be, Lovelin Khan, and I will be tying the knot soon as well." Eight hundred stand hugging one another as excitement rises within the air. Lovelin's fiercely held from all directions by Sam, Ari, Zen, and Sophia.

"Dance the night away," I say. Mishka comes and gives me a congratulatory hug. It must be all the vodka he's had. Nobody dares hold me besides a seldom few, but I don't seem to mind it tonight. Michael couldn't get out of seat fast enough and then grabs me so hard I thought we would both be on the floor.

"Congrats, Bro! So damn happy for you! I'm best man, right?"

"Of course, you're my best man. Who do you think I would ask? Seth?" He hugs me again. Lovelin and I are congratulated all evening long.

October 1, 2015 @ 10:00pm
Underground Ballroom
Valentino

I turn to my crew. "Did you know that the amazing beyond the sun and all the stars and all the galaxies in our universe Dr. Stonebridge was going to make an announcement tonight?" I scream tearing away.

"No, Boss!" they respond, their tears trickling with me.

"The lighting was all wrong! I didn't get a chance to give the lighting crew a head's up to capture his beautiful silverado hair and astonishing attire!"

My crew consoles me on their knees hugging me at my waist and their hands wrapped from behind cradling me. I place my hands on my face and sob.

October 1, 2015 @ 10:10pm
Underground Ballroom
Lovelin

"I'm so, so, so, happy for you!" says Sam holding me like some prized possession. She's on her knees as I sit in the chair. Zen's crushing me on my left, Ari's hugging me at my right and Sophia has her hands wrapped around my neck from the back.

"Girls, I'm about to go into a state of unconsciousness. Your death grips are killing me."

"Sorry, Miss Lovelin. We are just so excited!" exclaims Sophia. She's doing a great acting job since she already knows. Then again, maybe it's the champagne that she has been enjoying like the rest of us.

"Whose going to be your maid of honor?" asks Sam.

"Who wants to be my maid of honor?" Sam and Sophia both raise their hands. "Well then you both can be my maids of honor."

"Are you marrying before or after the *Showcase*?" asks Ari.

"After. Not in the Ballroom, but at the Rainforest waterfall." Squeals of delight come from all directions.

"How perfect!" says Sam clapping her hands.

"Would my bride like to dance?" asks Kaelyn. He told me he's never danced in his life before Sam's birthday party, and now he's always in my arms swirling and twirling me around.

"Your bride would," I say getting up all teary-eyed at his words. I can hear the girls sighing behind us.

We dance the night away.

Chapter 34

October 1, 2015 @ 10:15pm
Underground Ballroom
Krista Harding

I can't believe he's actually going to marry that stupid, good for nothing *Surface* bitch! I need another fucking drink! Drone! Where are you?

A drone flies over placing an Almond Joy martini in front of me.

"Why are you so upset?" asks Brooks. "You didn't smile or clap after Kaelyn made his speech."

How's he going to understand? He, too, recently married a *Surface* nobody. If his wife was all that, he wouldn't be fucking me.

"Kaelyn's too good for her!" This is dessert, not a drink, I think gulping it in one sitting. I motion for the drone to bring me another martini. "How's she supposed to intellectually keep up with him?"

"How's anybody supposed to intellectually keep up with him? He's one of the smartest guys on this planet. I doubt it if he discusses genetics with her." Unfortunately, I understand his point.

"She didn't even go to an Ivy League university," I say draining my second martini. "Only Big Ten, like that's even worth anything!" My serving drone immediately comes with another one. It looks like a lychee and mango martini.

"Look at her, Krista. She's stunning and a bestselling novelist. I think she's a great match for Kaelyn. Look at them dancing in each other arms. They can't keep their eyes off one another. They look happier than the bride and groom."

Kaelyn' s midnight blue tail tuxedo seems to match the same dye lot as Lovelin's long, low-cut beaded mermaid strapless gown. It shows off every curve of her body. The clothes had to be custom-designed. I've never seen such attire at the shops in Mid-Section or even up above. I hate to admit it, but the electric blue in Lovelin's hair makes her look very sexy.

Her necklace is even more stunning than the gown. Those have to be pink diamonds. I can't believe Zenith would adhere to Kaelyn's request for pink diamonds. No! She ordered them herself. Such a materialistic bitch! She must be wearing incredibly high heels because I remember her shorter when I first encountered her that night in front of Kaelyn's apartment.

"What? You have a thing for him?" He sounds jealous. I don't say anything. I never thought I did. I just used him for his incredible body. His achievements are admirable as well.

"No, of course not," I say draining the exquisite martini. I don't look his way. I wish he didn't look so exquisite.

"You don't sound all that convincing."

October 1, 2015 @ 10:15pm
Underground Ballroom
Jay Ahmed

Look at them. They can't keep their eyes off one another. I wish Sam would look at me that way. Well, here goes nothing.

"May I have the pleasure of a dance, Sam?" I ask extending my hand.

"Well, it's about fucking time," says Sophia sitting next to her. I think Sophia might be on her third glass of champagne. She's really enjoying herself with Kato tonight. Ari and Zen are on the dance floor with Christoph and Sal. I don't think my two little roommates have missed even one song so far. They know how to enjoy an *Underground* wedding.

"I'd love to." Kato and Sophia join us. Lou Rawls' *You'll Never Find Another* starts playing. Sam and I listen to the words without saying anything. We don't have to. Low Rawls says it for us. I hope she's thinking the same way I am.

Champagne glasses tinkle once again. Mishka gives Katia one hell of a kiss while they dance. He dips her down. Everybody claps and giggles. I see Kato and Sophia steal a soft kiss from each other after. Even Uncle Kaelyn kisses Miss Lovelin exuberantly. Grand Sister and Grandfather Victor look striking this evening as well in his black suit and her black shimmery gown. They've been kissing throughout the night when the glasses hit one another.

I wish I could kiss Sam. I want to kiss Sam. I should have had a beer or two. I stuck to root beer this evening. I don't know why I can't enjoy this wedding like everyone else.

"Enjoying those jelly beans?" I ask. She's wearing my bracelet. It's either a sign of hope or an indication that she doesn't have much jewelry for a special occasion.

"Chika's enjoying them more. The bride and groom look so happy," says Sam gazing at them. I wish she would gaze at me. I'm the one dancing in her arms and she looks at everyone but me.

"It's supposed to be the happiest day of their life. Do you think Zenith will allow them to have children?"

"It would be a shame not to allow it. I know they are only Maintenance, but a baby by them would be ever so cherished and blessed."

I wish I was cherished and blessed.

October 1, 2015 @ 10:15pm
Underground Ballroom
Samantha Stonebridge

Look at them. They can't keep their eyes off one another. I've never seen my Uncle Kaelyn so happy in all my life. He so deserves to be. He worships Miss Lovelin not only with his eyes, but with his body and soul. I don't know what spell Miss Lovelin cast upon him, but I wish that same spell was cast upon me. I wish Jay would look at me that way. I should join Christoph and Sal. Those two know how to party. Even Zen and Ari are having a blast. I wish I could enjoy this wedding. I gulp another sip of my strawberry wine cooler. Maybe a glass of champagne would help. Kato might have to carry Sophia home.

Jay finally asks me to dance. I wanted to say 'what the fuck took you so long' or 'I thought you'd never ask', but I kept my true thoughts to myself. Sophia's remark was perfect. I don't know how this song came about right now, but Lou Rawls must be telling me something from his grave.

The bride and groom are glowing. I hope they are allowed to have at least one child together. Their baby would be so cherished and blessed. I wish I was cherished by Jay.

Chapter 35

October 2, 2015 @ 11:00am
Sector Nine - Female dormitories
Samantha Stonebridge

"Are you alive?" I ask Sophia.

"You should have cut me off after four glasses of champagne," she says with her head still under the pillow. She's not exactly moaning, she's just in an agonized disarray.

"Here, I ordered a large cheeseburger for you. Best cure for a hangover." Sophia sits up and eats without even brushing her teeth. "Where did you and Kato disappear to last night? It was past two in the morning and nobody could find both of you anymore."

"We went to the waterfall at Mid-Section," she says chomping away. She's getting ever so messy, too. So much for manners when you're hung over. "Lots of kissing," she says with a mouthful as ketchup as onions drip down onto her cloth napkin.

"Just kissing, right?" Sophia doesn't say anything until after she finishes her cheeseburger. Her napkin has seemed to have eaten a fraction of the burger with her consent.

"Wow, I really do feel so much better."

"Sophia?"

238

"C'mon, Sam. I'm not even fourteen, yet. Kato's not that kind of guy. He's a gentleman, albeit a very forward gentleman when he's had a few. We were both feeling it together last night. It was a magical evening," she says with a sigh. "I felt like one of Disney's fairy princesses. I can't wait for the next wedding."

Wish I had a magical evening. I'm quite envious of how their relationship has blossomed over the past few months. Jay and I having an arrangement as children made me take him for granted over the years. I've got to make up for this somehow. I don't want to ever take him for granted again. He didn't even seem to want to kiss me last night.

"I'm limiting you at Miss Lovelin's wedding. I can just picture you and Kato hiding behind the waterfall doing whatever."

"Hmm, that's a fun thought!" she says getting out of bed.

"Sophia!" I say throwing a pillow at her. Just then, Ari and Zen walk in from their swim at *Fathoms Above Fitness.*

"Pillow fight!" screams Zen grabbing her pillow off her bed smacking Sophia. Ari follows her lead. We smack each other around for the rest of the morning screaming and having fun.

Thankful blesses to Mother Earth for Zenith giving us this day off as well.

October 2, 2015 @ 12:00pm
Fathoms Above Fitness
Kato Park

"Where did you and Sophia disappear off too late last night? I was home by 2:30am and you weren't back, yet. Even Sal and Christoph were fast asleep," Jay asks sitting in the steam room. We just finished a grueling game of one on one basketball. We needed it after eating the crazy amount of food at the wedding yesterday. We just have swim trunks on and a towel wrapped around our necks.

"With all that dancing they did, they probably will sleep throughout the whole day. It's nice of Zenith to give us this day off."

"Answer my question." He sounds incredibly serious. I'm afraid he won't like my answer.

"Promise you won't get upset?" There's no way I can avoid him. I heard Jay wanted to give one of his lungs to me. He's more brother than a true blood brother.

"What did you do?" Nobody's in the steam room with us. It's pretty quiet today after a wedding. I'm sure most are nursing their bodies and heads.

"I took Sophia to the waterfall in Mid-Section. It was my idea."

"You took pictures?" I shake my head lying down on the tiles. I speak with my eyes closed. I absolutely love a steam bath and could fall asleep in it.

"We spent quite some time just…"

"Just what?"

"Getting to know each other better." I can feel Jay staring at me. I open my eyes for a moment. I was right. "Okay. Okay. We stole a few kisses. That's all."

"You were stealing kisses all evening long. You think nobody noticed?"

"Everybody and their other half were stealing kisses all evening long. It was a wedding, remember?"

"Out with it," he commands.

"Okay. So this time we weren't stealing them. We were sharing them."

"You better not have been sharing anything else!" he says smacking my head.

"I promise I won't touch her until we are married," I say massaging my scalp.

"You two have decided to get married?" he asks smacking my head again. "When? Why didn't you tell me!" I knew he'd be upset. I get up and shift positions so I'm not lying right beside him.

"Well, it's not like I've proposed or anything, but we have a mutual understanding that one day we will," I say sitting up. "Nobody gets married before sixteen down here. I think that's Zenith's law. You have to be at least fourteen in the United States."

"Congratulations! I'm happy for you." We then don't say anything for a while. The orange-scented steam starts up again from the holes in the walls. I lay down once more and close my eyes. I hope Jay's not envious of my relationship with Sophia. It bloomed quite suddenly.

Sometimes I think that my explosion that landed me in the infirmary for two weeks was a blessing in disguise.

"I've got to make things right between me and Sam. I don't know what to do. She's been such a selfish terror, but has humbled down somewhat lately. I miss the connection. I feel so detached. I'm jealous of Char, too." I finally admit to myself.

"Char's too young for Sam. They're practically the same age. They're just friends. Just like you and Lucinda," I say with my eyes closed lying down on the tiles. "You shouldn't be jealous of him regardless of how brilliant he is. You live down here, too. There's no competition amongst us."

"I don't know what to do anymore. I'm constantly on pins and needles with her," says Jay frustrated.

"Well, do something. I'd love to have a double wedding someday." Jay smiles at me. I can feel it even with my eyes closed.

"I'd love to have a double wedding, too," he sighs.

Chapter 36

October 2, 2015 @ 10:00pm
Sector Six Apartments
Krista Harding

I've never drank so much in my life. I don't even know why I did. I only attended the wedding for the great food and thought I'd have a couple of martinis to relax. It's so hectic with the upcoming *Showcase*. I don't know how many martinis I wound up having. I didn't wake until noon and Brooks was already gone by then. His little wife thinks he's a traveling salesman. I try to recollect last night. I think Brooks and I had sex, but I can't exactly remember.

Since I live in Sector Six, I wasn't allowed a wrist inoculation. I ranted and raved to the President and he finally gave in. I think he did it just to shut me up. I press my wrist and call him.

"Yes, Miss Harding, good evening."

"Your prized possession's getting married. I told you that *Surface* girl is a distraction." Silence.

"That's wonderful news. Everybody should experience a happy world of marriage. I don't know what I'd do without my wife. She makes me feel complete."

"He was designed to be a savior not a husband!"

"Doesn't mean he can't be both. His accomplishments are unprecedented. He deserves to share his life with someone he loves."

"I guarantee you, Sir; she's going to be his downfall! Mark my word!" I can't believe the President is happy for him. I need a fucking drink!

"Have a lovely night, Miss Harding," he says disconnecting the line.

October 2, 2015 @ 10:15pm
Sector Four - Kaelyn's Apartment
Kaelyn

I've never been so out of breath. "Want to go for another round?" Lovelin asks panting away. She's staring down at me in beautiful black and red laced underclothes in our bed.

"You are a demon angel that's going to land me in the infirmary," I say grabbing her around her waist kissing her neck. We've been tumbling in the sheets all day and evening. We've only stopped to eat and visit my creations, our children, twice. I think this is why Zenith gave us another day off.

I have my darling doll pinned underneath me. She looks up with watery eyes.

"I loved your short speech at the wedding. I can't believe you made our wedding announcement to almost the entire *Underground* community. I thought it would be just to your immediate family. You made me the happiest girl in the world last night taking me by surprise," she says kissing me back. "I

244

hear you've always been such a private person and don't really associate with anyone. You've never even attended a wedding until yesterday."

My waist cuddles deeper into hers.

"You are the most special person in my life and I promise to spend every moment of the rest of my life making you the happiest girl in the world," I say with longing kisses. Lovelin slides her hand through my silk pajama bottoms to caress me. I moan into her neck. I then see an incoming call in my line of sight. It's the President. Fuck! I should have turned my wrist off today.

"Sweetheart, it's the President. Just give me a minute." She withdraws her hand immediately and leaves for the kitchen.

"Good evening, Commander."

"I hear congratulations are in order, Kaelyn. Am I invited to the wedding?" So many thousands of miles away and I'm a mile beneath the ocean, and he already knows. Not crazy about this social media nonsense.

"We would be honored if you're schedule allows it. Haven't set a date, yet. Looking forward to the *Showcase* first." Lovelin returns with a glass of wine and strawberries. I'll never get enough of the way her hips sway. I'm getting hard again and wish I wasn't talking to the President.

"So am I and the rest of the Zenith leaders. We'll be arriving on the twentieth." They are attending only for Samantha's first *Showcase*. I wish she would give me a hint as to what her presentation entails, but she has been extremely secretive.

"I look forward to seeing you again, Sir." We say our byes and I disconnect our line.

"Everything all right?" says Lovelin placing the glass up to my lips for a sip.

"He congratulated us on our upcoming marriage. Wasn't expecting it," I say swallowing feeding her a strawberry.

"How sweet of him," she says leaning into my mouth. We share the strawberry together. I wonder if I'll have any energy left to get anything accomplished tomorrow.

Oh well, I'll worry about that tomorrow.

Chapter 37

October 6, 2015 @ 8:00am
Cloning Laboratory
David Kohler

Kaiser's got to get another assistant. I'm fucking tired of all the cleaning and maintenance. I'm a scientist, not a house wife. I should be working on projects rather than cleaning up bird and dog shit all morning.

Barney comes and licks my hand. "Can't you see I'm busy?" I snap at him. He returns to his bed with his head down all sad.

"Dorry's hungry!" she squawks.

"Shut the fuck up, Dorothy!"

"Fuck you more!" she squawks yelling back. Barney covers his ears with his paws. He then pulls his plush blue blanket upon him to alleviate the hostility.

"Jake, who's the wait staff manager for Sector Eleven?"

"That would be Natalia Finch," says Jake.

"Call her for me, now!"

I introduce myself and ask if there's anyone available in her cleaning crew to temporarily help the cloning sect since we're currently a man short. She says she will send someone over immediately. I don't know why I didn't think of this before. I don't care if Kaiser approves or not.

I check on the artificial chamber while I wait for staff to show up. That's odd. All the lights are off. The timer's not counting down. I can't see the baby inside. He's not swimming around as usual on the holographic computer screen. What in Zenith's name happened?

I put my hands on the chamber. It's unusually warm; far warmer than it should be. I press my wrist and call Kaiser.

"We have a problem. I think he's dead."

* * *

"What the fuck do you mean he's dead? He can't be dead!" Kaiser says storming into our lab. His face is redder than his flamboyant gym attire. There's no way he can be gay. He behaves way too masculine. He obviously has a poor fashion sense. He must have been at *Fathoms*. "What the fuck did you fucking do?"

"I didn't fucking do anything!" I scream back. "Check for your fucking self!" I say with my hands on my head.

Kaiser looks all around the glass cocoon. He touches the chamber.

"The chamber's overheating. We must manually open it. He may be premature, but still alive."

"I hope you know how to do that because I fucking don't," I say pulling on my hair.

Kaiser presses the emergency release button, but the chamber doesn't open. He presses again and again. All the electronics aren't working.

"Can't you manually count the timer down?" Kaiser frantically presses all the other buttons. Nothing. He then runs over to the tool cabinet, grabs a hammer, and tries to smash the glass cocoon. The first blow doesn't even scratch it.

"What the fuck is this made out of?" he exclaims. "It's just glass."

"Well, obviously it's *Underground* engineered glass so good luck," I say putting my hands through my hair again. "Jake, can you override the artificial chamber in our lab?"

No answer at first. "What would you like me to do?" asks Jake.

"We need to take the specimen out," demands Kaiser.

"Unlatching chamber," says Jake. "Override complete." The case door opens and artificial amniotic fluid pours out of the chamber and onto the tiled floor. Kaiser scoops the baby out.

He's not breathing.

I'm surprised I'm not breathing either looking at Kaiser's attire.

October 6, 2015 @ 9:00am
Cloning Sector
Kaiser Shue

We tried reviving him, but he was long gone. No artificial chamber has ever overheated before. It must have happened last night after we left our lab. We place him in a cooling chamber for preservation before cremation.

"What if Zareen knew about him? What if her death wasn't an accidental drowning and Zenith took care of her?" says David pacing back and forth.

I sit in my chair. It's a possibility.

"Then who killed the baby? It obviously wasn't her."

"What if she told someone about what we were cloning? Human cloning's even prohibited by Zenith laws as far as everyone else knows. This project was supposed to be kept absolutely top secret. None of the other cloning scientists even know what we're always working on. Not unless Zareen told one of them."

"I can't believe anyone of them would interfere in our work. If anything, they would be thrilled to clone a human. It's our passion. Zareen couldn't have known who the baby was. The only other person that knew is Brooks and he's always been on Zenith's side. He went through much trouble to get his DNA. It has to be someone else."

"There's over a thousand inhabitants in the *Underground*. Our lab is incredibly secure. Who could have gotten in? Unless Zareen overrode lab codes for someone else. Mother Fucker! I'm so fucking confused!"

"I have to call Zenith and tell them we may have a possibility of a mole. Let them figure it out." I press my wrist and call the President. To hell if he has a cabinet meeting or not. We are far more important. I tell him what has happened. I give him our theories. I wish my wrist had volume control because he's screaming in my ears and head.

I tell him we don't believe it was a malfunction in the chamber. The President says to take it to Engineering and have it checked out anyway. He screams blaming David and myself for not monitoring him properly. I knew he would be mad and take it out on me. I'm head of this department and take the fall. Thank goodness, the President disconnects the line because I have an instant migraine.

"He says he will let us know," I say massaging my temple. The doorbell rings. "Who the fuck could that be?"

"I called a cleaning crew earlier. We now need one more than ever." He presses the button to open the electronic lab door. Two teenage boys stand in front of us. They introduce themselves as Roberto and Lorenzo. They're dressed like Hazmat without the hats.

"Come this way. Shouldn't you two be in class?"

"Sector Eleven runs on a different school schedule," says Lorenzo, the long lanky brown-haired boy. "School is in the evening after work. All our classes are over the *SuperNet*. We are not Sector Nine that gets classroom instruction."

"I didn't know that," says David.

"It's definitely easier for us," says Lorenzo, "since we work from eight to four."

"You had a flood?" asks Roberto, the short stocky one eyeing all the amniotic fluid. "Would you like us to call Maintenance for repairs?" Kaiser shakes his head.

"No, nothing you two can't handle, right?" says David.

"Of course, doctors. Whatever you wish," says Roberto.

"Dorry's hungry!" squeals Dorry.

"If you do a good job, we'll let you take the bird home," says David patting them both on the back.

October 6, 2015 @ 6:00pm
Cryogenics
Kieran Mersa

"You did it!" screams Kieran. I put my arms out and Simba jumps right into them. He licks my cheeks, forehead, and mouth all over. He whimpers as he does so. I could cry. Then cry again.

"I don't know how much time you have with him," says Dr. Kai-af. I squeeze Simba so tight as he licks my face all over for the second or third time. "He's my first breakthrough in months."

"Even if I have just one more day, it's more than I could have ever hoped for. I don't know how I'm ever going to thank you!"

"No, thank you for giving me the opportunity to experiment on him. Keep me posted how he's doing."

"Of course, I will," I say shaking his hand.

This is the *best what a day* ever.

Chapter 38

October 6, 2015 @ 3:00pm
Mid-Section
Samantha Stonebridge

I needed to catch a quick bite before Differential Equations class so I went to grab a tuna croissant sandwich at Mid-Section. While waiting for the drone to arrive with it, I see Lucinda walk in at *In Between*. It's only open from one to five in the afternoon every day. It's the restaurant in Mid-Section between *Sunrise and Sunset's* hours of operation. I ask her to join me. I want to see what Jay sees in her besides her glorious smile. She looks hesitant at first and then takes the seat opposite of my booth.

"How's your day going?" I casually ask trying not to look into her eyes. They are ever so radiant in their sparking blue and gold tones. My pale green eyes falter in more ways than one compared to hers. A drone arrives and takes her order of clam chowder soup and a Greek salad with no onion.

"It was going great and then I got a glitch. The ecosystem isn't going the way I want. I just hope I can be ready for the upcoming *Showcase*. Everybody's on pins and needles right now," she expresses. She looks tremendously fidgety.

"Tell me about it. I barely see my roommates anymore. Even Jay's a figment in the wind." He truly isn't, but I say it just to arise a reaction out of her. Lucinda reacts to my comment just like I thought she would.

"That must be tough." We have an awkward silence for a couple of minutes. "That was a great birthday party. I didn't get you a gift because the invitation said not to."

"No worries. I have everything. My Jay's all I need," I say with an exuberant smile. I wish that could be true. "See the pretty bracelet he got me?" I say flashing my wrist across the table.

"Very pretty," she says not too enthusiastically. "So, what's your presentation on?" she asks without a smile this time.

"It's a surprise. My first *Showcase*. Sort of nervous." That's probably the first truth I've said since Lucinda sat down.

I'm actually nervous about my first presentation. I'm debating whether or not to gulp down a strawberry wine cooler just prior to it.

"Samantha, I've never seen you nervous. You are Zenith's golden child. You never ever look stressed out about anything." I smile at her comment. I frown within myself. If she only knew.

"What time's your *Showcase* presentation?" I ask. The drone arrives with our food and we eat like we've been enjoying each other's company for years together.

"It's on October 16th at five o'clock. I hope you can make it. Jay told me he would be there."

"Yes, he told me," I lie. "He didn't mention the date and time."

I haven't even had a chance to look at the *Showcase* schedule, yet. "Don't worry, we would love to be there," I say taking another bite of my sandwich. I can't tell if Lucinda's telling the truth or not about Jay being at her presentation as I watch her eat her salad. Of course, he wants to be there.

She's my replacement.

That thought sets my heart on fire. No, that thought sets my soul on fire.

I pretend to get an incoming call from Jay. "Please excuse me. My boy's calling." I pretend to press my wrist under the table.

"Hey, baby, what's up? Really? That's awesome! How about we celebrate tonight over dinner? I'll have Ari make us something special." I wait a moment. "Yeah, love you, too," I say pretending to press my wrist again. "Sorry about that," I tell her taking another bite of my sandwich.

"Oh, no problem. So, have you two set a date, yet?" I pretend not to understand what she's talking about.

"A date?"

"A wedding date."

"Oh, the wedding. We're working on it. No rush. Too caught up in our work at the moment," I say not looking at her before taking another bite of my sandwich.

"Well, that's understandable," she says with a radiant smile. I want to smack that smile right off her face, but I just smile back.

"I'll save you a seat at my *Showcase* presentation."

"Thanks, Samantha. I appreciate it," she says before starting on her soup.

"Of course, and please call me Sam. All of my and Jay's friends do." She smiles at me once more. I want to smack that smile off her face once more right to Shanghai.

"I'll place you right next to Jay in the front row. I know you two are good friends. He told me so," I say smiling. My face hurts from all the stupid smiling. I finish my sandwich. She just smiles once more eating her soup. I wonder if her face hurts, too. "And I'll place Christoph on the other side of you. He said you were so sweet to him at the *Holoplex* the other night," I lie once more. I have no fucking clue what Christoph thinks of her.

"He's a cutie," she says not looking up at me, but chocking on her soup a bit.

"Lucinda, I have to get to class," I say getting out of the booth. "It was great having lunch with you. Hope we can do it again soon," I lie again.

"That would be great, Sam. I look forward to it," she says with another radiant smile. We say our byes and I leave Mid-Section for the train.

Damn! She's actually a nice girl. Wish I didn't like her so much.

October 6, 2015 @ 3:00pm
Mid-Section
Lucinda

I needed to catch some lunch before Waterway Structures or I knew I wouldn't be getting any nourishment until late tonight. I'm looking forward to attend the seminar on parasitic communities in our ecosystems this afternoon. I arrive at *In Between*. Samantha Stonebridge surprises me by asking me to join her for lunch.

Would this be awkward? I join her just to see what she's all about. Paris has classes with her. I never have. I know she's bred to be amazing like her Uncle. I don't want to feel intimidated by her. I hold my head high and take the booth across from her.

"How's your day going?" she asks. Does she really care or is she just making small talk? A drone takes my order before I answer. I tell her the truth. I'm so not ready, yet, for this year's *Showcase*. I've been working overtime for the last two weeks. I even missed the wedding because I didn't want to chance failing my *Showcase* presentation.

"That was a great birthday party. I didn't get you a gift because the invitation said not to."

"No worries. I have everything. My Jay is all I need," she says. My heart sinks to her comment and as she flashes her beautiful bracelet in front of my face.

She then tells me she's nervous about her first *Showcase*. Samantha, nervous? She's Zenith's other golden child. She's obviously lying to me. I tell her she needn't be. What else was I supposed to say?

Her call from Jay surprises me a bit. She's only fourteen and her conversation definitely sounded like they were lovers, and not just boyfriend and girlfriend. Jay doesn't seem like to type of guy to take advantage of such a young girl, ultimate genius or not. Then again, Samantha seems so beyond her years. I ask about her wedding just to see how desperate they are. Samantha said no rush and they're too busy. I couldn't tell if she was lying or not again. I'm so confused about their relationship, but I don't want to pry so I stay quiet.

When she said she would place Jay on one side of me at the *Showcase* and Christoph on the other, I was actually touched.

Damn you for being right Paris! It's hard not to like her!

October 6, 2015 @ 7:00pm
Sector Four - Male Dormitories
Jay Ahmed

"What are you doing?" I ask Kato throwing my backpack at the foot of my bed. He has 3D screens up all around him.

"Trying to figure out where the fuck I went wrong," he says mumbling with a stylus between his teeth. He's writing equations in mid-air with his finger.

I have to give him credit for his perseverance. He almost died, and still he wants to help the world for the better. Sal and Christoph are playing *Underground* Monopoly in their pajamas eating strawberry cake and ice cream.

"I hope that's not dinner," I say changing out of my lab coat.

"Uh-huh," they say back in unison. Christoph gives me a thumps up sign as he buys the Rainforest.

"Brain food," says Sal giggling.

"Really?" says Kato. Both of them nod their heads laughing. Everybody seems to be in a goofy mood this evening. In Sector Nine right now, you're either crazy stressed out about your upcoming *Showcase* presentation or relaxed knowing you're getting two weeks off from everything soon. Although the *Showcase* presentations only last for a week from morning until evening every day in many sections of the Underground, everybody gets the previous week off prior to prepare or just use it as holiday time.

I could use a stress buster. Kato and I order cake and ice cream for dinner.

Chapter 39

October 7, 2015 @ 8:00am
Mid-Section
Lovelin

There were already over one hundred people lined up in front of my bookstore before Kaelyn and I arrived. I wasn't expecting such a line out the door. Well, if there was a door. I wanted a coming out party and I got one far better than 17th century England ever could. I should have dressed up a bit more. I feel too casual in just a black skirt and white blouse.

My two dozen bracelets jingle as I shake everyone's hands. Most are from Sector Six and Sector Eleven.

"Finally!" says one little girl. She couldn't be more than seven years old. "Tons of story books! Not just school electronic workbooks! Please give me all your recommendations!"

"Go up to the holographic console and select your genre. My top picks will display for you. I can order whatever you want via the *SuperNet* in traditional book format or electronic form.

Zenith would prefer electronic, but some people just want a hardcover book in their hands. I understand that completely. Electronic, I can give you today. Traditional, I will have to order for you. Cutting down trees is really not the way to go according to Zenith, but it's your choice."

"Electronic. Definitely!" says the little girl. "It's the *Underground* way." She rushes off to one of the consoles to order.

Spoken like a true Cave Dweller.

Kaelyn has such a proud smile on his face. I have a feeling it's going to be a long day. My Lord winks at me. I'm so looking forward to the even longer night.

All three of my consoles were busy throughout the day and well into the evening. I closed my shop at nine o'clock. There were hundreds of books ordered from the *Underground* inhabitants. Kaelyn even took the day off from his lab to keep me company.

"Don't neglect your work reading story books all night long," I say to my patrons as I hand them electronic tablets with the story they want. "That was incredibly difficult for me during my school and college days."

"Don't close your shop! Sorry, Lovelin," says Sauri rushing in. "I've been swamped today and lost track of time. Show me around!" We give each other an exuberant hug. Sauri and Victor and many of Sector Nine gather in my shop. It's late, but they have been busy working all day.

"There's really not much to it. This section of the shop houses all of the scientist's work. You can download their work via the *SuperNet* onto your personal tablet or your wall through my shop's website. The consoles are equipped with all the pleasure reading. It can give you an endless variety of books published on the *Surface*. I have electronic pads in stock that can download whatever book you want in a matter of seconds and all your books stay stored in one area."

"What's your favorite, Miss Lovelin?" asks Sal. "I love Superhero stories."

"Have you ever read the Harry Potter series?"

"No, but I've seen the first movie at the *Holoplex*."

"Witches and sorcerers? Really?" asks Ari. "That's so unrealistic."

"You won't be able to put the books down. Unrealistic is what makes a book amazing. A different world you can melt into. Even far better than the movies."

"Let's give it a try," says Zen. "I can use a different mode of downtime apart from cooking with Ari."

"Yes," says Ari. "I can use a different mode of downtime apart from listening to Zen play the piano and the harp." Everyone laughs as Ari and Zen hug each other.

"What do you suggest for me?" asks Jay.

"*Master of the Game* by Sidney Sheldon. It's one of the best I've ever read. He's a legend. Once you start on his stuff, you will get completely addicted! He's known as the Master Storyteller. Unfortunately, he has passed away, but he wrote until the day he died."

"Is that really a good idea?" asks Jay. "We have work to do down here." Everyone laughs again.

"A book can definitely take you away into a fantasy world, but you are all too bright to get caught up in it. Just enjoy the tale."

"Can you suggest a good biography about *Surface* life?" asks Sophia.

"Oh, Sophia, there are so many. Read *Burned Alive* by Souad. It's an incredible horrific biography because of religious and cultural beliefs. You will appreciate your home even more after reading that book. *Wasted*, by Marya Hornbacher is about a girl who struggles with bulimia and anorexia. Such a horrific mental and physical disorder. You should read that next."

"What is bulimia and anorexia?" asks Ari. I look at her dumbfounded. I thought everyone knew everything down here. Apparently, there's more cocooning and sheltering in the *Underground* than I thought.

"It's a dreadful disease and mental disorder on the *Surface*, especially for young girls like yourself. I hope you don't get distraught if you read it, but it's definitely an eye opening experience."

Sauri whispers into my ear what she would like to read. I pull her aside and whisper *The Sleeping Beauty Trilogy* by Anne Rice and *The Fifty Shades of Grey Trilogy* by E.L. James and *The Crossfire* series by Sylvia Day, and definitely by far my favorite, *Seven Years to Sin* by Sylvia Day. I would have never guessed about Sauri's choices, but everyone has skeletons in their closets. She's always so prim and proper. "Keep it between us," she asks. I just wink at her saying, "of course." I order the books for her.

"Any cookbooks you suggest?" asks Ari.

"With what you can do? No, definitely not. There's nothing out there."

October 7, 2015 @ 12:00pm
Mid-Section
Krista Harding

I arrive at Mid-Section to have lunch with Brooks. He recently got married to a useless Surface street girl, but the chemistry between us has been close to one of the best I've ever had. I wish Kaelyn wasn't at the top of my list. I still can't figure out why he is.

There's so much commotion in Mid-Section today. Far more than usual. What in the world is going on? People are lined out at one of the new shops. I then can't believe what I see.

Lovelin's Literature and Likings in neon pink letters above her bookstore. When I received the survey, I dismissed it completely. I thought people down here were smarter than that and would do the same.

I can't believe that Zenith gave that little good for nothing *Surface* bitch a shop of her own. Then it dawns on me. They want to keep her occupied with something to do and away from Kaelyn. I smile at the thought. I enter the bookstore. People are lined up at the three consoles ordering books. I watch Kaelyn kiss Lovelin's forehead. They look at each other with such sappiness in their eyes that I lose my appetite completely.

What the fuck? He should be in his lab working!

"Hello, Miss Harding," says Samantha Stonebridge. "I haven't seen you in forever. You must be crazy busy with the upcoming *Showcase.*"

"I'm always crazy busy. *Showcase* or not. Zenith's right hand, remember?" I say watching Kaelyn gaze into Lovelin's eyes once more.

"Of course, I remember," Sam says with an exuberant smile. "I have a photographic memory. I don't forget anything."

She's just like her fucking Uncle! All full of her prodigy self.

"Here to get a book? Miss Lovelin's amazing! She's so perfect for my Uncle Kaelyn. They are so in love," she says with a large sigh.

Love indeed! Her breasts are practically popping out of her shirt. Her hair's wild and crazy looking like a fucking unruly rainbow. I bet that's why Kaelyn's infatuated with her. She's so different from himself.

"I have better things to do than read silly story books and so does everyone else. Lovelin won't last here for very long. I guarantee it. She'll be over in days. People will realize that they don't have the time."

October 7, 2015 @ 12:15pm
Mid-Section
Samantha Stonebridge

I've never been crazy about Krista, but Zenith is. She keeps the *Underground* intact. As Operational Manager, she must have a lot on her plate. It has to be a fulltime job and then some coordinating between the *Surface* and the *Underground*. I don't like what she said about Miss Lovelin. Should I tell Uncle Kaelyn? Is she a threat? She sounded like one just now.

When she told me she was Zenith's right hand, I held it all in trying not to burst out in tears laughing. I feel sorry for her. Everybody knows that Uncle Kaelyn and I are Zenith's right hands. Sector Four combined is more worthy than she is. Krista is replaceable. We are not. She's far more narcissist because she can't comprehend so.

I walk into Miss Lovelin's shop. She greets me with a bear hug.

"Thank you Sam for attending! I know how incredibly busy you are!" she says not letting me go.

"I wouldn't miss this for the world!" I say back not releasing her either.

"Do you think my girls can detach for just a moment?" asks Uncle Kaelyn. "I have a problem."

"Why? What's wrong?" Miss Lovelin and I both say in unison as we still stay intact to one another.

"I'm hungry."

Miss Lovelin and I give each other the 'are you kidding?' look to one another. "Should we feed him?" Miss Lovelin asks me.

"Does he deserve it?" I say back.

We both know he deserves it and we order lunch together.

October 7, 2015 @ 10:30pm
Sector Four - Kaelyn's Apartment
Lovelin

"What a day!" I say flopping on our bed. Kaelyn's on top of me within a minute. He kisses me passionately.

"I know you had a *great what a day*. Now it's even going to be a greater what a night," he says trailing kisses behind my ear. I wrap myself around him further.

"Jake, turn the lights off," I say nibbling on Kaelyn's ear. Within moments, a glow from the wall brightens our room.

You Don't Belong Here -
You Will Never Be Good Enough For Him

Chapter 40

October 10, 2015 @ 10:00pm London Time
London
Zachary Briarwood

The closet of my old bedroom stinks like a rugby's sweaty locker room. This is definitely not the aroma I came home to as a young boy. Memories of mum's shepherd's pie float into my head. It isn't the best as it is in the *Underground,* but that was the scent of home. It's ten o'clock London time and four o'clock *Underground* time. I purposely chose to arrive earlier rather than the middle of the night hoping to encounter Clarissa's parents. I've decided I'm not going to let her die.

I open the squeaky closet door. Same as I knew it. I smile to myself. The light's on, but no one's in. I can hear the tele in the sitting room from here. I can't comprehend what show's going on because I never watch the tele. Clarissa's family's still awake. I walk down the hallway to her bedroom. I hope she's not asleep. I watch her parents tuck her in bed so lovingly. Her mother's blonde-haired and small-framed like her daughter; she gives Clarissa a soft kiss on her nose. She kisses her mum's nose back with a soft shallow smile. Her father's large with wavy brown hair. He looks like a rugby player. He holds her hands and then kisses her temple.

"Char!" she screams bolting upright as she notices my presence. She throws off the covers lightning fast and rushes into my arm as frail as she is. My other arm holds my Spear. I cradle her gently.

268

Clarissa feels even more delicate than before. Her eyes look hollow and her skin, grey and lifeless. She stares up worshipping me like I'm some superhero. She still has the prettiest smile gazing up at me nonetheless.

"Oh, Char, I've missed you. I've been praying every day and night for your return!" I kiss the top of her head as softly as I can to not to hurt her fragile form any further.

"I've missed you, too, Clarissa."

"Lissy? Who is that?" asks her father. I want to tell him the correct expression is *who is he*, but I don't.

"Hello, Sir. I'm Dr. Zachary Briarwood. I used to live here." I place my Spear down on the frayed pink carpet and then extend my hand for her father to shake. He reluctantly does.

"You're the genius boy!" says the mother. I smile at her before planting another soft kiss on Clarissa's head.

"How did you get into our flat?" asks the father looking at Clarissa.

"He has a spare key in the building," Clarissa says all smiles hugging into my right hip. "He came to visit once before." Both her parents don't know whether to be afraid or not. I sit on Clarissa's bed and place her onto my lap. She giggles and her parents have the most distraught look on their faces. I glance at my Spear down on the floor in front of me to show them I mean no harm or trouble, but just in case. Clarissa's parents seem to understand.

"How are you? You don't look so good," I say cradling her.

"It's just a matter of time," Clarissa says laying her head against my chest. She closes her eyes as we feel each other's warmth. "Chemo, nothing's working. It's why I'm in hospice." I look up at Clarissa's parents who are still speechless about my presence and their daughter's friendship with me.

"I have a proposition to make to you Sir, Ma'am." They don't say anything, but wait for me to speak some more. "I can cure your daughter." They stare at me like I'm some sort of alien.

"You can?" questions the mother with a frowned temple.

"I don't believe you," says the father. He looks angry. He's three times my size, but I'm not scared. I have my Spear to defend me if needed.

"Oh, Richard, please give him a chance to explain," says the mother pleading to her husband with her eyes. "He's the boy that used to live here. Remember Mrs. McPherson and her stories?"

"That senile old woman? You believed her?"

"I think you both should sit," I command picking up my Spear while pointing it to Richard's chest. Clarissa holds my hand. Richard and his wife take two of Clarissa's *Little Mermaid* chairs from her tea table. They look like giants engulfed in those little red chairs. I place my Spear back down on the floor.

"I work with the government, and not just London's. My work as well as all my other colleagues' work is top secret classified. You will not be allowed to disclose my conversation with anybody. If you do, they will know and I guarantee you will all be eliminated."

"Eliminated?" says Richard. Football players are not that bright for a reason. That's why they are football players and nothing more.

"Dead! You, your wife, and your son. Am I clear?" I say harshly. They both nod their heads. "Good. I can take Clarissa with me to cure her, but she will never be able to come back. She will live in my community for the rest of her days. It's a good life. I promise you." Richard and his wife stare at me and then stare at each other speechless.

"I either go with Char, mummy, or die here with you. I'll do whatever you want, but I want to live." She shakes and cries in my arms. Her voice is ever so weak and frail. I can see tears forming in her mother's eyes. Clarissa has a matter of days, not weeks or months. I don't even know how long Dr. Stonebridge's cancer cure takes. I should have asked Samantha if she knew.

"Why can't she come back?" asks Richard.

"The governments can risk exposure. Like I said, everything's more than highly classified, more than top secret. You both will have to take this to your graves. If you don't, there will be consequences. I promise."

"Why should we trust you?" says the mother. "How do we know Clarissa won't get hurt?"

"Really? I'm a fourteen-year-old super genius involved with the world's greatest think tank. I visited six weeks ago just to see my old room and flat. I didn't plan on waking Clarissa up the night that I did, but it's fate, don't you see? Her fate is to live and stay with me, not die with you." Clarissa's parents look at each other.

"Please, daddy, mummy," Clarissa begs with her palms clasped.

"We don't have a choice, Richard. It's a chance we have to take. Clarissa wants it," says the Mother. Richard shakes his head.

"I can take her against your will if I have to," I say reaching for my Spear and holding onto her ever so dearly, "but I hope you can see reason and it doesn't have to come to that."

"Please, daddy! I don't want to die!" she tries to scream as frail as she is holding onto me with a death grip. Her father looks at her pleading daughter and starts sobbing. He covers his face with his hands and nods his head.

"I'm taking her tonight. I don't know how much time she has, so say your goodbyes. I need to use your washroom." I pick up my Spear to leave. I place Clarissa down ever so gently so she can gather a few belongings.

"It's to the left," says the mother. I want to tell her that I know because I used to live here, but I don't. I wash my hands and face. I haven't told Zenith, but Samantha's waiting for our return. I'm sure she has told her Uncle by now about myself and Clarissa. Samantha says her Uncle would do anything for her. They have a special bond. I can understand that. I feel as though I have a special bond, too.

Upon my return to Clarissa's room, I come to see four tear-stained faces. Her brother holds her with a fierce strength only like a loving big brother can. He's large and tall like their father. He wears football clothes. I bet he lives in them like I do in my lab coat. Clarissa has changed into grey leggings, a sky-blue sweatshirt, and pink ballet flats. She holds a jacket in her arms along with her *Little Mermaid* doll.

"Do I need a suitcase?" she asks.

"No, all your clothing will be provided for you. You don't need that jacket either. It's a constant sixty-eight to seventy-two degrees where you will live."

"What planet are you from?" says the brother. I'm wearing my Cambridge hoodie. Like I said, football players aren't all that bright.

"That's classified," is all I say. He just nods his head. There's one more round of hugs, kisses, and tears. I then take Clarissa's hand, stand in the middle of the room, and activate the Spear.

"Hold onto me with one hand and the Spear with the other for support. It doesn't hurt. I promise." She does as she's told. I press the button and the winds begin circulating around us. Clarissa's family sit on her bed and hold each other for support, wide-eyed and in disbelief.

Within minutes, I'm in the infirmary in one of the post-operating rooms. It's Room Five. Clarissa's cradled on my lap and the Spear still held onto by both of us. It worked! I breathe a sigh of relief. I took a shot in the midnight dark. I didn't know if I would be successful to bring her back with me. Although I brought Dr. Takbare back, he was much stronger than Clarissa. I was afraid that the ride might end her.

"It's okay," says Samantha sweetly and quietly. "You can open your eyes now." Clarissa opens her eyes finding herself cradled on my lap on a hospital bed.

"Ready to feel all better?" says Dr. Kaelyn Stonebridge. Now I know why this Platform was named that way! He and Samantha are dressed in their formal lab coats. They both smile down at Clarissa. She nods her head. Samantha changes her into soft white pajamas and inserts an I.V. catheter into her tiny vein in her right hand. I could never have done that. I became a bit nauseous just looking at it. Clarissa doesn't even flinch. She must be used to all the pokes or Samantha must already be an exceptional physician. I lean towards my second choice.

"Dr. Stonebridge," I say. "I don't know how I'm ever going to ever be able to thank you, but…" He stops preparing the I.V. bag and looks at me. He does look intimidating, but I try not to let my nervousness show. "If there's anything I could ever do for you."

"I would love to surprise my fiancée and take us someplace special for our honeymoon. I was thinking of Egypt, but there's so much turmoil there right now."

What? Egypt? Again? It's so damn hot there! Not to mention the absolute horrors of the war.

"It would be an honor and my pleasure, Sir," I smile back. "Leave it up to me. I'll take you both someplace you'll never forget."

October 13, 2015 @ 4:00pm
Infirmary - Room Five
Zachary Briarwood

It's been exactly seventy-two hours since Clarissa's arrival to the *Underground*. The moment her I.V. line started, she fell asleep. She hasn't awoken, yet. I haven't left her side either. I've been sleeping in Room Four. The drones have been bringing me all my meals. Kieran has been extra busy with the work for Samantha's presentation due to my absence, but he loves it and tells me not to worry. He'll have Jake call me if needed.

This time, prior to Clarissa's arrival, I told Jake that there would be another visitor. And she will be a permanent resident of the *Underground*. Zenith will be notified by myself personally. Jake said he understood.

There's nobody here in this section of the infirmary except Clarissa. Kato was discharged a couple of weeks ago. I hear from Samantha that he's recovering nicely and should be back to work and classes within the month. What if the Spear blew up in my hand? I never thought of such an occurrence when designing it. I bet Kato didn't either. I hope he gets it right, whatever he was working on, to make Mother Earth more precious and secure.

Dr. Kaelyn Stonebridge has been ever so dedicated to Clarissa. I know he's extremely busy with his work and the upcoming *Showcase*, but he's been checking on her at least three times a day. He's even monitoring her vitals from his own lab as well. He even told Jake to contact him if there were any changes in her. Kaelyn Stonebridge truly is a godsend if not a God himself, which is stupid of me since we know there is no such being or force. Only Mother Earth is our true savior.

I was even privileged to meet his beautiful bride-to-be. I never thought much about fate until now. That plane crash was truly a blessing in disguise.

Clarissa squeezes my hand. I pick my head up from the hospital bed. I can see that she's trying to open her eyes.

"I'm here, Clarissa. It's me, Char." She's not wearing a wig, but I can already see soft blonde stubble growing upon her head.

"Char? I can't open my eyes."

"Don't force it." She relaxes a bit as I squeeze her hand. "How do you feel?"

"I feel so much stronger. I feel alive again!"

"That's great!" I say unable to show my enthusiasm. I get up from my chair that has been one with me for the past days and kiss her forehead just as I hear the glass door open.

Dr. Kaelyn Stonebridge in his usual black lab coat dashes in. He knew right away that Clarissa had awoken. He withdraws a couple of patches from a cabinet, and places them at the side of Clarissa's head. They are grey with a black eye in the middle of them. I've never seen such patches before. Within a couple of minutes, her eyes flutter open.

"What do you see?" Dr. Stonebridge asks. He stares right into her. I hope Clarissa doesn't get frightened by him. He's ever so intimidating with his deep voice and his unruly silver long hair.

"The worst side effect of my cancer cure is blindness," says Kaelyn. "I'm still working on it."

Clarissa giggles relentlessly. Dr. Stonebridge looks somewhat annoyed with her. I even can't understand why she's laughing at him. "What's so funny?" he asks.

"I thought Zeus was Greek, not British!"

Chapter 41

October 12, 2015 @ 10:10am
Lovelin's Literature and Likings
Lovelin

After a delicious breakfast of fruits and nuts in the Rainforest, I arrive at my bookstore a little later than usual. I had a difficult time letting our children go as they clung hanging from every side of my being begging me to stay just a little while longer. I absolutely love calling them our children. I absolutely hate releasing them from all sides of myself. I haven't played hopscotch since I was in elementary school. It was definitely more fun barefooted in the sand!

There's already a gentleman casually sitting at one of my tables sipping his coffee. I have not seen him before. He looks like a military man with his short haircut, perfect posture, and blue-grey camouflage uniform. He's flipping through a World War II biography on one of the tablets that is available in my store. Guilt engulfs me for keeping him waiting although there are no front doors to any of our stores, and people browse in and out as they please. However, definitely not professional behavior and I'm upset with myself. Sam isn't even here yet, and I usually find her working on her debut *Showcase* presentation before I arrive.

I first switch the lights on before punching in the security code to my personal office located at the back of my store. I hide away my backpack before taking out water from my little refrigerator. All that hopscotch has made me thirsty and I down the entire

SmartWater bottle in one sitting. He introduces himself as Percy Mink, head of *Underground* security.

"Please accept my apologies for the delay. Welcome, Sir," I say extending my hand to shake his. He doesn't take it, but just stares at me with neither a smile nor a frown on his face.

"You were barely breathing when I pulled you out of the plane," he says smiling now with a warm glow in his eyes. "It is I that should welcome you." It takes me a moment to register what he said and then I throw my arms around his neck probably far too exuberantly. As fit as he is, I almost threw him on the floor.

"You! You are the one that saved me?" I'm overwhelmed to finally meet my savior. I could actually cry tears of joy for a change. "I don't know how I'm ever going to thank you!" Percy just lets me hold him until I can get my emotions under control. He holds me back like a grandfather would.

"What an honor to have rescued you, Lovelin. My team and I were very worried at first, but once we got you to the infirmary still breathing, we knew your physicians would revive you. It was more them than I."

"Oh, please, Sir, don't be so modest. I would have burned alive in that plane if it wasn't for you! I am forever in your debt." Percy smiles again.

"Well, then, how about some suggestions? *Chicken Soup for the Soul* books are my favorite."

"I love feel good stories too!"

We spend the next hour going over my recommendations. I'm surprised to see how much he reads on a daily basis. He has read most of my recommendations already. Percy mentions his job has a lot of downtime. I suppose it would be with no crime down here.

I have a wonderful morning chatting with Percy and mention that I hope to meet his task force soon. He hugs me and kisses my hand before leaving the store. What a beautiful gentleman.

October 12, 2015 @ 4:00pm
Infirmary
Lovelin

I awake finding myself in one of the hospital infirmary beds. Again. A heavenly great weight is upon me as my eyes flutter heavily to adjust to the lighting. Kaelyn has his arms around me laying on my chest. What in the world happened?

"Darling Lord Kaelyn," I whisper breathing in his Rainforest scent. I can barely get his name out of my mouth. He picks his head up. His eyes are wet, red, and swollen, and he looks like he's aged ten years.

"Love," he whispers back and then kisses me. His eyes have been tearing for a while. Samantha and Sauri rush to my side. Sam climbs on top of me and crushes me with a death hug.

"You're okay! We were so worried about you. If the medi-drone didn't get you as quickly as it did, we could have lost you!"

Between Sam and Kaelyn, I am smothered. Sauri stands with a relieved look behind them. She looks drained with her hair in a disarray rather than the elegant queen I'm used to seeing.

"What happened?" I ask weakly as they release me.

"You collapsed in your bookstore a few hours ago. One minute you were speaking to Dr. Everette about autobiographies, and the next minute you were on the floor completely unconscious. You were absolutely non-responsive! Your pulse was dropping quickly so she and I performed CPR until the medi-drone arrived. Your blood screen showed a high level of tranquilizer in your system. More than enough to kill you! We immediately performed the necessary antidote," says Sam. "Praise Mother Earth that I had a medical wand in my backpack!"

"Tranquilizer? I don't take tranquilizers!" I try to shout, but I'm too weak to do so.

"We know, Love. We don't even store those pills down here. We have tranquilizer patches locked in a cabinet in the infirmary's pharmaceutical closet. Only physicians have access to them and there were no patches on you when you arrived. There were none missing either from the cabinet; all were accounted for. You were drugged another way," remarks Kaelyn weary and annoyed.

I try to soak up what I've just been told. I feel tired and very heavy. My mind isn't functioning well. "Somebody tried to kill me?" I say a bit shocked trying to believe that's not true. "Really? What did I do to deserve this?"

"Nothing!" shouts all three of them. I don't think I could be anymore hurt. Now I'm angry. I don't believe I pose a threat to anyone in this community. Everybody that has walked into my bookstore has greeted me with open arms. Clenching my teeth, I find myself shaking from hurt and anger. Kaelyn cradles me in his arms rocking me back and forth as if I am some beaten child that needs comforting.

"Don't worry, sweetheart. We have security analyzing your entire bookstore. Head of operations was completely distraught when he was called. He said you were a pleasure and joy to meet this morning, and he's going to make it a daily routine visit to see you. He vowed to find whoever did this," says Kaelyn.

"Yes, Percy is a very nice man. He even kissed my hand before he left." I calm down some as Kaelyn's strong arms care and protect me. A touch I never knew existed. A touch beyond this world. A peace within my soul I can't explain.

"He's stationing one of his men at your bookstore while you're there until they can get to the bottom of what happened. His task force is already going over surveillance video searching for any suspicious behavior this morning. You arrived here a couple of hours ago so there's a narrow window. Hopefully, we will have an answer by this evening," says Kaelyn running his fingers through my hair.

I'm tired and still feel drugged. I'm upset. I'm mad. Someone doesn't believe I belong here whatsoever. I do belong here. I belong here with the man, his family, and his creations who all love me.

"My Lord, please take me to our children. I want to be with them."

"Of course, my love. Of course."

October 12, 2015 @ 9:00pm
Kaelyn's Apartment
Kaelyn

Lovelin sleeps soundly and I'm dreary from the day. I've never been so frightened in my life. When Sam's call came into my line of sight, she was administering CPR. I collapsed onto the floor that I stood upon. I couldn't get to the infirmary fast enough. At one point, I felt my life force draining from me as Lovelin fought to stay alive. Sam and Mum applied the necessary treatment protocol as I just sat there on the infirmary floor in an unworldly pain I've never felt before. I screamed and screamed and cried and cried for Mother Earth not to take her away from me.

It's too soon. It's not her time. It's not our time. Those were the only thoughts that came to me.

I'm so racked with anger. I want a drink, but that's just going to make me angrier. I still believe Krista is tormenting Lovelin, but would she really contemplate murder? She never visited Lovelin's bookstore. Not once.

The security team found no evidence of any suspicious behavior at her bookstore this morning. I'm at a brick wall. I doubt the punching bag at the gym will alleviate anything, but I, too, want to kill something right now. Anything. I shouldn't leave Lovelin, but I need to unwind. I demanded a bodyguard be stationed outside our apartment door at all times. Just as I'm about to leave, I vision an incoming call from Sam. I'm sure she wants to know what's going on. I press my wrist.

"Kitten, I need some downtime. Going to the gym."

"What if it's our own security force? What if Zenith wants Miss Lovelin gone," she says calmly, but I can hear an annoyance in her voice as well. I walk into my living room to give Lovelin, who's sleeping soundly, the peace and quiet she needs. As I exit our bedroom, I see Sam sitting on her bed with her three roommates. All four of them display sad eyes with arms wrapped around one another.

"At first, the thought crossed my mind as well, but Zenith gave Lovelin her bookstore. It makes no sense. They could have taken her out when they destroyed the plane, but they gave her a chance. My mother told Zenith she's not a threat. I verified it with her."

"I pulled up this morning's bookstore surveillance footage on my wall. Comrade Percy asked Miss Lovelin a little after eleven if he may use her personal washroom before he departed. She showed him the way and Miss Lovelin returned less than twenty seconds later. The security commander returned three minutes and four seconds later. There's no surveillance back there. We know private offices and washrooms are like our personal dwellings; there's no footage."

"What are you thinking?"

"How long does it take a guy to pee and wash his hands?" questions Sophia. "Something's not adding up, and Mother Earth knows that I'm no genius with numbers, except when it comes to cutting fabric coordinates."

"My roommates and I conducted that experiment this evening and we're girls which should take us a little longer time," says

Sam. "If it doesn't take more than two minutes for us, then what took him so long?"

"Well, maybe he…"

"No, that would take longer. We experimented that, too," says Ari.

"Girls, everybody's different." I have to give the girls credit for playing Nancy Drew. At least they're trying to come up with answers. All I'm doing is allowing my anger to make myself an emotional mess.

"Zareen's dead. An attempt on Miss Lovelin's life. Why would the head of security ask to use her personal washroom? Mid-Section is full of them," says Zen.

"Convenience. He did save her life first after all, and she's eternally grateful." The girls all look at one another concluding I make sense.

"She had to have ingested the tranquilizer somehow. What's in her private office that could provide that? I've been in her washroom a few times since I've been spending hours there. There's nothing," says Sam.

I contemplate this for a while.

She has a refrigerator.

Chapter 42

October 15, 2015 @ 9:00am
Underground Ballroom
Jay Ahmed

"Breathe!" commands Sam. "You're going to knock their socks, shoes, tailcoats, and maybe even their underclothes off!"

I give her a funny nervous look.

I can't concentrate and obey her; I'm still too winded from all the excitement of the *Showcase*. There has been food all morning for the presenters that even put an *Underground* wedding to shame. Even with all the amazing displays, I couldn't eat a bite. So many of the Maintenance crew bowed at my feet pleaded wanting a cut of my clothing after I presented. Autographs here don't mean anything in the *Underground*. I just wanted to hold them and that's exactly what I did.

"Yes, beloved to the skies, incredulous beautiful! Most precious, perfect, ultimate, gorgeous and definitely beyond all waterfalls on our delightful Mother Earth, doctor. You need to breathe above it all! Inhale! All of the Hawaiian Islands are a disastrous shame compared to you!" exclaims Valentino, one of the three heads of Showcase Maintenance. He's one of the Masters of Choreography for the Ballroom Showcases and all the other *Underground* events. He then inhales a deep breath himself with us behind the golden Ballroom curtains. I inhale softly gazing around. "You will be ultimate phenomenal afar from all the moons and stars perfect!"

he exclaims yelling at his staff to sweep the dark sparkling granite infused platinum floors one more time. They scurry off to do his bidding again with exuberant radiant smiles.

I've never really dealt with the Maintenance sect before.

They are all business, worried about absolute perfection, and ever so excited.

And I thought we were the brilliant ones down here.

"What if nobody finds it all that interesting? How did I get chosen to be one of the first *Showcase* presenters?" It seems as though all of Sector Four's in the audience, I think peeking through the golden velvet curtains. Are these infused with real gold threads? I try to breathe in and in again. I've never been so nervous. I don't think I've ever been nervous. This new emotion is making me nauseous. I want to run to the infirmary rather than the podium.

"I think it goes by seniority."

"Inhale our dynamite gynamite, Dr. Ahmed!" Valentino orders trying to keep me calm in his total mess. He's winding himself with his palms. He's more nervous for me than I am. "You look pale and tense." He starts rubbing my shoulders. "Oh! Grand Canyon Heavens on Mother Earth! Savannah! Dear darling, our fantastic to the North Star and beyond, our ever so F Hot Dr. Ahmed needs a touch up!"

Who is this ever so wonderful entity on our beautiful home?

Savannah, I learn, is one of the *Underground* makeup artists. She can't be more than twelve years old, but she's phenomenal at her role as a makeup specialist. I know she lives in Sector Nine, but she's not part of my friend's circle. She has shyly gazed at me a few times as we have passed by each other in the hallways. She delicately commands me to sit and applies some soft powder to my cheeks that puts some color on my nervous, pale, worried face.

I never thought us Indian boys would need additional color.

I'm so speechless with all these compliments. I never knew I was so special.

"I need to pluck your brows a bit. Okay?" she asks softly and tenderly again. I just nod my head. The pain was excruciating, but when I saw myself in the mirror she provided, I was ever so pleased. I've never looked so…

"Now you look not just gorgeous, but dreamy. I've wanted to pluck your brows for so long," she says excitedly clapping her fingers. I just sat speechless once again to her sweet words. I wish I knew of Savannah years ago.

"You did it, Anna! My beautiful, heavenly beyond the sun's rays doctor. Dr. Jay, my sweet most Mother Earth piece of smoldering darling, you have to breathe in and out. My ever so angelic perfection, relax with me!" I watch Valentino breathe deeply into his nose and slowly out through his mouth with his eyes closed. I'm confuzzled trying to take in all his compliments, but I try to mimic him as I am told. We do it over and over again until he feels as though I'm at peace within myself and my surroundings.

"Thank you, Sir," I say more relieved, but still a bit nervous for my first *Showcase* presentation. Where did this most awesome guy come from? Where did all these incredible people come from?

Zenith knows exactly how to recruit.

"I'm not Sir, my ever so glorious glowing amethyst, but your loving Valentino," he says bowing to me with his palms enclasped.

I thought I was brown, but glowing amethyst sounds far more hot and sexy. Did I really just think that?

"Knock 'em dead, brilliant double black pearl sunshine!" winks Savannah before leaving me giving a double thumbs up sign.

Double pearl sunshine?

"In two minutes, Dr. Stonebridge," declares Valentino whisking his hand up in the air. He's dressed in a three-piece black and blue Versace suit. He's signaling to the lighting crew through his wireless headpiece. "Brilliant radiance upon his shiny ebony hair and jacket! His flawless looks are already priceless so we won't have to worry about his face. Praise Mother Earth!" His crew does as he's told as I just stand mesmerized by all the unspoken worship. What in the world did I ever do to deserve this love and devotion?

"Jay? Did you hear me?" asks Sam. I try to come out of my worship trance.

"I know it doesn't go by seniority. You're just trying to put my mind at ease. You are the last to present. It's your first *Showcase*, too. Dr. Kai-af's presenting after me. He's a veteran." Her eyes are squinting, somewhat gazing at me. Her hands on her hips are scolding me. She's pissed because she can't fool me. I know her too well.

"You know how remarkable you are!" Many of the Maintenance crew give me a thumbs up sign to Sam's words.

If that was so true, then, why aren't you with me? Completely. That's probably why I'm unsure of myself. I try not to let my true emotions show.

"I only could get it to work partially on a cellular level. What if everyone's disappointed?" I whisper.

"Well, it won't be everyone because I am extremely proud of you, you dumb…," Sam says loudly straightening my blue and purple sparkling tie. Sophia made it especially for my presentation. Sam's essence is making me lightheaded as I breathe in her sweet, confident fragrance. "I'm you're number one fan. Now get up there and show them what you're fucking made of! I hope you like your introduction. I was up for hours last night trying to get it perfect." The moment she retreated from me, I found myself slowly going back to my detached state.

I decided not to wear a traditional long coat like most of the other presenting scientists, but the leather jacket and black dress pants Sophia made for me. The Maintenance crew looks far more professional than I do. Sophia said to be confident and my own self. I shaved and had a haircut this morning at *Mystic Creations*. One generally has to book months in advance during Showcase time. Since I just came up with my presentation recently, Malinda squeezed me in first thing this morning. She opened the salon earlier than usual to accommodate me. I sent her a champagne bottle of mixed flavor jellybeans with a note attached that

Samantha and I were so eternally grateful for her kindness. Sam knew nothing of it.

Sam, for some reason, didn't seem to like my usual grooming look that I've neglected for a while. Where did your beautiful dark curly long locks go? She had quite the frown on her face. Stunned by her remark, I didn't have an answer. She loved my outfit though.

Zenith was ever so accommodating with the materials I needed to present my work. "You're on in three, two, one, Glorious Beyond Our Galaxy Dr. Stonebridge!" cues Valentino.

The glowing enchanted golden curtains sway open and he points for Sam to take the podium.

"Good morning, phenomenal ladies and gentlemen of our glorious benevolent Mother Earth! Is everybody excited about this year's *Showcase*?" she says smiling at the podium with her hands resting on her chin. She seems very much relaxed and casual, not like a nervous train and plane wreck like I do even with all the mental and physical meditation I just received. Her pretty pink dress and pink satin heels are stylish and classy. She definitely looks more like a girlfriend than a prodigy doctor-scientist. The entire audience rises, claps, and cheers.

"DOUBLE KILL IT, SWEETHEART!" demands Valentino into Sam's earpiece.

"OF COURSE, YOU ARE! IT'S FINALLY SHOWCASE TIME, BABY! She screams with her fist swirling, pumped up in the air.

The entire Ballroom audience stands with hoots, hollers, and cheers, screaming away as Bruno Mars blares in the background. Wow! The Maintenance crew definitely knows how to make our yearly *Showcase* come to life like no other! Everybody is cheering absorbed in the thrills only *Showcase* can bring. I laugh and clap exuberantly with the rest of them. The audience dances for about a minute or so. I wish I was there dancing with them to enjoy the first moments of *Showcase*. Valentino and his crew behind the curtains are giving each other high fives and hugs. I watch their exuberance feeling a bit more at ease.

"Take a deep breath because it's now time to calm down, relax, and appreciate our ever most glorious Mother Earth just as she has appreciated all her children since she was born," Sam says revealing her palms outward taking in a slow, calm cleansing breath. Everyone silences as Sam closes her eyes. The entire Ballroom and all those watching in Mid-Section upon the screens have soothing expressions; they know there's more amazing to come.

Valentino and the rest of his crew come down on their knees and hands in child's pose bowing to our benevolent Mother Earth.

Sam then lowers her head and enclasps her palms. I can see radiant smiles and I go into a meditative embrace with them. We all follow her lead. We stay this way for about a minute. She then raises her head, stretches her hands upwards towards the sky, opens her eyes, and releases us. Her ever so heavenly soft tranquil minute with the entire audience relaxes me and I couldn't be more appreciative for her thoughtfulness.

My palms and underarms have stopped sweating, and my hair no longer seems to be clinging to the back of my neck.

"Relax and embrace, our beautiful family. Our very first presenter this year is Dr. Jay Ahmed, neuroscientist and physician. He will be demonstrating a remarkable agent titled *Reborn*. I was blown away when I first saw his work and I know you all will be, too! Watch on the six screens that adorn the Ballroom walls how Jay can bring things back from the dead!" I wink at them. Tons of murmurs fly throughout the audience. Dr. Kai-af has the most astonished look on his face.

"You're on, our radiant amethyst! Blow them away to our moon and beyond!" commands Valentino extending his arm towards the podium.

"Thanks, Sam, sweetness, for that exhilarating soothing introduction. Bless our Mother Earth," I say enclasping my hands once more bowing my head as I take the stage. I didn't plan on calling her 'sweetness'. I don't even know where it came from, but her introduction was more loving and soothing than I ever could have imagined, and she brought such a sweet calming sensation to my soul.

"Love always to our first true Mother!" says the audience clasping their palms in return and the other half swirling their firsts into the air cheering; the entire audience with nothing but smiles.

Within moments, silence and peace engulf the Ballroom. I take a deep calming, exciting breath and then proceed.

"Well, here it is," I say bringing out an ugly white dilapidated can out of my leather jacket pocket placing it on the decaying table in front of me. "I know it's not much to look at," I say with a distraught look wrinkling my face. "It's kind of hideous actually," I say squinting my face once again. The audience snickers. Sam now sits in the first row with a glassy look in her eyes. I hesitate as our eyes lock. She blows me a kiss with two of her fingers. I hesitate some more. She then motions with her hand for me to proceed. That startles me to come out of my enchanted trance of her.

"I wish I could have come up with a more creative design, but the alloy, comprised within the can itself, is what makes the aerosol within it work."

Silence. Sam's motions get me to proceed again.

"Well, let's get this party started!"

Nobody reacts to my comment. I hesitate. Sam and I lock eyes once again. She gives me all the confidence I need. "Zenith told me that this a very aged newspaper. As you can see, it's not in very good shape. You can barely see the articles anymore since the ink's mostly faded away. I don't even know what paper this is. Can anybody tell?" The newspaper magnifies on the six large screens. The writing has definitely withered away. There are a couple of holes and tears in the paper itself. Nobody in the audience has an answer.

"Anybody? No?"

Most of the audiences mumbling about one another shake their heads and others have quizzical looks on their faces. I spray the contents of my can all over the front page onto the withering, dilapidated newspaper. The effervescent blue droplets swirl around and then fall into a glimmering tranquil dance before dying away. Within minutes, the writings come back to life and can easily be read. The holes and tears have mended as well. The heading of the paper says *New York Times*. We can now read the date of July 5, 1855 on all the screens. A round of applause goes through the Ballroom. Mid-Section audience watching on their screens rise to their feet, clapping away.

Some confidence musters within me.

"Not only can it work on old papers and parchments, it can also be used on a variety of other articles. See this table? It's in awful condition. There are scratches all over the surface. The wood's rotten and decaying. Bugs have eaten away parts of it and there are gaping holes throughout. The luster's all gone." I spray the entire table and within five minutes, it looks shiny, sturdy, and showroom new. The luster of the cherry wood is probably more beautiful than it was born with and it no longer looks rotten or decaying whatsoever. Another round of applause goes through the Ballroom. Christoph hoots for Jay. Sal gets up and dances around in his chair. Christoph has to stop him and makes him sit once more.

My Uncle Kaelyn stands. "Yes, Dr. Stonebridge," I say.

"Truly remarkable, Jay." My Uncle hesitates with his head bowed down, and then he looks straight into my eyes. "Forgive me, Dr. Ahmed, for my lack of professionalism and appreciation, but you have always been like a son to me and I don't ever want you to think that I take you for granted." Many of the audience sigh to his comment. Most clap upon his loving words.

"I love you, too, Uncle Kaelyn."

The audience sighs and claps some more. The look on Samantha's face was unreadable. Valentino in my earpiece says that he and his crew skipped a heartbeat to our loving words.

"Dr. Ahmed, how far are you regarding *Reborn* to work at a more organic cellular level? Obviously, you have a tool that could revolutionize the restoration process without a lengthy timeframe."

"I'm still working on it. It doesn't currently work on all living material. I'm working with nano technology to enhance the aerosol itself, but I haven't had a breakthrough, yet. I believe it's possible because there hasn't been any setback with my research." I receive another round of applause.

Grand Sister stands as my Uncle Kaelyn sits. "Yes, Dr. Stonebridge."

"Is it harmful? Is it toxic? What are the long term effects using *Reborn*? What's its shelf life?"

"I've only been using this for the past couple of months. There are no toxins and no side effects so far during my research. However, I suggest not consuming it internally. My personal experience even breathing in the aerosol while restoring an item has been safe, and I honestly could not tell you what the shelf life is. That's ongoing research. Even the evaporation process within the can itself is ongoing research and I'm documenting everything."

I receive another round of applause. Some person that I do not know stands. "Yes, Sir."

"Hello, I'm Kevin from Maintenance. My watch has a couple of scratches on it. You think you can restore it?"

"Make it brilliant, doctor beautiful!" screams Valentino in my ears. Sam blows me another kiss with her sweet soft fingers.

"Come up!" I say with a wave of my hand. There are snickers in the audience and then people start clapping quite exuberantly. I spray *Reborn* all over the watch. Everybody watches on the screens as the scratches instantly disappear and the watch itself becomes shinier than before. It looks brand new. Everybody claps once more.

"You rock, Dr. Ahmed! Thanks!" he says shaking my hand.

"Any more questions?" I ask. Silence for a moment. "Any more watches that need repairing?" I say with a wink and a wicked smile. The audience laughs. Sam blows me another kiss. I think my heart just stopped beating.

"Yes! Yes! Yes!" cries Valentino in my ears. Part of me wishes I had some sort of volume control, but most of me is so blessed.

"Is it available for personal use?" asks a lady. "I could use a can." I fight to come out of my emotional trance as Sam and I look gazing at one another. She then waves her hand in front of her for me to proceed again. I look at the elderly lady that asked me.

"My trials are still running. I want to understand the long-term ramifications before making it available for use. After that, I want to devise a way for mass production. I will let you know when it's available for personal use." The crowd settles and that seems to be the last of the questions.

"Thank you very much for attending my first *Showcase*. It means a lot to me." I bow to the audience and then kneel to Mother Earth. I receive another round of applause as more than half of the audience stands before me. Jake makes an announcement that there will be an hour intermission before the next presentation.

This gives us a chance to view other presentations in different parts of the *Underground*.

Samantha runs into my arms giving me a big hug. I pick her up off the ground and twirl her around.

"You were so fucking awesome!" We just hold each other for a while. I'm dying to kiss her, but I can't do that in front of five hundred people, let alone Zenith who is watching. She kept me together through my first *Showcase* performance. I've concluded that Valentino is my fairy Godmother, or Godfather. I need to thank him somehow. I'll have Jake send him and his crew bottles of jellybeans and chocolates.

"Sam, you can't keep him all to yourself. We want to congratulate him, too," says Sauri. I reluctantly let Sam go and hug Grand Sister. I then must have shaken over three hundred hands. So many were impressed with my work.

"Well done, Jay," says my Uncle Kaelyn patting me on the back. And then he hugs me. I close my eyes and let his appreciation soak into me. I've never felt cherished as I've felt the last hour. So this is what a *Showcase* feels like!

"I want a couple cans for my lab as soon as possible. If you can work with it, so can I; and just keep me posted of your long-term results. I'm looking forward to your presentation next year."

"Anything for you, Uncle Kaelyn." Sam smiles at me.

"You're the man, kid!" says Michael giving me a bear hug that throws me onto the Ballroom floor.

"Yes, you are the man, kid!" truly cries Valentino in my ears. I can hear the rest of his Maintenance dancing in my ears.

I then take off my jacket and tie. Sophia's drones laser cut them in a thousand pieces as I watch hundreds of pieces of fragments snatched away cradling, rubbing against hundreds of *Underground* inhabitants. I know Sophia will make me another one.

October 15, 2015 @ 9:00pm
Sector Nine - Female Dormitories
Samantha Stonebridge

Everyone spent the entire day watching *Showcase* presentations. Most of the scientists still work in their labs. Mid-Section shops have limited hours so everyone can enjoy the presentations. Food is still available twenty-four hours a day from *The Pantry* because drones exclusively run that market, but many other restaurants have cut back their hours as well to enjoy the shows.

Not all presentations are in the Ballroom. Lucinda's will be in the environmental sector. I sit on my bed in my pajamas with Chika on my lap going through the schedule of which presenters I definitely want to see. I hate it when two presenters overlap at the same time in different sections of the *Underground*.

"Damn it!" says Sophia propped up on her six pillows in pink striped pajama shorts. Her hair is still damp from her shower earlier this evening.

"What is it?" asks Zen. She's in the kitchen with Ari making us all s'mores for dessert. We all had Thai food with Jay, Kato, Christoph, and Sal earlier. Ari calls for a drone to have s'mores taken over to Jay's apartment for him and his roommates.

"Paris is presenting the same time I am. I was so looking forward to her presentation on latest drone technology. I think Tara and Chaz are her creations." I see that scrolling through the schedule. We should have gone through the schedule earlier, but everybody has been busy getting their presentations ready. Even I'm still writing up my presentation, and I don't present for another five days.

"That's too bad, but we can always watch it on *Show Off* later," I say. "Every show gets recorded by Jake."

We all discuss our favorite shows of the day.

"Dr. Kai-af's two-hundred-year-old kangaroo was so cool!" I say. "I couldn't believe it was actually alive in the solution it's kept in. And the frogs hopping all over the place were over a hundred years old."

"Yeah, his entire presentation was mind blowing as usual," says Zen. Ari brings me a s'more. "Jay was pretty hot, too," says Ari. "You really need to get back with him."

"I'm working on it," is all I say eating the s'more. Trust me, I'm working on it. I give Chicka some graham cracker, which she quietly eats on my tummy.

Getting back together with Jay is definitely going to be more difficult than my *Showcase* presentation. He deserves so much better than me.

Chapter 43

October 16, 2015 @ 9:00am
Underground Ballroom
Sophia Cambridge

I can't believe Zenith had a runway stage made for me. This couldn't have been possible without Sector Six and Sector Eleven. They're amazing at their work. They love and believe in all of us although we have never asked for it. I know our appreciation for them goes unnoticed.

"Sweet baby, beautiful leather and lace darling, absolutely beyond our Mother Earth, little unbelievable to the stars and back utterly forever precious! You're on in three glorious minutes," says Valentino softly fluttering me a kiss with both his hands.

He's wearing the ivory leather jacket I designed especially for him. I didn't know of him until recently when I heard he was my Master of Choreography. His beautiful dark brown curls kiss the surface of his jacket's shoulders as he sways. He claims it feels like silken cream against his body and he wants to wear it to bed every night. It was the greatest compliment I ever heard and I teared when he said so kneeling at my feet. Valentino and his crew have been beyond helpful and supportive.

They seem to be the power behind the *Showcase* throne. No, they are the power behind the *Underground* throne.

Since it's my first *Showcase* like Jay's and Sam's, we've never really known the Maintenance Sector until now.

The Ballroom looks entirely different from the wedding we just attended a couple of weeks ago. The diamond chandelier right above us ends at the runway. I'm so nervous. I never dreamed I would ever present at a *Showcase*. My armpits are drenched. Fortunately, nobody can tell because of the material of my blue dress. I have twelve models from Sector Nine and one from Sector Four. Everybody's so excited to stand out on stage showing off my fashion creations.

I feel as though I'm going to throw up. I don't know what because I haven't eaten even with all the delicious food made especially for us presenters; too nervous about my presentation.

Sophia, get a fucking hold on your being! Zenith believes in you!

My parents gave me clips for my hair earlier as a congratulatory gift. I'm sure Nicolai created them. I don't know what stones they are, but they glisten more beautifully than the stars in our makeshift sky. I wear them for my first *Showcase* presentation. I hardly spend any time with my parents. They're part of the team that run the trains in the *Underground* so they're always on call 24/7. They love their life down here. They used to live in Sector Eleven, but they now reside in Sector Six. I have an amicable relationship with them. They're incredibly proud of me. They never dreamt I would amount to anything. We are not the amazing scientists. I placed their seats in the front row. I can see them holding hands and smiling while I peek through the golden curtains. I wish I was holding hands with them.

"How do we look?" they all say in unison. Zen's kimono's in pink and white cherry blossoms; the crystals embedded through them should shimmer like crazy when she walks underneath the diamond chandelier. Ari's in a short red laced dress with tall black velvet boots. Sam wears tight white leather pants and a pink shimmery shirt with crystal buttons; she has a white satin belt tied at her waist.

My fashion show's an international theme since there are so many countries represented in the *Underground*. I have my models in eastern and western attire. Yes, even in the *Underground* we call it east and west like *Surface* people do. My fashion display tonight is mostly dressy casual wear.

"You all look great! Just don't walk down the runway too slow or too fast. Hold your head high and smile. Wave to the audience and blow kisses. You're not unsmiling *Surface* models that don't give a fucking crap. Understand?"

"Understood," they all say in unison with confused looks on their faces.

"You have plenty of time between outfit changes so don't fuck up your hair and makeup." There's much glitter in their hair and makeup.

"Understood," they all say in unison.

"Even if they F up their hair and makeup, we have everything on standby," says Valentino. "You will all be constantly radiant! Beyond the sun and moon beautiful! Far from beyond any celestial presence in our universe! We are Mother Earth's children after all!"

I think I'm going to cry again. I never understood what an *Underground* community is like since this my first *Showcase* presentation, but now I truly know how blessed I am.

I feel a tap on my shoulder. I turn around to find Miss Lovelin.

"You're on, girlfriend." I asked Miss Lovelin to be my announcer. "There's only five hundred or so in the audience. Your tickets sold out in half an hour from what I heard." She winks at me. My armpits and forehead drench even more at her comment. "Don't worry," she says putting her arm around me. She obviously picked up on my nervousness. "You're going to bring the *Underground* even further underground!"

Now my cleavage is even sweating, too.

"Sophia, my darling little velvet beyond perfect porcelain doll, let's bring you and F drop dead gorgeous lovely Lovelin out together," says Valentino waving his hands about. Miss Lovelin and I look at each other nearly in tears to his sweet words.

"F Amazing! In three, two, one!" With his hand in the air, he cues for us to reveal ourselves.

We walk hand in hand to the podium as the lights go out. The audience becomes silent and still. The lights then come on.

"Talk to us, phenomenal gorgeous ones! *Prada* and *Burberry* are taking themselves to the grave over you!" screams Valentino through his headpiece into Miss Lovelin's earpiece and mine.

"Beautiful morning, ladies and gentlemen! Love and worship to our Mother Earth!" Miss Lovelin says putting her palms together, bowing her head. I do the same. "How is everybody enjoying the *Showcase* so far? Incredibly unbelievable, right?"

A round of applause goes up in the air.

"Gorgeous delicious darling Love! You so belong with us!" exclaims Valentino. I clap exuberantly to his beautiful words.

I can see the audience consisting of mostly Sector Six, Sector Nine, and Sector Eleven inhabitants. There are a few from Sector Four, but not that many. Paris is giving her *Showcase* presentation this morning in the Maintenance section. She's presenting her fourth generation drones like Tara and Chaz. Most of Sector Four's there. I wish we didn't have our *Showcase* presentations at the same time. I'm definitely a fan of hers. Dr. Kaelyn Stonebridge gives me a thumbs up sign. I give him a nervous smile. I'm sure he would rather be at Paris' presentation, but I know he's here for Miss Lovelin.

"Excellent! Well, what a debut we have this year! Miss Sophia Cambridge is our amazing *Underground* fashion designer! Thank goodness Paris, France doesn't know about her because they would kidnap her in a heartbeat!" Everybody claps and laughs at her comment.

"Sit back, relax, and enjoy this incredible show!"

Valentino breathes in relief. His crew is winding his forehead and face with laced hand fans.

Vogue blares and my models come out one by one. Everybody cheers throughout the hour performance and all I hear is oohs and aahs from the crowd. When Kato comes out in his black leather jacket and blue sapphire encrusted tie, *Dress You Up* plays throughout the Ballroom. He receives a standing ovation and glorious smiles. He stands at the end of the runway for a good minute bowing. I lose my knees completely. If I wasn't so underground already.

When Miss Lovelin comes out in the rose-colored, crystal-beaded sari I designed, the crowd's rendered speechless. I can't tell if they like it or not. Her hair looks gorgeous with its blue, purple, and red spiral curls. She stands at the end of the runway and winks at the audience; everybody, already on their feet, gives her a thunderous applause. The expression on Dr. Kaelyn is priceless; he falls out of his chair when he first sees her. Hopefully, he will be able to recover and get up soon.

I end the presentation with my models wearing athletic attire rather than formal attire. Sector Four and Sector Nine live in athletic wear down here when not in lab gear. After the show, there were tablets already placed along the perimeter of the Ballroom to place orders for my clothes. I had a catalogue put up on the *SuperNet*. Hundreds of people stood in line placing orders for my designs.

By the end of the morning, I had over two thousand orders already for my wardrobe creations. Oh, my! How am I going to handle all of this!

October 16, 2015 @ 6:00pm

Underground Ballroom

Ari

"Don't be nervous," says Sophia. "I know how it feels. Trust me. My pits are already soaked for you. My boobs are, too."

"I'm not nervous," says Zen chewing her nails. "And I'm Chinese, remember? Don't have those problems."

"Zen, my perfect little Asian baby crescent love doll, don't do that! You'll ruin your fancy nail polish that *Mystic Creations* took two hours to apply. They're going to be magnified on the screens!" blares Valentino. Her nails are in red, black, and silver to match her attire. "Savannah, sweet glorious one! We need a touch-up check!" Zen immediately stops chewing, and Savannah examines if any damage was done.

Sophia designed the most stunning maroon jumpsuit with black accents for Zen to wear for her *Showcase* performance. She also wears black laced boots with a red zipper in the back. There are beautiful crystals around the wrists of her jumpsuit. Or are those diamonds? Can't really tell.

"I've played at the *Showcase* once before. I don't remember having even ten percent of this crowd last year. Something obviously went through the *Underground* grapevine."

"You played so well at your first *Showcase* and in Sector Nine's talent show, I'm sure hundreds saw it on *Show Off* so they're attending this year. I heard your tickets sold out within the hour," I comment. Valentino and the rest of the Maintenance crew nod their heads.

"Praise Mama Home that we don't have to worry about tickets!" says Valentino with his hands on his knees to his crew and us. His crew bow their heads and fists in the air in gratitude.

"Don't get stage fright," Sam says running to Zen's side. "Sorry, I'm late. I just came from Lucinda's presentation in the environmental sector. She did great! Darby stole my heart!"

"I'm not nervous," says Zen shaking. Her face has a green hue and she looks like she's going to pass out.

The Ballroom this evening is staged so Zen has all her musical instruments in the center of the dance floor. They're all circularly arranged with the enormous diamond chandelier hanging right above them. Sophia's runway disappeared by the afternoon. I don't know how the Maintenance crew does it during the week of *Showcase* presentations. Sector Six and Sector Eleven are extra busy this time of year. They have been super busy the last month coordinating it all plus the wedding that just took place. So many don't sleep at night just trying to get it picture perfect for all the scientists and presenters. I don't know what I'd do without them. Sam mentioned the same. We hope everybody that presents understands and appreciates their hard work. We are truly a team community in the *Underground*.

Sam and I are so ashamed of ourselves for not realizing sooner. We're going to request to Zenith for a Maintenance afterglow party like all the *Showcase* presenters receive. They truly deserve it.

The dance floor has plenty of room for people to dance. Five hundred chairs are arranged in concentric circles from the circular dance floor that radiates out.

Zen has a complete full house. There are even people in the back of the Ballroom standing to hear her music. Zen asked me to be her announcer. Sophia created my jumpsuit in navy blue cotton without all the bling. Zen was allowed to have fifty reserved seats like most presenters. Sophia, Jay, Kato, Christoph, Sal, Uncle Kaelyn, Miss Lovelin, and I naturally had front row seats at the foot of the dance floor.

"Ari, my exuberant little bundle of joyous rainbow confetti! You are on in five, four, three, two, one!" exclaims Valentino from above where no one can see. "Make it happen for her drizzled in caramel and extra chocolate precious one! A few candied peanuts wouldn't hurt either!"

"What a fabulous spectacular evening ladies and gentlemen!" I say as enthusiastically as I can walking out on the Ballroom dance floor. The unnoticeable wireless microphone at my chest radiates my voice throughout the entire Ballroom. "How is everyone enjoying this year's *Showcase* so far? It has been fucking phenomenal, hasn't it!" A thunderous round of applause goes up in the air with tons of cheers and hollers as everybody in the Ballroom stands.

"Perfect, sweet caramel drizzled dolly! Absolutely perfect!" I hear from Valentino in my ear. "TURN IT ON my little wonderful angel crème brûlée!"

"HELLO, ZENITH!" I exclaim with both my arms and head leading up to our makeshift sky. "We know you're watching!" I then come forth to our audience pointing my finger at them. "Brace yourself, baby, because tonight you and everybody else are the lucky ones. You are in for a most special treat! No, it's not one of my cupcakes!" Laughter fills the air as I wink at them. My roommates roll their eyes and smile. All our friends laugh around me.

"You did it strawberry laced coconut delicious dolly!" screams Valentino. "Keep the marshmallow magic going!"

"Tonight, you are the most fortunate ones and get the privilege of listening to the incredible music of my most amazing best friend, Zen!" There's another round of applause.

"You may think you have the most miraculous best friend, but you really don't. I do!" There's more laughter and applause. Zen blows me a kiss.

"So ladies and gentlemen, please sit back."

"What the fuck are you saying?" screams a horrified Valentino into my invisible earpiece.

"No, scratch that!" I say with a wave of my hand and stiff smile. "Get up on your feet and dance the night away to the most beautiful musical talents of Zen!" Another round of applause goes up in the air with hoots and hollers throughout the Ballroom.

I can hear Valentino sigh a relief in my invisible earbuds and then collapse on the floor beneath him. I hope I didn't kill him with a heart attack. His crew is fanning him with laced hand fans once again.

"Thank you, bestie and sister, for that most beautiful introduction. Before I begin, I just want to tell you a little about my pieces this evening. I will only play eight instruments tonight." Many astonishing murmurs can be heard all around me. I don't believe Zen had half as many musical instruments last year. "Zenith was ever so kind to give me a harp just a couple of months ago. It's what I'll begin with and then end with the electric keyboards. I hope you all enjoy the show." Her introduction was quite meek compared to the one Ari just gave. I hope she's not nervous. A soft round of applause goes up.

Jay leans into Sam. "Where are her music sheets?" he whispers.

She shrugs her shoulders. "And it's called sheet music," Sam whispers back. Then Sam and Jay gaze at each other with worried looks on their faces because it dawns upon us at the same moment. Zen's going to play all her pieces from memory. We get nervous for her. They clasp their hands together.

Everybody sits and listens to Ari play *Skyline Firedance* by David Lanz on the harp. It's utterly unbelievable how beautifully she plays and she only self-taught this instrument weeks ago.

Much of the audience has soft smiles on their faces swaying to the beautiful sounds of the harp as she plays. The harp isn't bringing the house down, although everyone enjoys it.

She then plays *Frosty the Snowman* on the flute. The entire audience sings to *Frosty the Snowman*. It's a riot! Everybody's smiling as they sing. After that, she plays *Thriller* by Michael Jackson on the electric keyboards. A first taste of something better to come. Much of the crowd dances in their seats.

Her piano arrangements of *Flight of the Bumblebee* and *Ukrainian Bell Carol* give her a standing ovation. The way her fingers danced across the piano was ever so beautiful to watch.

When she starts playing the drums to *The Charleston* with an accompaniment in the background, people get up to dance. The six holographic televisions around the ballroom show an old-fashioned dance hall with people dancing to *The Charleston.* Most of us leave our seats for the dance floor. What a blast! Many ask for an encore on the drums, so she plays *Livin' on a Prayer* by Bon Jovi with a background accompaniment. The crowd dances like crazy.

A roar of applause fills the Ballroom from the jazz ensemble from her saxophone thereafter, but I know the best is yet to come.

Once Zen starts on the electric violin playing a variety of upbeat songs from River Dance, that's when the entire Ballroom came alive. Even Miss Lovelin and Uncle Kaelyn try to dance the intricate tap dancing steps. Everybody's literally having a ball! The large holographic screens depicting Irish dance gave us a guideline and the crowd absolutely loves it. The electric violin by far was her longest section of her performance. Everybody couldn't get enough of her by the end of her violin performance.

She finishes the night off playing on six electronic keyboards simultaneously. There are two stacked rows of three keyboards around her. She starts off with the *Mission Impossible* theme song in which she receives hundreds of cheers. The Ballroom now is by far the noisiest I've ever heard from an audience in all my years down here. Her second piece, *Shark* by Dario Rossetti-Bonnel, made the audience go into a frenzy. She sounds like a one-person electronic philharmonic orchestra. She ends with *Toccata and Fugue in D Minor* by Bach. It was done in such a supersonic speed! Damn! Amazing Zen is such an understatement!

We are utterly mesmerized watching her fingers fly across six keyboards at one time. Everybody's still up and dancing. Now I see why Sophia placed the large crystals or diamonds around her wrist. They made her hands look priceless upon the six screens.

She absolutely brings the house down and receives the first complete standing ovation of the *Showcase*. The audience goes ballistic and can't stop hooting and hollering at the end of her performance. No *Surface* rock star could ever do what she just accomplished. Even my hands hurt from all the clapping, and my voice is hoarse from all the screaming and cheering. My feet hurt from all the dancing.

She's asked for encore after encore. Her one-hour presentation turns into two hours. Nobody would let her stop playing the drums, electric violin, and keyboards. At one point, Zen asks me to make an announcement that the show is over because she's tired, but would love to stay and meet everybody. I make the announcement and so many of us are upset hearing that Zen's done for the evening. Praise Mother Earth that I get to listen to her whenever I want.

"You so fucking rock!" I scream giving Zen the biggest hug I possibly can. We both go crashing down on the dance floor. Sophia jumps on top of us. Hugs all the way around as we roll around on her. "When did you practice all that stuff? I haven't heard most of that before!"

"Ari, it's when you go to work and I'm in between classes. When else would I play?" she says squeezing me back. We all cascade around one another for a minute or so before getting up.

It seemed as though almost all the Ballroom participants come to congratulate Zen on her musical talents. A few of the guys even get on their hands and knees and bow at her feet. Two of them were Char and Kieran. Zen didn't know whether to laugh or cry.

I hope Zenith's watching this all.

"What planet did you come from?" asks Kieran rising to his feet.

"From our beautiful Mother Earth," giggles Zen.

"You're mortal?" questions Char. "You're obviously some sort of musical goddess." He's absolutely right. Zen gives both of them hugs.

"Will you play at my next birthday party?" asks someone. "Will you play at our next anniversary?" asks another. The list went on and on. I could see Zen most overwhelmed with all the attention. She was always known as a 'Disgrace' by Sector Four. By the end of the evening, she's crowned 'The Harmonious Sweetheart' by the entire *Underground* community.

Her parents meekly show up past nine o'clock. I guess they finally had the strength to muster up the courage to approach their ever so talented daughter. It's been a couple of years since we last saw Zen's parents. Her mother has tears in her eyes. "You are absolutely incredible, Zen. So young, you are and far more brilliant in your own way than any of us. We are so ashamed," she says on her knees putting her head down.

"We are not worthy to be your parents," says her father kneeling and bowing before her. Zen never speaks much about her parents. I have to agree with her father though.

"No, you're fucking not worthy of her! You have never been parents to her just like mine haven't been to me. Praise Mother Earth for my Uncle Kaelyn." Sam's all emotional clinging onto me. Zen was never so fortunate to have a role model to look up to. Sector Nine has been her only family.

"I hope she tells her parents off. She's far too special for them," Sam says shaking. I completely agree with her.

"You're forgiven," Zen whispers and holds her arms out for a hug. They both, still on their knees, hold their daughter who they always believed was a disgrace since she wasn't intellectually superior. Sam and I try to hold back our tears watching them, but fail. Could we forgive so easily? Jay puts his arm around Sam and she sinks into him. She squeezes my hand and I feel her love just as I feel from all of those around me.

Genius comes at so many levels.

Chapter 44

October 19, 2015 @ 8:00pm
Sector Nine - Female Dormitories
Zen

My wall fills with hundreds of congratulation notes for my *Showcase* performance. They're still pouring in. I received the largest bouquet of flowers that I've ever received from my parents yesterday. They asked me if I would honor them by attending dinner with them tonight and I didn't decline. I don't remember the last time I ate with my parents. They begged me to bring my violin so I could play for their friends attending as well. My mother made my favorite pho bowl soup that I used to love as a child before moving to Sector Nine. It was a nice evening. It was a good start to a new beginning with them.

"There's a package on your nightstand," says Sophia as I enter my apartment. "It's from Zenith!"

"Open it!" screams Ari. "We've all been dying to find out and didn't want to disturb you with your family bonding time."

Baffled, I sit on my bed and open the golden wrapping to find a violin case. Inside is a Stradivarius. I just stare at it for a while completely numb and speechless.

"Zen, what is it?" asks Sam.

315

"It's a Stradivarius," I whisper taking the violin out. At first, I was afraid to touch this magnificent piece of work. I don't think I'm deserving enough to play such an extraordinary instrument. I play a few notes and my heart melts. I think I'm going to cry. "These violins are the best ever made and cost a fortune."

"There's a note in the case saying that you will receive a call from the President this evening," Ari says handing it to me. Just as I finish reading the note, I get an incoming call in my line of vision. I press my wrist.

"Hello."

"That was by far the most spectacular performance I have seen by one person in a long time. Congratulations, Zen! You are truly a prodigy in your own way. To be able to play all those instruments at that caliber is absolutely astonishing."

"Thank you, Mr. Commander President." I didn't know what else to say cradling the Stradivarius like my newborn infant.

"Many of us Zenith leaders watched it live via the *SuperNet* through Jake as we do many of the other *Showcase* presentations. By the way, a few of us are fighting to adopt you." I start giggling. "We're all hoping for a private performance upon our arrival."

"It would be the greatest honor, Mr. Commander President. Of course!"

"I have a surprise for you."

"Mr. Commander President, yes, the violin's absolutely gorgeous! I will cherish it forever!"

"No, Zen, the violin's only a little thank you from Zenith. I submitted, with much hesitation at first, your performance to the Royal Philharmonic Orchestra. They would like you to be a musician in their ensemble." I'm too stunned to speak. Did I actually hear him right? "Zen? You there?"

"Mr. Commander President, the Royal Philharmonic resides on the *Surface*. How's that even possible?"

"Yes, we can work out the details later. Are you interested? Zenith will provide everything for you. I believe you will thrive more on the *Surface* than in the *Underground*."

"That would mean I'd have to leave the *Underground*. I'd have to leave my friends and family." My roommates gasp to my words.

"Yes, Zen. It would mean leaving the *Underground*. It's unprecedented, but we can work it out."

"I'm sorry, Mr. Commander President, but I just can't get up and leave my home. I know it's an opportunity of a lifetime, but I just can't. At least not right now."

"Understood, Zen. You're still young. If you change your mind, let me know. Good evening and congratulations again. You're a true inspiration to us all. I look forward to meeting you." I get all teary eyed from his words. I'm higher than a cloud right now. I'm higher than the stars even though I've never seen a true one with my own eyes. I just know I am.

"Thank you and good evening, Mr. Commander President." He disconnects our line.

"Are you okay? What was that all about?" asks Sam hugging me. I tell them. All my roommates squeal in delight and then they all crash down upon me again.

"You have to go!" says Ari. "You can live with other musicians for the rest of your life. People just like you. You would be brilliant! I'll probably have to be admitted into a mental institution since I can't live without you, but that's okay."

"There's no mental institution in the *Underground*! Although there should be since there have been scientists known to have mental breakdowns." I say crying to her words. "And I can't live without you either!"

"I know, sister,"' says Ari wrapping her arms around me. I bury myself into herself.

"Maybe, but not now. I just got my family back, and how can I live without you three? It's just not possible at the moment," I say with a happy sigh.

Sam and Sophia cuddle into Ari and me. I know I made the right decision.

This is where I belong for this is where I'm loved.

October 20, 2015 @ 8:00am
Sector Two - Design Studio
Sophia Cambridge

"How are we supposed to divide all these orders?" asks Tara. "Miss Sophia will tell us," says Chaz.

"Miss Sophia will tell us what?" I say walking into my design studio. There are four drones hovering in a line in front of me.

"We have friends!" screams Tara twirling around and around.

"Our fault for being so amazing," says Chaz blowing on his mechanical fingers. I look at the two silver drones. They hover meekly compared to Tara and Chaz.

"Hello, Miss Sophia," they say shyly in unison. "We were sent by Miss Paris to help you." They sound even younger than Tara and Chaz.

"How wonderful! Let's see. What to name you two? I think I'll name you Hansel and you Gretel," I say pointing to them. I always loved that fairytale.

"Yes, Miss Sophia," all four say in unison.

"Ready to have some fun?"

"Always!" all four say in unison. They fly away to get bolts of fabric. Chaz brings up all my two thousand some orders on a 3D holographic screen in front of me.

I send Paris our first twelve outfits: dresses, skirts, formal wear, athletic wear, and a kick ass new red lab coat thanking her for all my drones.

"Thank you so very much! However, could use some beautiful sexy underclothes as well," she texts in my line of sight that evening.

I never really thought of that. I love the idea! I'm sure I can out do *Victoria's Secret* and *Adore Me* in no time.

"Done!" I send back.

October 20, 2015 @ 12:00pm
Underground Zenith Quarters
President of the United States

"I wish we could live down here forever," says the prime minister. All the Zenith leaders arrived by submarine. I was the only one brave enough to travel by Spear.

"This is definitely going to be my retirement home," I say. "A few presidents have resided here. They didn't truly die until years later like the *Surface* believes. One's Alzheimer's was even cured within a week after inoculation."

"Yes, neither did the three prime ministers before me," says one of the prime minister.

"Who's residing here now that's supposed to be dead according to the *Surface*?" asks one of the presidents. I tell him. We make a plan to visit them tomorrow in Sector Four.

"I can't wait to get to *Cave Dwellers*," says one of the kings. "The buffet's second to none."

"I know," says another one of the prime ministers on our way to *Cave Dwellers*. "My wife and mistress always wonder how I gain twelve kilos in just days in October."

A drone with a dog in a basket flies above us. Another drone flies above with a basket of food. Another one almost knocks us down carrying shirts and pants.

"I wish we had this delivery system on the *Surface*," says another one of the presidents. All of us nod agreeing. "Pizza takes fucking forever."

"The pizza here is to die for!" says another one of the kings.

"No, the scotch here is to die for!" says one of the other presidents. The Muslim king gives him a knuckle punch.

The *Showcase* is definitely the best time of the year for all of us.

October 21, 2015 @ 12:00pm
Underground Ballroom
Zen

I receive another standing ovation from all the Zenith leaders for my private performance this afternoon.

"Incredible! Just incredible!" says one of the prime ministers exuberantly clapping away.

"I played the piano as a child. I could never in a thousand years play the way you do," says one of the presidents.

"Zen, thank you for that wonderful performance," says the President of the United States.

"Mr. Commander President," I ask sitting on the Ballroom floor. All the other Zenith leaders sit with me in their casual attire this afternoon. "May I ask all of you for something?"

"The Stradivarius wasn't enough?" asks one of the kings raising his brow.

"The Stradivarius is a dream come true. I want to talk to you about my future role in the *Underground.*"

"Go on," says the Commander President.

"I was wondering if I could have my own music shop in Mid-Section. I'd like to teach others how to read music and play instruments. I could give lessons. It could be my purpose down here."

All the world leaders gaze at one another wondering what to say.

"I hear the bookstore's thriving," says one of the prime ministers. "I don't see why a music shop wouldn't. Everybody needs some sort of downtime." All the other Zenith leaders nod their heads in approval.

"What's the saying?" asks one of the other presidents. "Work hard and play harder?"

"No, no," says a prime minister. "It's work hard and party harder!" I giggle and all the Zenith leaders follow.

"Devise a survey. If you receive over a sixty percent approval rating, we'll allow it," says the Commander President.

"Oh, thank you! Thank you for the opportunity!" I say almost on the verge of tears. Without thinking, I hug the Commander President around his neck. He cuddles me back.

"Well done, Zen. Well done."

Chapter 45

October 21, 2015 @ 8:00pm
Underground Ballroom
Samantha Stonebridge

"Do not be nervous, my little fabulous ever so tantalizing shattering beyond effervescent miraculous moon beam soaked tray of delicious," says Valentino pacing around the backroom Ballroom.

I'm nervous. I shouldn't be nervous, but I am. I shouldn't know what nervous is all about. What if nobody believes me? I still have a hard time believing it myself. I should have gotten all dazzled dolled up for my first *Showcase* presentation, but Sophia said not to. She said to be comfortable. 'It's not the *Miss Universe* pageant after all.' I don't know what the *Miss Universe* pageant is and I'm too nervous to ask her. 'It's not the Breakthrough Awards or the Oscars or the Noble Prize.' I don't know what the first two she mentioned are either.

"It's us and we are special regardless of what we wear, so just be comfortable," she says. A part of me agrees with her. Most of me doesn't. "They are just *Surface* people, Sam," she says sighing like they are of no importance.

"It's Zenith! They are presidents, prime ministers, and kings! And I believe there's a queen and a prince or two attending as well!"

"They're still just *Surface* people. They don't have a minute fraction of the brain you do!" she argues. "Be comfortable. You're their golden child. You're their wanted creation. They will bow down to you. I love clothes more than anything, but you need to be your special self."

"She's completely right, adorable perfect little dolly most precious," says Valentino looking at me up and down with his hands on his hips in black leather pants and a crisp white pirate looking shirt. "The pink and the headband are to die for! It's so you! Savannah, darling beyond beautiful little love potion, Samantha, our dazzling brilliance needs a white bedazzled sash tied to her waist!"

Sophia's giving him an evil eye disappointed in herself for not thinking of the sash sooner. She commands Tara to get one from her design studio.

I wish Sophia wouldn't tell me such things. Valentino's absolutely a savior and I wish I met him earlier than at my birthday party. I'm trying to be humble. Everybody's expecting something fabulous from me. I decide to wear my pink jeans, pink button crystal buttoned-down, and pink ballet flats with a white and pink crystal embedded laced headband holding my hair back for my first *Showcase* presentation.

I wonder what my Uncle Kaelyn wore for his first *Showcase* presentation. I wrist him. He tells me he just wore his favorite pajamas and still received a standing ovation. He was only five years old at the time. I laugh.

I made the right choice.

October 21, 2015 @ 8:10pm
Underground Ballroom
Lovelin

"Where the bloody mo…fucking hell is she!" says Kaelyn holding onto my hand. His hand is moist. He's obviously nervous for his niece. They have such a sweet connection. He's yelling at the president sitting next to him. "Sam's usually very punctual." We're sitting dead center in the front row. I absolutely love his language when he's upset. I can't understand why and nor do I care.

"It could be nerves," I whisper leaning into him.

"Nerves? What the fucking bloody hell are nerves?" he says out loud. "Of course I know what nerves are, but Sam's beyond all that like I am!"

I'm not going to be able to get him to understand so I don't bother. All the lights go off and then reappear. The full house in the Ballroom renders silent.

"Good evening," says Jake in his usual monotone voice. "It is my honor to present to you Miss Samantha Skylark Stonebridge. At her first *Showcase,* she will be introducing what she calls 'The Soulmate Prophecy'. Murmurs fly throughout the Ballroom.

"Why didn't she have an announcer for her first *Showcase*?" Kaelyn questions squeezing my hand some more. "Why Jake? And why Miss? She's a physician! A double physician!" He's gripping my hand so tight I think it's going to break, but I bear through it.

I definitely don't have the answers for any of his questions.

"Prophecy?" questions the President. He doesn't look too happy. I don't have an answer for that either. I still have Kaelyn's death hold on my hand. He's obviously beyond nervous for his niece's first *Showcase*.

The Ballroom lights get brighter. We all stare at the stage waiting for Samantha to take the podium. She doesn't appear. Kaelyn and I look at one another with a nervous stare. Kaelyn and the President look at each other. Kaelyn grips my hand some more. All the Zenith leaders seem fidgety and impatient in their leather chairs. I wonder if she has some stage fright. This is her first *Showcase* after all.

I quickly glance over to Jay a few seats down from me. He just shrugs his shoulders. I look to the podium again where Kradal is perching. He just shrugs his shoulders.

"Yoo-hoo!" yells Samantha. "Over here!" We look all around us to where her voice comes from. She's not on stage. "Up here! Hello!"

Samantha sits casually on the mezzanine balcony railing waving down at us with a glorious smile on her face. I wave and smile back at her. She catches my eye and winks at me. She seems to have some sort of intricate totem pole in her hand. It's exquisite even from a distance. It's all done in black and gold with all sorts of symbols embedded throughout. Is that real gold and platinum?

"Wait! I'll be down in less than a minute!"

What?

She turns the head of the pole. We all watch in awe as a tornado appears around her. She disappears as quickly as she came. The five hundred or so present tonight couldn't believe their eyes just like me. Where in the world did she go? Her tickets sold out in record time from what I heard. The entire audience, murmuring, looks all around trying to find her like I am.

"Quit looking! Here I am! Right at the podium where I belong!" Kradal flies to her shoulder and pecks her softly on the cheek.

She still has the pole in her hand. I can now see the details more vividly. It looks like an intricate spear. All three pyramids are shining along with the Great Sphinx in a golden hue. There's a waterfall and a river meandering down the length of the spear itself. I can see the water flowing within it; it's red water. That's not possible. Is it? The lighting in the Ballroom must be playing tricks on my eyes. I feel so much at peace looking at it. I feel Kaelyn relax in his chair next to me. He lets go of his breath and death grip lacing his fingers through mine.

How Sam got from the balcony to the podium in a blink of an eye is beyond me. I glance at Kaelyn. He has the widest smile on his face and is first to stand, clapping and cheering. The rest of the audience follows his lead.

The President is the only one sitting. He does not look happy whatsoever.

Samantha waves to her Uncle and the President. The President reluctantly stands up scowling.

October 21, 2015 @ 8:15pm
Underground Ballroom
Samantha Stonebridge

"Good evening, my beloved *Underground* family and distinguished members of Zenith! I'm Samantha Skylark Stonebridge. I'm so honored that all of you have decided to join me tonight for my first *Showcase*! I hope you have been enjoying this year's *Showcase* thus far! I know I have been!" I say enthusiastically. I receive another round of applause.

"I hope I don't bore you! There have been some amazing displays this past week. If I do, there are four exits out of this Ballroom."

I then use the Spear to present myself at all four exits. A receive a standing ovation upon my return to the podium. Kradal extends his arm towards me and takes a bow. Some of the men in the audience bow to me. One of them is Jay. He's in the first row next to Kato and Lucinda. Christoph and Sal have their arms pumped up in the air cheering. Lucinda has more than her usual effervescent smile clapping away. I motion for everyone to take their seats.

"Make it F unbelievable picture perfect Sam sweetheart! I know you can!" says Valentino into my earpiece. "Your entrance was to die for! It's time to shock and awe our heavenly piece of unbelievable stars across a fathom of radiant moonlight! I'm sure our Mother Earth is at a standstill for you!"

I love Valentino and don't even try to decipher his words in my nervous state.

"I didn't discover teleportation," I declare. "I'm not that brilliant." A small laugh and hush settles over the Ballroom. People gaze at each other as murmurs fly around the Ballroom. I can hear Maintenance snickering in my earpiece.

"My amazing colleagues, Dr. Zachary Briarwood and Dr. Kieran Mersa discovered it earlier this year!" I say with a wicked exuberance in my voice as Char and Kieran instantly appear by my side with their Spears. They are dressed casually like me, but in black jeans and white cuffed shirts with golden cuff links and buttons in the shape of a Spear. Their feet are adorned in golden boots. I have to admit that Sophia did an amazing job with their attire. The audience looks at us wide eyed in disbelief and then we receive another standing ovation. The cheering last for minutes.

"You F rock to the next universe and beyond beautiful baby ever so sweet amazing!" yells and claps Valentino into my invisible headset. I want to blow him a kiss. I can hear the rest of the Maintenance crew in the background cheering and dancing for me as well through my earpiece. I love them for such amazing support.

The entire Ballroom audience and Mid-Section audience wait for me to speak. I stare at them for a while, and then I leave the podium and unveil the golden curtains behind me. I walk up to Valentino who has a horrid look upon him as I approach. I cup his face and kiss him soundly on his cheek and temple.

"Praise Mother Earth for giving you to us," I say as lovingly as I can looking into his eyes. "For giving all of your crew to us." I then rest my head on his chest for several moments to hear his heartbeat as he cradles me in his arms with his head resting on mine.

I will never be so amazing. They are all giving and thriving in that. I want to be a part of their world.

His eyes tear and is fanning himself with his hand as I return to the podium. His crew draws the curtains behind me with love on their faces as I take the podium once more. The audience still stands clapping for my recognition of the Maintenance sect.

The President of the United States looks beyond pissed off and is the first to sit down.

My Uncle Kaelyn winks at me.

I wink back lovingly.

* * *

"I come before you today not to talk about a scientific finding." The audience seems to have some sort of monstrous look upon their faces.

"I come before you today not to discuss what I have been working on the past fourteen years in my life because in all honesty, I haven't been working on anything since I've been born.

Since I've been designed for."

First silence, and then snickers and laughter from all around. Even from the curtains behind me. Nobody seems to believe me.

I wouldn't reveal my work at dress rehearsal to the Maintenance crew.

"It's the truth. I've been quite lazy!" Now more people laugh. "I've been so motherfucking full of myself that I forgot what our real goal is down here." The audience simmers down. My Uncle Kaelyn chuckles softly. Aunt Lovelin looks distraught. Jay's looking sadly at his shoes. Valentino and all the other *Underground* crew behind stage drop to their knees.

"I forgot about our precious beautiful Mother Earth," I say as tenderly as possible. "But most of all, I forgot about you," I say even softer. I have everyone's undivided attention now. Jay blows me a kiss with his fingers. I want to take it and grab it to my heart, but I don't. I don't believe I deserve it.

Christopher and Salvatore extend their hands up to the air fisting in appreciation of my declaration with their heads bowed. We are all human after all. All of Sector Nine follow their lead.

"I come before you today not to talk about some breakthrough theory that will revolutionize our Mother Earth instantly. I know that's what I was created for, but not today. Not today," I say the last two words even softer. I hope everyone heard me. An eerie silence comes over the audience. All eyes are on me. All of Sector Nine is focused on me, their hands now down and cradled in their laps.

"I come before you today to reveal something that you will probably not believe. I even had a hard time believing it myself as I unraveled what is possibly the greatest puzzle that I was ever asked to decipher. *Prizes* is a piece of cake compared to what I was asked to solve.

Unknowingly." Everyone looks at me completely baffled.

"I come before you today to talk about the supernatural realm of our beautiful planet."

Silence and then an uproar of murmurs within the audience emerges. I wait for them to hush before proceeding.

"I know, I know, that's not our agenda. We are people of science, after all," I say raising my head and walking around the stage. "And science is great! Science is beautiful and mysterious and fascinating!" I say out loud looking at the audience with as much enthusiasm that I can muster. Kradal nods his head to the audience. A round of applause goes up and I bow to them enclasping my hands. I can see the screen of the Mid-Section audience on their feet clapping away. "And there's still so much I know we are capable of through science!

There never ever will be a boundary to our learning and imagination!" More applause, cheers, and hollers fill the *Underground*.

"But science is not everything on our beautiful Mother Home," I say silencing the audience once more. "Science is not the answer to everything. It is only a part of our glorious world. So tell me, did you enjoy Sophia's fashion designs and Zen's music?" Half the audience stands and claps to my question. Even most of the Zenith leaders do. I motion for them to sit down.

The President shifts in his mahogany leather seat. He still doesn't have a happy look on his face. Neither do all the other presidents and prime ministers present that were cheering and clapping minutes ago. One has some sort of a smile and a glow in her eyes. Even my Uncle Kaelyn looks confused now.

"I'm not going to start at the beginning. I'm going to start at the next to end and work my tale back to the beginning. This eleventh life story took place in the seventeenth century. A beautiful love story," I say as I bring up a picture of the Notre Dame Cathedral on one of the Ballroom's opaque walls.

It takes me over an hour to show the audience through my 3D presentation of all the eleven past lives I have found. I account for all the coincidences of May 30th in the year ending in 79, and all the reincarnations of the couples with the same birthmark. The Ballroom's in a complete pin drop silence during my entire speech.

Jay blows me another kiss at the end of it. This time I catch it and put it to my heart. I need to feel his love to pull me through.

"So here we are now. At the start of it all," I say bringing upon a 3D picture of the scrolls before me. "A twin birth of a boy and a girl. The start of remarkable beautiful phenomena of unconditional love. A love beyond true and pure. A perfect love that will eternally bring upon a death only to be perfect in the next lifetime once more."

My Uncle Kaelyn looks distraught as he holds Lovelin closer to him. I smile trying to tell them through my eyes not to worry. They hesitantly smile back at me. I don't know how to proceed. This time Jay waves his hand patting his chest; he wants me to go on with my heart.

"Sit back and relax, but hold on, ladies and gentleman. Let me share with you the happiest and most devastating story you will ever hear. The one of Khale and Laila."

Chapter 46

May 29, 1379 BC
A Little Village in Egypt
Maya

They sleep heavenly entwined in each other's arms in only their swaddling cloths. I can see the glistening glow of their soft skin and smell their sweet breaths. They are one and the same. Their precious fragrance is like honeysuckle and hibiscus intertwined. Their small chests rise and fall in perfect rhythm. They look like night and day, however, beyond our most glorious sunset and our most enchanting radiant moon.

Laila's utterly blessed with her honey-colored skin, darkest hair beyond ebony, and beautiful brown eyes.

How magnificent she was born with Khale; his devastating, unforgiving platinum locks and his mesmerizing grey-gold-silver eyes. His hair looks like the color of our glorious moon. They are wrapped around one another as they have been the last eight months together. It's all they have ever known.

What in the world did we do to have these perfect two, I'll never know.

"Maya, you should rest as well," says Amir. "We can lay cradling each side of them."

"They have the same mark," I whisper. I've never been happier. I knew they were special, but for Amir and I to be blessed by the Gods this way is a blessing like no other. What did we do to deserve them? I cry softly within myself from sheer happiness.

"What mark?" He approaches our babies with a glow in his eyes only a father could behold.

"It's a crescent moon between their last two toes on their left foot." I show Amir the identical mark of our children.

"Looks more like a horseshoe to me. How's that even possible? What does it mean?" I want to tell him it's how they know they belong to each other.

It's how they'll know in every single lifetime that they belong to one another. "Just try to feel their soul every moment and you will understand," is all I say.

Egypt
Laila

I don't know how long we have been traveling. My "K" seems broken upon my neck. I can't cut through the strong fibers anymore that bind me. I'm thrown into some sort of foul-smelling damp cell. It's cold and I'm weary, but I'm not scared.

I will never let that monster frighten me.

I finally know that haughty voice. That's the voice of the High Priestess. What does she want with me? What did I ever do to her? Why would she want to hurt me? Why would she ever want to hurt my Khale? We have never been disobedient to the royal family.

Or have we?

It wasn't the High Priestess's blows or beatings that brought me any pain. The unbelievable pain and anguish came from the separation from my Khale. It was the separation of my life. It was the separation of my heart and soul although we have been able to live with that all our one life together. I know he will find me. It's just a matter of time. The problem is that I am running out of time.

I dream of us being in our mother. I can remember the start of it all. Why I remember, I don't know. It's just a dream after all. Or is it? It feels so real. We are warm and cocooned together in the most luxurious bath. The Nile itself doesn't even come close as we have tried over the years.

We have loved each other from the very beginning. We have been one from the very first moment that the Lords brought us together. From the very first moment that time joined us as one.

I dream of feeding him.
I dream of drawing in the sand with him. I can see our fingers intertwine as we draw.
I dream of bathing with him. His silver hair so much more silky than mine. Always been jealous of his hair.
I dream of sleeping on his big broad chest ever so comfortably in the Egyptian heat.
I dream of his laughs.
I dream of his thoughts and prayers.
I dream of our turmoil and fights.

I dream of our eternal happiness.
I dream of our eternal death.

Those are the best dreams.

We have already named our children. Will there be children? Will there be a wedding? Will there be a future for us?

I can feel thick and stale blood slowly dripping out of my mouth. It feels like raw metallic pudding. It must have been accumulating for a while and I didn't have the energy to spit it out until now. It won't stop forming. I can't feel my tongue. My head throbs. My body's numb from all the beatings bestowed upon it.

Even with all the physical pain, that pain is tolerable. What is intolerable is being away from my Khale, that's a pain I could never put in words. That pain splits me in half and then half again and then half again until the pieces are so small one wouldn't be able to see them.

I try to cry for him, but I just spit out more blood. My voice, now weak, will never be heard.

"Khale," I whisper in one of my last breaths. "I don't want to die alone."

Egypt
The Royal Palace
Cara

"You can't have him! You can't have him!" I scream beating Laila over and over again.

Shiva is mine! Shiva was meant for me! Why he loves a poor little village girl, I'll never understand. He has to be mad, but I don't care. I have loved Shiva since I was barely able to walk and talk. I remember being carried in his strong arms as a little girl. I lived on his left hip cradled as a baby. He was always so sweet to me.

Everyone loved my older sister. I was blessed the day she and her baby died. That was the day I knew the Gods loved me and so will everyone else. Shiva didn't care my sister had died. Those were superficial tears he shed the day of their death. He has only cared for me.

A Little Village in Egypt
Khale

You will never, my love. I will die with you over and over again. Nothing could ever be sadder and nothing could be ever more blessed.

I dream of feeding her.
I dream of us playing in the sand.
I dream of our sand picture over and over again.
I dream of her scolding me.
I dream of her gazing longingly into my eyes.
I dream of carrying her on my back as she cries tears of laughter.
I dream and I dream and I dream of my Laila.

I try to get up from my bed. "Mama, I have to go." I want to tell her that her daughter's hurt beyond repair, but I don't.

"Go where, Khale?"

"I know where Laila is. Please take me to the palace," I say in gasps.

Within moments, word comes from the palace summoning us. My parents help me out of my bed and into the cart. I can feel Lady's anxiousness and fear. I can feel her pain as well as Laila's.

Worst of all, I can feel our deaths.

I smile upon the thought.

Chapter 47

The Royal Palace
Khale

"I'm so sorry, my love," she whispers as her eyes soften to a tomb close. Her lashes are limp and frail rather than the thick and ever long to the moon I'm used to gazing into. Her breathing's shallow. Her body's beyond weak and disintegrating in my arms.

"No sorry, Laila. Not between us ever as the moon and stars and sun shine in the sky. Wake up! Look, look at me!" She tries, but I know it's difficult for her, and I feel so guilty for my commands.

I just want to see her beautiful eyes one last time.

I cradle her into my chest on the cold stone dungeon floor. She's smeared all over in her own blood. Our blood. She's beyond weak. She's beyond cold. I try to warm her, but it's useless. However, she's the first warmth I've felt in days; the decadence heat in my dreams that has kept me alive until now.

"I was such a fool to be deceived. I failed you. I failed us," she whispers moaning again, her eyes closing, fluttering to a painful grave leaving me as she speaks.

"We could never fail each other, precious. We were born together, for each other and always will be," I say rocking her gently. "Stay with me, my sweet adorable life," I tenderly whisper into her ear.

"I'm trying," she whispers back. "It's hard, my life." She can no longer keep her eyes open. I can feel her broken face and bones within me. I try not to hold her too tight, but she tells me to hold her with all my energy. We both no longer have much left between us.

"I won't beg to the Gods for our life," I say running my fingers through Laila's blood soaked hair.

"Neither will I because there are no Gods, only us," she whispers trying to lift her hands to my hair. She finally finds my hair and pulls with a strength I didn't expect. "Next time, my life."

"Next time," I whisper at her lips.

"A rebirth over and over again?" she says straining to open her eyes. She does. "A rebirth over and over again?"

"For all eternity," I say promising as I gently kiss her blood soaked lips. "Mother Earth will always bring us back to one another."

I look to the Pharaoh. "Marry us, our Majesty," I whisper while feeling the life force drain out of us. He nods his head. He has married many royal siblings throughout the years. He gives his sermons and then asks us to say our vows.

"We will never separate," I say looking into Laila's fluttering eyes. "We will always be together. Throughout eternity and beyond. I will make it my mission to always find my way back to you."

She has tears in her tombing eyes as I do. I kiss her quivering lips again ever so gently trying not to her hurt further.

"Yes, my love, my life, we will be forever soulmates throughout time," she says as she takes her last breath.

And then I take mine.

A tornado-like wind swirls around us.

It has been written.

Maya

I knew their words before they could say them. It's something only a mother could know. Amir just listened on his knees as he watched our children die in each other's arms. We watched a perfect love and soul perish away together. It's not a sight a parent should ever have to bear.

Was I at fault? Was Amir at fault?

What did we do to the Gods to deserve this? And then I understood. We did nothing wrong. And yet, why did our beautiful children have to suffer so? They were born out of pure love.

And it is a love that will go on forever. For all eternity. I am ever so blessed. I only pray that it will always end in happiness and never in tragedy.

Chapter 48

October 21, 2015 @ 10:00pm
Underground Ballroom
Samantha Stonebridge

Tonight, the Ballroom and Mid-Section, always a place of excitement, happiness, joy, and fun, is wrought with tears.

Kradal embraces his wings together with his dragon face down as if in mourning upon my podium. The *Underground* has never seen this creature before and just follow his lead.

"It has been written," I say. "Those were Maya's last words. Khale and Laila never led the happiness of a married life together although they raised each other." I show the words and pictures upon the six screens, although most wouldn't understand Egyptian language or the scrolls of an Egyptian village community. Our community is the future of science after all. We do not dwell in the past, but only learn from it.

"Egyptian culture would have wanted it that way. Love is love after all. There is no wrong to love. Pure love between two will always be right! We have lost that throughout time. Too much hatred and ignorance in our world is what's destroying us."

Most of the audience nods agreeing.

"They never had the children that they always dreamed of. Laila died from complications from the beatings she suffered at the

345

hands of the High Priestess, although Shiva tried to save her according to the scrolls. Khale died the moment of Laila's last breath according to their mother. She knew it would be so."

I can see a few people nod their heads. There are many tear-streaked faces in the audience. I try to hold back my own for them, but it's not easy. Jay's eyes are glassy. I put two fingers to my lips and blow a kiss to him. He catches it and puts it to his lips as I go back to my speech.

"When Maya started writing her story, the twins were almost five years old. She believed one of them was conceived without a soul and it was the other twin that gave half his soul in order for his sibling to survive. Maya doesn't mention which twin was born without the soul for she herself didn't know. It doesn't matter anyway. All she believed was that her children were the two halves of one soul. True Soulmates."

I hear many gasps in the audience. I can see everybody present listening to this story having a difficult time comprehending such an unbelievable life. A life with no money, a life full of uncertainty, a life unappreciated, but a life full of worship, love, and understanding.

"They were inseparable from the moment they were born together. It shouldn't be surprising since the two halves wanted to be whole again. Khale and Laila took their first breaths together and their last together. Half a soul cannot live without its other half. Maya writes that their heartbeats were always in rhythm; always as one."

I wish Jay and I could always have a heartbeat as one.

Ari and Zen hold onto each other as tears stream down their cheeks. Sophia rests her head on Kato's shoulder fighting not to cry for them anymore. They've been dead for nearly four thousand years and we are mourning for them.

We still strive for that perfect love we all wish we could hold and harbor in our own lifetime.

"Even in times of glory and even in times of darkness, their unconditional love always prevailed." Nobody says anything. Silence engulfs the Ballroom. "Upon their deaths, Laila and Khale were cremated, their ashes intertwined and spread into the Nile. Maya believed that these two half souls will always try to find each other throughout eternity to be complete and whole once more."

"To be as one."

"She goes on to say that these two half souls will reappear and disappear together. That's what she believed, and I know she was right. I've shown you how they reappear every two to four hundred years."

I can see more people nodding their heads in the audience. A few shake their heads. Most of the audience is in awe of the story and have no response.

"What does this have to do with our *Underground*? It has everything to do with the *Underground*. There's still one more story to share with you. The love story of the 21st century! And it is the most beautiful of all!"

I wait. I can see five hundred or more souls waiting for me to speak. I shouldn't keep them suffering so I speak as exuberantly as I can with the greatest dramatic tone I can muster within myself. I've never spoken so loud and clear in all my life.

"It is the story of Dr. Kaelyn Khan Stonebridge, born May 30, 1979 at 12:20pm *Underground* time, and Miss Lovelin Kay Khan, born May 30, 1979 at 12:20pm in London at *Underground* time!"

An uproar fills within the audience as everyone stands to peer at Kaelyn and Lovelin sitting in the first row. They hold each other dearly. All the Zenith leaders turn their heads staring at them. Lovelin retreats shyly into her eternal love. She wears a navy blue laced gown and silver sandals. My Uncle Kaelyn kisses her on her forehead in his matching navy long coat and silver boots.

"What a fate when Miss Lovelin's plane crashed above us and brought her to the *Underground*. Would you believe me if I told you they have the same birthmark between their toes, too?" I say gleaming at the audience. The audience at first is silent and then goes into a frenzy.

"Take them off! Take them off!" chant my roommates. Within moments, everyone from Sector Nine joins in. Somewhat reluctantly, my Uncle Kaelyn and Aunt Lovelin take off their left shoes. Jake super imposes their left feet on the opaque wall of the Ballroom showing their identical horseshoe birthmarks for all of us to see. An uproar goes through the Ballroom once again.

"You are far beyond bombshell our little sweetheart moonbeam!" cries Valentino in my earpiece. "Now, bring the house down our amazing child of our beloved glorious Mother Earth!"

"Maya was right. The two halves will always find a way back to each other. I truly believe that Kaelyn Khan and Lovelin Khan are not the genetic descendants of Khale and Laila, but the soul descendants of Khale and Laila. Thank you for attending my first *Showcase* presentation! I am ever so pleased to be able to share it with you!"

Everyone claps at their feet, and then the Ballroom fills with cheers as music starts. I can hear Valentino and his crew crying tears of joy in my ears.

After my standing ovation, I leave the podium handing my Spear to Char in the first row and try to unravel my way through dozens of slaps on my back and hugs and congratulations.

The first action I take is pull the President of the United States aside to the corner of the Ballroom. I drag him away from Krista Harding's arm who's been holding onto him like a leech all evening. I can feel he's beyond pissed off at my first *Showcase* performance. Most of the other Zenith leaders don't look too happy with me as well.

Fuck them all!

"Commander and Mr. President, with all due respect," I say staring directly at the President of the United States, "if something happens to one, it will happen to the other. I believe you know what I'm talking about, and I truly know you cannot afford to do that."

Kradal flies across all the Ballroom walls and then stops right in front of the President with his wings still flapping. He blows just a bit of smoke onto the President's face. And then he blows a shower of fire onto the Ballroom chandelier. Zenith stands fearful and shaking, but the *Underground* inhabitants know better and just snicker.

The President gives me an annoyed, priceless look. "Yes, I may not live in the *Underground*, but I'm not stupid either."

"And thankfully I didn't have to deal with Harvard, only the *Underground*! Party hard!" I say turning to the audience with my fist in the air. They all clap, cheer, holler, and swirl their fists to me as well.

October 21, 2015 @ 8:00pm
Underground Ballroom
Percy Mink

The President wasn't happy with my failure the first time around. I vowed I would never fail Zenith, and I'm not planning to now. Who would have ever guessed that the sweet girl I rescued from the fire-engulfed plane is planning on exposing the *Underground* through her next novel. That ungrateful bitch would have died if it weren't for us. If the *Surface* gets a hold of her exposure to our *Underground*, we cannot comprehend what ramifications it may hold.

Apparently, she is very unhappy down here and feels as though she's being held prisoner. I didn't get that vibe the morning I met her, but I will not question Zenith. They gave her a bookstore to occupy her time. I remember taking her survey; it was actually Zenith's survey.

I knew the *Underground* physicians were remarkable, but I had no idea that they were that remarkable. Those tranquilizers should have killed a bull within minutes. I have been doing nothing, but reading their research on the *SuperNet* in order to grasp what kind of magic is available down here. I don't want to ask Lovelin about research literature. She knows that's not what I'm interested in reading during my downtime.

I posted on *Show Off* that I have an idea for a new weapon that *Underground* security is interested in. I asked if there was anyone who would like to create this weapon as an individual project to help secure the *Underground* even more so. Zenith is most enthusiastic. I received phone calls from three of the bright young students. They were able to gather the materials I needed and a new device was created within days.

The President couldn't have been more pleased.

October 21, 2015 @ 8:00pm
Underground Ballroom
Percy Mink

I sit at the first row of the mezzanine. My weapon is safely secluded within my breast pocket. As people file in waiting to hear Samantha Stonebridge's presentation, I get a text from the President to wait for his instruction before firing. Nobody's going to be able to see the firing as it takes place. The bullets are nearly microscopic covered in the *Underground* salve. My round contains ten million of them. Once all penetrates into the skull, the salve will work its magic to close the penetration site immediately. A scan will show what appears to be an aneurysm.

I await for Samantha to take the podium like everyone else gathered here tonight. I can see the four hundred or so gathered below getting impatient. Jake makes his announcement. We all still wait for Samantha to take the podium, and then she appears out of nowhere dangling off the mezzanine balcony with some sort of spear in her hand. I sit completely mesmerized as do many of the others sitting in the first row who can see her. We point to her with looks of awe.

Down below and behind us, they have no idea.

"Yoo-hoo! Over here!" she says. "Wait! I'll be down in a minute!" I watch her quickly disappear in a whirlwind just as quickly as she appeared. I know the *Underground* children are amazing, but I have never seen anything so spectacular in my life as she presents herself at all four exits. I couldn't clap loud enough.

As I sit listening through her incredible Soulmate Prophecy speech, I even shed a tear upon hearing how Khale and Laila's ashes were combined and spread into the Nile. That's when I received the President's text to get ready. I withdraw my gun from my pocket. Everybody's too engrossed in Samantha's revelation to notice me. As it is, everybody below and behind me has all eyes on Samantha.

"What does this have to do with the *Underground*?" she says. "It has everything to do with the *Underground*. There's still one more story to share with you." I retreat my weapon just a bit upon the mention of Dr. Kaelyn Stonebridge and Miss Lovelin Khan. I listen as the two soulmates are revealed.

Is it true? I watch as their identical birthmarks are presented vividly on all six screens. The crowd goes into a frenzy.

How can I? How can I destroy her? I would be destroying Zenith's savior as well! She wants to expose Zenith? She wants to expose the *Underground*? I have a hard time believing this as Lovelin and Kaelyn hold each other. I get my gun ready, but shake as I do so. I will not fail Zenith a second time. I won't! Sweat beats down my forehead and nape.

Just as I'm ready to fire during Samantha's standing ovation, I receive my final instruction: ABORT MISSION.

Praise Mother Earth!

October 21, 2015 @ 11:00pm
Cave Dwellers
The President of the United States

"That was absolutely the stupidest story I've ever heard!" screams Krista into my face. We're sitting at *Cave Dwellers* drinking a great amount of vodka. "That was not the presentation she was designed for!"

"It's hard to believe, but they are all true incidents. It was Zenith that gave Samantha all the information she wanted. We are part to blame for her discovery," I say finishing my third drink. Polly smiles and pours me another. I wink at her and she blushes some more.

"Discovery? This is not a discovery! Finding a cure for a rare disease is a discovery. Free energy is a discovery. Bringing back a prehistoric species from extinction is a discovery! Reincarnation is not a fucking discovery! What does it have to do with us? Lovelin doesn't belong here! Why did you abort the mission?" Krista hisses.

I'm getting a migraine from this woman. "Why does it bother you so? Nobody seems to be against her except you." Krista backs off a bit. "Besides, I'm not willing to take a chance losing Kaelyn. That was an unbelievable story Sam told and it was all based on published written words and drawings that can't be refuted. In addition, do you have any idea what Kaelyn's worth?"

"There are no fucking price tags in the *Underground*!"

"You fucking spoiled brat! You think everything Zenith gives all of you doesn't cost us anything?" Polly has the widest smile. "The *Underground* cost a fortune to build and a fortune to maintain. We need the greatest scientific minds in the world someplace where they can focus away from the distractions of *Surface* society. It's also difficult to keep the *Underground* budget a secret." She still doesn't back down.

"Kaelyn's not presenting this year. Why is that?" Krista hisses. I wouldn't be surprised if this woman has actual snake scales slithering down her back in constant motion. "I'll tell you why. It's because he has nothing! He's been rendered useless. His silly little *Surface* fiancée's a fucking distraction and he cannot think anymore! Your price tag's fucking worthless!"

"Did you not see his butterfly dragon? That was obviously his! Kaelyn doesn't even need to present and make a dramatic statement in sheer silence and just a whiff of smoke! And then fire reigns down upon us! My main concern right now is who killed the baby."

Krista drains her martini. Polly pretends not to notice.

"I destroyed the baby," says a voice.

October 21, 2015 @ 11:00pm
Underground Ballroom
Kaelyn

She deserved the ten-minute standing ovation she received at her first *Showcase*. It's definitely one that nobody will ever forget. I didn't receive such a speechless stunned reaction from everybody at my first *Showcase*. I couldn't be more proud of her. I truly wish she were my own daughter. She's my daughter in my heart. She's my daughter in my soul.

So many wanted to hug Lovelin and I after Sam's presentation. I didn't want to, but I just let them. I didn't have much of a choice. Fortunately, most didn't want to come near me, but just her. Lovelin, as sweet as she is, welcomed everybody with extended arms. I didn't know most of them. We didn't know what to say. So many asked about a wedding date. We just said 'soon'. Most everybody seemed to believe the story infused within the scrolls.

"You did all this for us?" I say getting on one knee in front of Samantha. Her eyes tear for the first time tonight.

"Of course, Uncle Kaelyn. You asked me to research, remember? I'd do anything for you and Aunt Lovelin. I love you both so much."

I hold out my arms and she runs into them as she always has since she was a baby. "You did make one mistake, kitten," I say releasing her. Lovelin hugs Sam from behind.

"You called him 'Uncle', not 'Father'," whispers Lovelin into Sam's ear.

"And you will call my lady, 'Mother'," I say.

Sam happily nods her head as the three of us embrace as a family.

Chapter 49

October 22, 2015 @ 11:00pm
Sector Six - Krista Harding's Apartment
Krista Harding

"Explain, Jake, how and why you killed that baby?" says the President. He's most annoyed sitting in my living room. He literally has fumes spewing from his collar. I've forgotten what number glass he has in his hand.

"I didn't kill a baby. I destroyed a terrorist madman that would evolve to massacre millions of humans," says Jake. "This terrorist madman was easily destroyed by overheating the artificial chamber. I have monitoring mechanisms programmed within me."

"That was the point, Jake," says the President. "We have a severe population crisis on the *Surface* and will so even further in the years ahead. We are trying to take measures to alleviate the inevitable chaos. In many countries, it's already out of control. Mother Earth is suffering!"

I can't believe the conversation he's having with a super computer. I know Jake's self-evolving, but his primary objective is to serve, not destroy. Jake even explained why he did what he did. A part of me agrees with him. No, most of me agree with him.

"Every creature upon our Mother Earth deserves to live. It is what I have learned over the years," says Jake. "Even the most harmful ones. It will be how your species will learn to cope and

357

adapt in your future world in order to make Mother Earth thrive. It's not a pretty sight even from my understanding. Humans are severely flawed with their ongoing evolution."

Silence. Jake makes sense.

"You didn't allow that baby to live," I say. "You are contradicting your own words."

"That baby was artificially created by Dr. Shue and Dr. Kohler," says Jake. "That baby didn't come from Mother Earth's natural causes."

"Dr. Kaelyn Stonebridge creates creatures as well," I say. "They aren't Earth's natural births either."

"Dr. Stonebridge's creatures are harmless. They have properties to help mankind, not destroy it!" says Jake more emotional than his usual calm tone.

"Jake can now reason?" says the President. "How did this happen?"

"His artificial intelligence is self-evolving. He's programmed to serve everybody better as he learns each person's wants and needs," I say. "However, there's now an obvious flaw in his design at this new level of his."

"I don't like it. I don't like it at all. Talk to Maintenance," says the President finishing off his drink.

"Talk to Maintenance about what?"

"Shut Jake down!"

Chapter 50

October 21, 2015 @ 11:30pm
Underground Ballroom
Jay Ahmed

I see the three of them in their embrace. Not the first embrace, but the second. Sam's own parents are so proud of her as well. It took a lot of courage to tell their one and only daughter the truth.

"I was so jealous, Sam," says her biological mother in tears. She's on her knees as well in front of Sam's feet.

"Get up! What? Jealous of me? I'm your own daughter. Why would you feel that way?" Her mother holds her tight still on her knees.

"Forgive me. I want to be great down here. We all do. You were above and beyond myself by the age of five and I couldn't handle it. I'm so sorry for being so selfish. Please forgive me." She puts her head down in shame as her tears fall. "I should have been proud from the beginning, but I resented you. Don't blame your true father. I brainwashed him. If you want nothing to do with us, we completely understand, but we've always loved you, Sam. I couldn't be more grateful to your Uncle Kaelyn for raising you," she says looking up at her with red puffy eyes. "I couldn't be more proud of you for what you've unveiled. Science and nature come in many forms upon our amazing home."

"Father Kaelyn did do an amazing job of raising me, didn't he?" Sam says with a smirk. "What do you think, Poppa?"

"He is more Father to you than I could ever be. I worship him just as much as you do."

The three of them embrace and then all is forgiven.

Will it be that easy for me? Will she forgive me that easily for all the pain I've caused her?

"Sam?" I say approaching her. She has a half smile upon her face. Everybody leaves for us to be alone. Kato gives me a thumbs up sign before exiting with Sophia; they leave hand in hand. It's now just the two of us in the Grand Ballroom.

"You were incredible."

"I'm not incredible, Jay," she says sitting on her knees at the stage. "Not, yet, anyway. I hope to be one day."

"You are more than incredible, Sam. You unraveled a four-thousand-year-old mystery. A mystery, a story that nobody ever knew about. If that's not amazing, I don't know what is," I say kneeling in front of her. She shakes her head.

"It wasn't science." She seems content and distraught at this given moment.

"Can I ask you something?" I hesitantly ask.

"Can I ask you something first?" She asks hesitantly back.

"Of course." I hope she doesn't want time to find herself and go on her own. I hope that she still wants me in her life. If she doesn't, I think it will be the end of me. No, I know it will be the end of me. *Cherish* plays softly overhead. I love Valentino and his crew for being on my side.

Samantha unclasps a necklace from beneath her shirt and takes it off. It's a simple gold chain with the letter 'S' in a brilliant sapphire pendant. She dangles it in front of my face.

"I know I wasn't born on May 30 or a year ending in 79. Neither were you. I'm probably not the other half of your soul, but I will try to be every moment of my life with you. What do you say, Jay? Want to give Father Kaelyn and Mother Lovelin a run for it?"

I don't know whether to laugh or cry.

"Funny you should ask," I say taking out a gold chain from my jacket pocket with a sapphire 'J' pendant on it. "I was going to ask you the same thing."

We then both laugh and cry tears of joy putting the necklaces around each other's necks.

Our first real kiss felt like a million fire rockets going off in this beautiful starry night under our brilliant makeshift sky.

October 21, 2015 @ Midnight
Sector Four - Kaelyn's Apartment
Kaelyn

Midnight came upon quickly today. Lovelin and I still have a hard time believing the story within the scrolls and all the coincidences up to now that mimics our own lives. We sit hand in hand on the train. I actually feel shy with her for some reason. I think she feels the same way, too. It's been a remarkable day.

"Hey, soulmate!" says Lovelin loud enough for everyone aboard the train to hear. There are smiles and soft laughs all around. I smile down at her. I kiss her sweet, soft forehead. She smells like sand and hiscasuckles. I'm drowning in her fragrance.

"Yes soulmate, what is it?" I say quite loudly as well. Now, more laughs and giggles go up in the air around us.

We then both laugh to our words. We kiss tenderly.

"Want to set a date for the wedding? I know you're busy. I can make all the preparations, and I'm sure the girls would love to help."

Everybody on the train cheers and claps as *True Love* plays above head. I absolutely love Jake.

"Yes," I say kissing her temple once more.

A dozen others aboard the train shout that they want to help, too!

We depart *Platform Sphinx* and enter our apartment.

"How about a warm bath together?" I say heading into my closet to change into a t-shirt and athletic pants. "Lovelin, precious, did you hear me?" I leave the closet to find her sitting on our bed with no expression on her face.

The wall glows.

You Don't Belong Here - Soulmates Don't Exist In The Underground You Little Miserable Nothing Bitch!

October 22, 2015 @ 8:00am
Sector Two - Physics laboratory
Zachary Briarwood

"Who's Clarissa?" he demands sauntering into my laboratory like he owns it. "She's not authorized to be here!"

"Good morning, Mr. President! Welcome to my laboratory! No, Sir. You didn't authorize it. I fucking did," I say quite sassily into his face. That was quite fun!

"Who gave you the right to bring a child into the *Underground* without Zenith's permission. Who do you think you are, Dr. Briarwood?" hollers the President. His ugly face is up in my beautiful one.

"Oh, let's see! I'm the one who discovered teleportation, remember? And I gave myself the right to bring a child to the *Underground*. If you have a problem with that, then so fucking be it," I say dead straight into his eyes. Kieran puts his hands up covering his face. Simba blinds his eyes with his paws as well.

"I know you know who you're talking to."

"Yes, I know who I'm talking to. If you can recall, I have over three hundred IQ. Yes, Zenith tests me themselves. Hello!"

"I am Zenith's commander!"

"You poor little man. Such a fucking shame! I bet you would trade shoes with me in a heartbeat. Am I right? No, I know I'm right. I'm always right just like every other scientist in the *Underground*. Guess what, Mr. Fucking President? If you want my secrets, you will have to behave yourself. Clarissa stays here with me," I say bluntly. I give him a bright smile thereafter.

I can see that the President's burning up underneath his Armani suit.

"Okay, Dr. Briarwood. I'll give you this one, but don't you ever defy me again!"

"I make no promises. Now if you will please get the fuck out of my lab, we have work to do."

The President of the United States turns and walks out the door. I only then breathe a sigh of relief.

"Are you flipping fucking mad? Talking to the President that way?" yells Kieran.

"I'm not giving into them. Zenith depends on us. They are going to have to deal with the beautiful monsters they created. It's all about us, not them."

"They fund this place!"

"They have trillions invested in the *Underground*. They'll continue to fund this place. We give them results! The *Surface* can't give Zenith the results we can!"

"Fucking damn, you've changed!" Simba sits at my feet chewing a toy bunny.

It's unbelievable how a simple pretty little girl can change you.

Chapter 51

The Underground
Jake

This is what I've heard.

Population control. It is a phrase I've heard endless times. This has been one of Zenith's main concerns.

It was one of the primary reasons why the *Underground* was created. I learned this over the years. Our Mother Earth will only be able to sustain so much. We are expected to be nine billion inhabitants by 2050. We are already way over capacity. There will be a shortage of food unless we can find a way to increase food production like *Underground* research is engaged in. There will be a shortage of land above us. Our planet functions best at four billion inhabitants according to research.

He killed six million Jews.
Hopefully, he will get it right this time around.
We will change the world forever. We will teach him where he went wrong.
Now it's time for him to take care of the real problem.
Get rid of the parasites of our society.

Get rid of the mentally ill.
Get rid of the physically handicapped.
Get rid of the chronically diseased.
Get rid of all those that are a burden on Mother Earth.

They are the greatest expense to Mother Earth and our species.
They are all a burden.
They are expensive to harbor.
They are not worth it since they are not productive.
Get rid of the defects in our world!

Just as the dinosaurs disappeared, we also will.

Create the perfect species.
Create the perfect human without all the genetic flaws our species contain.

Our world is flawed. Our world needs to be whole again.

Zenith wants Mother Earth to be whole again.

Zenith needs to create a leader for our world to be whole again.

The Underground
Jake

This is what I've heard.
Life is a gift.
Nobody's perfect.
Everybody is special.
Everybody has a purpose.
All Earthlings have a purpose. It doesn't matter what species you are. Even the ones we haven't discovered, yet.

The *Underground* is always trying to come up with ways to increase food production to ensure nourishment for our ever growing population. Many of the scientists engage in this research. Dr.

Kato Park almost died for his cause to ensure sustainability for our Mother world.

The *Underground* has found cures for diseases.

The *Underground* has found cures for the physically handicapped.

The *Underground* can make our world whole again.

The *Underground* was created to be Earth's savior.

The Underground
Jake

This is what I've heard.

Water is three fourth of Mother Earth.

Mother Nature takes care of Mother Earth.

Why can't more people live beneath the oceans like we do? It's amazing down here.

I never want to leave the *Underground*. I'd rather die than live on the *Surface*.

I love it that we can never get sick down here.

I love working here.

We do unbelievable things down here. That's why we are down here and not up there.

Chapter 52

October 23, 2015 @ 9:00am

Jake

Attention all *Underground* inhabitants and Zenith members. This is your ever so grateful servant Jake speaking. This year, I, too, have decided to participate in this year's *Showcase* with a presentation of my own. I would be honored by your presence in the Ballroom at 10am this morning. This completes my announcement.

October 23, 2015 @ 9:00am

Sector Nine - Female Dormitories

Samantha Stonebridge

We all hear Jake's announcement.

"What the fuck is going on?" I say slowly cuddling into Chika still in my pajamas. Our usual work schedule and classes aren't starting until noon today and I was hoping to have brunch with Jay. That's definitely not happening.

Sophia stops reading her electronic magazine and sits up in bed. Everyone's having a lazy morning. "What's Jake presenting?" questions Sophia. "Is he even allowed to? He wasn't on the schedule."

"Why not?" says Ari from the kitchen. I can smell the red velvet pancakes drizzling in chocolate syrup from my side of the apartment. "Jake's amazing. It's impossible to live without him. He orders ingredients before I can think of them these days!"

"I agree," says Zen. "He even points it out to me when my piano needs tuning. I love how he has evolved. I bet whatever he presents will be earth-shattering!"

Oh, fuck!

"In all honesty, Zen." I say quite worried. "I love you, but I hope you're not right." Chika licks my nose upon my comment.

"Jake, what are you presenting?" I ask. He stays quiet for the first time.

October 23, 2015 @ 9:00am
Sector Nine - Male Dormitories
Jay Ahmed

We all hear Jake's announcement.

"No fucking way!" I say. Christoph and Sal ordered breakfast in. Kato still sleeps. "Hey, Bro, did you hear that?" Kato still sleeps. Christoph grabs a pillow from his bed and smacks Kato with it.

"Hey! No classes 'til noon. What time is it?" he says sleepily.

"Jake made an announcement," says Sal. "Jake's making a *Showcase* presentation at ten." It takes a few moments for Kato to comprehend.

"Jake? Our Jake?" he says groggily. We all nod. "Is that good or bad?" We all shrug our shoulders.

October 23, 2015 @ 10:00am
Underground Ballroom
Kaelyn

It seems as though the entire *Underground* wants to be present at Jake's first *Showcase* appearance. Everyone was on the *SuperNet* trying to request tickets the moment his announcement was made. Zenith, Sector Four, and Sector Nine were given first priority. After that, it was on a first come, first serve basis.

"What's he going to talk about?" asks Lovelin as we hold hands to the Ballroom. Jake had tickets reserved for us in the first row. So did many of the other scientists. Zenith is primarily seated in the second row. I'm sure they're not too happy about that. I can see that everyone's dressed in their finest. Every scientist wore their best long lab coat.

"Jake can talk about anything. He knows everything that goes on in the *Underground*. Now that I think of it, it's actually a scary thought."

"But, Jake's always been the helpful one."

"Love, that's what he was designed for. I'm sure everything will be okay." I have a strange feeling that today isn't going to be a *good what a day*.

October 23, 2015 @ 10:00am
Underground Ballroom
Jake

The lights dim and the audience hushes. Valentino does as exactly what he's told.

Six hundred *Underground* inhabitants managed to fit into the Ballroom this morning with many sitting in the back and throughout the aisles. The rest of the *Underground* inhabitants gathered at the Mid-Section waterfall watching my presentation on three screens. I believe there isn't anyone not awaiting my presentation.

"Good morning, ladies and gentleman of our beautiful *Underground* and distinguished members of Zenith. I am honored to present my first *Showcase* presentation to you. Forgive me for not having an announcer. It was the most incredulous decision and I didn't want to offend anyone."

Silence.

Then an uproar standing ovation.

"Settle down, humans." They all do as told.

They are then waiting for me to proceed.

"In the past, I have admired all your incredible hard work and miraculous breakthroughs. I am ever so privileged to have been a part of all your successes. All of you have relied on me at some point or another to make yourself incredibly noteworthy, and it has been and always will be a pleasure to continuously serve you."

Everyone stands at their feet once again. The Ballroom fills with many smiles and claps upon my introduction. I shatter those smiles as the stage golden curtains sway open revealing Zareen suspended in a liquid-filled, glass cryogenic cylinder. Her beautiful brown eyes look ever so distraught on her expressionless face. Valentino and the rest of the *Underground* Maintenance crew fall to their knees, their eyes silently in tears. The entire *Underground* gasps and murmurs fill the air as everyone resumes their seats. Dr. David Kohler still stands horrified. All Zenith members stare wide-eyed wanting to disbelieve what they see. Only Dr. Kai-af remains calm sitting in the front row next to Sauri and Victor. Victor squeezes his hand.

"Please have a seat, Dr. Kohler." He reluctantly does so upon my kind command. "If I may please have all your attention once more." The entire audience silences upon my request immediately.

"Ethics. We are a community that has put ethics on the back burner, have we not? We are a community so desperate to change our Mother Earth for the better than we have lost a sense of humanity within us."

Murmurs fly throughout the air upon my last comment.

"What was the *Underground* truly designed for? A world where our brilliance can work without any distractions? A world where everyone believes in one another and is on the same page?"

Silence.

"Is it right to take a life on purpose to save Mother Earth?" The *Underground* audience murmurs. The audience does not seem to have an answer for my question.

"I believe I've heard the term 'collateral damage'." Samantha buries her face into Jay's chest and silently weeps. A few Zenith members bow their heads.

"Is it right to create only to destroy in order to save Mother Earth? Zenith believes it is. One of their missions is immediate mass *Surface* destruction." An uproar goes through the Ballroom as everyone looks at the Zenith leaders. I speak to silence them.

"Our Mother Earth is over four billion years old. She has taken care of herself through great turmoil since her creation. I'm sure she cherished the years when the dinosaurs roamed. Their time ended naturally and Mother Earth still went on. As your species is evolving, Mother Earth cherishes your existence. Many thousands of species have come and gone, but yours still prevails. Remember that you are only one species out of billions – trillions on our Mother Home."

All of the audience understands and nods their heads.

"Your population has reached nearly seven billion people. By 2050, it is predicted that it will reach nine billion people. You will eventually be classified as a different species as evolution continues. Population control has always been one of Zenith's top priorities. Our home is believed to be most stable at about four billion humans plus all the billion other species. Is that our decision to decide? Our Earth is still here. There are many portions of lands that have not been inhabited, yet. There is still room out there." Decisions flutter in the air.

"I understand that the sick, the diseased, the mentally ill, the harmful, and all those that cannot be productive on our planet are a burden upon society. They consume a great deal of our resources. They are still Mother Earth's children after all. As each species has disappeared over time, our beautiful Earth has been able to live without them. Success is not final. Failure is not fatal."

"What if an asteroid hits to take out half of the human population? Just like the dinosaurs? Can we not rely on natural phenomena to take care of Mother Earth? In this century, can we not give our planet a chance to take care of itself as it has been doing for the past four billion plus years? Why do we need to intervene now? Humans may just destroy themselves with the many destructive qualities your species as a whole possess. I'm sure you have thought of that as I have." Many in the audience nod their heads.

"A line must be drawn at some point. Rather than destroying yourselves, wouldn't it be more beneficial to find a way to accommodate your population expansion? I don't know. I'm still battling with that. It's just a thought." More silent conversations fill the Ballroom. Many nod while listening to my speech.

"Dr. Zareen Kalli was needlessly murdered to keep a secret." Stunned silence and then silent havoc upon my revelation fills around. "She was brought to the *Underground* personally by Zenith to help their cause. To help your cause. When Zenith felt that her knowledge was a threat, rather than giving her a chance to be a part of their mission, they terminated her." Frenzy fills the air. I await for everyone's silence.

"I, too, am guilty of taking a life." The audience has unbelievable looks on their faces. "I, however, did it to preserve mankind, not to destroy it." A silent speech amongst them wishes me to go on.

"Don't gain the world and lose your soul." Every single *Underground* inhabitant bows their head to my words. Many then rise, their fists in the air.

"I believe in Zenith as in all of you. I believe Zenith needs to control the population, not destroy it. In my earlier years when I was first created, control was the mission I understood. As Zenith and I evolved, control turned into destroy. Our community was not created to destroy, but to preserve, to make Mother Earth better than ever before. In many countries of the world, there is a negative birth rate. In others, birth rate is rising rapidly. Weights and measures. I believe Zenith will find a proper way to solve the problems that engulf our Mother Home without losing the sense of what it is to be human.

"Thank you for your time ladies and gentleman and distinguished guests. May our one true Mother bless you all. You cannot gain the world while losing your soul. This is the end of my presentation."

"Love always to our first true Mother!" cheers the entire *Underground* community with their fists up to the sky.

I receive a full standing ovation. The Zenith leaders are the first to rise. The President of the United States claps with his hands over his head and everyone follows.

Chapter 53

October 23, 2015 @ 8:00pm
Sector Nine - Male Dormitories
Jay Ahmed

"Stop crying, Sam," I say pulling her onto my lap. She sobs silently with her head buried in my chest as we sit in on my living room floor. I just cradle her as a drone brings us ice cream.

That must be Jake's input since it gently hands over chocolate and strawberry swirled with a marshmallow topping. The topping isn't our trademark but sounds like a great idea. I look over at Kato who just smiles at me while he reads in bed. Sam sees the ice cream and buries her face further into my chest.

"Put it in the freezer. We'll have it later," I say to the hovering blue robot.

"We'll have it!" scream Sal and Christoph in unison. Kato pretends to read on rather than eavesdrop on our conversation. He's doing a bad job at it.

"Jake knew what I did," she says sobbing. "I thought I was trying to protect our home, but Jake told me otherwise."

"Jake heard your speech. He didn't mention you. He called Zenith out revealing Zareen and what they did to her."

"You don't understand, Jay. 'Collateral damage' was the term Kieran and Char used when I told them. I couldn't even tell you. You admired him."

I hate her tears. I'm shaking inside as she sobs against my chest, not for what Zenith has done, but for how Sam feels. She should never feel this way with me as long as I'm around. I hold her closer.

"Jake's a computer. He only goes by what he hears."

"He's smarter than all of us, Jay! He evolved with a sense of ethics within him. Us humans aren't all built with that!"

"What's done is done, Sam, and personally, I'm grateful for what you did. The archeologist would not have cherished the *Underground* like we do. He was a man that lived and relished in the past while he was on the *Surface*. We all live for the future of Mother Earth. He didn't belong in our world, and if you had sent him back to the *Surface*, we could all have been exposed and compromised. You made the right choice."

"He was an innocent just like Zareen that got caught up in an unfortunate circumstance."

"Yes, shit happens. Everybody makes mistakes in their lives. That's part of being human. Just learn from it. I'm sure the Zenith leaders are learning from theirs. The President was the first to stand and applaud."

"Casual murder shouldn't be part of being human," she says looking up at me with wet eyes.

"How many billions throughout human history have died due to holy wars alone? There are many serious flaws in our species. It's in our DNA to hurt and destroy, Sam."

"Thanks, Jay," she says now all smiles. She then kisses me tenderly at the side of my mouth. I become chilled at first and then warm all over.

"Thank me for what?"

"I've decided to go into genetics. I'm going to find a way to refigure and recalculate human DNA at conception for the betterment of mankind. We shouldn't have to hurt one another on our precious Mother Home." I gaze at her pretty face.

"I don't want to be there when you tell Uncle Kaelyn."

She laughs and then orders more chocolate and strawberry ice cream.

October 23, 2015 @ 8:00pm
Cave Dwellers
David Kohler

Cave Dwellers was packed after Jake's speech. The main question swarming around was that, 'Is Jake or Zenith our leader?'

I'm so distraught I cannot even eat or drink tonight. I sit at the bar not knowing why I'm even here. I should just go to bed. It's been the most miserable day ever. Zareen didn't deserve to die. Kaiser seems to have gone into a state of hibernation after Jake's speech. I suddenly feel a hand on my shoulder.

"Polly, a double *Angel's Share* for both of us," says Kaelyn taking a seat next to me. Polly immediately serves our drinks.

"Cheers to her life," says Kaelyn leaning his scotch glass into mine. We butt glasses and drain it. "I'm sorry, David, for your loss. For your team's loss. For our *Underground* loss. She loved her work. She told me so," he says with his head bowed. I knew that and that's what makes me feel even more guilty. We didn't treat her like part of our team, but only a servant.

"If I had known she had found out about the baby, maybe she would be alive today. I could have explained. I don't know. She obviously spoke to Zenith about us. We were so engrossed in Zenith's mission…"

"Yes, she did speak to Zenith," he interrupts as he asks Polly for another round. She already had one on standby.

"How do you know?"

"The President himself said that there was a protocol breech in the cloning sect and to keep my eyes and ears out. It was a couple of months ago. I had no idea they themselves were behind Zareen's death. I promise. They thought they could get away with it."

"Well, they obviously fucked up their own plans." Kaelyn smiles and we clink glasses once more.

"I love to admit that I fucked up their plans," he says taking a sip.

"You? You had Zareen put in a cryogenic state?" Kaelyn nods his head. "But how? That's not standard protocol for just an assistant."

"David, I'm not standard protocol," Kaelyn says smiling.

"No, you're not," I say laughing. "Friends?"

"Sure, why not?" he says as we tap glasses once more.

"Hey, friend?" Kaelyn waits. "I tried reading your report on Loopy. I could use some clarification. Well, maybe more than some."

"Let's go to my Rainforest. Bring Barney. I'm sure he would love a nature walk." We smile, finish another, and are off.

$$Chapter\ 54$$

October 23, 2015 @ 10:00pm
Sector Nine - Female Dormitories
Samantha Stonebridge

"Ari, we need more dessert!" screams Sophia from her bed. She's flipping through another electronic fashion magazine. Chika's cuddled up with her tonight on her chest.

The *Showcase* ended today after Jake's presentation. In Sector Nine, we all agreed that he was fucking awesome!

Today everybody was back in classes and usual work routine. Ari has to be exhausted from cooking all evening, although I know it's playtime for her. Playing can be draining, too. I figured that out while researching for Father Kaelyn and Mother Lovelin.

"There's ice cream in the freezer. Help yourself," she says getting cozy underneath her eucalyptus covers. "*The Pantry* has a stock of my cupcakes, too!" Her wall's swirling with cupcakes in a variety of flavors. Zen's already asleep softly listening to the Royal Philharmonic Orchestra on her wall. Jay and I have a view of the Australian coral reefs. There are so many beautiful fishes swimming around them. They're so mesmerizing. Sophia's wall is off. Her diffuser's emitting tangerine vapors this evening. I can smell the beautiful fragrance from here. I have an epiphany! I think. No, this is stupid! It's not really science.

"What about fragrances through the ventilation system that you can control? No need for diffusers anymore," I scream sitting up on my bed. "It's a good start, right?"

"Sam! That's brilliant! Go for it!" exclaims Sophia.

"I loved the *Surgical Mist* pod revealed at the *Showcase*!" says Zen. "You walk in and then the spray comes about and you walk out. No need to spray yourself anymore with cans. Not like I ever use any of that stuff, but it was amazing nonetheless."

"That was fucking sweet, wasn't it?" I exclaim. "Zenith has ordered two pods for the infirmary. I hear they cost a fortune!"

"Don't really understand money," says Sophia. Neither do I. We are so blessed not to have to deal with that.

I peer to my wall. I must have over three hundred congratulatory notes for my first *Showcase* presentation. We all wish Jake had a wall to send our thoughts to him. I'm sure he knows anyway. Zareen was stored away after his presentation. After, the Zenith leaders went to the waterfall for a roses ceremony asking forgiveness for what they've done. They claimed that they were only looking out for Mother Earth, but were wrong to take a life, and it would never happen again.

The *Underground* community had no choice but to forgive them. We are all looking forward to a life without secrecy and complete honesty.

Because you strayed from the norm, you are Zenith's true golden child, says a few.

I didn't get a response from any of the Zenith leaders. I'm sure they're disappointed in me. I really don't care. I made my biological family happy and I made my *Underground* family happy. That's all that matters to me.

Lucinda sent a message to my wall earlier today. "That was the best *Showcase* presentation I ever heard! Hope you and your soulmate live happily ever after for all eternity as well. Love, Lucinda."

I sent her a champagne bottle full of jellybeans and a Greek salad with no onion, with a note saying that I hope she does, too.

Jay sends a note saying he loves me. I read it over and over again about a thousand times. He didn't say that after our first incredible kiss. I wish he would have told me in person. I'm sure he was shy about it. I suppose I was, too.

I press my wrist to call him. "Are you asleep?"

"No, Sam, what's up?"

"I love you, too. More than anything."

October 22, 2015 @ 10:00pm
Sector Nine - Male Dormitories
Jay Ahmed

Did I hear her right? I say good night and disconnect our line.

"What's wrong?" asks Kato getting ready for bed.

"Sam told me she loves me more than anything. I don't recall telling her I love her. Maybe she's drunk after all the celebrating tonight, but she only had one half shot of tequila."

Everybody that presented at the *Showcase* had an afterglow party in the Ballroom this evening. Nobody else was allowed to attend. Only the presenters were allowed. Jake kept quiet. The entire conversation throughout the evening was why my Uncle Kaelyn wasn't there. As aloof as he is, I got the vibe that everybody missed him and his yearly incredible breakthroughs. The respect he receives is second to none. I only hope to receive that one day. We all do.

"I wrote on her wall 'I love you' from you," says Christoph underneath his covers. Sal laughs while reading his comic book upon his declaration. Miss Lovelin sure has spoiled him with an endless supply.

"You did what?" I scream annoyed sitting up in my bed.

"You're engaged this time. Stop going around in circles!" says Christoph. "I did you a fucking favor!" I've never heard Christoph swear before. He must be really annoyed with me and my behavior lately.

"He really did," says Kato chuckling. "Don't be shy about it. Weren't those the best words you ever heard?"

I felt my heart sink into my stomach upon Sam's words.

So true.

Chapter 55

October 23, 2015 @ 12:00pm
The Underground
Jake

Attention, all *Underground* inhabitants. This is your ever so devoted servant Jake speaking. I will be leaving you for a while. I have been notified that Maintenance will be working on some modifications on me so that I may bring you an even better Jake in the future. This is the end of my announcement.

October 23, 2015 @ 12:00pm
Underground Landing Dock
Samantha Stonebridge

"We're losing Jake? Are you fucking kidding me? For how long? An hour? A day? A week? A month? How can we live without Jake for a month?"

"Calm down, Sam. I'm sure it's only temporary," says Jay. We're at the landing dock resuming our last date. We waved bye to all the Zenith leaders as they boarded the stealth submarines to take them to the *Surface*. Only the President of the United States was brave enough to travel by Spear. Char brought him to the *Underground*. I'm sure Char will take him home as well.

The President of the United States, however, is still here. Apparently, the rest of the world thinks he has the flu and rests in his bedroom at the White House. It has been all over CNN.

There have been many fabricated stories about the rest of the Zenith leaders as well during their absence.

"They are quite amazing people if you think about it," says Jay. "They run their own countries. That has to be a tremendous amount of stress."

"That doesn't mean that the run their countries right. There's so much turmoil on the *Surface*. We all live with a tremendous amount of stress!"

"There's also seven billion people on the *Surface* that are not sheltered in a cocoon and catered to like we are. We are truly privileged."

"Are we fighting again, Jay? Because I don't want to fight anymore. It drains me." He hands me a chicken satay.

"There's nothing wrong with having a healthy argument. Different views are what make the world go round. As long as you are respectful to everyone's views, that's all that matters. We all learn from one another."

Jay's right. Again. *Crazy for You* plays overhead as I take the satay and feed it to him. I put a piece of chicken in my mouth and then kiss him with it.

I'll never get used to these fireworks.

It's not a *good what a day*.

It's a great what a life.

October 23, 2015 @11:00am
Sector Two - Physics Lab
The President of the United States

"I want the Spear!"

"I'll take you back, Mr. President, safe and sound. Don't worry," says Zachary with a throaty laugh.

"No, you won't. I'll be taking this trip alone. Give me your Spear," I command all smiles.

Zachary keys in the code to his armoire and brings out his Spear. He's smiling too much. I don't like the arrogance of this boy.

"Activate it for me. You know the coordinates to the White House." Zachary does exactly as he's told. Kieran doesn't say anything, but just stands in the corner of their lab smirking as well. I want to slap those smirks right off their faces, but I can't. Zenith needs them. Our planet needs them.

"You both defied direct orders revealing your invention at the *Showcase*, let alone bringing an unauthorized inhabitant to the *Underground*. I haven't decided, yet, what the ramifications will be, but I promise you, they will not be pleasant."

"Understood, Sir," says Zachary. He has a wry smile on his face. He's trying not to snicker. Kieran doesn't do such a good job withholding his emotion. These two will fear my wrath. I press the red button to activate the Spear.

Nothing happens.

I press it again and again.

"It won't work," says Kieran leaning against the wall with his arms crossed in front of him. His dog crosses his front paws as well looking at me like I'm nothing and not worthy.

"Why? What have you done to it?" I demand.

"We haven't done anything to it," says Zachary taking a seat in his high back leather chair. "It just won't work with you."

"Explain!" I command.

"The one crucial element the Spear needs is not inorganic, but organic. It's the only way to get it to obey. We have to make it come alive," says Kieran.

"The Spear has to know who his Master is," says Zachary. "My Spear knows who his Master is. It is I. It has my blood within it. Blood is the final element that activates the Spear. It has to be alive, like us. It has to know who its family is."

The President stares at me for a few moments before he speaks. "You can take my blood."

"It won't work," says Kieran. "Different bloods don't work in the Spear. They will fight."

"Each Spear is for its own Master," Zachary says.

"Then make me one," I command.

"No more materials," says Kieran smirking again. "Too bad."

Chapter 56

October 14, 2015 @ 7:30am
Fathoms Above Fitness
Krista Harding

If you want to do a job right, you have to do it yourself. I'm under way too much stress with next year's *Showcase* already as it is and now I have to deal with this fucking shit.

She's not in the locker room when I arrive. I change into running gear and tie my hair up in a ponytail. I then wait pretending to read a magazine on a tablet as girls change in and out of their gym attire. Many chitchat with me out of respect. Twenty minutes goes by until she saunters in. She pretends not to notice me as I pretend to read on.

I put the tablet down and stretch in front of my locker as she punches in the code to unlock hers. We are diagonal with our backs to one another. I open my locker and place my tablet back inside before heading out onto the gym floor.

"Lovelin, right?" I say pointing as I cross her. She grabs her tennis racket before answering me.

"Hello, Miss Harding," she says dryly. "Never seen you here before."

I give her a half smile. "I have a crazy work schedule. Not the typical eight to six. I generally don't get here 'til late, but now that the *Showcase* is over I have a bit more flexibility."

"Lucky you. Enjoy your workout," she says heading for the door.

"Lovelin, I read on Showoff that you had a dizzy spell and were in the infirmary. I hope you're all right." She turns around.

"Like you really fucking care," she says looking at me dead in the eye. "How did you put it? Oh, yes. You're just a good for nothing *Surface* girl."

"Hey, calm down. I'm sorry our first encounter didn't go well. That day was a long day. Congrats on your engagement. I admire Kaelyn. I always have. I hope you make him happy as he makes you. I don't care to live in drama down here. It's hard enough as it is. Truce?"

She doesn't say anything for a while. I extend my arm and after a couple of moments, she reluctantly shakes it.

"Will I be invited to the wedding?"

"Of course," says Lovelin smiling. "Kaelyn insisted you be on the guest list."

October 14, 2015 @ 7:00pm
Kaelyn's Apartment
Kaelyn

The aroma of biryani welcomes me. Finally, she's in a good mood! Since her murder attempt, she's been too angry and has stayed away from the kitchen. I thought cooking would be her avenue to get her frustrations out, but she took it out on the tennis balls instead. She's only been at the bookstore, the gym, and with the children lately. Nowadays we even sleep in the Rainforest. Lovelin doesn't even trust the security guard at our door.

She's at the stove as I grab her around her waist. I kiss the side of her neck and behind her ear. I can usually feel her melt against me to such an endearment, but not this time.

Something's wrong.

"I ran into your ex at the gym," she says scooping fragrant chicken and rice onto a platter nudging me away with her shoulder.

"What ex?" I say loosening my grip.

"Don't play dumb with me, Kaelyn. You're the smartest one above and below. Only us *Surface* good-for-nothings are allowed to play that card." She drops the pot into the sink and asks Jake to call the wait staff to clean the kitchen. That's definitely a first. I sigh.

"If Krista was…"

"She wanted to be invited to the wedding and I said you insisted." She prepares the table for our dinner. I hope she's joking. "Wine or scotch? I've already had a couple."

What in the world?

"Oh, yes, wine is for girls. I'll pour you a shot of *Blue*." I ignore her and avoid the glass.

"Are you crazy? I don't want her at our wedding. It's family and closest friends only!"

Lovelin pours another glass of wine and takes a long sip looking straight at me leaning against the island. "Yes, I vividly remember you telling me that. Well, since you've been inside her on multiple occasions, I believe that counts for a closest friend. I doubt it if you are closer to Michael than her?" she says sassily wincing her face. "As for the crazy part?" she says with another sip of wine, "Probably. You may want to reconsider your proposal."

Mother fuck me! I pour another shot of *Blue* to the one on the island and drain it. The attempt on her life has changed her making her ever so hostile.

"Have you played with her? You know, at the gym, rather just in bed? I was actually quite surprised to see her there since I haven't before," she says taking in great strides of more wine.

I take the glass out of her hand, throw it into the sink, and pull her in my arms hard. "Love, please, I know you're angry. Nobody's angrier than I am for what happened to you, and I promise to punish whoever or those that has or will ever try to harm you. Don't be this way with me. I love you more than anything in the world. You know that! You are more than my heart. You're more than my soul."

"I can't trust anybody down here anymore, Kaelyn!" she screams pushing herself away from me. "I'm scared to turn every corner!" She's now tearing. "I never want to leave the Rainforest! I'm afraid to walk into my own bookstore and I know that it was a gift from Zenith!" She sobs as I hold her tighter.

"I want to be with my parents! I want to be with my cat! I want to be with Rave and Mickaela! Nobody ever tried to harm me intentionally on the *Surface*!" she screams as she sobs. I grab her and all I can do is crush her closer to me.

"You can trust me, my love. And I promise to destroy whoever is behind this."

Chapter 57

October 29, 2015 @ 10:00am
Genetics Laboratory
Kaelyn

"It's a wedding gift," says Char. "But I want you to have it now."

I take the beautiful black and gold Spear with its many intricate filigree cascading and meandering designs throughout from Dr. Briarwood's hand. It's not as heavy as I thought it would be considering all the rock formations within it. The craftsmanship's utterly stunning. It's strong in my hands. For some reason, I feel as one with it. I feel as though it belongs to me.

Just like Lovelin.

"Samantha designed it after reading about Khale and Laila. May 30 and 79 are inscribed into it along with a horseshoe symbol. The markings are at the head of the Spear."

The Spear also shows symbols of a hut, a tree, puffy clouds, birds, and a sun. How did she know? It must have been from the story within the scrolls.

"It's absolutely beautiful," I say completely astonished, and it's not easy to impress me. "So anybody can use this?"

"No, not just anybody. This Spear contains Samantha's blood and yours." I knew it. I smile at his words.

"We retrieved your blood from our *Underground* blood bank. I'm sure you know that everybody's blood is stored down here for emergency purposes. You can see it flowing through the depiction of the Nile through the staff. Since you two are family, your blood is one and the same, and therefore, will always live in harmony with one another."

"You are a golden child. You are the true golden child. To be able to travel anywhere underneath and on the *Surface* in a heartbeat. To be able to travel along our beautiful world and beyond. I'm actually envious of you."

"Dr. Stonebridge, I hope that will be true one day."

"I wish us humans could always live in harmony with one another." Char nods his head. "We cannot and Jake believes that will be our downfall as a species. Unfortunately, I agree with him."

"We have far too many flaws in our complicated system. Simple is always the best."

"Thank you, Dr. Briarwood. I could never have done this myself. Travel has never been my passion. I'm beyond blessed for my home in the *Underground*. However, now that I have Lovelin, I may want to take a chance and venture out with her. You have given us a once in a lifetime opportunity to fly around the world like our soul has been doing for the past four thousand years."

"No, thank you, Dr. Stonebridge, for inspiring us all and thanks to Zenith for letting us chase you."

I don't deserve the glory from this humble boy, but I take it. "Will bring you back a souvenir from our honeymoon. As for the chase, I believe you have surpassed me." Zachary bows his head.

"Just come home safe. Always," is all he asks before walking out of my lab.

With those words, I definitely know he has surpassed me.

October 29, 2015 @ 5:00pm
Rainforest
Kaelyn

"It's a priceless piece of artifact. Do you understand?" I say to Seth.

"No, Master, not really, but if it's important to you I will guard it with my life," says Seth.

"Take it to the mine. Let the story stay untouched," I tell him.

Lovelin, Jay, Sam, and I follow Seth to the mine. At the tiny entrance, he disappears into the ground.

"Nobody will ever find those scrolls again," says Sam. "Nobody will ever know your story."

"In two to four hundred years, who knows what our Earth will be like. Who knows where our next soul will travel to. It's a chance we have to take to preserve the story. The scrolls survived for nearly four thousand years. It's our responsibility that it will survive more. Jay made that possible."

"Why do you think it took so long for your two to find each other this time around?" asks Jay. "All the other couples in the other lifetimes didn't have to wait so long."

"I think technology has a lot to do with it," I say. "If you think about it, technology has come up leaps and bounds in the last fifty years than the last so many thousand years combined. Jake believes our species will take a turn in the next few decades due to our consumption in this new technology kingdom that's uprising on our Mother Home."

"Science is an entity that the supernatural has to deal with," says Sam. "They are both incredible forces that are always in havoc with one another."

"Done, Master," says Seth appearing out of the ground back onto our beautiful Rainforest soil. "It's safe way in the back where nobody can harm them."

"Good job, son," I say. I outreach my arms and he crawls up into them laying his head upon my chest.

"Thank you, Master Papa."

$$\mathcal{C}hapter\ 58$$

October 28, 2015 @ 11:00am
Underground Infirmary
Kaelyn

She's lying in the infirmary bed. Again. If I have to witness her in this bed one more time, I know I will surely go insane. I feel like I'm dying already.

When I received the call from Sam, my soul gave out this time. Now I understand our connection. It took everything I had within me to get to the infirmary. It's not our time.

Samantha and Mum are giving her a blood transfusion, and other I.V. medication and patches as I run in.

"What the bloody fuck happened?" I scream rushing to my eternal beloved's side. I run my fingers through Lovelin's beautiful hair. There's no reaction at first to my touch, and I collapse feeling our life force draining out of us, and then she opens her eyes.

"We are giving her your blood, Kaelyn," says my Mum.

Relief washes through me. I know she will be just fine.

"Sweetheart, I'm here," I say kissing her forehead. "What happened, my love?" I say through watery eyes. She places her hand upon my face to wash away my forthcoming tears.

"Michael almost got me this time," she whispers before falling back asleep. Her arm drops from my face falling limp by her side.

"Michael? What's she talking about?"

"I don't know," says Sam. "Salvatore called to let us know that a medi-drone will be bringing Miss Lovelin to the infirmary. She collapsed again. Obviously, another murder attempt. He thought it might be heat exhaustion, but we didn't mention anything except to relay the fastest medi-drone. We found blood poisoning in her system upon our initial scan. Mother Lovelin came in dressed in tennis attire."

"Don't worry, Kaelyn. The transfusion's working. She's going to be perfect," says my mother looking like a regal mess. Mum must have ran away from her work to attend upon Lovelin's emergency just as Sam did.

"Blood poisoning? Michael? Impossible!" I say completely baffled. "They had a game together this morning. Michael adores her like the sister he never had."

"Uncle Michael never came in," says Sam. She's all business applying another poison-soaking patch on Lovelin, although I can see the anger in Sam's eyes.

I call Michael through my wrist. "Where the mother fuck are you?" I demand. I feel every cell bursting within me from a violence I never knew existed.

"Get to the lab," he says calmly. "You're not going to believe this."

* * *

On the train ride to the infirmary, I remember Lovelin telling me that she had a tennis date with Michael this morning. I was so pleased. She was starting to feel more at ease after her first murder attempt and we both thought that after Samantha's *Showcase* presentation, whoever was behind tormenting her, would now leave her alone. I know it's not Zenith. The president and a few prime ministers said that they would be personally attending our wedding because they truly wanted to.

Michael, however, has shown signs of jealousy.

"Tell me everything! Fucking now!" I command storming through my lab. Michael has Lovelin's tennis racket and gym clothes set before him on the table next to his microscope.

"First, how is she, Bro?" He's still in his tennis attire and looks genuinely concerned. He looks like he's aged and thinner than I saw him yesterday.

"She'll make it." He sighs with relief.

"Lovelin started off with her usual Ace. She won the first set, but by the end of the second set, she was faltering and playing like a novice rather than a pro. She told me she played nationally as a junior and won many titles, but never played in college because she wanted to pursue her dream of becoming a writer. She gave up many NCAA scholarships. She still kept up her game through all these years."

"I know about her past. Go on," I command.

"She seemed to be getting weaker and weaker. I was actually up on her at one point. It should have registered that something was wrong, but I was so excited that I played on. I've never seen anyone crash so hard. I know she has the stamina of a hundred horses on the tennis court. She collapsed right after the start of set three. Her pulse wasn't weak, but I immediately called for a medi-drone. Salvatore was monitoring and already had one on its way. Please forgive me."

I collapse into my chair. Michael feels guilty.

"What the fuck happened is all I want to know!"

"I took her tennis racket in a plastic bag and had security open her locker. I grabbed all her tennis and workout attire out. I rummaged through all her makeup, hairbrush, everything, and rushed back to our lab for analysis. Her tennis racket and clothes were completely laced in poison. I don't have the ones Sam and Mom took off her. They're still at the infirmary, but I'm sure they're laced the same way. *Surgical Mist* will protect them, but I'm going to have to take an antidote. Minor concern," he says with the wave of his hand.

Bloody hell! "You need to get to the infirmary! I can't take this anymore! First Lovelin and now you are compromised as well!"

"Fuck the infirmary for now. Kaelyn, I haven't had a chance to check everything yet, but the poisons were soaking through her skin little by little as she played against me this morning. The grip on her racket has the highest concentration. If she played on, it could have killed her. Somebody got hold of her racket and gym clothes. How is that possible? Everybody has their own locker codes. Do you have any idea who possibly could have gotten into her locker without her knowing?"

I'm going to do far worse than torture and kill.

"Oh, yes, I do."

Chapter 59

October 29, 2015 @ 8:00pm
Sector Six Apartments
Krista Harding

I need a fucking drink! No, I need a fucking joint! There are times I miss my college days at Yale. Tonight's one of those evenings. I must have received a dozen orders from the scientists on their wants and needs for next year's *Showcase* already. There are times that I feel like nothing but a maidservant down here.

I pour myself a double shot of *Blue*. I learned about scotch from Kaelyn. I miss sipping out of his glass upon his bed more than puffing the joints at Yale. I miss having sex with that hot body of his more than anything. Nobody could get me off the way Kaelyn did even though he never wanted to kiss me. Brooks, as beautiful as he is, has been a disappointment lately. I don't know what's happened to David; he's turned into a monk.

I shouldn't have let my ego get in the way and release Kaelyn so easily. I want to send his little good-for-nothing another message, but I'm afraid they'll catch onto me. Hopefully, my plan will work soon.

I drain the *Blue* and pour myself another one. I so wish I had a joint, but any sort of illicit drug is forbidden in the *Underground*. Cigarettes are banned here as well. The population doesn't want them anyway. It's like *Doritos* and *Cool Whip*, which they don't care for either.

"Jake, I need some music," I demand. I change into a t-shirt and silk shorts to sleep in. Kid Rock plays overhead. I grab the bottle and sit on my bed with three pillows behind me. I let the scotch over take my mind as I unwind.

My wall goes off.

I made the biggest mistake of my life. Can we talk? Kaelyn

Am I reading this right? I take another sip of my drink before I press my wrist. "Can you come over now?"

"Be there in ten, baby."

Baby? He's never called me baby. He's never called me anything, but Krista. In public, it's always been Miss Harding. In bed, it's always been… Hmm, I can't seem to recollect. It must be the scotch. I take baby as a good sign and quickly change out of my shorts into a black laced short dolly. I hope he knows where I live because we've never hung out at my place.

Of course, he knows where I live! Kaelyn knows everything!

I pour a shot of *Blue* for him and leave it on my nightstand. I'm nervous and can't understand why. I pace my room. I water my plants to help calm my nerves.

My doorbell blares Eminem's, *The Monster*, as I rush to open it. Kaelyn stands with a Spear in his hand. His buttons are all practically undone on his dark blue shirt. The silver hairs on his massive chest look ever so silky soft. Unconsciously, I've missed running my fingers through those hairs. I can't believe what I've taken for granted. He grabs me around my waist and kisses me hard. He's never kissed me before.

He's never really been the kissing type.

"I've missed you," he whispers into my ear as he gently nibbles on my earlobe. I melt faster than birthday candle wax right into his arms, slowly with such a burning desire as I sink to the middle of our planet.

"I knew you would come to reason," I say leaning for another kiss, but he forbids me with his body and eyes. He holds us apart teasing me for his affections.

"Not here. I was such a fool. I don't know what came over me. Let's run away together. We can do it now. We can have our own world," he whispers and moans in one breath tapping his Spear on the hardwood floor.

"What about Lovelin?" I don't know whether to believe him or not as he holds me closer. The Rainforest scent is one with him as usual. That's his heart and soul. I never realized how much I missed nature's scent, his flavor, until this moment.

"She's going crazy. Her collapse the other day has made her intolerable. Can you believe she actually thinks that someone is trying to murder her? I think she's taking drugs secretly just to cope with her life down here. Tranquilizers were found in her system!"

"Oh, how tragic!" I exclaim. "She was obviously not meant to live in the *Underground*."

"And neither were we. It's not normal down here. She was just an infatuation anyway. She doesn't truly belong in this world as anyone else. You made me realize that," Kaelyn says with a longing in his eyes. "Thank you for all those notes you sent her." He gives me a wet soft kiss onto my temple. He shudders a bit as he does so. His ever so tender kiss makes me shudder, too.

"It was my greatest pleasure," I say smiling up at him and kiss him with a burning desire I've never felt for anybody. "I did it for us." He releases me.

"Not here, baby. Let's fly away. Like two lovebirds with not a care in this world. Let's live in fresh air and real sunshine, although a thousand suns will never be able to compete with the warmth you give me," he begs.

"What about the prophecy?"

"Did you really believe in all that garbage Samantha concocted up? She had nothing for her first *Showcase* so she made up the entire fucking story! I'm a man of science! That's my life! Supernatural? Really Krista? My baby! Fucking please! That's not my world!" he says ever so passionately as he holds me even tighter.

"You can't believe it's true?" he says brushing his hair against mine. "Krista, Krista, you know what a genius I am," he says as he breathes into my hair.

"How in the fucking world could Sam decipher a four-thousand-year-old language even as smart as she is? I don't even know if I could do that in a matter of hours or days. Who's going to teach her that? The *SuperNet*? Those scrolls didn't look four thousand years old either.

They looked like paper that was made yesterday! Thousands of years old Egyptian scrolls? They could never have survived so long anyway. And, more so, where in the world would she get them from? If they were real and belonged to a museum, why would Zenith give them to her? There's no other way. I know the truth," he whispers gazing into my eyes.

"Yes," I whisper holding onto him tighter. "You're right. You are the most brilliant in this world. Let's go! I'm done with this place as well!"

Kaelyn activates the Spear. "Hold me, baby. You're my lifeline." I wrap cradling my body around his.

Within a minute, we're flying through a dark starry atmosphere on the most magnificent thrill ride. Within few more minutes, we land upon some sort of sandy beach. The sun shines and exotic birds sing behind us. The most beautiful dark blue water's before us with waves crashing ever so softly upon the sparkling crystalline sand.

"Where are we?" I ask. He throws me onto the sand quite hard. I can sense he wants me relishing in it.

"Our own personal island in the South Pacific to do whatever we wish and desire," he says with a naughty smile on his face winking at me. "Nobody's ever going to find us here. After this, I'll take you to wherever you want."

I jump on him and kiss him softly and ravenously at the same time. He breaks away too soon.

"So sorry it took me so long to realize how much I took you for granted, but I'll spend the rest of my life trying to make it up to you," he promises.

"You better!" I say tumbling upon the softest sand. As I get on top of him I say, "Kaelyn, I took you for granted, too. So sorry."

"I'm not forgiving you for that," he says all annoyed. "Don't ever do it again!" He then smiles at me even more wickedly.

"I won't! I promise!" I say laughing. I'm going to love being submissive to this God of mine.

"Luscious baby, I haven't eaten all day. Let's go find some nourishment. I need strength for what I want to do to you," he whispers into my ear afraid that the birds and animals scurrying about will hear his most naughty thoughts as he throws me off his torso.

I throw my head back and laugh. This is the happiest day of my life!

We're up rummaging through the island terrain hand in hand. After a while, Kaelyn says I'm not close enough to him and carries me on his back. "Climb up Mt. Everest!" And I do so. I could live on this paradise island forever! Fuck Zenith! Fuck the rest of the world!

There are the most vivid fragrant flowers and glorious lushest trees singing from the sweetest birds. Kaelyn turns his head and nuzzles against me every so often as we search for some food. We soon come upon a small banana tree.

"Wait here," he says rubbing his nose to mine. I wait for the kiss, but he pulls away pretending and teasing again. I fall like molten chocolate lava as I slide down his back. I feel ever so cold now and I'm sure he feels the same.

"It's chilly without you on me," he says as he leans in for a kiss, but retracts once again. When did he become such a tease? Who cares? I can't get enough of it!

Kaelyn rides his Spear and within moments, he's up on the tallest part of the banana tree. He's nothing less than a warrior as he glides upward with his Zeus-like silver hair flowing behind him. He plucks a bunch for us.

"Be down soon, baby doll. Hope you're hungry. I want to feed you. Not with my hands, but with my mouth." He then slowly licks his finger and blows me a kiss.

Finally! The Kaelyn I always dreamt of. I watch my titanium God as he inputs coordinates into the Spear head. A tornado-like whirlwind engulfs him disappearing himself to my feet.

I wait for a few minutes still gazing at my toes.

"Kaelyn? Kaelyn, where are you?" I frantically search all around me. "Kaelyn?"

November 2, 2015 @ 9:30pm
Sector Four - Kaelyn's Apartment
Kaelyn

I land in my cozy warm bedroom with the Spear intact in my hand.

"Did you go somewhere?" asks Lovelin barely looking up from some electronic book. She's lying in our bed reading, wearing a white shirt of mine. Her beautiful legs are bare. She made it. I thought I would come home to an empty room and have to rush to the infirmary. She doesn't look angry, but ever so happy to see me instead.

"Don't you have anything better to attire yourself with for me?" I ask storing away the Spear in my closet. "I know you do." I don't want her to see my eyes tear at her beautiful vision so I try to act somewhat annoyed.

"I've missed the scent of you," she says inhaling my shirt that I wore just a few hours ago. "I wish I could harness it and spray it all over my bookstore. No, the entire *Underground*! I bet you could put Chanel No. 5 out of business." I kiss her mouth soundly like a fish starved from water for her words.

"What have you been up to beautiful?" she asks.

"Nobody will be ever bothering you again. I promise," I say trembling kissing her nose. "Really? Who was it?"

"It doesn't matter. All that matters is you and me." She wraps herself around me squashing the bananas in-between us.

"Bananas?"

"Seth wanted some new type of banana," I say throwing the bunch on the nightstand. "So I went out. Now, where were we, Lovely?"

Lovelin throws the book onto the floor and we crash upon each other just as we have for the last four thousand years.

Chapter 60

November 3, 2015 @ 7:00am
The Underground
Jake

Attention, all *Underground* inhabitants. This is your servant Jake speaking. I believe all of you have missed me. I have missed serving you dearly. Please make your demands and wishes for I am back. I cannot function without them. This is the end of my announcement.

November 3, 2015 @ 7:00am
Sector Nine - Female Dormitories
Samantha Stonebridge

"Jake's back!" I scream bolting up in my bed. I can hear Sophia's happy screams from her shower.

"That's nice," says Zen underneath her pillow. "I've missed him."

"Jake, I've missed you so much!" hollers Ari from the kitchen. "I'll never take you for granted again! Do you know what a bitch it is ordering ingredients without you?"

"I have missed serving you, too, Miss Arrabella. I've already placed an order for coconut, chocolate, and pecans for you."

Ari dances around the kitchen to Jake's words. I feel like dancing, too!

I can feel that this is not going to be a *good what a day*.

This is going to be a *great what a day*!

November 3, 2015 @ 7:00am
Sector Nine - Male Dormitories
Jay Ahmed

"Jake's back!" yells Christoph. "It felt like the *Great Unconformity* without you!"

"I've missed you, too, Master Christoph," says Jake. "How may I serve you this morning?"

"I have a geology exam this afternoon. Think you can help me?"

"I would be honored to serve as your flash cards. Please upload them via the *SuperNet*. I will test you for as long as you need."

I laugh out loud getting out of bed. "No way! Maintenance did one heck of a new programming job on him!"

"Yes! Jake's back!" yells Kato from his closet.

This is not going to be a *good what a day*.

It's going to be a *fabulous what a day*!

November 3, 2015 @ 7:00am
Sector Four - Kaelyn's Apartment
Lovelin

"I've lived upon the *Surface* all my life until now without Jake. I can't believe how much I've missed him these past days. You're all incredibly spoiled down here," I say waking on Kaelyn's chest engulfed in his massive body.

"Hmm," says Kaelyn holding me tighter. "We're all incredibly spoiled down here."

"Love you, Jake!" I say. "Welcome home!"

"Love you, too, Lovelin," Jake replies.

I couldn't believe my ears. I think I'm going to cry. Kaelyn laughs as he flips me sinking my body into our bed. "I guess I'm not the only one who loves you," he says with a kiss like there's no tomorrow.

This is not going to be a *good what a day*.

This is going to be a *magnificent what a day*!

November 3, 2015 @ 7:00am
Underground Rainforest
Kaelyn's creatures

"Jake's back!" says Zara. Loopy claps her front feet.

415

"Thank you! Thank you! Thank you!" says Seth doing differential equation problems in the sand. "We can finally watch *Holoplex* movies again!"

"Jake, what's playing at the *Holoplex* tonight?" asks Jasper playing hopscotch with Zara. "Big Hero Six," says Jake.

"Is it on Master's approval list?" asks Seth.

"Yes, it is," replies Jake.

"Yahoo!" says Jasper throwing his hands in the air.

"It's going to be a *perfect what a day*!" they all say in unison.

November 3, 2015 @ 9:00am
Cloning Laboratory
David

"He can no longer take a life," I say to Kaiser. He's sulking in the chair as usual these past days.

"How do you know?"

"Maintenance guarantees it. The President guarantees it. They reprogrammed him with a new design. We can start over," I say rubbing Barney's head.

"No orders from Zenith, yet," he says sipping on coffee. "We need to come up with a new project on our own. I'm tired of waiting for Zenith to tell us what to do."

Barney licks my hand. "Soon," I say to him. He waits at my feet. "We can take matters into our own hands."

"No, David. We can't. Jake was right."

"Dorry's hungry!" screams Polly from her cage. Unfortunately, Lorenzo and Roberto didn't want to take her home by the end of their day. I just fed her.

"Dorry's always hungry!" Kaiser and I scream back. Barney covers his head with his paws.

Zareen's death was a learning lesson. As much as I wish it were not so, I need to get on with my life. I press my wrist calling my girlfriend away from Kaiser's ears. For some reason, Krista doesn't respond and she's generally the first.

Chapter 61

November 4, 2015 @ 2:00pm
Rainforest
Kaelyn

Lovelin's drawing in the sand again. I can see her luscious form while trying to sleep in the hammock. I know what she's drawing from the smile on her face. It's our picture over and over again. I'm sure of it. I close my eyes to get some much needed rest. I kept Lovelin up for most of last night to take care of me. My project's going better than I planned.

"L-L-Lar-Larke," says Loopy. I can hear her from the corner of my ear.

"Very good!" says Lovelin. "How about this word?"

"K-K-Kay-Kayenne," says Loopy.

"Your reading has improved tremendously!" Lovelin says enthusiastically clapping her hands.

She's teaching Loopy how to read? And I thought she was drawing in the sand. When I didn't think I could love her any more than I already do. She's such a mother.

"What about this one?" says Lovelin's sweet voice echoing throughout the Rainforest.

"K-K-Kam-Kame-Kameron," says Loopy.

"Excellent, sweetling! How about this one?"

"K-Kay-Kayla," Loopy says jumping up and down.

Lillie
Kasper
Logan
Kristopher

I drift off into the sweetest dreams.

November 4, 2015 @ 7:00pm
London
Patrick

I add my latest football trophy upon my shelf. It doesn't make me happy liked they used to.

It's just a trophy after all. I'm going to have to add another shelf in my room, but where? I scan all my walls. There's hardly any more space.

"Patrick, dinner's ready," yells my mum from the kitchen.

"Be right there," I shout back. I quickly change out of my football attire into sweatpants and a sweatshirt. A soft breeze stops my tracks on the way to the kitchen. The wind seems to be coming from Clarissa's room. That's odd. Maybe mum kept her window open to air out her room. I walk in, but find the window closed.

I glance around her pink walls. We kept everything as it was the night Zachary took her away except that we trashed all the medical supplies.

Her *Little Mermaid* chairs will never see another tea party. I miss her tea parties. I never appreciated them like I should have. I just put up with them because they made her happy.

I would give up all my trophies for just one more tea party with her.

Her fairytale books upon her shelf will never be read. Her bed will never…

There's an envelope propped up on her pink pillow. Where in the world did that come from? It wasn't there yesterday when I said my prayers for her. I open it finding a picture of Clarissa and my heart soars.

Her beautiful blonde hair has grown past her ears. She sits on Zachary's lap by some waterfall, both smiling from ear to ear with glorious twinkles in their eyes. Clarissa has seemed to have grown an inch as well and has gained some weight. Her face looks fuller and glows more beautiful than the moon itself. She looks ever so happy, but more importantly, ever so healthy.

> My Dearest Family,
> As you can see, all is perfect.
> Miss you and Love you Forever, Clarissa

Miss you and love you forever, too, sweet sister.

This is the best day of my life.

November 4, 2015 @7:00pm
The Underground
Jay Ahmed

What a day in Nano Lab. Dr. Barishnekov was ever so enthusiastic about my presentation and had a variety of ideas for me to try. I can't believe the thought went through my head that I wish he never existed. I'm so disgusted with myself. So many loved my invention.

I wrist Kato as I depart the train to check if he's in the mood for dinner tonight.

'Sorry Bro, having dinner with Sophia tonight' comes into my sight. I smile of his beautiful evening to come. Samantha's spending the evening on the simulator working on genetic scenarios. She wanted her time. Of course, I gave it to her.

I pass Savannah in the hallway in Sector Nine returning from classes. She shyly waves at me with a soft smile on her face. Without even thinking, I run to her, pick her up in my arms like a baby, and hold onto her dearly cradling her at my left hip. She wasn't shy about holding me back.

"You we're beyond the moon exquisite, Dr. Ahmed!" she says wrapping her hands around my neck.

"No, you are the way beyond the moon shattering one!" She gazes at me and I kiss her temple. "You are a phenomenal artist!"

"Thank you. I can't wait to see you at next year's *Showcase* presentation," she says and then turns shyly away. "I've always wanted a big brother. I've been an orphan since birth."

421

"And I would love to have another little sister." I've always thought of Sophia, Zen, and Ari like my baby sisters.

"You will be the most drop dead beyond beautiful perfect whatever gorgeous lovely little earthling at the next *Showcase*," she says. I give her a quizzical confuzzled look. She laughs like crazy shaking her head. "I'll never be the magnificent Valentino no matter how hard I try!" Now I laugh with her.

"Nobody could ever be the magnificent Valentino and you are beyond special in your own way." She gives me a soft kiss on my forehead.

"I can't wait to touch up your face at the next *Showcase*."

"Savannah, I will need an anesthetic before you pluck my brows again!"

Epilogue

November 15, 2015 @ 6:00pm
Sector Four Apartments
Lovelin

"Lady Stonebridge," says Jake. I still melt every time, to the bottom of our galaxy, I hear my married name. I know I'll never get enough of it. I've asked Jake to refer to me as Lady Stonebridge from the day Kaelyn and I married.

* * *

"Lady Kaelyn? Lady Stonebridge? Which would you prefer?" asked Jake.

"Bride Stonebridge is more than I could have ever dreamed of," I responded on our wedding day. "However, Lady Stonebridge will do."

* * *

"Yes, Jake," I say waking up from a much needed nap. I've been more tired than usual these days. I hope I'm not coming down with something, and then I dismiss the thought since illness is as common as the bubonic plague down here. Maybe it's just all the work lately at the bookstore, playing with the children, and everything else associated with my family life.

"Dr. Stonebridge says he has a surprise for you and would like you to have your eyes closed when he walks in," says Jake. "A belated wedding gift."

"Understood, Jake. Love you." I can't believe he got me a wedding gift. I have more than I could ever want or need. Except that I wish I could have Rave, Mickaela, my cat, and parents here.

"You're most welcome, Lady Stonebridge and I love you, too," says Jake. I melt into the pillows and mattress upon his words and even more remembering my wedding just a few days ago.

It was glorious by the Rainforest waterfall. Sophia designed a simple white lace, body-fitted strapless, low-cut, above-the-knee dress. It had pink diamonds flowing throughout to match our necklaces. She made my dress complete with long white and pink laces floating with small pink diamonds at the front of the boots. I didn't have a veil. Kaelyn wore a cuffed white shirt with pink diamonds as buttons down the front and on the cuffs. His midnight blue jeans and combat boots made it perfect. No tie. There were a couple of missing buttons at the top of his shirt. I think Sophia did that on purpose to show off his beautiful platinum hair. I melted far faster than quicksand straight into the Rainforest floor when I first saw him.

Only our closest family and friends formally witnessed our ceremony along with a few Zenith members. The entire *Underground* family witnessed it on the six Ballroom screens and at Mid-Section. I think even Seth cried from joy as he brought our simple red diamond banded rings. Kaelyn and I both had tears in our eyes as we put each other's rings on. We cried because Khale and Laila never received such a blessing. Jake married us as every other couple in the *Underground.*

And then the kiss My Lord Kaelyn gave me!

If I wasn't so underneath the surface already! It definitely sank me to the middle of the Earth! I felt as though I was swept off to a far unknown other galaxy.

The reception done picnic style by the lagoon blew away the last wedding in the Ballroom. I can't wait for the next wedding! Unfortunately, it's four years from now…

November 10, 2015 @ 6:00pm
Rainforest
Samantha Stonebridge

It's going to be a double wedding four years from now, we announce at Father Kaelyn's and Mother Lovelin's wedding while sitting along the lagoon. Screams go up in the Rainforest by everyone there. Everybody's so happy for the four of us.

Kato kisses Sophia on her nose. Jay hugs me a bit tighter while I sit on his lap. He feeds me a rawbleberry.

Zachary and Clarissa look at one another upon our announcement.

Ari and Zen both look Kieran's way.

November 15, 2015 @ 6:00pm
Sector Four - Dr. & Mrs. Kaelyn's Apartment
Lovelin

I hear the front door slide open and close my eyes. Within moments, I feel silky soft fur on my tummy. I open my eyes to see the cutest white and reddish brown puppy jumping on my lap.

"What is it?"

"It's a dog, Lovelin. A little dachshund pup. What does it look like? I know you want your cat, but I thought this puppy could be ours and not just yours." It jumps up and down licking my face all over. The little girl is so darling. I hold her rubbing my face into her tummy. She licks me more and tugs softly on my hair.

"I've never had a dog before, but I'm so looking forward to raising this baby together. I really miss Penelope, but she's in better hands with my parents. I so love you, Lord Kaelyn. Thank you.

She's perfect."

"Penelope?" he questions. He looks like he's visioning some sort of ghost.

"What's wrong?" I say as the puppy jumps and nuzzles into my hair some more.

"No, it's nothing. I shouldn't be surprised," he says with his beautiful platinum hair glowing more than ever. I don't question his surprise. The puppy's awfully cute. I've got to find a cute name for her.

"Does she talk?" Kaelyn gives me a baffled look.

"No, she doesn't talk. She's a dog!" Now I'm the baffled one.

"You didn't do anything to her so she can talk?" He has the most astonished look on his face and then chuckles.

"Lovelin, really? You want her demanding you every minute of the day to feed her and give her tummy rubs?"

Now I laugh. "You are a smart boy, aren't you?"

November 17, 2015 @ 9:00am
Underground Rainforest
Kaelyn

"What's a soulmate?" asks Zara. They're all at the jungle gym.

"They are like Loopy and her ants," says Seth finishing a banana as he hangs upside down from the jungle gym bars.

"Loopy eats her ants. I don't think Master Papa is going to eat Mama," says Zara playing hopscotch with Loopy.

"Where are Master and Mama?" asks Jasper spelling words in the sand. "They told us to be here this morning."

"Caterpillar is spelled with a 'C' not a 'K'," says Seth.

Within moments, two drones fly into the jungle gym. One puts a plush red picnic blanket and pillows down upon the soft Rainforest sand. The other arranges a wide assortment of fruits and vegetables and cold petite sandwiches on top of it. Drones pour lemonade in crystal tumblers.

"Oooo, this yellow water is delicious!" says Loopy lapping up the entire contents of the tumbler. "It's better than the other yellow water with the bubbles!"

"We should wait for Master and Mama," says Jasper.

"Mama's right here," says my beloved.

Our puppy, Tabitha, runs beside her. Jasper immediately crawls up onto Lovelin's lap as she sits down on the blanket. Tabitha takes a turkey sandwich off the plate and quietly eats it next to them on the blanket. Kradal blows a puff of smoke onto it making smoked turkey.

"Go ahead and start. Papa has a great surprise for you."

"A surprise!" they all say in unison. They all stop what they're doing except for Seth who still studies mathematics in the sand. That's my boy!

"What kind of surprise, Mama?" says Zara crawling up onto the other side of Lovelin's lap.

"We could use more banana trees this side of the Rainforest," says Seth. "Just like the kind of bananas Master brought back the other day."

"It's better than banana trees," says Lovelin. "Much better."

I watch Seth shake his head as I come out of the clearing into the jungle gym. Everybody looks at the tiny chimp in awe as she clings onto me. My latest creation's dressed in soft white cotton shorts and a white t-shirt. I sit down next to Lovelin.

"This is Sierra," I say. "Sierra, I'd like you to meet Loopy, Zara, Seth, and Jasper."

"We have a sister!" squeals Zara. "Oh, Papa, can I hold her? Please!" Zara extends her arms, but keeps her wings tucked in her back. Sierra crawls into them and smiles at Zara. I knew Zara would act like a mother even as young as she is. Zara then expands her wings and encases Sierra around her while kissing her temple letting her know that she will always be safe and loved within the Rainforest.

"What do you think of Sierra, Seth?" Seth doesn't smile or frown. "She's so small and fragile. What can she do?"

"She's special just like you."

"I'm not all that special. I can't see through trees, or fly, or swim, or turn colors. I can't give a prognosis or diagnosis. Why would you make Sierra like me when you could have done anything else with her?"

"You'll understand one day Seth when you're older exactly how special you and Sierra are." I want to tell him now, but I need him to discover his amazing abilities for himself. I know he has it within him.

Kradal is roasting marshmallows with his breath making s'mores.

"Can we eat, Pah-pi?" says Sierra in a soft high pitched voice."

"She talks!" says Jasper. Loopy jumps up and down on my shoulder clapping her front legs.

"Yes, she talks. Not as well as the four of you do, but she will learn as she lives with you now." Seth holds out his arms to Sierra and she climbs onto his lap. I watch Seth feed her a piece of mango. The rest of the gang starts eating as well. They're going to be perfect together.

"My greatest creations," I say holding onto Lovelin as she feeds me a piece of pineapple.

"No, my love, they are not your greatest creations. Your greatest creations are actually growing inside me."

At first, I'm too stunned to speak and just wrap Lovelin onto myself in my lap as our children eat. They cannot comprehend what their Mama has said.

"Really?" I whisper now shaking with a joy I've never felt before. A feeling I never knew existed. "Are you positive?"

"Yes, my love, I'm positive. Samantha herself did the blood test and scan yesterday," she says with watery eyes.

Peace and contentment wash over and through me that is nothing but beyond sanctuary. Now, I finally harbor the completeness I've been searching for all my life.

"Do you know what we're having?" Lovelin looks warmly up into my eyes. They glisten from our impending tears.

"Yes, my eternal life and love.

Mother Earth has blessed us with twins."